The Last Scion

by Richard Reed

To my wife Jayne, without whose belief and constant encouragement
this book would never have been written

Second edition

"This is the disciple who is bearing witness to these things, and who has written these things; and we know that the testimony is true."

John 21, v24

Chapter 1

The old priest shuffled across the cluttered room clutching his arms around himself nervously, picking his way unseeingly through the piles of books that littered the floor.

She should be here by now .. She should be here. Where was she?

He stumbled against a bureau, reaching out wildly with a withered arm to steady himself. His hand found a pewter jug and sent it flying, the contents spattering his dishevelled clothing.

A key turned in the lock. "C'est toi, Emilie?" he called hoarsely, a fleck of spittle hanging from his unshaven face.

"Oui, c'est moi," came the reply. "Uncle Jean!" she exclaimed, entering the room and seeing his wine-stained chemise, the crumbs of food on his jacket and trousers. "Come, let's tidy you up."

The priest shied from her ministrations. "My spectacles... I cannot find my spectacles," he muttered.

"Why, they are here on your desk, under all these papers. You must take more care – if a candle were to fall..." She handed him the spectacles before leaning across to scoop up the scattered documents.

Her arm was grasped in a tight, bony grip. "Leave those be, Emilie," he said, glaring at her. "You know it is forbidden to touch my work."

She stared back angrily, rubbing her arm where his fingers had left livid marks. "That was unnecessary, uncle; I was merely trying to help. If you don't keep this place tidy, it will be the death of you. Here's your supper, and some more wine." She stooped to pick up a wicker basket and thumped it down on his desk before heading for the door. "Just don't get drunk again."

"You'll not stay?"

"On All Hallows' Eve? Everyone will be out celebrating."

"All Hallows already?"

"If you went outside the presbytery occasionally you would know what month it is – and what your flock are doing. They've barely seen you in two years. How will you answer to the bishop when he asks why you've been absent from mass? You're lucky to have Abbé Saunière to help."

A dark shadow crossed the priest's face. "Don't mention that man's name," he said angrily. "He haunts me, day and night."

"Such gratitude, after all he has done for you! Enough, I must go. I will see you in the morning." She left the room abruptly, and he heard the key turn in the front door.

Gelis picked up the basket, placed it on his desk and sat down wearily. He broke off a hunk of baguette and slowly started chewing on the rubbery bread, absent-mindedly leafing through the files Emilie had picked up.

The heavy clock on the wall ticked away the hours. Gelis ate more bread and cheese, then poured himself some wine, slurping greedily at the rich, blood-red liquid. After a while, he began to doze.

He awoke with a start. It was dark outside. In the distance he could see the flames from the village bonfires; hear the singing and chanting. Peasants! Still clinging to their pagan customs. He picked up the wine bottle and drained the dregs into his goblet. A noise made him stop abruptly, and he turned in his seat. There it was again; a strange scraping sound at the door. He got up from his seat and shuffled into the hallway.

"Is that you, Emilie?"

There was no reply and he turned back towards the study.

He heard the latch turn and a cold blast of night air entered the house.

"Emilie?" he called out again.

A heavy body cannoned into him and hurled him to the floor.

"Emilie! M'aidez, m'aidez!" He tried to shout out, but the air had gone from his lungs and his voice was feeble.

"You think anyone will hear you, tonight of all nights, old man?" A powerful hand tightened around his throat. "Now, tell me where you have hidden the papers."

"Papers? I don't know what…"

"Don't play dumb with me, Abbé. One way or the other, I want the papers. Anything and everything you have written about it. About her. I can make it easy or I can make it hard. It's up to you. But you will tell me."

"I cannot – the secret must survive, it cannot die with me or Saunière. The truth must be protected. The Church must be told, when the time is right…"

"The time will never be right for this… this heresy."

"Heresy or truth, that is for His Holiness to decide."

"Do you think the Pope wants this sacrilege to spread? This will go no further. Saunière is on borrowed time – he is lucky he has friends in high places. Now show me the evidence." The man dragged Gelis to his feet by the scruff of his neck and frogmarched him to the study. The Abbé tried to peer round at his attacker and glimpsed a clerical collar beneath the heavy cloak. The man gripped his head and turned it away.

"Mon dieu! You are a man of the cloth?"

"A true believer! Not a worshipper of Isis."

"She is not Isis! How dare you blaspheme against…"

A hand grabbed his throat once more. "Enough! Give me the papers." Gelis

2

held out his hands palms upwards in supplication and the hand released its grip.

"Very well. Now find them."

Gelis moved unsteadily towards his desk and began leafing through the untidy piles of papers. His eye rested on the candle that stood at one corner. Emilie had been right. They would burn easily.

With a sudden movement Gelis knocked the candle to the floor, where it fell among the scattered documents. They caught light instantly.

For a second the stranger hesitated, taken by surprise, then picked up a heavy poker from the grate and smashed it over the Abbé's head. Not waiting for him to fall, he pulled off his cloak and beat out the flames. He stood, panting, turning his attentions once more to Gelis.

The dazed priest was dragging himself forward towards the fireplace, his eyes focused on an axe that stood beside a pile of logs. The stranger leapt forward, and grabbing the axe from the reach of his outstretched fingers, brought it down on the priest's head again, and again and again.

He stood trembling, staring at the mutilated body before him, appalled at what he had done. Struggling to control his emotions, he made the sign of the cross before crouching down over the body.

"I am sorry, Abbé," he muttered. "I had no wish for this." He dragged the priest into the middle of the floor, straightened his limbs and placed his hands on his chest as if in prayer. Reaching under his own shirt, he pulled out a crucifix and signed himself once more. "*In nomine patris et filius et spiritus sanctus. Misereatur tui omnipotens Deus, et dimissis peccatis tuis, perducat te ad vitam aeternam. Indulgentiam, absolutionem et remissionem peccatorum nostrorum, tribuat nobis omnipotens et misericors Dominus.* Amen."

"It is for the greater good," he said quietly when he had finished, as if seeking absolution for his actions. Starting out of his reverie, he began rummaging through the piles of documents, throwing aside those of no interest.

An ever-bigger heap grew at his feet – scribblings, scrawlings, the ravings of a maniac, but not what he had come for… There was nothing, nothing. He looked frantically around the study and his eyes fell on a heavy, brass-bound Bible on a chest of drawers in the corner. Could that hold the key? It would be suitably sacrilegious. He struggled across the cluttered room, stumbling past tottering towers of books and grabbed the Bible, holding it open upside-down. Several loose pieces of paper fluttered to the ground. Remembering what he was holding, he placed the Bible to his lips and placed it reverently back on the chest before stooping to pick up the fallen papers.

"No. No, No, NO!…" He discarded the sheets with increasing frustration. Then he paused at one folded parchment much older than the rest. He opened it slowly and began to read.

His skin went pale and he began to tremble. "This cannot be… In the name of God, this cannot be!"

Chapter 2

"And as I was saying, this programme will shed dramatic new light on the mystery of Rennes-le-Château, and exactly what it was that Bérenger Saunière, the local priest, discovered there that made him so fabulously rich."

The interviewer turned to the attractive 30-something woman sitting at her side. "Rachel Spencer, you're leading this investigation for National Geographic. What is it you claim to have found?"

"Well, first let me give the viewers a little background about Rennes-le-Château," said Rachel, artfully tossing her mane of chestnut hair and smiling winningly at the camera. "There have been so many theories about this beautiful little village perched on a hill-top in south-west France... that it was the hiding place for treasure plundered from Rome by the Visigoths; that it holds the riches of the Knights Templar, who hid some of their immense wealth there; or that it is somehow linked to the mysterious Priory of Sion, which is claimed to have been guarding some dramatic, world-changing secret for centuries."

Rachel smiled at the presenter conspiratorially. "The story begins in the late 19th century, when the parish priest, Bérenger Saunière, a man of previously modest means, mysteriously started spending huge sums of money – he would have been a millionaire by today's standards.

"He renovated the village church, dedicated to St Mary Magdalene, at vast expense, and in the process included some unusual – one might even say bizarre – features. For instance, over the new porch there is an inscription that reads: '*Terribilis est locus iste*'. That's Latin for 'This place is terrible'. An odd inscription for a religious building.

"Then he built a stone tower that looks like something from a fairy-tale castle just to house his extensive book collection. He called this building La Tour Magdala, after Mary Magdalene. Her name means 'tower' in Hebrew, which is an odd coincidence, to say the least.

"He also built a grandiose new house for himself, the Villa Bethania, again, at considerable cost. The name is another Magdalene reference – Bethania is where the gospels say Mary lived with Martha and Lazarus. As well as restoring the church and building his quixotic tower, Saunière created some unusual gardens, laid out in strange geometric patterns. The total cost of his elaborate building programme is estimated to have been in the region of three-quarters of a million dollars in today's money, at a time when labour was cheap.

"Legend has it that Saunière's tale of rags to riches started when he was renovating the church and found a parchment hidden in a pillar under the old pulpit. According to one theory, this led him to find an ancient buried treasure – perhaps the lost treasure of the Templars, hidden when their order was outlawed by the King of France in 1307. Saunière later dug up half the graveyard looking for something.

"According to another theory, the parchment revealed a shocking secret about the Catholic Church which paid him to keep his silence. Saunière is known to have made a number of long-distance journeys, including several trips to Budapest – one of the twin capitals of the once mighty Austro-Hungarian empire – allegedly returning with a suitcase stuffed full of cash.

"The theories have become even more wild in recent years, with claims that the hidden treasure is none other than the Holy Grail or the Ark of the Covenant.

"The number of parchments Saunière is supposed to have discovered multiplied as the story spread – some have subsequently been exposed as fakes.

"There was also a tombstone in the churchyard of a noblewoman, Marie de Blanchefort, which appears to have contained a coded message. I say 'was' because Saunière deliberately destroyed it. Luckily, unknown to him it had already been recorded by a local historian. But even though the text is so odd it must have some hidden meaning, so far no-one has successfully deciphered it – at least, not in a way that makes any sense.

"What we do know, however, is that shortly after finding the original parchment in the pillar under the pulpit, Saunière found a hidden tomb inside the church. The discovery is recorded in his own diary on September 21st, 1891, six years after he took up his post as parish priest. He instructed two workers from the village to remove a stone slab in the floor in front of the altar, and underneath was a tomb.

"It seems he knew exactly where to look, so he must have been led there by a clue in the parchment. Two workmen saw him climb down into the tomb and return with a small pot of gold coins and jewellery. Saunière claimed they were worthless souvenirs from the nearby shrine of Lourdes – but he immediately dismissed the locals and completed the job with men from outside the area. All the evidence suggests Saunière found something pretty spectacular down there – but his obsessive behaviour was only just getting started. He was later censured by the mayor after villagers complained about him digging up the graveyard.

"To add to the enigma, the Church authorities did eventually discipline him, but for selling masses. There does seem to be some basis for this accusation, which, while not unusual for a priest at the time, was frowned upon. However, this could only account for a fraction of his wealth. After this censure Saunière resigned, but many villagers went to mass at a makeshift chapel attached to his villa, rather than attend church with the new priest.

"Where it really starts to get interesting, at least from the conspiracy theory point of view, is that Saunière allegedly told his secret to another local priest, Abbé Gelis, who became so paranoid about his own safety that he would only let his niece into the presbytery. Despite his precautions, however, he was murdered on All Hallows' Eve – but although the house was ransacked, nothing of value was taken and, bizarrely, the body was laid out by the attacker according to Catholic ritual.

"Saunière's long-serving housekeeper, Marie Dénarnaud – whom villagers referred to as his 'bit of skirt' – is also thought to have known the secret. The two were inseparable, and Saunière left everything to Marie in his will. It's claimed that after Saunière's death in 1917, she told local villagers they were 'walking on gold, and didn't know it'. According to some stories, when the French currency changed after the Second World War, she was seen burning heaps of banknotes so she didn't have to account for the origins of her wealth.

"Marie later suffered a serious stroke and was unable to talk before her death in 1953. However, her wealthy benefactor, Noel Corbu, whom she may have confided in, was later killed in a mysterious car crash."

The camera cut sharply to the presenter. "Fascinating stuff," she glowed. "I can see why you were able to persuade National Geographic to fund your research – it's going to make great TV. Now you told me before we came on air that you had made a ground-breaking new discovery that shed some light on all of this. What is that, exactly?"

"Well the dramatic news is that, thanks to the latest archaeological techniques, using ground-penetrating radar, we have found hard evidence of a crypt beneath the church. We think this is what Saunière discovered during his renovations, and we're hoping the crypt will contain some of the answers researchers have long been looking for. We know the original building dates back to the eighth or ninth century AD, and we also know it was at one time the official manorial chapel for the château.

"There are several historical references to local nobility being buried there, and one of Saunière's predecessors as priest of Rennes-le-Château, Abbé Bigou, referred directly to a crypt beneath the church 'dating to the times of the ancient kings' which he had deliberately sealed up so that 'documents did not fall into the wrong hands'."

"Mysteriouser and mysteriouser," said the presenter. "And what do you think those documents could be?"

"We can only speculate," said Rachel. "Perhaps they contain clues as to the whereabouts of hidden treasure, as some believe – or perhaps it's something more spiritual; some information the Church didn't want to get out."

"Obviously you're hoping to discover some treasure – to have your own Howard Carter moment!"

"That would be fantastic. But from an academic point of view, written treasures can be worth far more than any amount of gold – we're hoping to find clues that could lead to an even more spectacular discovery than hidden

Templar treasures. A discovery that would explain the hold Bérenger Saunière appears to have had over the Catholic Church."

"Tell us more!"

"I can't tell you too much at this stage – all will be revealed when the programme goes out this autumn. And we still haven't finished the excavations. But we have every reason to believe it will be pretty earth-shattering."

The interviewer turned back to the camera. "Well, it sounds as though the mysterious village of Rennes-le-Château is finally about to be give up its secrets. Will they find Templar treasures – or perhaps a shocking revelation that will rock the Church?"

The screen cut to a trailer of the National Geographic programme, with a stunning view of the hilltop town set against the looming presence of the Pyrénées, and a voice saying dramatically: "Is one of the last big mysteries of our times about to be laid bare?"

Rachel winced at the over-the-top production on the trailer, then flicked off the TV on the remote and started pacing up and down her hotel room.

It was way too cheesy, and she hated it – but he who pays the piper calls the tune... Bill Krakovitz from National Geographic had insisted on the interviews to raise the profile of the programme before it aired. "I want this on the front page of every newspaper in the western world," he had said in his clipped east coast accent. "And don't under-sell it. I've put a lot of faith – not to mention cash – into your pet project. Now it's pay-back time."

The phone rang on her bedside table. She hesitated before reaching over to pick it up. "Rachel Spencer..."

"Hi Rachel! That was pretty impressive!"

"Oh hi, Jon. Thanks. Actually I thought it was a bit gung-ho, but I suppose they've got to grab people's attention."

"They've certainly done that! Listen, how long are you in London for?"

"I'm heading back to Rennes tomorrow – we've got a deadline to meet. They want this to go out in the second week of September, at the start of the autumn season. You know what it's like."

"Sure. Look, what are you doing tonight? Fancy meeting up for a bite to eat?"

Rachel hesitated. She still felt guilty about leaving Jon, despite his oppressive, manipulative behaviour. He wanted to control her every move, to know where she was going and what she was doing. While he, of course, could do whatever the hell he wanted. It had come to a head over the contract with National Geographic in France. It wasn't the first time she had picked up an overseas assignment, but this time Jon had been totally bloody-minded.

In the end, she just snapped; walked out with Emma, their ten-year-old daughter, and went back to her mother's house. She knew it wasn't a good idea to meet up again so soon; that she had to go through with the split, for the sake of her own sanity. But she knew, too, that she had a duty to Emma. Whatever Jon's flaws as a husband, he was a loving father – when he chose to be around – and Emma needed that. It was something she herself had missed dreadfully when her own father had left home and returned to the States, a loss compounded by his sudden death in a plane crash just six months later.

"Rachel?"

"Sorry, just working out if I've got time. OK, I'll pop over, but I can't stay out late – I've got an early start tomorrow. But I suppose we could meet up in town for a quick curry, or something."

"Actually, if you can get yourself down here, there's a great little Italian place that's just opened. Family-run – a really friendly bunch."

"It's a bit of trek from Mum's…"

"Come on, it's ten minutes on the train from Waterloo. You can be here in half an hour."

* * * * *

Rachel fumed as she sat on the train while it crawled its way out of the station. Why had she agreed to meet up? It had been a nightmare getting across London on the tube. Why did she still feel so guilty about leaving him? There had been so many times when he had failed to come home after a night out with his mates. He claimed, of course, that he had crashed at a friend's house, drunk out of his mind, but she had nagging doubts. He was a good-looking guy; he wouldn't find it difficult to pick up women while he was out on the town.

Making her trek across London so they could meet close to his home was typical; unwilling and unable to put himself out for her, or anyone, for that matter – except, perhaps Emma.

Yet she knew the guilt would never go away. This was the guy who had supported her while she did her doctorate in archaeology – three years when she hadn't contributed a penny to their bills. The guy who had made her believe she really could be a TV researcher, and not just put up with the lame secretarial job she had drifted into after the triumph of getting her PhD dissolved into the drudgery of job-hunting. Guilt, too, that she was consciously and deliberately breaking up her family. Hell, why did he have to change? Was that just what happened after the sex fizzled out? God knows, she had tried to make an effort in that department.

Now he was making an attempt to win her back – something she had absolutely no intention of succumbing to. But he was comfortably familiar, and a big city could be a lonely place if you were single. She also felt obligated, on a purely practical level, to try to persuade Jon to ease the burden on her mother while she was away in France. There was that guilt again – Emma was his daughter, for God's sake; he had a duty to help look after her.

No doubt Jon would be quizzing her about Rennes. He was paranoiacally jealous about the men she worked with, so she would have to tread carefully. David Tranter, the lead archaeologist in Rennes, was a big name, and not just because of his undoubted skills. With his mane of golden curls and polished English charm, his first appearance on a TV documentary had quickly earned him the sobriquet of 'the thinking woman's crumpet'.

This was her big moment, and she didn't want Jon ruining it for her in a fit of petty jealousy. With a little luck, the programme might lead on to fame and fortune. She smiled at her own irony. She might be fleetingly famous after the documentary went out. But certainly not wealthy. That didn't matter, though: she was living out her passion: making history come alive.

She had grown up on a diet of National Geographic and the History Channel, and she had been obsessed with the HBO drama series on ancient Rome – though that might have been something to do with the hunky male actors. She just loved the past – the complex histories, the mysteries, the revelations. The more she had learned about past civilisations, the more she realised how little humanity had really advanced in the past few thousand years. Take technology out of the equation, and were we really that much more 'civilised'?

She fished her cell-phone out of her bag. "Jon? I'm on the train now. It took forever to get to Waterloo – problems on the Jubilee Line, as usual. Anyway, you're going to be there to meet me at Queenstown Road station, right? I'm not wandering through Battersea on my own at night."

"South Chelsea these days, darling – the next best thing to Notting Hill. But yes, I'm nearly there now."

"Right. See you soon."

Queenstown Road station was like something from a 1950s black and white movie; the taxpayers' money allegedly spent modernising the railways seemed to have passed this one by. She trudged down the worn steps in the dingy interior and emerged from a dilapidated doorway under a railway bridge.

She looked around, but could see no sign of Jon – late as usual. She stood there feeling lost and vulnerable, trying to blend into the background as a gang of adolescent males in hoodies walked past, leering at her.

"Rachel!"

She spun round and saw Jon waving at her from the other side of the street. She waited for a gap in the traffic and started to cross. As she neared the other side she became vaguely aware of the sound of a car gunning its engine and a screech of tyres. Something cannoned into her hard and fast, flinging her across the tarmac. She heard herself scream, saw a large granite kerbstone racing to meet her. Then everything went black.

9

Chapter 3

Bérenger Saunière, curé of Rennes-le-Château, took another long swig of Marie's famous home-made herbal liqueur and stared out of the window of La Tour Magdala, the quixotic faux medieval tower he had built next to his new villa. It was an icy January day with a biting north-easterly wind, and despite the blazing log fire in the study, he needed the potent liqueur to keep the cold from his bones.

He was weary. The war had made life difficult. No longer could he make his trips to Budapest to draw on the money deposited there by the Hapsburgs. Instead, he was living on the savings accrued from saying masses – quite legitimately, as far as he was concerned – for far-flung members of the Catholic flock who needed intercession with the Almighty. He grimaced as the word came into his mind: his view of that had certainly changed over the past 30 years.

He pushed his stamp album to one side, eased back his chair and moved stiffly across to the window. How he resented this increasingly infirm body; he who, as a young man, had walked many kilometres across the rugged terrain around Rennes-le-Château. Even that trip to Lourdes had proved a waste of time. Perhaps it was hardly surprising under the circumstances, but he found it hard to change beliefs so deeply ingrained during the formative years of his life.

His frown faded as he looked down from the window onto the countryside below. From here he could see the rich tapestry of hills and valleys that surrounded the village, and, beyond, the snow-bound peaks of the Hautes Pyrénées, glittering in the bright winter sunlight. It was a magnificent panorama, one that had inspired him to create the walkway between the two towers of his chessboard. Let someone figure that one out in years to come, he thought to himself with grim satisfaction.

A sound at the door made him turn, and he was surprised to see a well-dressed stranger enter the room.

"Do I have the pleasure of knowing, you, monsieur? I'm afraid my memory is not what it used to be…"

"No, you do not, Father Saunière," came the curt reply, in a clipped Germanic accent. "But I think you know who sent me."

"Ah! In that case we are indeed friends. Will you take a seat and have some liqueur? I can thoroughly recommend…"

"I did not come here in the dead of winter for a cosy fireside chat," interrupted the stranger brusquely. "I have come to tell you that our little arrangement is formally at an end. The war has changed everything, and it is no longer prudent or practical to let this charade continue. You will not, of course, have been able to get to Budapest, since France is at war with Austria-Hungary, but even if that had been possible, you would have found no funds in your account. The war is not going well, your prime minister Clemenceau is conspiring against us, and the new Emperor has bigger fish to fry. There will be no more 'donations' to your cause."

Saunière's gaze hardened, and he defied the rheumatism that plagued him to pull himself to his full height. "In that case, sir, you will not object if I share our little secret with my flock?"

The stranger crossed the room and stood in front of the priest, his eyes inches from his face. "I would not advise that, Saunière. You are not a well man – we heard about your trip to Lourdes, and rumour has it you are a little too fond of your housermaid's liqueur…" He turned his head to let his gaze fall on the half-empty bottle. "Not to mention her affections," he added, pointedly.

Saunière was visibly startled. "That's just salacious gossip," he blustered.

"Do you really think we would let you carry on your life as if nothing as happened – that we wouldn't take steps to ensure you kept your side of the bargain? How naive you really are, Saunière. You were once a well-read priest with a keen mind. Now you are reduced to trafficking in masses and playing with your little stamp collection. It has got beyond the point of embarrassment. You have been more than well paid for your services. If you will not, or cannot, keep your silence then steps will be taken to ensure your compliance."

"Are you threatening me?" said Saunière thickly, unable to take in what he was hearing.

"If you cannot hold your counsel, then yes, I am threatening you."

Saunière eyes misted red, the years of frustration and humiliation surging up in him. He lunged at the immaculately coiffured man and grabbed him by the throat, the huge strength of his youth momentarily returning as he exerted every sinew to keep his grip on the struggling man. The red mist grew darker, and a loud thrumming began in his ears. His head began spin, and as the noise in his ears grew, so the strength began to ebb from his limbs.

Slowly, centimetre by centimetre, the stranger prised apart the ageing priest's hands, then staggering to one side, slammed Saunière hard against the wall of the library, where he slid in a crumpled heap on the floor. The stranger doubled up, clutching his bruised throat, a thick string of saliva hanging from his mouth, his breath rasping. Slowly he regained his composure, and stumbling across to Saunière's desk, grabbed the liqueur bottle and took a deep swig.

He gasped and shook his head as the fiery liqueur burned his throat, but there was a jolt of awareness as the alcohol hit his bloodstream. He walked across to where the priest's body lay slumped on the cold, tiled floor and bent down to feel his pulse. Still alive. That would not do. Time to be rid of this meddlesome curé once and for all. He splashed some of the liqueur on Saunière's shirt, then put the bottle back on his desk. Grabbing him under the arms, he started dragging him across the floor. The priest was a big man, grown heavier through years of self-indulgence, and it took several minutes to haul his body to the door. The stranger paused momentarily for breath, then heaved Saunière's body over the step into the glass porch and let it fall by the doorway to the promenade.

He stood up, breathing heavily, and straightened his neck-tie. Then, leaving the door wide open, he stalked out into the bitterly cold January afternoon without so much as a backward glance.

Chapter 4

Pain punctuated every waking thought. An intense, throbbing pain that gripped her skull like a vice and threatened to crush it. When she tried to open her eyes it felt as if a knife were being twisted in her brain.

It was too much. There must be somewhere she could go, somewhere far away from this torture. She gave up the struggle and let her mind wander. That was better; the pain was going away now; far, far away. As she drifted towards the light, a feeling of great peace spread slowly through her being. All her cares, all her troubles, all the stress, all the pain, all the heartache… she was leaving it behind as surely as a receding tide leaves its detritus on the beach. She was heading out to sea; floating; bathed in that glorious white light. Far back on the land she could see vague outlines of people, places she had known, growing further away, becoming blurred.

She was vaguely aware of a man's face getting closer; a caring, loving face, full of compassion. It was her father, she realised, in a detached kind of way. As the realisation sank in, her spirit soared with delight. To see him again! How she had missed him… This time, she knew intuitively, when they met again there would be no parting.

But her father's face was changing; slowly morphing into someone else. "No!" she shrieked in a voice no-one could hear. "Not again! I can't lose you again." The face was becoming recognisable, now; not someone she had ever met, but a face she knew, nonetheless. It was as if in a painting, a life-drawing; not a photographic image… But why did she know that face? Where was it from? It had the look of a religious icon… Something she had seen in a church… A young woman… But not the Virgin Mary – there was no baby Jesus. Instead the woman seemed to be holding a white jar in her hands.

The Magdalene! A sudden realisation dawned, and as it did so it seemed as if the woman spoke to her, though no words passed her lips. A thought entered her mind; a thought given voice. "Find me," it seemed to be saying. "Find the truth. The time has come for my story to be told."

"Quick, we're losing her!"

The words cut through her ecstasy. She became aware of a hive of activity around her body as it lay stretched out beneath her. She could see nurses rushing around frantically – one grabbing a syringe, another wheeling a trolley laden with a large instrument towards her body, a third person in green surgical coveralls standing over her, doing something with the syringe. Strange pads with trailing wires were being placed on her naked chest… Why could she see her body lying beneath her like that? Interesting… but so much

13

nicer back where she had come from. Let me go back, she thought, to no-one in particular. And then the pain returned, this time ripping into her chest like a projectile, her body arching off the trolley as 3,000 volts of electricity punched into her heart. Her eyes jerked open and the stabbing in her skull returned, doubled in intensity. She heard herself scream.

"She's back! OK, keep up the adrenalin, but no more morphine – we can't risk losing her again."

"Rachel." A woman's voice echoed around her head as her face loomed in front of her half-open eyes. "I need you to stay with us. You must stay awake."

"I'll try," she mumbled through bruised and swollen lips. "I'll try…"

Chapter 5

Marie Dénarnaud couldn't stop herself from worrying. It was not like her Bérenger to be late for supper – especially when he knew she had been preparing one of her rabbit stews, for which her reputation had spread throughout the village. Bérenger was certainly a man who enjoyed his food and drink – perhaps a little too much, if truth be told.

It was nearly dusk, and he should have been back by now for his usual pre-dinner pastis. He had probably dozed off in front of the fire; too much of her herbal liqueur, no doubt. It wouldn't be the first time he had nodded off in the afternoon with a few glasses inside him, but she couldn't help feeling a little uneasy.

Another half-hour passed, and Marie could wait no longer. Bérenger didn't like to be disturbed, and he could be an impatient man, but it was now well past the hour when they would normally eat. She put a thick woollen shawl over her black dress to guard against the cruel wind that whipped around the village in winter and went out of the presbytery. She stumbled as a fierce gust caught her unawares, and pulling the shawl closer around her, bent her head and walked purposefully across to La Tour.

She was still some yards away when she noticed the porch door banging in the wind, and knew instantly that something was wrong. She hurried forward as best she could against the strong gusts, and reached the porch to see Bérenger's body lying just inside the door. She put her hand to her mouth with a gasp of dismay, and crossing herself, stooped down beside her beloved priest. Hesitatingly, fearful of the worst, she reached out her hand and touched his face. He was cold and clammy, but perhaps there was still some life there. She picked up his hand and felt at his wrist: there was a pulse; feeble, but a pulse nonetheless.

She grasped him by the shoulders and desperately tried to drag the big man back into the library where the fire was still flickering, but it was a hopeless task for the petite housemaid. She put her hands to her face once more, fighting back the tears. What could she do? She must get help. She stood up and went into the study, where she found the blanket Bérenger put over his knees on a cold winter's day. She draped it over his body, then shutting the door behind her, hurried across the presbytery gardens to the village.

"Jacques, Jacques!" shouted Marie hoarsely as she ran in through the back door of the boulangerie. The baker's wife was clearing the table after supper and looked up startled as Marie stumbled breathlessly into the room. "Annette – where's Jacques? He must come quickly; the curé's had a fall. He's lying in the porch of La Tour – the door was wide open, and he's frozen half to death.

I can't move him – please, please, get Jacques to come right away."

Annette collected her senses. "He's next door, making the dough. Sit yourself down – don't worry, Marie, I'm sure the curé will be all right." She went out of the room and returned a few moments later with her husband. Marie grasped him by the hands agitatedly. "Please, Jacques, you must help – it's the curé…"

"I know, Marie, Annette told me. He turned to put on his thick winter coat. "Venez! We'll grab Jean-Luc on the way. The curé is no featherweight – it will take two of us to carry him to the house."

With the wind now at their back, it took only a few minutes for the three of them to reach the tower, where the priest still lay stretched out under the blanket, his face a horrible shade of pale.

"Mon dieu – he looks in a bad way," muttered Jean-Luc, the village odd-job man, crossing himself. "Perhaps we should put him in front of the fire for a while," he said, nodding in the direction of the open door to library, from where the warmth of the fire could still just be felt. It had probably kept Saunière alive.

"No, no!" protested Marie. "We must get him to the presbytery. I cannot care for him here! He needs to be in bed."

"She's right, Jean-Luc," said Jacques. "Let's get him to his bed – and then someone had better get down to Rennes-les-Bains and fetch Dr Courrent."

* * * * *

For more than 36 hours, Saunière lay in a coma, teetering on the threshold of life and death. Then, finally, on the third day, the ministrations of Marie and Dr Courrent began to bear fruit, and the priest stirred into consciousness.

"Bérenger, Bérenger – I've been so worried." Marie reached across and stroked his face gently. She had rarely left his bedside since they had brought him back, except to refresh the warming pan with coals from stove.

"We found you on the floor in the porch of La Tour! The doctor says you've had a seizure – you were almost frozen to death. Were you heading back for supper? What happened, chérie – can you remember anything?"

The room slowly came into focus and Saunière saw the terror in Marie's eyes. He forced his face into smile to reassure her. This was the woman he had loved for 30 years; the woman who, despite his calling, had become his most intimate companion, and partner in everything he did. He could not bear to see her so distraught.

He struggled to move his lips, but could only mumble incoherently. His mind was clear, though. He knew he would not be long for this world – but Marie? As the memories flooded back, his mind raced. What would become of his beloved Marie? She knew too much… they had done everything together. Would the Hapsburgs stoop to killing her, too? To kill a woman – they could not... they would not – surely. Nonetheless, it would pay to be prudent. He couldn't risk the truth getting out now, not in Marie's lifetime; they must destroy the evidence. And as for future generations... well, he had left plenty of clues for those with inquiring minds. Saunière allowed himself a wry smile.

Over the course of the next day, village gossip ran wild as the diminutive figure of Marie Dénarnaud was seen tending a small bonfire of papers outside the curé's ground-floor bedroom, from where he could keep an eye on proceedings. But what was she burning – and why? Were these secrets that Saunière would take to his grave, or did Marie know, too?

Finally, on Sunday, January 21, 1917, Saunière sent for a fellow priest to hear his last confession. When Abbé Rivière of Espéraza arrived, however, the tongues began to wag even more. Here was a priest whom Saunière was known to dislike – and the feeling was apparently mutual. Yet he had called on him to perform the final sacrament. What was going on in the poor man's mind?

Marie ushered Rivière into his colleague's bedroom. "Saunière! I'm sorry to see you this way," he said with genuine sympathy.

"I am dying, Rivière," said Saunière hoarsely. "I would be confessed."

"Nonsense – I'm sure you will be well again soon, Bérenger..."

"Don't waste your breath, Rivière! Death is stalking me, and you know it. Now will you confess me, and give me the final sacrament?"

"Of course, if that is your wish."

"Then sit, and let me talk. This may take a little while."

An hour passed before the door to the bedroom was flung open, and Abbé Rivière emerged, pale and shaken. "This cannot be," he raged, slamming the door behind him.

"Monsieur l'Abbé, what is it?" said Marie, jumping up from her chair by the stove.

"That man – he is the Devil himself! I will not give him the sacrament, I will not!" He stood in front of her, visibly agitated. Then a sudden realisation dawned. "Did you know this, Marie – did you know this... this... blasphemy?" he exploded.

"Blasphemy?" she queried. But her voice was too measured.

"You know! You're in on this, too."

"We cannot pick and choose the truth," she said obliquely.

"You're as bad as Saunière," snapped the Abbé, snatching his cloak from the stand. "I'll not stay in this Devil's house a moment longer."

A small crowd of villagers had gathered close to the presbytery, partly out of loyalty to the dying curé, partly out of curiosity. As Abbé Rivière stormed out of the building, a murmur went up.

"Is the Abbé dead?" asked one villager, as the angry priest pushed his way through the throng.

"He is not, madame, but he might as well be," replied Riviére. Climbing into his trap, he motioned the driver to start on his way.

Chapter 6

For several days, bruising and swelling to her brain left Rachel's life hanging in the balance. The doctors fought hard for her, inducing a coma to minimise brain injury, while her mother, brother and Jon took turns keeping a vigil at her bedside. They talked to her, holding her hand and chatting as if she were still listening to them – which the doctors told them was theoretically possible.

It was the visits from her daughter, however, which helped her turn the corner, and as the doctors eased back on the sedation, it was Emma's face she had seen first through drug-hazed, half-closed eyes.

The consultant later admitted she had been concerned about the possibility of long-term brain damage – particularly short-term memory impairment – but it was soon obvious that Rachel's mental acuity was unaffected. "You're one lucky girl," the doctor had told her. "I have to admit, I didn't rate your chances of making any kind of recovery very highly, let along a full return of all your mental faculties in such a short space of time. You're obviously made of stern stuff."

It had taken four weeks in hospital and a month of recuperation at home before Rachel was well enough to consider returning to France. She had stayed with her mother at first, still in need of practical help, but after a couple of weeks with her mum endlessly fussing around her, she succumbed to Jon's entreaties to stay with him for a few days. Since he was looking after Emma, it had given Rachel the chance to spend some time with her daughter.

Jon had never been far from her side throughout her stay in hospital, and while before the accident he had been hinting at a reconciliation, he now put the idea firmly on the table shortly before she was discharged. If truth be told, in her vulnerable state, the possibility of 'turning back the clock' on their relationship had its appeal.

However, just a few days of enduring Jon's pompous, arrogant preaching was enough to remind her why she had left him in the first place. OK, she was being a bitch. Jon was concerned; he had been there in her hour of need. But his self-centred attitude to life was goddamned annoying, and as a couple they were completely incompatible. There could be no going back.

Of the driver who so nearly cut short her life, there was no sign. "I'm afraid we get so many hit-and-runs these days," the police officer had told her while she was recovering in hospital. "Unless we get a definite 'plate', it's hard to track them down – and even then, half the time the car's been stolen. By the time we find it, the culprit's long gone."

Because of her fractured skull, Rachel was under strict instructions not to go back to work for at least four weeks, and to take extreme care in everything she did. For a woman as active as Rachel, it was a frustrating time. The dig was continuing without her under David Tranter, and National Geographic had been sympathetic about her plight. The TV schedule was pushed back a month to October, and since the dig was progressing more slowly than expected, they were quite relaxed about the situation. Of course, as a freelance she wasn't getting sick pay – but that was the least of her worries.

Then in July, just a few days before she was due to fly back to the Languedoc, Rachel received the news she had been dreading.

"Hey babe, how are you doing?" David Tranter's cheery voice immediately brought a smile to her face and lifted the gloom of being virtually housebound for the past month. "Hope you're feeling a bit better than last time I saw you. I have to confess you had me worried, there."

"I'm good, thanks, David – the doctors say I'm making great progress. Champing at the bit to get back out there – going out of my mind with boredom while you're having all the fun."

"Well, there's not too much excitement going on here at the moment, just lots of cataloguing and other boring stuff – you know what it's like. The big excitement was finding the crypt with the ground-radar when no-one was even sure it existed – you were here for that…" His voice trailed off.

"What's the matter?"

"You're not going to like this."

Rachel's heart sank. "Like what?"

"We've had a bit of a setback. It seems the Church is getting a bit funny about letting us into the crypt."

"Well that's hardly a surprise – we're only digging outside the church because they wouldn't let us excavate the interior. We'll bluff them. That was always the plan – they can't turn us down with the whole world watching."

"I know. But it seems that having failed to stop us digging outside, they're determined not to let us into the crypt – at least, not without going in there first themselves. And I don't just mean the local clergy; this is now being taken up at the highest level."

"But that's outrageous – we've done all the hard work, now they want to go and steal our thunder!"

"Actually, that's my biggest fear – that they might try to steal or cover up any evidence they find. Anyway, I've set up a meeting with them next week, so we can discuss a plan of action when you get here."

Chapter 7

Rachel wriggled uncomfortably on the hard, stony ground. Beads of moisture clung to the inside of the tent wall over her head as the pounding rain permeated the canvas, swelling slowly before bursting and dropping onto her damp sleeping bag. The forecasters had predicted glorious sunshine for the Languedoc; the gods, it seemed, had other ideas. A brilliant streak of lightning lit up the sky, followed seconds later by a deafening peal of thunder. Rachel started to feel a little nervous.

She had only been back for two days – now this. It was not supposed to be how things turned out. With the dig running behind schedule, the tourist season at Rennes-le-Château was now in full swing, and the team's lease on the gîte they were using had run out.

The ancient hill-top village, with its derelict castle, narrow, winding streets, old stone houses and stunning views across to the Hautes Pyrénées, was a natural magnet for holidaymakers at this time of year. Add to that the legend of a mysterious priest, buried treasure and the enduring myth of the Templars and the Holy Grail, and it was a formula for a mass influx of visitors, who arrived daily by the coach-load.

The team had been faced with the choice of taking lodgings further afield or camping on site. In the end they had done both; finding rooms at a guest house in nearby Rennes-les-Bains for showers and somewhere to keep their spare clothes, but also pitching some tents next to the churchyard so they could keep an eye on the dig now their goal was in sight.

The more extreme treasure hunters who had plagued Rennes for the past 40 years – in some cases even using dynamite when they found a promising site – would have dismantled the church stone by stone, given half a chance. They wouldn't think twice about robbing an archaeological dig.

Another crack of lighting split the sky, closely followed by the sound of running feet. Then the zip to her tent suddenly ripped open and a body tumbled inside.

"What the hell?" said Rachel, rolling away from the flap.

"It's OK, it's only me," came a male voice. "I just wanted to check you were OK."

"David! I'm not exactly sweet 16 any more – I can look after myself. What if someone saw you? The bush telegraph will be working overtime."

"In this?" he said, grinning, shaking the moisture from his shock of golden curls.

"Well, since you're here, I suppose you might as well stay a moment," said Rachel. Still feeling vulnerable after the accident, she was secretly pleased to have his reassuring presence at her side. "Just don't get any ideas."

"I used to be terrified of thunder when I was a boy," said David, ignoring her jibe.

"Really? And there was me thinking you were the new Indiana Jones."

"Ah, that's only the superficial me. Scratch the surface and you'll find I'm quite a sensitive soul."

"Hmm. I'll bear that in mind."

Another bolt of lightning lit the skies with an eerie brilliance.

"So how did you lose your fear of thunderstorms?" asked Rachel quickly.

"My mother told me to listen for the time gap between the lightning and the thunder. The bigger the gap, the further away the lightning. She said it was a mile for every second, though I've no idea if that's true. Anyway, concentrating on counting the seconds takes your mind off things. And then when you notice the delay increasing, it's reassuring because you know the storm's moving away."

"Clever mum. So where's the storm right now?"

A shaft of light lit the tent as if it were day, followed a split second later by a deafening peal of thunder that made the ground shake underneath them.

Rachel threw herself, sleeping bag and all, into David's arms.

"I'd say that was right overhead," said David softly, his lips brushing her hair. "Don't worry. You're going to be fine."

Rachel woke wearily the next morning to find herself alone in the tent, the sound of activity all around her. She looked at her watch. 10 o'clock! She struggled out of her sleeping bag, pulled on her clothes and stumbled out of the tent to find the camping field had become a quagmire.

She spotted David's tousled head near the portable building that housed all their tools and equipment and plodded across to him, the mud sucking at her loosely tied boots. "Hey!" she said. "You started without me."

"We haven't all got time for a lie-in. Anyway, you're still recuperating."

"I'm fine!" she said indignantly. "But thanks for last night," she added, sotto voce. "Just don't think it gives you an open invitation to come into my tent in the middle of the night."

"You're welcome! And I wouldn't dream of it. Now grab yourself some breakfast, and I'll see you in the museum in half an hour."

The team had negotiated space at the Villa Bethania, the luxurious mansion built at considerable expense by the secretive 19th century priest Bérenger Saunière and now owned by the town council, where they stored their finds and carried out the tedious process of cataloguing. The council was more than happy to have the National Geographic team on hand, throwing an even greater spotlight on a story that had proved a veritable money-spinner for the village over many years.

The villa also acted as a ticket office and bookshop for the museum, which now occupied the old presbytery where Saunière had lived and died. Despite building the grandiose villa, which he used for lavish entertaining, the priest always slept in the presbytery.

Rachel snatched a quick coffee and croissant from the makeshift canteen and was in the finds room 20 minutes later.

"Hi Rachel," said David, looking up from an artefact he was examining. "I've just had an interesting phone call. You'll never guess who it was from."

"It's too early in the morning for guessing games," said Rachel, irritated. "Are you going to enlighten me?"

"What if I told you it was from the Vatican?"

"You've got to be kidding me!"

"Absolutely not. As you know, so far I have been liaising with the Bishop of Carcassonne, Monsigneur Billard, over the dig. But who should I get a phone call from while you're munching on your croissant but the Pope's personal private secretary."

"No way!"

"Indeed. Not only that, it seems that the person coming to inspect the crypt is none other than a papal legate. He's going to be here at 10am on Wednesday morning. It shows how seriously they are taking this whole thing. I guess with an arch-conservative pontiff holding the keys to the Holy See, they aren't taking any chances on what might be inside that crypt. Apparently the official's title is legatus missus – literally 'sent legate', possessing limited powers for the purpose of completing a specific mission. He will decide whether we can go into the crypt or not, and if so under what conditions."

"And what if we can't agree terms?"

"As we've said before, it all comes down to who blinks first. But the Vatican seems to be playing hard ball on this one. They're used to accusations of being reactionary, and may not care about the media storm that would follow if they refused us permission to go in there. If we're not careful, there's a risk they could end up calling our bluff."

"Damn! That only gives us today and tomorrow to come up with a solution," said Rachel, thumping the door frame of the finds room in exasperation. She paused, her eyes screwed up in frustration, before exhaling sharply. "OK, we need to change our game plan here, and fast. In case we can't get into the crypt, let's go around the church while there's still no-one watching and make sure we haven't missed any vital clues."

"Clues? What good will that do us?"

"I don't know exactly, I've just got a gut feeling there's a way through here; something we may have overlooked."

"Female intuition? Well, I suppose we've nothing to lose."

They went out of the Villa Bethania, a classic Second Empire double-fronted mansion, and walked the few yards to the church that Saunière had so enthusiastically restored and redesigned at vast expense. Little evidence remained that the building dated back to the eighth or ninth century save for the semi-circular Romanesque apse at the eastern end of the building, so typical of the ancient village churches of the Languedoc.

They stopped in front of the porch with its gaudy yellow frieze around the edge of the roof.

"What wonderful taste this guy had," said Rachel scathingly.

"You can say that again."

"You know one thing that I don't understand is why Saunière spent so much time and money remodelling the church. I mean, the hideously distasteful redecoration one can understand, in the context of the times. He had the cash, from where we know not, and he obviously had some kind of epiphany as a result of what he discovered here. But why rebuild the altar and move the pulpit?"

"Trying to make his humble village church look more grandiose – part of the renovation scheme?" ventured David.

"Possibly," said Rachel. "But I'm still not convinced. And then there's the sacristy – why did he build that little semi-circular extension on the side? No-one ever went in there apart from him, if comments by local villagers at the time are to be believed."

"I've heard a theory from some French archaeologists that the sacristy was built after Saunière discovered the crypt. They think it contains a hidden entrance so he could go down there whenever he wanted."

"I suppose that's a possibility. But if that's the case, why did no-one find the crypt before now? And why are there no signs of an entrance to the crypt inside the church, either from the sacristy or anywhere else?"

"I agree it's odd," nodded David. "It was one of the first things we looked for. But then we've not been allowed to dig inside the church, whereas Cholet did uncover the start of a stairway leading downwards during his excavations. But for some reason he didn't explore further."

"Perhaps he wasn't allowed to."

"Perhaps. But wouldn't he also have been pressurised not to even mention it in his report?"

"The whole thing's odd," mused Rachel. "The more I find out about this place, the less I know. What was it Churchill said about Russia? 'It is a riddle, wrapped in a mystery, inside an enigma.' That describes Rennes perfectly."

"But he also said, 'Perhaps there is a key'."

"Well talking of keys, let's start with the obvious – the keystone in the door arch. *Terribilis est locus iste* – 'This place is terrible'. An odd welcome for church-goers, don't you think? I know it comes from the Old Testament, and some people say it simply means 'this place is awesome', in the old-fashioned sense of the word. But does that fit in with the pattern of Saunière's thinking? There are little idiosyncrasies scattered all over this church, and the domain he built around it – the gardens, the towers, the villa itself. Nothing is quite what it seems. That phrase isn't there by coincidence. Could it be that the church is guarding a 'terrible' secret?"

"Well, it's clearly a possibility. If he discovered something that would embarrass the Church, and they were paying him to keep his mouth shut, it could explain where the money was coming from."

"But he didn't want the information lost forever," said Rachel, thinking out loud, "so he left clues. If we could piece them together, it might give us an idea what is hidden in that crypt."

"As an atheist, religious symbolism isn't my strong suit," said David drily.

"I should have guessed you were an atheist – you're just the type."

"What type is that, then?"

"I don't know – heavily sceptic; always reducing things to their empirical basics; refusing to accept the possibility that something might not conform to the laws of Newton and Darwin."

"Sounds pretty much like me!"

"Oh. I guess I misjudged you, then," said Rachel, a hint of disappointment in her voice.

"Being an atheist isn't a crime, is it?"

"No, it's just… Never mind. Let's get on with this. Is there anything in that stone relief of Mary Magdalene above the door that looks odd to you?"

"Not that I can see. You would expect to see a statue of Mary on the front of a Catholic church dedicated to her, and all that 'cake icing' around her is pretty much what you would expect from a 19th century neo-Gothic restoration."

"That 'icing', as you put it – it's a bit unusual to have a turret popping up out of the corner of the statue, isn't it?"

"Doesn't Magdala mean 'tower' in Hebrew?"

"Sure, but it's totally out of place in that relief – and it also looks just like La Tour Magdala across the way."

David stared at the sculpture, shielding his eyes from the bright sunlight. "Now that you mention it, it does seem a little odd. Maybe it's a reference to La Tour. But why? I guess we'll have to see if it ties in with anything else. It's a start, anyway."

They walked inside the church they had come to know so well, trying to look at its exotic array of statuary with fresh eyes.

"Well, the first thing that hits you is our friend here," said David, gesturing towards the hideous statue of the crouching Devil immediately inside the door. "A rude welcome for parishioners, don't you think?"

"Yes – though it was all about fire and brimstone in those days, wasn't it? There's a church in Barcelona with a similar statue, where the Devil is being defeated by the archangel Michael. Here you've got a group of angels above him with the cross – all female, I might add – and the inscription Par ce signe tu le vaincras, 'By this sign you will vanquish him'. But isn't the usual phrase found in French churches just Par ce signe tu vaincras – without the 'him'?

25

That's what over the door outside, above Mary's statue."

They went back out and had another look. "Actually, it's in Latin here," said David. "In hoc signo vinces, 'By this sign, you will conquer'. It's what the Roman emperor Constantine is alleged to have heard when he saw the sign of the cross before the Battle of Milvian Bridge, which led to his conversion to Christianity. But you're right, there's no reference to the 'him' in the inscription above the Devil."

"I wonder if adding the two letters 'le' in French is part of a code, or something," said Rachel, counting out the letters on her hands. "The extra two letters bring the total to 22… Does that mean anything to you?"

"Not that I can think of."

"There's something else I can't figure out – the 'BS' seal stamped on the crest above his head. Are those really Bérenger Saunière's initials, as most people seem to think – or is it some kind of code?"

"Bull Shit, perhaps?" said David, with heavy irony. He wandered into the nave, gazing around the flamboyantly decorated church. His eye caught the Stations of the Cross placed at regular intervals on both sides. "If there are any clues here, it's a given he will have done something with these," he said, turning to Rachel. "Not to mention the statues of the saints. We should be writing this down and cross-referencing it. And I'd like to mark out on a plan where all this stuff is" – he waved a hand at the garish statuary – "so we've got a contextual reference. I'll go and get the Nikon and take some close-ups of these oddities. Perhaps something will come to us. Don't go away, I'll be back in a second."

Rachel mooched over to look at some of the 14 Stations of the Cross. They seemed pretty typical of 19th century religious art – over-the-top, sugar-icing artefacts. David returned to find her poring over Station IV, where Jesus meets his mother. "This is odd," she said, glancing round. "What's that behind the soldier's spear? It looks like a sail to me."

"Odd shape for a sail," said David, threading his way along the pew to join her. "Sails from that era were square, not diamond-shaped," he said, peering over her shoulder. "Are you sure it's not some kind of banner attached to the spear?"

"If that's the case, why don't the spears that appear in some of the other stations have a banner, too? If you look closely, it seems to be attached to a tall wooden pole by some rigging."

"Maybe. But even if it were, what's the relevance? Ah, you're thinking of the French connection, aren't you?" he said with heavy sarcasm. "The legend that Mary Magdalene came to France to escape persecution."

"Yes," said Rachel defiantly. "It's perfectly feasible. If Mary had fled Palestine, she would have wanted to escape to the further reaches of the Roman Empire – Gaul, now France, would have been ideal, just across the Mediterranean. One local tradition has it that Mary and several companions crossed the Mediterranean in a small boat and landed in France. So maybe Saunière is hinting at something here."

" 'Just across the Mediterranean'?" said David incredulously. "It's the best part of 2,000 miles from Palestine to France! It would have taken them at least three weeks if they sailed non-stop, longer if they stopped off en route to pick up supplies and shelter from storms. It's a pretty long shot."

"We know merchant ships travelled those routes in that era – there's evidence of Mediterranean trade with Britain going back to the Bronze Age, let alone France in Roman times."

"Yes, but the legend is that she came in a small boat, not a cargo vessel! Come on, let's be scientific about this."

"Maybe she was on a merchant ship – maybe they put her off in a small boat when they reached France to avoid awkward questions from the Roman authorities. Legends often get distorted, but there's usually a grain of truth in them. OK, you want to be scientific, let's be scientific. You've got the writing pad – let's mark down all the statues, stations and paintings around the church, annotate any irregularities against each one, and see what we get."

It took them the best part of an hour to carefully measure out a floor plan and mark down the relative position of the statues.

"Look," said David, "we're not going to have time to go through all the Stations of the Cross in detail before the church closes. Let me photograph them now, while it's still light, and we can go through them this evening."

Rachel took the A4 pad and studied their notes, while David started walking round systematically, taking photos. Why this obsession with saints, she thought? She had never understood the need for the pantheon of saints when the central message revolved around just one person. Was it a throwback to pagan times; a substitute for the myriad gods and goddesses that fell victim to Rome's new monotheistic religion?

Looking at the sketch of the floor-plan, she noticed that the statue of Mary Magdalene inside the church was situated half-way along the wall, next to that of an obscure local saint, St Roch, rather than nearest the altar. Instead, pride of place was reserved for St Anthony of Padua. She looked at the other saints to see if there was any particular order. Opposite St Anthony, at the back of the pulpit, was St Luke. Next was St Anthony the Hermit, then St Germaine, then back to the other side again.

She picked up David's pencil and idly started sketching lines between the statues to see if there was any kind of pattern to their positions. After a few minutes she froze, digging the pencil into the pad in astonishment. "Hey, look at this," she shouted at David, who had disappeared behind the altar. "David!"

He reappeared a few moments later. "What's the panic?"

"These statues that we've marked down – look at the way they're arranged."

"What about them?"

"Look! "She turned the pad around. What shape is that?"

"An M, I guess. Oh, please tell me you're not thinking of the Magdalene again… It could just as easily be a W."

"But look at what's at the apex of the M! It's the statue of Mary herself – it has to be this way up. Saunière left nothing to chance – we know he was a pedant for detail, micro-managing the entire restoration process. He had the Calvary cross in the churchyard taken down and rebuilt twice before he was satisfied. Why isn't Mary at the front of the church? It's dedicated to her, after all. Instead, we've got St Anthony of Padua up by the altar. There's a reason for all this."

"Even if it is an M, what does it prove? The guy was obsessed with Mary Magdalene; that much is pretty obvious."

Rachel looked crestfallen. "Maybe you're right. Perhaps I'm just getting carried away, like everyone else who comes here."

"Don't beat yourself up. It's pretty easy to start jumping to conclusions in a place like this – hell, it's a real-life computer game. Come on, I think we've got everything we need, and they'll be locking up soon. Let's go back to the chambre d'hôte, get scrubbed up and download these pictures to the laptop. Then we can go through them over dinner."

"Sounds like a plan. And I don't know about you, but after last night's firework display, I'm staying at Rennes-les-Bains. I'm sure Guy can keep an eye on things."

Chapter 8

It was a 20-minute drive to the chambre d'hôtes at Rennes-les-Bains, the small spa town nestling in the valley below Rennes-le-Château, that had sprung up around the thermal springs that bubbled up from volcanic strata far below the surface. The site of an extensive Roman bath-house, the town acquired a reputation in the Middle Ages as a place where lepers could come to bathe and be cured of their disease. It reached its heyday in Victorian times with the arrival of the railway just a few miles away at Couiza, and rapidly became popular as a station thermale, with the waters said to be a cure-all for everything from TB to gout. Sadly it had now seen better days, the faded facades and peeling paintwork of its grand old buildings a testament to the town's steep decline in prosperity.

Rachel squeezed her car across the tiny bridge over the Sals river and managed to find a space outside the little guest house, Au Coeurs de Rennes. Feeling grubby and tired, she headed straight for the shower, then poured a generous glass of red wine. After a few gulps she felt ready to return to the fray.

She fired up her MacBook and started scouring the internet, trying to find as much background information as possible on the interior of the church.

They had carried out several weeks of preliminary research on Rennes-le-Château before starting the assignment, and knew many of the theories – some downright wacky, others more plausible. But there was such a web of confusion it was almost impossible to separate fact – or at least, serious theories – from fiction. Historical accounts had become exaggerated and conflated with conjecture, while new theories appeared out of thin air without any reliable sources – and were subsequently reported as fact. It was almost as if there were a conspiracy to hide the truth.

It was for this reason they had decided to focus the documentary on the excavation of the crypt. There had been little doubt as to its existence, or National Geographic would not have gone ahead. There had, after all, been that excavation in 1967, when French archaeologist Professor Cholet had been given permission to carry out excavations inside the church on the strength of an 18th century document in which Abbé Bigou referred to a 'Tomb of the Lords' under the church.

Bizarrely, however, despite finding the entrance to three passages – one under the stairs to the pulpit, one in the sacristy and one in Saunière's Secret Room, Cholet decided to block everything up again without going further, claiming to have run out of funds. He returned a few years later, thanks to a wealthy benefactor, but mysteriously confined his excavations to the area

29

in front of the altar, where nothing was found. He made no attempt to re-excavate the staircases he had discovered. Just another strand in the enigma that was Rennes-le-Château.

Rachel opened her translation of the Cholet report to remind herself of what he had found. Most of his typewritten findings, amounting to nine pages, were devoted to recounting the historical background to Rennes-le-Château and its transition from the site of an ancient Gaulish temple to a stronghold for the Visigoths after they sacked and plundered Rome. Its population was estimated at some 30,000 inhabitants – an incredible number for such a tiny hilltop location. It was claimed that when the Saracens attacked from Spain, the Visigoths escaped through underground passages. Had they taken their treasures with them, or were they still in the crypt? But she was convinced there was more than just gold buried under the church.

She read on, refreshing her memory. Rennes, then known as Rédé, did not come to light again in the history books until the Albigensian Crusade, when it was a Cathar stronghold. However, it fell early in the campaign to the armies of the sadistic baron Simon de Montfort in around 1212. The town was destroyed at least twice more after the crusade: once during the 100 Years War with the English, and again during the Wars of Religion, when it was razed to the ground by Calvinists.

Rennes-le-Château rose from the ashes, this time as nothing more than a small village, under the ownership of its new overlords, the wealthy Hautpoul de Blanchefort family. Cholet recounted the legend of how it was believed that Saunière had discovered an ancient Visigoth temple under the church.

Cholet then speculated on the likely source of any possible treasure. Was it indeed Visigoth in origin, or rather a sacred relic left by the Cathars – though they were known for their renunciation of worldly goods. Or something hidden by the Templars, perhaps, who had a powerful presence in the region, and escaped the initial round of arrests by the King of France when the order was disbanded in 1307. Blanche de Castile, regent and mother of Louis IX, had visited Rennes with a sizeable baggage train while her son was away on a crusade – had she hidden a hoard of royal gold? Or was it the treasure of her daughter, Blanche de France, whose gold had been stolen and allegedly hidden in the underground passages?

Then came the really interesting part – the route by which Cholet believed Saunière had gained access to the temple or crypt. The general consensus was that on the first occasion Saunière discovered the tomb, apparently based on information contained in one or more parchments, the entrance was situated underneath the flagstone in front of the altar. The flagstone, which had been laid upside-down, turned out to feature a ninth century Carolingian bas relief of knights on horseback. Such was the hysteria surrounding Rennes-le-Château that some treasure hunters believed the stone, now known as La Dalle des Chevaliers, was a depiction of the famous Knights Templar symbol, even though it appeared to pre-date the order's foundation by some 300 years.

How could they be sure the bas relief was Carolingian? She had seen the stone herself in the museum. A piece of solid rock that was impossible to carbon-date. It was certainly Carolingian in style, but did art really change much in medieval times? The image of two knights mounted on one horse was strongly tied to the Templars. Was it really just a coincidence?

She returned to Cholet's report. Saunière, it seemed, had moved the slab out into the grounds and retiled the church floor, presumably blocking off the entrance to the tomb – at least, Cholet was never to find it there. But as the archaeologist himself said, the priest must have had continued access to the crypt, possibly by more than one entrance. There were several eye-witness accounts of Saunière apparently 'disappearing' while in the cemetery. And then there was the 'Secret Room', which could only be reached through a false door Saunière had installed in a cupboard in the sacristy. Was this where he had gone to visit the crypt? Again, according to eye-witnesses, he spent some considerable time in there. What other reason could there be for such secrecy?

Rachel found the text relating to Cholet's discovery of the hidden stairways.

"Beneath the stairway leading up to the pulpit there is another staircase leading downwards towards the cemetery… In the little structure to the left of the sacristy [the Secret Room] it appears that the stones of the wall adjoining the apse may be in the form of a relieving arch. Beneath the floor of the sacristy I found the beginning of a staircase leading south. The treads are rough-cut and of the width of the entrance to the sacristy."

She was puzzled, however, that in the Secret Room, Cholet had found nothing more than an arch in the stonework. If the room had been Saunière's access to the crypt, what had happened to it? Cholet had dug the place up, but to no avail. Had Marie Dénarnaud filled it in after the priest's death? It was hard to believe Saunière himself would have removed the access to something that had so clearly become an obsession for him.

She tried searching the internet for 'Cholet and Saunière's Secret Room' to see if anything new had come up. Not much, surprisingly. Just two pages of entries, while a search on 'Rennes-le-Château' yielded more than 26 million results. It seemed people were more interested in wild theories than an archaeologist's official report.

One Google result seized her instantly – a claim that someone had made an attempt on Cholet's life by suspending a heavy oak beam over the church door with invisible nylon wire. The trap had failed to work, but it had been enough to scare away the quiet academic for several months.

Fact or fiction? It was hard to say – there was no citation, and there were so many 'urban myths' flying around. As a professional researcher, she had to discount claims that lacked the evidence to back them up. Nonetheless, if it were true, it would explain a lot. .

A knock on the door made her jump.

"Who is it?"

"Me – who else are you expecting?"

"Oh hi David, come on in."

David gave her a concerned look as he entered the room. "Are you OK?"

"I'm fine, I was just buried in some research. You startled me – this whole thing spooks me a little sometimes."

David smiled at her indulgently. "There's nothing down there – or anywhere else in Rennes-le-Château, for that matter – that isn't explained by the laws of physics," he said. "Hopefully just some nice, juicy historical finds that will make us both famous."

"Oh for God's sake, don't be so patronising. Scientists keep changing the 'laws' of physics every five minutes. What is it they say in quantum physics? You can't separate the observer from the observed – matter is materially affected by the very action of being observed, and every observer will see it differently. Basically, nothing is what it seems. And I see things differently to you – that doesn't make me wrong."

"Well, if you've finished the lecture, come and look at these pictures I've downloaded. I think you'll find them interesting."

Rachel followed David into his bedroom on the other side of the landing.

"Right, take a look at this," said David, sitting down at his laptop. "I've already spotted one or two anomalies. Firstly, the statue in the churchyard opposite the Calvary depicting Jesus on the Cross."

"The Virgin Mary, or as she seems to be known round here, Our Lady of Lourdes?"

"That's what it says in the museum pamphlet that we've all seen. But look again – why is she wearing a crown composed of little towers? And why does the canopy above her head contain more turrets? We're back to La Tour Magdala again, if you ask me: an homage to Mary Magdalene."

"That's astonishing. I must have walked past that countless times over the past few months and I hadn't noticed the tower symbolism. Pan the image out a little… Look, she is directly opposite the Calvary, almost as if gazing at Christ forlornly from a distance. It could be his mother, but given the way the scenario is played out, it's begging you to assume it's Mary Magdalene, his closest disciple – and, as the gnostic gospels hint at, perhaps his wife…"

"Funny you should say that," said David. "Normally I'd tell you to stop jumping to conclusions. But look at this." David zoomed in on the bas relief of Mary Magdalene over the porch. "Does anything strike you as odd about that statue?"

Rachel gasped in amazement. "She's pregnant!" she said, without hesitation.

"Exactly my thoughts. That's the swollen belly of a pregnant woman if ever I saw one. And it's definitely not the Virgin Mary, because underneath there's a plaque giving her name: St Maria Magdalene."

"Damn!" said Rachel, putting hands to her face in disbelief. "This is almost literally incredible. And look at the way her cloak parts around her stomach. That's the way clothes hang on a woman when she's pregnant!"

"This would have been earth-shattering in Saunière's time," said David. "Which brings me back to that statue of Our Lady of Lourdes in the churchyard. I've discovered that the pillar it's mounted on is Carolingian – that's around 750-950 AD, around the time the original church was built on this site. Saunière is believed to have found the pillar under the original altar during his restoration work, and used it as the base for the statue. But why did he turn it upside down? Look closely at the alpha and omega symbols: they're the wrong way up. As a cleric, he would have known that. The stem of the cross, too, is slightly longer – but at the top, rather than the bottom, as you would expect. Is Saunière trying to tell us he found something that turns religion upside down? A pregnant Magdalene would certainly do that: no prizes for guessing whom most people would assume the father to be."

"Indeed not," said Rachel distractedly, still staring at the photo of the bas relief of Mary Magdalene. "Look at the cross she's holding in her arms!" she said, abruptly.

"What about it?"

"Doesn't it strike you as odd?"

"Slightly, but I didn't attach any significance to it."

"That's exactly the way a woman would hold a baby. It's hard to believe no-one's noticed these things before."

"Well, it takes a good camera with a zoom lens. And I guess most people are more interested in hunting for buried treasure – Mary Magdalene is much lower down the agenda… Rachel?"

She was staring across the room, lost in thought, an intense look on her face.

"I'm just thinking… I've seen the Magdalene in that pose somewhere before, but I can't think where… Got it! My thesis for my Art History master's was on the Baroque painters. I can picture an image in my head right now… I think it was Caravaggio, but I'm not sure… Here, give me the laptop." She sat down as David vacated his seat, and started a new search. "Yes, here we are – I was right! Caravaggio's *The Repentant Magdalene*. Look at this!"

"What about it?" said David, peering over her shoulder, studying the painting.

"Her hands – look at her hands. It's like the statue at Rennes, she's cradling a baby in her arms, but in this case, her arms are empty."

"Maybe you're on to something," said David. "So is this the secret Saunière was hiding all his life? That Mary Magdalene was pregnant – presumably with Jesus's child. Is this where all the money came from – was he really blackmailing the Church?"

"It looks like a distinct possibility, doesn't it? Now, while I'm on an art website, I'm going to have a quick look at *The Last Supper*."

David groaned. "God, not that hoary old chestnut again, please…"

"I know we've had this discussion before, David, but some of Dan Brown's comments about *The Last Supper* are right on the money. I mean, that figure to Jesus's right, which all the so-called experts claim to be John, just has to be a woman. You'd have to be blind not to see it, especially in the newly restored painting. Earlier restorers were obviously uncomfortable with it and made the figure more masculine. But now we're back to what Da Vinci actually painted, there's no question about the gender."

"Yes, but as an art history grad you must know that Da Vinci was gay and used a female model for some of his male figures…"

"Goddamn it, David, it isn't a boyish man, or a womanish boy – it's a woman," said Rachel. "Come on, let's get it up on screen and I'll prove it to you."

The image of the painting on the art website turned out to be quite small, and she searched the web again, eventually finding a Milan tourism site that allowed her to zoom in to high resolution close-ups of the mural at the city's Santa Maria Delle Grazie church.

"There – look at that," said Rachel. "How in God's name is that supposed to be a guy? I mean, if you saw this painting for the first time, and knew nothing about it, would you think it's a man or a woman? Look, there's Da Vinci's idea of a 'boyish' man – James Minor, five places to the right of Jesus. But he's still easily identified as male from his jaw and forehead, and even the size of his skull. The figure of 'John' is distinctively different – look at that delicate, feminine face and chin; the pale, feminine hands that are obviously not used to hard work; even the passive body-language is feminine, at least for the era. And she is wearing a necklace – some of the others have clasps on their cloaks, but only she is wearing a necklace; you can see the chain clearly."

"I hadn't noticed the necklace. Zoom in closer."

Rachel took the website zoom function up to its highest setting, and a clear picture of the necklace appeared. "There's some kind of symbol on that pendant. Can you work your magic on it?"

They swapped seats again and David took a screen-shot of the section of painting. Then he opened it in Photoshop and digitally enhanced the contrast and sharpness.

Rachel gave a sharp intake of breath. "It's a crown – a four-pointed crown! David, this proves Mary was of royal blood! The anointing of Jesus, who the Bible says was from the royal house of David… this was a dynastic marriage that produced a holy bloodline. Everything points in that direction – and Saunière obviously found some kind of proof!"

"I hate to disillusion you, but it's a painting, not a photographic record."

"Yes, but look at the facts. Da Vinci was probably the world's greatest ever genius – art aside, he came up with everything from the theory of plate tectonics to engineering designs for helicopters and hang-gliders – and this in the late 15th century! He was big on symbolism – he wouldn't have included anything in this mural without a reason. And look at the massive V-shape created by the space between Mary and Jesus, as they lean away from each other! Yes, it gives the painting structure, but it's so dramatic there has to be more to it than that. Is it a coincidence that the 'V' is an ancient emblem for the feminine – symbolic of both the womb, and the female genitalia?"

"I think you're stretching things again, but I have to admit the figure on Jesus's right does look every inch a woman. It's a while since I've seen a copy of the fully restored fresco."

"He knew, David, he knew – Da Vinci was privy to some kind of secret that had been handed down over the centuries. Let's do a search and see if we can find anything more on that…" She typed in 'Leonardo da Vinci The Last Supper hidden symbols' and waited.

"There certainly won't be a shortage of theories out there," observed David drily. "Do we really have to waste any more time on this?"

"Just bear with me… Here we are. Hey, this is interesting – look: 'Templar figures hidden in *The Last Supper*'." She clicked on the link. "It seems some Italian researcher by the name of Slavisa Pesci has found some hidden images in The Last Supper by manipulating it… a baby and two Templar knights. Seems he copied the painting, mirrored it, and laid it over the original as a semi-transparent layer. You can do that stuff in Photoshop, right?"

"Yes, but…"

"Just humour me?" she said, jumping out of her seat and smiling sweetly at him.

David sighed and sat down in front of the laptop. He opened a copy of The Last Supper, created a duplicate layer, flipped it, then reduced the transparency to 50%. "Leonardo may have been a genius, but he didn't have access to computers," he grumbled as he did so. "There we go. Can't see a baby, I'm afraid," he added, scrutinising the composition carefully. "What's the matter?" he asked, as he heard Rachel gasp.

"Look at the end of the painting, on the right," she said in a strangled voice.

"Good grief," said David. "Some kind of knight wearing a chain-mail helmet!"

"There's not just one – scroll to the other end of the painting."

"Well there would be two of them, since we've duplicated the layer," said David.

"True. But they are perfect images – because the top layer is reversed, all the other characters in the scene are jumbled up, yet these two are just sitting there, perfectly formed. And it fits, because we know Leonardo used mirrored handwriting. We also know he used glass as tracing paper to create landscapes and study perspective. But why the Templars – what's the connection?"

35

"You're assuming they are Templars – we don't know for certain."

"Their reputation as a mysterious order guarding secret knowledge or an ancient relic is pretty well established," protested Rachel.

"'Reputation' is the right word. They were certainly secretive, and they may well have had a 'holy' relic – just about everyone returning from the Holy Land did in those days; the locals were churning them out on a production line. But the rest is just pure speculation."

"Maybe," said Rachel. "But clearly Da Vinci knew of some connection. And is it a coincidence that the original figure this is based on, Simon the Zealot, appears to be explaining something to those two other disciples?"

She paused, deep in thought. "Do you remember that mysterious 'Lost Leonardo' they found in Scotland a few years ago?" she asked suddenly.

"The one that the owner nearly threw out with the rubbish?"

"Yes – I wonder if it's another piece of the Da Vinci puzzle? A painting of a woman with a baby on her lap, and an old papal bull stuck on the back with the word 'Magdalene', clearly visible."

"I heard they thought it was a portrait of the Magdalene."

"Well it's can't be the Virgin Mary – she was always painted wearing blue, by order of the Church. And the papal document seems to bear out the theory that it is Mary Magdalene. But why is she holding a child? Let's have a quick look." She made a quick search. "Here we are," she said. "Oh my goodness!"

"What?" said David peering closer at the screen.

"Well as with many of Da Vinci's paintings, John the Baptist is in the scene, and here he is pointing at the lamb. Remember the phrase '*Ecce agnus dei*'? 'Behold the lamb of God'? I think I've seen in the church somewhere – it's taken from the New Testament and it's a common Catholic motif. So if this is Mary Magdalene, why is she holding a baby next to the symbolic Lamb of God that John is pointing to – unless Mary is holding Jesus, or his bloodline…" her voice trailed off.

"Well it would tie in with the pregnant Mary over the porch, but as for the idea of a bloodline I'm pretty sceptical, I'm afraid."

"And look at all this symbolism," said Rachel, ignoring his comment. "How do you explain the fleur de lys just below her neck, coming out of the back of the baby's head?"

David took a closer look at the screen. "OK, I have to admit that's about the weirdest thing I've seen in any painting of this era, bar none."

"The fleur-de-lys cropped up a lot in my research on this place," said Rachel. "In France it's strongly linked to Clovis, founder of the early French Merovingian dynasty. And, of course, in *Holy Blood, Holy Grail*, the 1980s book that inspired the *Da Vinci Code*, there are claims the Merovingians carried the bloodline of Jesus."

"Come on Rachel, that's nothing but speculation created by the Priory of Sion.

I'm not buying into the hysteria that some shadowy organisation has been guarding this knowledge for centuries – that particular group has been proven to be a complete bunch of scammers. They planted fake evidence in the Bibliothèque Nationale, for God's sake! Even their former president said the Priory was nothing more than a 'club for boy scouts'. Now, let's leave the realms of fantasy and get back to Saunière, and the photos I took inside the church."

David scrolled down to the next series of images. "OK, after the statue of Old Nick ready to meet visitors just inside the door, next up is the statue of Jesus's baptism by John the Baptist. It's right opposite the entrance. See anything unusual?"

"Nothing at first glance," said Rachel. "Hang on a minute – look at the banner John's carrying!"

"*Ecce agnus dei*, again." His voice trailed off. "Are you psychic or something?"

She smiled smugly. "Look at the shape of it."

"I was – it appears to be a large capital M."

"There's no way that's random. Then there's the 'M' pattern around the statue of Mary Magdalene..." She grabbed the pad to have another look at the layout. "Is there anything else in those statues? Working from the back of the church, we've got St Germain, St Roch, St Anthony the Hermit, the Magdalene, St Anthony, St Luke..." She scrawled the names on the pad as she read them out, underlining the initial letters for emphasis. "G-R-A-M-A-L," she said slowly, with an edge of disappointment in her voice. "Not much to go on there. I was hoping there might be another clue... Hang on!" Rachel leapt out of her chair in excitement. "Take M for Mary out of the equation – after all, she's the focus – and look what you've got! G-R-A-A-L! The old French word for 'grail', as in the Holy Grail. You know all about theory that the Holy Grail wasn't the chalice from the Last Supper at all, but that Mary herself was the grail; or more specifically, her womb, carrying the holy child of Jesus."

"Hmm..."

"Oh for God's sake, David, don't be so sceptical!"

"OK, I'm not ruling it out. Given all these other clues it has to be a possibility. Though the whole san graal/sang raal thing that they also raked up in *Holy Blood, Holy Grail* – that 'holy grail' should actually have been written in old French as 'royal blood' – turned out to be nothing more than a spelling mistake by an illiterate monk."

"We don't know that for certain, David – the change might have been made deliberately. Monks were well educated and went to painstaking lengths when copying books. I'm not sure I accept the glib theory that such a crucial change was just a 'mistake'. How do these self-appointed myth debunkers know? Anyway, we're getting off the point. Is there anything in the statues themselves that might give us a clue? What about him – St Anthony of Padua? Why does he take pride of place in front of the altar?"

"Ask me another."

"OK, let's Wiki him." She sat down again at David's laptop. "Here we are." She scanned down the Wikipedia entry. "Born in Lisbon – seems he was related to royalty. Joined a local abbey against the wishes of his family. Went on to join the Franciscans because he was impressed with their simple lifestyle. Became known as a famous preacher... Spent a lot of time in southern France – Montpelier, Toulouse, Arles. That's the reason, I suppose – a saint with local connections..." Again, she could not help feeling a little disappointed. Why give him pride of place? She was missing something. She scanned on down. "Patron saint of Padua in Italy and many cities in Portugal..." She stopped in mid-sentence, her mouth open in disbelief, as a flash of intuition hit her.

"Well?" said David impatiently. "Don't sit there like a goddamn goldfish! What is it?"

Rachel was barely able to speak. "It says he is especially invoked for the recovery of lost things."

"So?"

"My God, don't you see? She's here! Saunière found the tomb of Mary Magdalene! That's why he went so potty about her, that's why there are so many nods and winks to the Magdalene everywhere. It's a shrine to the Magdalene – a Magdalene pregnant with Christ's baby. That statue over the porch proves it. That's why St Anthony of Padua has pride of place – Saunière is giving thanks for finding such a precious relic – and leaving another deliberate clue in the process!"

"I suppose you might have a point..."

"Might have a point? How much more evidence do you need?"

"OK, keep your hair on. Let's have a look through the rest of these photos and see if anything else jumps out." Rachel glowered at him but he carried on obliviously. "We've done pretty well so far. Here's the eastern end of the church; the semi-circular Romanesque apse containing the altar. There are some more of the altar itself, but this is worth a quick glance..."

They both studied the photo intently. "Not much there," said Rachel with a tinge of disappointment.

"What about the altar itself? There's a painting on the front of that." They peered down at the screen as David brought up the enhanced image of the altar. "Hmm. Just the usual picture of Mary with the skull and the Bible – the triumph of the Scriptures over death. You can see that imagery in several Renaissance paintings."

"I agree. Nothing obvious there at a glance – though I've always wondered about the credibility of that explanation. I mean, why connect that specifically with the Magdalene? Could it be a reference to *The Gospel of Mary*?"

"That's an interesting point," conceded David. *"The Gospel of Mary* was found in 1896, the year before the restoration of this church was completed. It came up in my research – the codex turned up in Cairo and was bought by a German scholar by the name of Carl Reinhardt. The translation wasn't published until the 1950s, but it's interesting that it showed up in Egypt – a melting pot of illicit archaeological relics – only five years after Saunière made that enigmatic entry in his diary, 'Discovered a tomb'. Officially, the codex was found in a niche in the wall of a Christian burial site in Egypt, but there's considerable doubt about that among academics. Left out in the open, it would have crumbled to dust, yet it was in remarkably good condition. It makes you wonder…"

"You're not kidding. There are just way too many coincidences here." Rachel turned back to look at the laptop again. Something caught her eye and she frowned, zooming in on the photo. "What does that look like to you?" she said, pointing to the top left-hand corner of the altar painting, which now occupied most of the screen.

"Looks like the ruins of an old castle."

"Look more closely."

"Good God! The ruins form a perfect 'M'!" enthused David. "And that stump on the left is a cross, set back slightly, as if it were on a gravestone. I'm beginning to agree with you – it looks like yet another clue that Jesus and Mary were married. A Catholic priest doesn't make those sort of allusions all over his church without having some pretty strong evidence. I wonder if there's anything else we've missed?" He scrolled slowly around the painting. "That area in the bottom right looks pretty murky – let's see if I can enhance it." He selected the area in Photoshop and boosted the contrast. "What on earth is that?" he exclaimed. "It looks like a sword lying among the rocks."

"Hey, you could be right," said Rachel, peering at the screen. "And is that a coronet or something underneath it? That band of gold? In fact there are several blobs of gold there, though it's hard to distinguish anything else. You know what I think? I think Saunière hit the jackpot here at Rennes. All his numbers came up – he found the Magdalene, or something closely associated with her, that proved she was Jesus's widow, and he also found some hidden gold. That would explain everything."

David ran his fingers through his unruly mop of blond curls. "You're stretching things, Rachel…"

"Hell, by the law of averages, every once in a while, someone hits the jackpot. Vegas is built on that dream. Look, you know all the legends about the gold that's supposed to have been stashed here over the centuries…"

"I've heard the stories."

"Right! And we know there's some truth in that. What about that shepherd boy in the mid-1600s who came back to the village with his pockets stuffed with gold?"

"Ignace Paris, I think, was his name. He was looking for a lost sheep and fell into a ravine crammed with skeletons and huge amounts of gold. Unfortunately no-one believed him and he was stoned to death for theft."

"That's the one! Not to mention the gold objects that farmers reputedly keep finding in their fields round here. As I said, maybe Saunière just got lucky. I've been focusing on the religious side, but perhaps he found both spiritual and literal treasure. Any other pictures worth a look?"

"Obviously there are the 14 Stations of the Cross, but it could take some time going through all those, and we need to find something conclusive before morning." David sat drumming his fingers on the table in frustration.

"Is there anything in the windows?"

"The stained glass windows? Good call – let's look at that big rose window in the apse. If Saunière's putting clues here, there and everywhere, he wouldn't have missed a chance to leave a hint there when he replaced the window." He pulled up the image – a stunning tableau of richly coloured glass depicting Mary Magdalene at Jesus's feet. "Here we are – Mary kneeling beside Jesus, washing his feet with her hair…"

"I think you mean anointing…"

"Whatever…"

"There's a big difference! That vase Mary is using contained pure nard – an incredibly expensive perfume. That's why Judas criticised her for wasting money that could have been given to the poor – it was worth a year's wages. The word Christ means 'the anointed' in Greek, yet he was only anointed once in the entire New Testament, and that was by Mary Magdalene. Some scholars see it as a symbolic act; anointing Jesus as king before his sacrificial death. It's only in Luke's gospel, the most heavily edited version of events, that we have mention of a sinful woman washing Jesus's feet with tears, rather than oil. It's also Luke who describes Mary as a woman from whom seven demons had been cast out. A classic piece of misogyny by Christian elders in Greece, who wanted to undermine Mary's position as his chief disciple."

"OK, as I was saying… is there anything unusual about this scene? Anything out of the ordinary? It seems odd to me that only Jesus and Mary have haloes. None of the other disciples have any."

"I agree, normally they would all have haloes. But that doesn't really tell us much that we haven't already guessed – that Saunière placed Mary above all the others." She frowned, tilting her head as she studied the window intently. "Hang on a minute. Don't you think she's sitting in a slightly awkward position? I mean, if she were washing his feet she would be sitting with her back to the viewer, surely – not sideways on?"

"Artistic licence – he wanted to show her face."

"Possibly. But from here it looks as if she's almost under the table!"

David peered at the screen.

"My God!" said Rachel, clutching her mouth in disbelief. "It's the altar

– the table is a representation of the altar! Saunière is trying to tell us that Mary's body is actually here in the church, under the altar!"

Chapter 9

Rachel and David stared at each other in disbelief. "Maybe that's why Cholet didn't find the entrance when he dug up the floor in front of the altar," said David. "Saunière moved the altar forwards to cover the entrance and stop anyone else from going down there! It's obvious, with hindsight – we know he demolished the old altar; that's when one of the parchments was allegedly found. When he had the new one built it gave him the perfect opportunity to cover his tracks."

"And he created a new entrance in his Secret Room so that he could still go down into the crypt himself. That's got to be the way in, David. We've got to find it!"

David looked at her quizzically. "You know we haven't got permission to dig in here…"

"I wasn't planning on asking permission."

"You can't be serious! We could get into all kinds of trouble. And how do you propose to carry out a dig, without anyone noticing, in just 24 hours?"

"At night."

"And how do we get into the church at night?"

"Hide in the Secret Room late in the afternoon, while it's quiet."

"We've got to get into the sacristy first, and that's usually kept locked."

"Perhaps we could just ask to have another look round?" said Rachel brightly. "They gave us an official tour when we first arrived, but that was months ago. We'll just say we need to check something. We know the museum staff pretty well now; I'm sure they won't mind."

"Yes, but they are going to want to lock up afterwards!"

"We'll just ask to borrow the key, and say we'll bring it back when we've finished. They won't have any reason to be suspicious. Trust me, I can be very disarming when I want to be."

"Yes, I've noticed that particular quality. Usually when you want something…" He jumped aside to dodge the punch.

"OK, I know there's a risk of failure. But what have we got to lose? You can bet your bottom dollar than when the Monsignor turns up on Wednesday to witness the break-through, he's going to insist on going in there first – alone. And if Mary's tomb is down there, or some other significant artefact, we're not going to get a look in. The Vatican will stall us for months, and remove anything incriminating – anything that might suggest she was pregnant. It would bring the whole Catholic Church crashing down; not just on theological grounds, either. The male-only hierarchy would be completely undermined. There would be a huge vested interest in keeping it all under wraps."

"I don't disagree with you on that one. Well, I guess it's worth a go – you're the one calling the shots on this project. It's going to be like something out of Tomb Raider!" he said, with a boyish grin. "So now we know what we have to do. Let's go and get something to eat."

* * * * *

The next day seemed to drag. They didn't want to ask Hélène, the museum curator, about seeing the sacristy until late afternoon, as they didn't want to risk her going back into the church to check the door had been locked.

By 4pm Rachel could wait no longer. "I'm going to go and ask her," she announced, as they sat in the Finds Room staring at their empty coffee mugs. "Stay here – you might give the game away. Subtlety isn't your strong point."

She strolled into the museum and found Hélène sorting through some newly arrived boxes of books for the gift shop. "Bonjour!" she announced.

"Bonjour," replied Hélène, looking up with an armful of books. "Ça va?"

"Très bien, merci – et toi?"

"A little busy, as you see. I have to put all these out – we have two coaches of tourists from Japan who arrive tomorrow."

"I guess you've got your hands full, then," said Rachel, struggling to disguise her good fortune. "I wonder, would it be possible to borrow the key to the sacristy? We wanted to check some measurements…"

"Mais bien sûr," replied Hélène without hesitation, picking up a box of brochures. "It is the second to last key on the right, over there" – she gestured with her head at a key rack behind the counter.

"Ah – merci beaucoup!" said Rachel, plucking it off the rack.

"You will return it before I go, yes? Or I will get into trouble."

"Of course!" said Rachel over her shoulder, as she disappeared out of the door. "I promise!"

David, who had been listening in to the conversation through the open door, followed her into the courtyard that lay between the villa and the church. Rachel gave him a triumphant smile and waved the key in his face. "See?"

"I never doubted you for a moment," said David. "You usually get your own way," he added, darting out of reach of her punch.

Rachel marched on ahead of him into the church. She went down the aisle until she reached the door to the sacristy, just in front of the choir on the right-hand side. "Here we go," said, putting the key in the lock. It failed to turn. "Damn," she exclaimed in exasperation, still struggling to turn it.

"Here, let me," said David. "You'll break the key if you're not careful, and then we really will be in trouble." He stepped over to the door, and after jiggling the key backwards and forwards to no avail, stopped with a frown on his face. Rachel was about to make a sarcastic remark, but David returned to the door, this time lifting it bodily by the handle before trying to turn the key.

43

The lock moved with a satisfying clunk and the door opened smoothly onto the dark, dusty chamber beyond.

They had seen it briefly when they first arrived at Rennes. Areas of the church that were normally out of bounds had been shown to them as a special courtesy – with the exception of the Secret Room beyond the sacristy. When they had asked about it, the curator had given a typical Gallic shrug and said it was "not possible". New on the site, they had not wanted to argue with her.

The sacristy itself offered little of interest. Bare, apart from a plain wooden stand on which stood an ornate, multi-coloured Victorian pitcher and bowl for the curé to wash his hands, it gave up no clues. Taking up the entire width of the far wall stood a large cupboard where Saunière would have kept his robes.

"According to some of the books I've read, the entrance to the Secret Room is through a hidden doorway in that wardrobe," whispered Rachel.

"Why are we whispering?" asked David.

"I don't know," said Rachel, trying to force herself to talk normally. "This place has that kind of effect on you."

"Let's shut the door. We might as well have a look for the entrance while we're here – it will save time later."

They opened up the two pairs of doors and stared at the back of the empty wardrobe. There were no obvious signs of a hidden doorway. "This is going to be tricky," said David.

"No-one said it was going to be easy," said Rachel. She climbed in and started tapping on the panels at the back.

"Someone will hear you," said David.

Rachel ignored him and continued tapping. After a few minutes, she crossed to the far side of the cupboard. As she worked her way down, the sound changed from a dull, flat tap to a deeper, hollow echo. "Got it!" she exclaimed.

She started pressing on the back panel, upwards, sideways, downwards and around the edges, but to no avail. She stood back and studied the panel from a distance. A piece of raised beading ran around the edge of the cupboard-back – part of the joinery, she surmised. But on closer inspection of the mitred corners, she noticed a small infill about an inch long. It was hard to spot, as everything had been covered with several layers of varnish, but on close inspection, the grain was noticeably different. She pushed on the small section of beading and it slid smoothly up out of sight with a satisfying click. As it did so, the back-panel swung open to reveal a small opening to the Secret Room beyond.

Chapter 10

Corba de Péreille shuddered. The cold mountain breeze bit into her olive skin and chilled her to the bone. She stared down at the deeply wooded valley below, the jagged limestone outcrops jutting through the forest canopy. At another time she would have been captivated by the rugged beauty of her surroundings. But now the bleak landscape represented her only hope for safety, and with winter fast approaching, it was not a prospect she relished.

It had been hard since the crusade started; hard on them all. Still she could not comprehend that a 'Christian' Pope would declare war on his own people – yet he had, and the powerful barons from the north had not been slow to heed his call. There were rich pickings in the Languedoc, that was for sure. Or there had been.

For ten years the invading armies, under papal authority, had pillaged their land, laying waste to whole towns and villages in their frenzied zeal to eradicated the Cathar 'heresy'.

Ten years of brutal, savage attacks by armed soldiers on defenceless men, women and children, masterminded by that evil zealot Simon de Montfort. Ten years of torture and mutilation; ten years of misery.

The outrages were indelibly seared upon her mind. Béziers had been the first, one of the foremost towns of the Languedoc, famed for its tolerance, independence and learning. Their Catholic brothers and sisters had refused to give them up and fought alongside them against the armies of the Pope.

She closed her eyes and shuddered, the scenes still vivid in her mind. And it was her fault. They were fighting to protect her; her and her mother. Had they not been there – if she had not been sent there to finish her schooling; had her mother not chosen to accompany her to bring enlightenment to the people… They should have left as soon as Pope Innocent – hah! there was an irony – had declared his vile war. She could not believe such atrocities could be carried out in Christ's name… She choked back her tears. Was it possible that such a noble message from such a man could be so twisted and distorted that people would murder in his name? Pope 'Innocent', the supposed vicar of Christ, had the blood of tens of thousands on his hands.

The townspeople had rallied to protect them; the outcome had been inevitable. And so, on St Mary Magdalene's feast day, of all days, while she had been smuggled out, Cathars and Catholics alike had mounted that fateful sortie to distract De Montfort's men. Driven back inside the walls by the heavily armed crusaders, they were put to the sword without mercy – even those who took refuge in the churches. Thousands had sought sanctuary in the cathedral, and the church de la Madeleine – among them her mother, who had refused to leave the people to face their persecutors alone. But the cathedral was set ablaze, and all those sheltering in the church were brutally butchered.

According to the pitiful handful of those who managed to flee the doomed town, when Arnaud-Amaury, the papal legate commanding the crusade, was asked how soldiers could distinguish Catholic from Cathar, he replied: "Kill them all, God will know his own". Twenty thousand people had died that day.

Outrage had been followed by outrage; scarcely had there been rumours of one act of unspeakable cruelty than another, even more heinous, had occurred. At the sacking of Bram, De Montfort had rounded up the survivors, gouged out their eyes, cut off their ears, their noses and their lips, and sent them on to the next village as a horrible warning.

It was hard to comprehend such savagery. And for what? This 'heresy' they railed against... Did it deny the Christ? No! Did it deny his teachings? No! But the Pope did not have a monopoly on truth. Peter had been a coward. He had denied Christ. He had loathed Mary, hated her sex. He was a simple fisherman; he did not begin to comprehend the true meaning of the Lord's message. And here was Peter's supposed ecclesiastical descendant insisting that his was the only truth. If he but knew...

Corba shivered again as the increasingly bitter wind found its way through the folds of her cloak. She could not shake the memories of that vicious campaign, however hard she tried. The evil De Montfort might be dead – how her heart had leapt at the news – and his son, Amaury, finally defeated by the southern lords, but the armistice that followed had proven but a lull in the storm. The few, brief years of peace and happiness she had spent with her husband and children had offered false hope. King Louis of France would not be deterred from seizing control of the Languedoc, and hell had been visited upon them once more.

As if that were not enough, the papal Inquisition had started its evil work, systematically rooting out and destroying the Cathar faith through fear and persecution, its interrogators spreading terror throughout the land.

Now the Cathar faithful were fleeing towns and villages, seeking safety in the hilltop strongholds still held by Cathar nobles. It was a double-edged sword, however – the dramatic fortresses perched high on their craggy hill-top sites might seem unassailable, but the Church knew exactly where they were.

"Corba". She sprang to her feet, startled. "It's time we were moving on, my lady."

"Must we keep up this punishing pace, Benoît? I am tired and cold, and Philippa is so young. Cannot the Lord's work wait a little?"

"You can answer that question, better than I, my lady. But this world must be endured, and you must be protected at all cost."

"I have seen that cost, Benoît. Sometimes I wonder…"

"This world is but a sham, my lady. It matters not what we suffer here. The truth – the real truth – must survive; and the Word must be spread by any means, even if it is left to troubadours to tell the tale. But for now, our need is more urgent. We must flee further into the hills; once we reach the château at Puylaurent we shall be safe, for the winter at least. In the spring you can journey on to Montségur and rejoin your husband."

"We were safe at Peyrepertuse," countered Corba.

"Perhaps for a time, but Guillaume de Peyrepertuse cannot defy King Louis forever. And now that even Count Raymond of Toulouse has proclaimed an edict against the Cathari we must seek safety in numbers."

Corba wandered over to where her seven-year-old daughter Philippa lay sleeping under a pile of rugs. Her face was a study of innocence, framed in a cascade of dark curls. Corba's heart nearly broke; it seemed so cruel to force her to endure yet more hardship. Yet she must if they were to survive the year.

"Wake, ma petite," whispered Corba. "Come, we must be on our way."

Philippa opened her deep brown eyes and smiled back at her mother as she stirred. "Don't worry, Maman. Everything will be all right. You'll see." She scrambled to her feet, rubbing her eyes sleepily. "May I ride with you, Father Benoît?"

Benoît de Termes' worried, craggy face broke into a smile. What a blessing this child was! Procreation was frowned upon by his faith – the only Christian church to believe in reincarnation – as an evil act that chained a soul to another tortured existence on Earth. It was expressly forbidden among the parfaits, the lay preachers who lived and worked alongside their parishioners. Then Corba had arrived with her infant daughter at Quéribus, fleeing the Inquisition, en route to the safety of the formidable fortress at Peyrepertuse. Drawn to his gentle wisdom and understanding, the two had become close: Corba had found a man in whom she could confide her deepest secret, while for Benoît, she was the daughter he had never been able to have. And here was her beautiful daughter, standing before him. Despite his faith, it was hard to see how anything about her could be remotely evil.

"Father Benoît?" Her voice broke into his thoughts.

"Of course you may, Pippa. Of course you may."

The journey to Puylaurent took another two days. They avoided the main route through the Maury valley, and instead cut across country through increasingly rugged and inhospitable terrain, riding their horses through steep ravines alongside rivers swollen with heavy autumn rainfall.

Winter was fast approaching, and at times during the day the temperature in the foothills of the Pyrénées barely rose above freezing. They made camp where they could, halting for just an hour to eat at noon, and spending the night wherever they could find shelter; once at a remote farm belonging to a bon homme, a respected member of the Cathar faithful; and once in a shepherd's deserted shelter. As the wife of Raymond de Péreille, commander of Montségur – now declared the official seat of the Cathar church – Corba was very much on King Louis's wanted list. Benoît, the Cathar Bishop of Razes, was sought by the Inquisition, so to avoid detection they travelled as husband and wife.

Those few years' respite from the horrors of war had made them soft, thought Corba, as she struggled to make herself comfortable in the saddle; soft, and complacent, too. She had enjoyed her stay in the hidden villages of the rugged Aude hills, and the occasional visits by her husband, moving from place to place to ensure her safety. The unexpected arrival of Philippa, more than ten years after the birth of her elder sister Esclarmonde, had brought her much joy at an age when she had not expected to have more children, but now those idyllic summers seemed but a distant memory.

As they headed further west the hills became steeper and more rugged, and the valleys more tortuous. In the distance the jagged peaks of the high Pyrénées appeared fleetingly through the clouds like gaping fangs.

On the third day they found themselves following a stream along a narrow valley overshadowed by towering limestone cliffs. Little Philippa, perched on the pommel of Benoît's saddle, made even the hardest soldiers smile as she sang catches from a minstrel's song about the Holy Grail she had learnt over the winter at Peyrepertuse.

The bandits struck shortly before noon as the small group of riders slowed to negotiate a narrow defile created by a rocky promontory. Seemingly from nowhere, an arrow flew across the leading horse and embedded itself into a gnarled old willow that had taken root beside the water.

The outrider reined in his horse sharply and spun round, looking for the assailant. Benoît urged his horse alongside Corba's mount to shield her with his body as a small group of bowmen slid silently from the dense chestnut woodland, arrows nocked on strings.

"What do you want with us?" cried Benoît. We are simple folk; we have no gold."

"We'll be the judge of that," said a tall, disfigured man with a badly scarred face in which an empty eye socket stared horribly. "Are you in the service of the king?"

"No, we most certainly are not," said Benoît emphatically.

"Reckon you're right," retorted the bandit, eyeing the party. "Reckon you're Cathars headed for Montségur. And judging from your apparel, my friend, you must be a clergyman – the Inquisition will pay handsomely for you. After we've had a little bit of fun," he added, eyeing Corba.

"You'll have to kill me first," said Benoît furiously, pulling his sword from his smock in one swift movement. In an instant, a bowstring twanged and an arrow thumped into his thigh with such force it knocked him clear out of the saddle. Benoît hung down as the horse skittered nervously, his foot caught in the stirrup, his face contorted with pain.

"Benoît!" shrieked Corba, flinging herself out of the saddle and running to his horse. "Help me get him to the ground," she snapped. Benoît's squire was already at her side, and together they gently laid the priest on the ground as the bandits stood watching, bows at the ready.

"There are more where that came from, mistress," said the man, who appeared to be the leader of the group. "The next one will be in his heart. Or, perhaps, the little girl is more precious to you?" he added after a pause, swinging his bow up to where Philippa still clung, petrified, to the saddle of Benoît's horse.

Corba summoned her last ounce of courage and drawing herself up to her full height, looked the robber directly in the eye.

"If you do us more harm you will pay for it dearly," she said fiercely.

"Says who?" he sneered.

"Those who gave me this ring," she said, pulling a large silver signet ring from her finger.

"A little silver? Good, that will add to our takings." Stepping forward, he snatched the ring from her hand and squinted at it, before looking up, startled. "Here, François," he said, turning to the man nearest him. "Is this what I think it is?"

The man walked across and taking the ring, held it close to his face. His expression grew grim, and he crossed himself swiftly. "We'd best not interfere with the likes of them," he muttered.

The leader took back the ring and eyed Corba speculatively. "Friends of yours, I take it?" he said sarcastically.

"You could say that."

He hesitated, turning the ring in his hands, then stepped forward, holding it out to her. "Well then you had best be on your way, my lady." He paused, looking down at where Benoît lay clutching his thigh in agony as his squire bound the wound. "He'll live," muttered the robber, nodding in his direction. "I've seen worse – there's not much blood. You won't mention this? We weren't to know…"

"Weren't to know?" exploded Corba. "Never mind that you attacked a priest or threatened an innocent girl!"

"We must make do as best we can, my lady," said the man stubbornly.

"They have burned our homes and killed our women and children. I have no liking for priests, but I wouldn't have hurt the lass; she has a likeness to my daughter Ariane – raped and skewered on a Crusader's sword these ten years' past."

Corba's face softened. "I am sorry for your loss. But I beg of you, if you have no choice but to remain outside the law, then at least avoid harm to those who share your plight. Life is precious; do not allow them to take away your dignity."

There was something about her eyes that made him look down humbly. "What is your name, my lady?" he asked quietly.

"Corba," she responded simply. "Some know me as Myriam."

"I've heard tell," he said, wonderingly. "Men say they sacrificed Béziers for you. I'll not trouble you further, my lady."

"Thank you," she said. "And please, if you value my life, do not tell anyone that we have passed."

"Of that you have my word, my lady," he said, bowing his head.

Chapter 11

Rachel gave an involuntary gasp as the door to the Secret Room swung open. Here, possibly, lay the answer to all the secret hopes she had fostered over the past two years since the project's inception. They had made their first real 'find' – and one they had never thought to see.

The tiny, quadrant-shaped room, with its bare stone walls and dirt floor, was even more empty and unkempt than the sacristy, lit only by the small, circular window in the outer wall and the feeble light filtering through the hidden door. Cobwebs festooned the ceiling and the ground was covered with a thick layer of debris that had found its way through the loosely fitting roof tiles. Here and there broken tiles lay discarded. Devoid of a ceiling, the room would be cold and draughty in winter – this was plainly not a place where Saunière intended to spend much time. Yet anecdotal reports suggested he regularly disappeared into the room for long periods. That could mean only one thing – whatever his destination, it was not the Secret Room itself. This was just a portal, a doorway to whatever lay in the crypt.

Rachel gingerly stepped up into the wardrobe and climbed down through the doorway into the room beyond. As she stepped down, she turned to look over her shoulder and gave David a girlish grin of excitement that sent a delicious shiver through his body. Mercurial she may be – but he found her quite intoxicating.

She stared around her. The room was utterly bare, and gave no signs of the purpose for which it must once have been used. She shivered, and not just from the cold.

"Rachel, we can't stay here," said David through the open door in the wardrobe. "Someone might come in at any moment to check on us."

"You're right. Let's take the key back and go and get some things for later."

"There's something you haven't considered in all this," said David, as she climbed back through the cupboard. "What are we going to do when they lock up the church?"

"We'll have to hide inside beforehand, of course."

"And how do we get out again?"

"The same way – wait until they open up in the morning, then sneak out."

"With our stash of loot in plain sight?"

"I'm not planning on doing any grave-robbing – it's information we need; information and photographs to prove it. So don't forget your camera. And by the looks of it, we're going to need a spade in here, too, to prise up those slabs and dig out the dirt floor underneath."

"And how do you propose to smuggle a spade in here?"

51

"I don't. You're going to do it."

David was almost apoplectic.

"Don't worry," said Rachel quickly, "All you have to do is stick it down your trousers…"

"You've got to be kidding me!" he exploded.

"Look, just poke the handle down your trouser leg and hide the blade under your jumper. No-one will notice with all that flab," she giggled.

David burst out laughing. "You cheeky minx – I'm not that fat! A bit too much good French cooking, maybe. Well, I suppose we've nothing to lose – it might just work. Promise me one thing – if we get caught, you do the talking."

"Absolutely," said Rachel.

Leaving the sacristy door unlocked, they returned the key to rack behind the museum counter. Hélène, who was still knee-deep in cartons of books, acknowledged them with a brief nod before returning to her task.

There was now only about half an hour to go before the church closed, and most of the tourists had left. Those that remained had completed their tour of the church, and were now traipsing round the adjacent presbytery.

David and Rachel went into the small portable cabin where the dig team kept their tools and overalls. "OK, what do we need – apart from a spade?" asked David.

"Not much – a couple of carrier bags, in case there is anything we need to smuggle out – supermarket bags won't look suspicious. And a dustpan and brush; or at least a brush."

"What on earth do we want that for?" asked David.

"We need to leave the place looking as though no-one's been in there. We are going to have to sweep all that debris to one side, then scatter it back over the floor afterwards to cover our traces."

"Smart thinking – I'm pretty sure there's one round here somewhere. And, of course, the camera and tripod. It's going to be pitch black down there, and cold, too; we need warm clothing. On the subject of lighting, we need a good, strong torch; you bring one, too, just in case. I'll see you back here in five minutes."

Rachel looked David up and down curiously when she returned to find him standing nonchalantly outside the cabin. "Have you got the spade?" she asked, intrigued by the lack of bulges under his clothing.

"Absolutely!" said David, mimicking her own buzzword with the same, humorous inflexion. He laughed. "OK, I'll let you out of your suspense. I remembered I had a folding shovel in the back of the Range Rover – I keep it there in case I get stuck in the winter."

"A bit of overkill with a car like that, isn't it? Still, on this occasion your caution seems to have paid off."

"Why thank you, my lady," said David ironically, bowing from the waist. "Shall we proceed?"

They wandered into the church trying to look as casual as possible. Rachel gave a quick backward glance as they crossed the threshold, but no-one seemed to be around. The church itself was empty. They walked quickly down the aisle and into the sacristy, closing the door behind them.

"I think we ought to wait in the Secret Room, just in case someone looks in here," said David.

"Good idea." Rachel climbed up into the wardrobe and pressed the catch in the far corner, as David had done earlier. The door to the Secret Room swung open invitingly. She climbed down inside once more, and turned round to face David. "Hand down your things," she said. He passed her the camera, then reached under his jacket and pulled out the folding spade, before retrieving the floor-brush from the waistband of his trousers. He was about to climb through the opening when she stopped him. "Haven't you forgotten something?" David looked puzzled. "The cupboard door!"

He tutted at his oversight, and pulled the outer door shut. As he did so, they heard steps ringing out on the flagstones in the church. Quickly, he stepped down into the Secret Room and shut the hidden door behind him. They stood frozen in silence, waiting for the visitor to leave the church. Instead, through the thin partition they heard the door to the sacristy creak open. They both held their breath. After a few moments they heard it close again – and a key turn in the lock. The footsteps receded into the distance, and then there was a deep thud as the heavy oak door to the church was pulled shut. They could just hear the dull rasp of its ancient lock turning, then silence.

They looked at each other aghast in the fading light. It was Rachel who spoke first.

"We're trapped!"

"No shit, Sherlock," said David.

"How are we going to get out of here?"

Panic shone momentarily in her eyes, and he relented. "Don't worry, we'll find a way out. If the worst comes to the worst, we'll just have to holler out of the window tomorrow morning. But then, of course, everyone will know what we've been up to."

"Why did they lock the door?"

"Hélène knew we'd been in here. She probably checked to make sure we had locked up properly."

"Those didn't sound like a woman's footsteps."

David shrugged. "It hardly matters. We're here now – there's no going back."

Chapter 12

Languedoc, south-west France, February 1233

The long winter passed without incident at Puylaurent. Corba and Benoît had been greeted warmly by the ageing châtelain Pierre Catala and his son Roger, who had made them their honoured guests and extended every hospitality. Corba and Benoît had been given their own tower at the north-western end of the château, which had been hewn out of the living rock at the summit of the pog, as the Occitans called the steep, volcanic mounds that jutted up from the valley floor.

Benoît's party had been sworn to secrecy to protect Corba's identity, but despite the precaution, rumour abounded, and as word spread Corba came to be regarded with awe by the many Cathars who had taken refuge at the château. The faydits, the nobility dispossessed of their lands by the Pope's crusade, showed her particular reverence, and by the time of their leaving, their lodgings had become known as Our Lady's Tower.

Corba tried to ignore the gossip as best she could without appearing rude, focusing her attention instead on trying to continue the important task of educating her daughter. It was not easy.

"But Maman," protested Philippa one day, after reporting back one of the rumours she had heard. "Why don't you tell people who you really are?"

A fleeting smile crossed Corba's face at Philippa's naivety. "I am afraid, ma petite, that if that became known, the Pope's men would not stop until they had torn this place down, stone by stone, to capture me."

"But why?"

"You are too young to understand the evil that drives these people, Philippa," said Corba quietly, "and I have no wish to upset you by telling you of their misdeeds. Suffice it to say they have done unspeakable things in the name of God, and they will stop at nothing to see us all eradicated like so much vermin," she said vehemently. "That is how they see us. Nothing we can say will change their minds. They take our words and twist them to suit their purpose."

She turned to look out of the turret's narrow, arrow-slit window, fighting back the tears so that Philippa would not see her grief. She stared out across the valley, where the tiny houses that comprised the village of Puylaurent clustered around the foot of the pog, to the scrub-covered mountains that rose dramatically from the valley floor just a short distance beyond, their dark green flanks broken with sheer limestone outcrops, rising in serried ranks to the snow-covered peaks in the distance. How, in God's name, in the midst of so much beauty, could such evil exist?

"But Maman…"

"No more! Back to your studies," she scolded. "Have you finished reading that book? So tell me, what have you learned about the Madeleine?"

"Well, what I don't understand is why her teachings are so different to those of St Peter."

"He was a simple fisherman, Philippa. He did not fully understand the Lord's teachings, any more than some of the other disciples. Mary was a well-educated woman – she was of royal blood and came from a wealthy family. She could not only read and write, but she would have studied many ancient texts. Look at the anointing of Christ – none of them understood that it was a sacred ritual that only she could perform, anointing Jesus as king, the rightful heir of David. They just accused her of wasting precious spikenard, the simpletons!"

"Did all the disciples hate her?"

"Not all, though many were mistrustful. You have to understand that women had no respect in Jewish society – you're lucky you have grown up among the Cathars, where women are treated as equals. The Church of Rome is not so open-minded – it does not even allow women to be priests, unlike our parfaites. But as for your question: yes, others were less hostile; Levi, for one, but especially John. Jesus, John and Mary were very close. But the men were all cowards; they would not stand with Our Lord at the crucifixion. Only the women stayed until the end." A surge of anger ran through her. "Hah – and they think only they are fit to be priests!"

"Why did they run away?" queried Philippa.

"They feared the Romans would crucify them, too. Do you remember how when Peter was challenged, he thrice denied that he knew the Lord?"

"So why did Jesus choose Peter to lead the Church?"

"He didn't, Philippa. At least, not exclusively. I'm afraid many of the gospels have been changed and added to over the years to increase the power of the Church. Rome wanted a Bible without room for contradiction, so they simply threw out texts that differed from their agreed position, and excommunicated anyone who dared continue to use them. Take those verses in the gospel of John – the Catholic gospel, not the Cathar one – in which Jesus asks Peter three times if he loves him. They were added later to counteract Peter's denial of Jesus. And that passage in John where Jesus intervenes to save an adulterous woman from being stoned to death? That was added later, too. And although the woman wasn't named, they no doubt hoped people would link it in their minds to the Madeleine – which many did.

"Our Lord said he wanted Peter to be a cornerstone of the Church, but a building has four corners. He was never meant to be the exclusive leader after Jesus's death. Mary, John, Peter and Paul – they were meant to be the four leaders of the new Church. Peter's role was to preach to his fellow

Jews; Jesus knew his limitations. Paul, a more educated man, had the role of converting the Gentiles – principally the Greeks; the philosophers whose ideas have shaped the civilised world. Mary and John were to focus on the spiritual side; to explain Jesus's higher teachings to those who would listen. But it didn't happen that way. The power of Rome was too great. Constantine saw the chance to unify the empire under one god, with himself as the Church's ultimate leader. And now the Bishops of Rome, who claim their role is descended directly from Peter, are trying to impose their version of Christianity on everyone else. In fact, the first Bishop of Rome was not Peter at all – there is not even any evidence he went to Rome – but a Briton called Linus, son of King Caractacus.

"Don't think we are the first 'heretics' to be persecuted; we are not. Many others have been put to death by their fellow Christians in the name of Christ since they first decided what to put in their Bible – and more importantly, what to leave out." Her throat tightened as she thought of the horrific suffering she had witnessed, multiplied many times over the centuries.

"And so, ma petite, that is why you learn what you learn; that is why we seek refuge among the Cathars, who respect us and care for us. Their truth is not the whole truth, but the parfaits follow the Lord's teachings more closely than any corrupt Catholic cleric. And as long as we have them to protect us, the ultimate knowledge you and I carry with us will be kept safe for future generations."

* * * * *

Early that spring, Benoît heard the news he had been dreading. The dreaded inquisition, set up to extract confessions from the Cathar faithful four years earlier, was redoubling its efforts to bring the people of the Languedoc back into the Catholic fold. They had the choice of confessing their heresy willingly, confessing under torture, or dying for their faith. For the simple peasants and even the merchants in the towns, there really was no choice. Despite the Cathar belief that death was a release from an evil world, it was not easy to give up life when faced with the unknown.

"Between them, the Pope and King Louis are determined to exterminate us," Benoît said wearily one evening, after Philippa had been put to bed.

"The final solution: the Pope gets his flock back and Louis gains control of the Languedoc," said Corba. "Will we be safe even at Montségur?"

"It is more remote, and better protected. Besides, you will be with your husband, and I will be with my brothers and sisters in faith. Better to die together than alone."

"Better not to die at all!" reprimanded Corba sharply. "Have you forgotten my bloodline? I fear not for myself, but now that Esclarmonde has chosen to become a parfaite, Philippa must be kept safe, at all cost. The message must be kept alive."

"Montségur is the safest place to be. If things don't go well, we can smuggle you over the border to Aragon. King Louis has no power there. The alternative is for you both to flee there now. But I cannot come with you – my place is with my fellow Cathari."

"And my place is with my family," said Corba quietly.

They left at the end of the week, with just four men-at-arms. Roger Catala had tried to insist on a larger escort, but Benoît had categorically refused. "We don't want to draw attention to ourselves," he said. "Four men are sufficient to ward off robbers; any more and we become a target for the king's men."

They rode across the flank of the Pic d'Estable, which towered over Puylaurent, and skirted the main highway at Axat to take a tiny track that led up into the mountains. The highway, a quicker route, would have taken them close to the former Cathar stronghold at Puivert, which had fallen to De Montfort's men at the start of the crusade.

The mountain track – so narrow they had to ride single file – followed a raging stream through a narrow, steeply wooded valley that had gouged its way through the massif west of Axat. They made good progress, however, and spent the night at a small village called Joucou, where they found lodgings at a farmhouse.

In all her wanderings, Corba had never failed to find a warm welcome in the Cathar homesteads. They had now endured two decades of persecution and were a close-knit community, used to the comings and goings of wandering parfaits, bringing their gospel and teaching the true word of the Lord. The faydits, too; the dispossessed nobles who had refused to recant their faith, were made welcome under the roofs of many a simple commoner – though Cathar society was much more equal than under the Catholic nobility.

It was but a few hours' riding the next morning until the rocky outcrop of Montségur came into view on the horizon, the 400-foot limestone pog pointing dramatically skyward like a finger, a reminder of the heavenly realm so desperately sought by the beleaguered Cathars who fled to its sanctuary.

"Look, Philippa," said Corba excitedly. "The château of Montségur. We will be there by nightfall."

"It looks scary," said Philippa.

"Nonsense! It's a magnificent place – the views are even better than Puylaurent. And you will get the chance to meet your father, at last."

"How do I know he'll like me?" she asked, diffidently.

"Trust me, he adores you."

"How do you know? He's never seen me."

"Yes, he has – he came to see you when you were very little. Don't you remember? He has asked about you many times in his letters, ma petite. And don't forget your sister, Esclarmonde, will be there, too."

Philippa stared at the distant hill, a faraway look in her eyes. "I don't like it," she said stubbornly. "Something bad is going to happen, I can tell."

Chapter 13

Time dragged as they waited for darkness to fall, and the temperature started to drop rapidly. As they sat in silence on the cold stone floor, Rachel couldn't stop herself from shivering. She jumped as a strange noise echoed through the church. "What the hell was that?"

"You know what it's like with old buildings – you often get creaks and groans as the timbers expand and contract with the change in temperature."

As darkness finally enveloped the room, Rachel began to feel even more jittery. Her imagination was working overtime, but it was more than that. There was a presence here; something malevolent. She could feel it pressing in on her skull; a darkness; an eternal darkness. Someone or something didn't want her to be here tonight. Her skin began to crawl and her heart raced.

"David!"

"Yes?"

"Can we start digging now, please? I don't think I can take any more of just sitting here doing nothing."

Without waiting for an answer, Rachel clicked on her torch and a beam of brilliant white light cut through the gloom.

"For God's sake, Rachel, keep that pointed at the floor – someone might see it through the window! Now let's clear this crap off the floor and get to work. We'll take it in shifts."

David took the brush and gently swept aside the detritus of years of neglect – dust, leaves, cobwebs and bird droppings – revealing the hard dirt floor underneath, embedded with lumps of stone and old tiles.

"I'm guessing this had a tiled floor at some stage," he said. "I wouldn't mind betting it's not just Cholet who's been digging this place up. The question is, where do we begin?"

"Cholet reported seeing a relieving arch in the outer wall of the church," said Rachel. "So I guess that's the obvious place to start."

David pulled an archaeologist's trowel from his jacket pocket and started breaking up the surface in the corner of the room, digging out the rubble as he went. Although the surface was hard, the ground a couple of inches down was soft and crumbly, and it wasn't long before he had loosened an area roughly three-foot square. "That was easier than I thought," he observed. "Let's hope the rest is just as straightforward."

He set to work once more, and soon a mound of earth was piling up in front of them.

"Right, your go," said David sotto voce, picking up the shovel from the floor and handing it to her.

"You've hardly started!" she hissed. "Go on, get digging."

David put his foot on the top of the shovel blade and tested the soil. The blade bit easily into the ground, and he hoiked out a spadeful of loose sand-earth mix. "This is too good to be true," he remarked. "Cholet's mixed sand with this backfill to make re-excavation easier." It wasn't long before a large pile of spoil had formed between them.

"What's that?" whispered Rachel.

"What?"

"Over there, near the top edge of the hole – it looks like a piece of wood."

David scraped along the side of the trench with his trowel.

"You're right. Looks fairly modern – well at least, within the last 150 years… Oak, I would think, or it wouldn't have lasted in this damp soil." He pulled a paintbrush out of his top pocket and started dusting along the side of the timber. "Shine the light a bit closer, will you? Ah-ha! The earth reveals its secrets! Look – can you see those rebates, one on each side? They would be for hinges. This must be part of the framework for a trapdoor. I'm surprised Cholet missed that."

"Maybe he didn't," said Rachel. "Maybe he left it out of his report for a reason."

"Then why mention the relieving arch?"

"A throwaway mention, perhaps. No-one would have believed him if he said he found nothing under the Secret Room. So he just included enough vague information to satisfy people's curiosity, without giving too much away. It gave him the excuse to come back later – but someone or something stopped him from digging in here again."

"I'm beginning to agree with you – there seems to be some kind of conspiracy to hide the truth." David resumed his digging. "Here we go," he said at length. "There's the top of the arch Cholet mentioned." More and more of the arch slowly came into view, though the stone wall continued underneath it. David stood up to take a rest and looked askance at the stonework. "I'm not sure about this being a relieving arch – an arch built into a wall to spread the load. But the stonework underneath this is just rubble. It looks to me more like infill – someone has blocked up an old doorway. Look, you can see a smooth vertical line of faced stonework going downwards on both sides of the arch, then this jumble of rubbish in between."

He paused, hand on shovel, scratching his head. "Hang on a minute – I've got it! You know last week we found the edge of what looked like some steps? I didn't want to waste time, since we were so close to our goal, but supposing there was originally a staircase outside the church, leading down into the crypt? After all, this was a manorial chapel – it's not unusual to have an external entrance, so the nobility could come and admire their ancestors' tombs without having to go through the church."

"Brilliant, David!" enthused Rachel. "Obviously Saunière originally got down into the crypt through the tomb he found in front of the old altar – but when he realised what he had discovered, he had to find a way of getting in where no-one could see him coming and going. This blocked-up doorway must have been obvious from inside the crypt. That's why villagers reported seeing him digging up the churchyard – he was looking for a second entrance! He built the Secret Room right over the top of it, then moved the altar to hide the original entrance from prying eyes."

"It's beginning to add up," agreed David. "Right, back to work."

"Do you want me to have a go?"

"Be my guest," said David wearily, handing her the shovel and climbing out of the hole.

Rachel clambered down and starting digging, but the trench was getting so deep she found it hard to lift the spoil over the lip. "We need a bucket," she observed.

"I'd already figured that one out. But as you've probably noticed, there isn't one to hand."

"Give me your jacket."

"What?"

"Just give me your jacket!"

"So you can fill it up with mud?"

"Do you want to get in the crypt or not?"

David grudgingly removed his parka, and Rachel zipped it up, folded in the hood, and lay the bottom open in front of her. Soon it was bulging with spoil, which she heaved up to David. They kept up the process until around three feet of stonework was exposed under the arch. "You're right – it's just in-fill," said Rachel, poking the shovel blade into the pointing. "But the mortar's quite hard, and this shovel is way too unwieldy."

David pulled a long screwdriver out of his pocket, its tip worn almost to a point. "Try this."

"What else have you got stuffed in your pockets?" asked Rachel in astonishment.

"I wouldn't be much of an archaeologist if I didn't come well prepared. I'll save the bullwhip for later."

"You're not exactly Harrison Ford, so don't get any ideas." She took the screwdriver and started to claw out the pointing, but it was slow progress.

"Here, let me."

Rachel gladly pulled herself out of the pit and let David go to work once more. His powerful arms, acclimatised to long days working on digs, soon started to lever out chunks of mortar, which proved quite soft once the hard outer crust had been broken away. "Once we've got two or three stones out, the rest will be easy," he muttered between clenched teeth, as he drove the blade between the stones.

Eventually he had loosened one stone enough to make it wobble. "Assuming we're right, and there's a void behind here, this should push right through," said David. He tried shoving the rock with his hands, but the six-inch piece of limestone refused to budge.

"OK, time for brute force and ignorance," he said. He stood back as far as he could within the confines of the small pit, lifted up his foot and pushed hard on the stone with heel. It still wouldn't budge, so he kicked with his heel time and again until the stone abruptly disappeared from view in a cloud of dust, revealing an inky black darkness beyond.

Encouraged by his success, David set to work again feverishly, gouging out the pointing from the surrounding stones. "Right. Let's see if we can make this any bigger," he said, wiping the beads of sweat from his head.

Again, he pushed himself back and gave the stonework a kick. There was a little movement, but nothing else. The rocks appeared to be jammed together by their own weight. Exasperated, he pulled his leg back as far as he could and gave the wall an almighty stomp. The result was more dramatic than either of them could have predicted. With a echoing rumble and a cloud of dust, the top part of the wall underneath the arch tumbled inwards, revealing the straight edges of what had obviously once been a doorway.

For a moment they froze, terrified someone might have heard the noise.

"There's no way people in the village didn't hear that," whispered Rachel.

David put his finger to his lips, and they waited, but there was complete silence, save for the sound of their own breathing.

"We must have got away with it," he whispered back. "I've heard people are always digging around the village looking for gold – apparently, one treasure hunter even used dynamite. I guess they must get used to strange goings-on. Right – hand me the torch. I'm going in."

David squirmed his way through the opening and shone the torch inside. Through the cloud of slowly settling dust he could see a stairway descending underneath the church. He handed back the torch to Rachel. "There's a staircase behind here – it must be a continuation of the one we found in the trench. I'm going to need to go in feet-first so I can drop down inside. Once I'm in, hand me the torch and follow me down."

David turned round and backed into the hole he had created, lowering himself down inside until he was hanging from edge of the stonework. "Shine the torch down here," he gasped. "I can't reach the stairs – I don't want to break a leg."

Rachel did as she was bidden, and David could see that because of the steep angle of descent, the staircase was at least a metre under his feet. Moreover, if he dropped straight down there was a danger he could fall backwards. "Saunière must have had a ladder here," he muttered. "Oh well, here goes." With that he swung his body as far away from the wall as possible before letting go and throwing himself forwards onto the steps. He slithered down a little way and grazed his knee, but was otherwise unscathed.

"OK, hand me the torch." Rachel leaned through the opening, but the torch was out of reach. "You're going to have to throw it. Just let it drop into my hands."

"What if you drop it?"

"Got a better idea?"

"Yes," said Rachel, putting the torch in her teeth before turning round and lowering herself through the entrance. David reached up and held her tightly by the legs before lowering her to the ground. She ended up pressed against him, his hands around her waist, and for a fleeting second she allowed herself to enjoy the feeling. "OK, let's go David," she said abruptly. "Let's see what's down here."

She led the way down the steep flight of worn steps. "I can't believe we're finally in the crypt at Rennes-le-Château – we must be the first people down here since Saunière..." She broke off as she was confronted by a heavily studded oak door barring their way. "Well I guess that's predictable," she grumbled.

Rachel turned the rusty iron ring-handle and pushed hard. Surprisingly, the door slowly squealed opened to reveal more stairs continuing downwards. She glanced up at David with raised eyebrows, then turned back and started carefully down, brushing aside the accumulation of debris on each step with the side of her foot before proceeding to the next, wary of slipping.

After a short descent, she found herself standing on level ground in what was obviously the crypt. She looked around slowly, her powerful LED torch stabbing the murky gloom like a wartime searchlight. Around the periphery of the chamber were niches containing, she presumed, the tombs of ancient nobles. A heavy layer of dust covered everything in sight and cobwebs hung thickly across the entrances to many of the niches. Again, she felt a strange, brooding presence; something deeply dark and terrible, and she gave an involuntary shudder. This, then, was the place that had sparked so much speculation.

She shook off the pervading sense of foreboding and slowly walked forward, her torch picking out tombs surmounted by effigies of knights that had lain undisturbed for centuries

"I assume that's another way out," she whispered to David, pointing to another flight of stairs on the opposite side of the crypt. "According to eye witnesses, Saunière was seen going into the church several times, not coming out, then appearing in the graveyard some hours later."

"Assuming it does lead into the graveyard, it would surely have been blocked up, too," said David doubtfully.

"No harm checking it out."

They climbed the short staircase to find another oak door, identical to the one they had passed on the other side. Rachel tried turning the handle, but this time it refused to budge.

"We're clearly not getting out that way," she said. "It would take a battering ram to get through that thing."

They retraced their steps to the crypt. "If the tomb of Mary is here," observed Rachel, "it's clearly not going to be under one of these guys." She lifted a veil of cobwebs from the nearest tomb and peered at the inscription on the effigy of the knight that surmounted it. "François d'Hautpoul," she murmured. "Décédée 15th May 1753. Wasn't he the husband of Marie de Nègre d'Hautpoul, the noble-woman whose cryptic, mis-spelled tombstone caused all this furore?"

"I think you're right."

"Why was she buried in the churchyard rather than down here?"

"Only the male nobility were buried in manorial crypts. Women weren't considered important enough."

"Careful…"

"Hey, you can't change history. It's just the way things were."

Rachel sniffed and moved on. "Where is she? She has to be here somewhere, after all the clues we've discovered," she muttered. She shone the torch to the far end of the crypt. "What's that up there?" The brilliant white torchlight reflected off a veil of dust particles cloaking the scene. As they made their way down the chamber she began to make out the shape of an archway, guarded by a barrier of spear-headed railings. Beyond was a large white limestone sarcophagus roughly three feet high. The effigy surmounting the tomb, hands raised in prayer, was that of a woman. And, quite clearly, a pregnant woman.

Rachel felt giddy. She took a deep breath and grabbed hold of the railings to steady herself. "Is this what I think it is?" she asked quietly.

"Let's look at the inscription before we make any judgements," said David. He draped his muddy coat over the sharp railings and clambered over. He turned to offer Rachel a hand, but she was already straddling the railings and dropping down lightly beside him.

She turned to the sarcophagus and started brushing away the dust and cobwebs that festooned it to reveal the capitalised lettering running along the edge.

CI GIT LE CORPS DE MARIE CONNUE COMME LE MADELEINE ~ BÉNI PAR DIEU ~ |||||||||||||||||||||||||||||||||||||||||||||||||||||||||||||||||||||||||||||||||||||||||||
|||||||||||||||||||||| *~ AGÉE 55 ANS ~ ENTERRÉE ICI LE XVII JANVIER CMLII*

Rachel turned to look at David, an expression of awe on her face. "I think we've finally found her," she whispered.

Chapter 14

A shiver ran down Rachel's spine at the enormity of what they had discovered. She paused, tilting her head to one side as she took in the dimly lit scene. "But why was she buried here in 952? If she was 55 years old, she would have died in 60AD or thereabouts, given the vagaries of the calendar."

"I imagine she was originally buried elsewhere and reinterred here some centuries later. It was quite common to move saints and other notable figures to a burial place that was deemed more fitting – often a church was built around them. The dating ties in with the original church built on this site."

"I guess…" said Rachel slowly, still staring at the sarcophagus with a mixture of reverence and fascination as David began taking photos. "I wonder why someone has chiselled out part of the inscription. Was the tomb just too controversial?"

"The tomb itself wouldn't have been that controversial. After all, they claimed to have found Mary's grave at St-Maximin-la-Sainte-Beaume in Provence in the Middle Ages, and it became a major shrine for pilgrims."

"True – but she is shown as being pregnant. There's huge symbolism there, and it doesn't take much figuring out to guess what's been erased from the sarcophagus. This is Mary Magdalene we're talking about, after all – was she pregnant with Jesus's child?"

"Oh come on, Rachel," said David exasperatedly. "Let's stick to the facts, not go flying off on a wild goose chase. I accept there is a possibility that Mary came to France after Christ's death, but anything else is just pure speculation. Leave the crackpot theories to the fantasists. Heaven knows there are enough of them out there."

Rachel bit back her rejoinder and forced herself to focus on the tomb. "And the 17th of January? That's the date Marie de Blanchefort died, according to her tombstone. It's also the date Saunière suffered his fatal stroke in La Tour Magdala. Coincidence?"

"I'm not even going to answer that one."

"Whatever you may think about my ideas, there are plenty of people out there who would have a field-day if this tomb became public knowledge. When the papal legate sees this, he's going to seal it off for all time."

"There you have a point," he said grudgingly. "If that happens, we're going to need some hard evidence for TV. The photos will be pretty damning, but photos can be easily faked. We need to open the tomb – there may be something inside we can get carbon-dated, assuming Saunière hasn't beaten us to it."

Rachel gave a sharp intake of breath. "Open the tomb of Mary Magdalene? That would be sacrilege!" she gasped. "It's almost like opening the tomb of Jesus! This sarcophagus contains one of the most important figures in the history of mankind. It's not a game of Tomb Raider – you of all people should know that."

"I'm open to suggestions, but it's your TV show on the line. Photos on their own won't cut it, but if we can get something carbon-dated, it's a whole new ball-game. I'm certainly not suggesting we disturb her remains, but there may be some sort of artefact in there we can remove. Archaeology is about hard facts. If there were even a slim chance of carrying out a proper analysis of this tomb, it would be different – but you're right, there's no way the Church would allow it, given their track record."

Rachel wrestled with her conscience. The hard-nosed journalist in her wanted to expose the truth, but there was something else here, something she had never felt before – a deep sense of mystery and awe, coupled with an intense spiritual awareness. Opening the sarcophagus seemed like sacrilege. But David was right – people had a right to know the truth. "Go on then," she whispered. "May God forgive us."

David gave her a startled look before turning his attentions to the sarcophagus. "This lid is going to be heavy. That's odd, it's not on straight," he mused. "Looks as though someone has already tried to move it – Saunière, I guess."

He grabbed the lid by one corner and heaved with all his might, but it barely moved. "I'm going to need a hand," he said, breathing heavily, but Rachel continued to stare vacantly at the tomb. "Rachel!" he snapped, as she remained rooted to the spot. "Give me a hand, will you?"

She looked up, dazed. "Sorry – this is all really weird. I just had a flashback to the crash – at least, to an experience I had just afterwards while I was on the operating table."

"We don't have much time. It's 3am already."

Rachel threw her weight in alongside David and together they slowly inched the heavy stone lid half way across the sarcophagus.

"That should do it," said David. "If it comes all the way off it might break, and we'll certainly never get it back on again. It makes you wonder whether Saunière did actually open it – I know he was a big guy, but it would have been a struggle single-handed. OK, what have we got here?" A grim look shadowed his face as he shone the torch into the dark interior. "Nothing, it would seem. Well that's a let-down – an empty tomb. It seems history is repeating itself – at least, in Biblical terms."

Rachel scratched her head. "Why would they have gone to all this trouble to build a church over the tomb and then move the body? It just doesn't make sense – unless someone was trying to hide the evidence." Rachel stared thoughtfully at the bottom of the sarcophagus three feet below, trying to make sense of the jumble of debris. "There's certainly a lot of junk down there. It looks as if the body was removed in a hurry. I think those are shroud fragments – they could be dated."

"But probably only to the tenth century. The body would almost certainly have been rewrapped when it was interred here. We'll take some anyway, but I don't hold out much hope.. ."

"I know. I wonder if there's anything else down there?" Rachel peered down inside the tomb again and gently sifted through the debris. She knew they were breaking all the rules of archaeology, but she was determined to find something conclusive. "Ouch!" she exclaimed.

"Are you OK?"

"I've just cut my finger on something sharp."

She reappeared, blood dripping from her hand, clutching several large fragments of white pottery, including a circular base about three inches in diameter. David took them and examined them carefully, turning them over in his hand. "I'm afraid this looks medieval – still, we can carbon-date pottery pretty accurately. Anything else down there?"

Rachel reached down into the tomb once more and continued to sift carefully through the detritus in the coffin until she felt her fingers brush something dry and brittle. "Ah, what's this? My God, it looks like a parchment scroll – it must have been in that jar. It looks pretty fragile – I'm frightened to move it."

"Let me take a look," said David, squeezing his shoulders through the narrow gap and peering down into the coffin. "You're right," he said. "It's parchment, and it will certainly be fragile. We can't unroll it without treating it first – it would just crumble."

"How are we going to get it back in one piece?"

"I'll pop it in my lens case. As long as we're careful, it should be OK. Pass it over, will you?" Rachel handed them down to him, and putting his screwdriver carefully through the centre of the scroll, David lifted it up and placed it gently into the case. "That was tricky," he observed, straightening up and massaging his back. "Now all we have to do is get this coffin lid back on and find a way out of here."

"Cholet mentions the possible existence of a secret passage leading from the château to the church," suggested Rachel.

"With the emphasis on the word 'possible'," said David. "He was merely setting the scene. But we've got to find a way out of here, and since the only alternative is retracing our steps and owning up to what we've done, we might as well explore every option. We're going to have to comb every inch of this place, so let's get going."

For the next hour they methodically examined the walls of the crypt, scrutinising every nook and cranny for a possible exit, but to no avail, and eventually they slumped down wearily on the ground near the staircase they had entered by.

"I guess the game's up," said David bitterly. "We'll have to go back up to the sacristy, wait until they open up the church, and shout until someone hears us. I'll leave you to do the explaining."

Chapter 15

They stood despondently staring at Mary's tomb; their moment of triumph soured by the prospect of imminent defeat.

"If we cover up the excavations, perhaps we could get away with saying we just went back to look at the Secret Room and got locked in," suggested Rachel.

"Do you really think they would believe that?" sneered David.

Rachel turned away angrily. "Goddamn it, why do you have to be such a self-righteous prick sometimes?" she said, stamping her foot on the ground in temper. She abruptly turned back to David, a glimmer of hope in her eyes. "Did you hear that?"

"What – you having a tantrum?"

"No! Listen…" She stamped her foot again.

"I don't get it…"

"It's hollow, you dummy! God, why are men so dense sometimes? Listen…" She stamped again, harder.

"You might have something," said David, finally showing some interest.

Rachel hunkered down and started brushing away some of the debris on the ground. "Hell – look, I was sitting on it!" she said, grabbing hold of a rusty iron ring set into one of the flagstones. "Come on, give me a hand!"

Together they grasped the ring and heaved as hard as they could. Slowly but surely they lifted the heavy flagstone from its bed to reveal a flight of stone steps leading into the inky blackness beneath. David looked enquiringly at Rachel. "Do you really want to go down there?"

"Do we have a choice?" she snapped, betraying the fear slowly creeping up her spine. The palpable sense of menace had dramatically increased; it was as if they had opened a door to the underworld. Abruptly, she grabbed the torch and started gingerly down the stairs. "There's a tunnel down here," she said, reaching the bottom. "From the way it's been hacked out of the rock, it looks pretty ancient. Are you coming down?"

She didn't wait for a response, but turning on her heels, marched off down the tunnel. They had only gone a short distance when the passage forked in two. "Now where?" she demanded, not expecting, or receiving, an answer. After a moment's hesitation, she took the right fork, but it wasn't long before the passageway forked again.

"If we're not careful we're going to get lost down here for all eternity," said David tersely.

"I've got an idea – do you remember your Classical history?"

"I should hope so."

"Remember Ariadne's thread? The princess who gave her lover Theseus a ball of red thread so he could find his way out of the Minotaur's labyrinth?"

"Great idea, but no balls of thread handy, as far as I am aware."

Rachel took off her loose-knit woollen jumper and unpicked a thread. "Here we go. It's not red, but it will do." She unravelled a good length of yarn, tied one end round a piece of rock, and set off down the right fork again, paying out the yarn as she went. They passed another fork, and this time the tunnel they entered appeared to have been created naturally by an underground stream, enlarged here and there where necessary.

"I don't know where this leads, but we've gone way beyond the château," said David's voice behind her.

"We might as well find out where it goes – it may come out further down the hillside..." Rachel's voice trailed off as the passage opened out into a vast underground chamber, and her heart faltered. In the middle of the cave stood what was clearly a stone altar, an iron spike driven into each corner; a goat's skull placed at its centre, leering at her eerily. As the torch cut a path through the darkness, she could just make out what appeared to be bloodstains on the altar-stone. A palpable sense of evil pervaded the chamber, and panic surged inside her; she desperately wanted to scream as the blackness seeped into every fibre of her being. With a huge effort of will, she screwed up her courage and pushed the rising fear back down. "OK, I don't know what this is, but I'm getting out of here," she said, brushing past David and walking rapidly back up the passage.

He caught up with her at the next fork and grabbed her by the arm. She pushed him away fiercely and stumbled on, trying to keep the tears from her eyes. He grabbed her arms with both hands and shook her, forcing her to look at him. "Hey, Rache, it's me – don't be scared. We mustn't let this place get to us – we've got to keep our heads." He paused as he felt her relax slightly. "If it's any consolation, I felt that, too... whatever it was. It wasn't something I've ever experienced before or want to again – it certainly wasn't anything in my scientific lexicon."

"*Terribilis est locus iste*," said Rachel, struggling to keep her voice steady. "The quotation above the church door says it all. This place is evil, David; I've felt it ever since we went into the Secret Room. I don't know what it's got to do with Saunière or the tomb of Mary Magdalene – maybe it's just a coincidence. But there was – or is – something terrible going on down here."

"I agree – let's find a way out of this place. You go on ahead."

They went down the other branch of the fork, but after a short distance were met by a rock-fall.

"Let's hope that wasn't the way out," said David grimly. They retraced their steps to the previous fork, then followed Rachel's woollen thread back to where the passage had split. "OK, let's hope this one gives us more luck," he said. "We're running out of time – it's 5am."

They had followed the passageway just a few yards when it veered sharply to the left and started to double-back on itself. After a few more twists and turns the tunnel ended in a smallish room, obviously man-made. A few odds and ends were scattered around the floor, while in the ceiling was a wooden trapdoor.

"We could be under the château," said David. "That's got to be the way out."

"The castle is still inhabited," said Rachel.

"Only partly – the wing round the back is in ruins. Anyway, inhabited or not, we don't have much choice but to try it. If we're discovered we're no worse off than by giving ourselves up. Here, jump on my shoulders and let's see if we can open it."

David knelt down and Rachel put her legs around his neck while he heaved himself up. "My dad used to carry me like this when I was a kid," she teased. "It was great fun. Now, let's try this hatch." She reached up and pushed hard against the trapdoor, but try as she might, she could not get it to budge. "There must be something on top of it," she said dejectedly, as David set her down on the floor. "Now what the hell do we do?"

David paused a moment, trying to gauge her state of mind. "I don't know what your reaction is going to be to this, but there was another passage leading off the far side of that cave with the altar – and we were going downhill. If it's an old water-course, it should lead out somewhere."

The same thought had already crossed Rachel's mind. It was a terrifying prospect, but there seemed no alternative. "OK, let's do it," she said abruptly.

David was surprised, but said nothing. Rachel could be infuriating sometimes, but she was certainly plucky. They walked swiftly back towards the large cave, David again letting Rachel lead the way. As they neared the chamber, Rachel could feel the fear rising in her throat. There was a presence here, something as old as time, something evil and remorseless. She marched into the middle of the room, walked straight past the stone altar without looking, and headed for the dark shape that marked the passage on the far side.

"Hang on a minute, Rachel," called David. "Take a look at this."

Rachel turned round, clenching her fists tightly. "What!" she exclaimed, her nerves jangling. "This had better not be one of your stupid jokes – I'm not in the mood."

"No Rachel, it's not," said David gently. "I wouldn't do that to you; not here. But look at these sarcophagi around the edge of the cave."

Rachel gazed around the chamber in astonishment. "Hell – why didn't we see those before?"

"I think we were both a little freaked out," said David diplomatically.

Seven or eight stone coffins were arranged around the edge of the chamber, lying parallel to the wall. Rachel walked over to the nearest one and knelt down in front of it. "Come and take a look at this," she said, fascination momentarily overcoming her fear. "It looks pre-Christian to me – what do you think?"

"I don't recognise the language," said David, kneeling down beside her. "It's certainly not Latin or Old French. I wonder if these could be Visigoth tombs? Cholet mentions that Rhedae was once a major Visigoth settlement. That would fit in with the bloodstains on the altar – we know from the Roman writer Tacitus that Germanic tribes carried out animal and human sacrifices before their conversion to Christianity."

Rachel shuddered. "It doesn't bear thinking about," she said. She walked across to the adjacent tomb, but finding nothing new, went on to the next. "Hey, come here," she called. "Look at that," she said, as David joined her. The tomb lid was split, and the corner had broken off and was lying on the floor. The yellowed, skeletal bones of a foot could clearly be seen in the light of her torch.

"That breakage doesn't look like an accident," said David. "Look at the marks on the edge. Someone has been at this with a hammer and chisel."

"Saunière?" queried Rachel.

"Probably, though these tombs have been here for nearly 2,000 years, so it could have been anyone. It does make you wonder, though…" He shone his torch into the coffin, and gasped. "Good grief – I think we may have found the source of Saunière's wealth – or at least some of it." He reached into the coffin as far as he could go. "Look at that!" he exclaimed, opening his hand to reveal a gold coin.

Rachel could not believe her eyes. "How much more of that stuff is in there?"

"A few more, though I can't see much through this narrow opening. We'll leave the rest where they are – this will do for dating purposes; I don't want to disturb the archaeology any further. This must have been some kind of royal burial chamber. In its way, this rivals the Valley of the Kings – if not in grandeur, at least in terms of historical importance. After all, the Visigoths sacked Rome. The world ought to know about this place."

"But Saunière wanted it all to himself," said Rachel, thinking out loud. "And even if he had wanted to reveal it, he couldn't, because of the tomb of the pregnant Mary in the crypt above. It seems he didn't want that to become public knowledge, even though he clearly venerated Mary as a result of his discovery."

"The gold seems to blow the theory about him blackmailing the Church," observed David.

"Not necessarily. For a start, it might not have been Saunière who took the gold. And don't forget he was getting complaints from the villagers about digging up the churchyard – they even went to the bishop. And we know he had a highly extravagant lifestyle. Maybe he just got greedy."

"The pieces of the jigsaw are beginning to fall into place," said David. "I'll take a few pictures, and then we'll get out of here. Here, take this, will you?" he said, holding out the coin.

Rachel froze. David's hand seemed somehow tainted – it was almost as if she were being asked to take poison. "I'd rather not," she said, speaking with difficulty. "Can't you just stick it in your pocket?"

David shrugged, put the coin away and started to rattle off some pictures. Rachel hugged herself as the flash repeatedly lit up the dark chamber with an eerie brilliance. "Are we done?" she asked at length, as David previewed some of the pictures he had taken. "If so, can we get out of this place?"

"Yes, I guess so."

"You do realise the treasure from this place hasn't exactly brought people much luck," commented Rachel, as they walked towards the opening on the far wall of the cavern. "The shepherd boy, Paris, stoned to death when he turned up in the village with pockets full of gold; the deaths of Gelis and Saunière."

"I'm not superstitious," said David. "They obviously thought Paris was a thief, and while I agree about the deaths of Gelis and Saunière, I suspect it's more to do with someone trying to cover up the truth about the Magdalene."

They turned to enter the passage, which started to run steeply downhill, and they had to scramble their way over a number of rocky outcrops. This section of the old underground watercourse had clearly not been enhanced by human hand, and at one point it narrowed to such an extent they were only able to squeeze through with difficulty.

David, who was now leading, wriggled through the gap, one foot catching as he did so. He pushed forward hard with the other, only for it to fall away beneath him, leaving him hanging precariously over a large chasm.

Rachel lunged forwards and grabbed him, finding unexpected strength as she hauled his body back from the brink.

"Christ, that was a close call," gasped David.

"Cholet says there were rumours of man-traps in the tunnels," said Rachel, still holding him, her heart beating like a steam-hammer. "Like you, I dismissed some of that stuff as bunkum, but these old stories often have a grain of truth in them. If you covered up that pothole with some sticks and bracken it would certainly keep the treasure hunters at bay."

"Well, we've got to get across it," said David grimly, peering over the edge of the rock. "It's OK," he called over his shoulder. "There's a narrow ledge on one side. It's only about 18 inches wide, and there's an overhang, but we should be OK."

Rachel blanched, but followed him forwards. The ledge would have been wide enough to walk across safely but for the curved roof of the tunnel, requiring them to shuffle across on all fours. Fighting the vertigo, she tried hard not to look into the looming pit just inches from her hands and feet, but by the time she reached the far side her legs had turned to jelly.

"Thank God that's over," she said.

"I'll tell you what Rachel," said David, look at her seriously. "Thank God you weren't leading – luckily one of my big feet got wedged in a crevice, but you could have gone straight down."

"Thanks for that, David. You certainly know how to cheer a girl up. Now come on, let's get out. It will be dawn soon."

She switched on her torch and pushed in front to prove she wasn't afraid, but an icy fear still gripped her, and it wasn't until she saw a faint patch of starlight punctuating the gloom ahead that she felt herself relax.

She waited for David to join her and switched off the torch. "We're out," she said, pointing at a window of sky a few yards ahead. "Thank God, we're out."

Chapter 16

Rachel and David stumbled out onto the hillside below Rennes-le-Château through a narrow fissure in the rock that was all but invisible from more than a few feet away.

Dawn had already broken in the eastern sky, and professional formalities momentarily forgotten, they trudged wearily hand in hand up the hillside to the narrow mountain road leading to the village. They had been up all night and were exhausted from the mental strain of the past few hours, but they were also elated at their discovery – near-certain proof that Mary Magdalene was buried in the church. Proof, too, that below the crypt at Rennes-le-Château lay an ancient Visigoth burial chamber whose existence would stun the archaeological world.

As they turned off to cut up a goat track into the village, David stopped dead in his tracks. "I've just realised something," he said, a shocked look on his face.

"What?"

"The Secret Room! We haven't covered our tracks. When the papal legate arrives on Wednesday, tonight's little high jinks will be completely exposed – assuming Hélène doesn't discover it first. We'll be thrown off the dig."

"Don't beat yourself up, David – what were we supposed to do, anyway? We had to get out of there. Anyway, it doesn't matter after what we've found."

"It most certainly does! I'll have my credentials withdrawn by the French authorities – I would never be able to work on a dig over here again. Come to that, the British authorities would take a pretty dim view of it, too. I could lose my licence."

"I'm really sorry I've got you into this mess."

"Don't be daft – I wouldn't change a thing. What we've just seen down there is every archaeologist's dream come true. It makes up for all the months of working ankle-deep in mud in the middle of winter, sifting through pottery shards with a trowel."

"If the worst comes to the worst, I could probably get you some work as a resident expert on TV shows," said Rachel. "You'd be famous – whatever you may say about the media, they understand the selling power of a famous name."

"Thanks, Rachel, that's sweet of you. Let's hope it doesn't come to that." David paused, his mind working overtime. "Hang on a minute – I've had a brainwave!"

She resisted the temptation to tease him. "Tell me!"

"The dig – we were planning to break through into the crypt by creating a temporary hole in the stonework, since we weren't sure where the original entrance was, right? But now we know where it is, I can divert the trench under the Secret Room and take it right up to the stairway. We'll hit the hole we've dug, and say there's been some subsidence. I'll have to let Guy know – I can trust him to keep a secret. We've worked together for years. I'll make sure there's no-one else in there when the time comes."

"And Hélène?"

"We'll cross that bridge if and when we come to it."

"Won't digging directly under the room undermine its foundations?"

"Not if we're careful and shore it up. There's not much weight on that outer wall – it's only a small extension on the side of the church. I'm not going to ask anyone, I'm just going to do it – say we found some steps, which is true, and we felt it would do less damage to follow them than burrowing through the church foundations. Hopefully the papal legate will buy it – I will certainly get into far less than trouble than I would for our secret expedition last night."

"Will you have time to extend the trench that far? You've only got till tomorrow morning."

"I'll go and talk to the team now. We can do it if we get a move on – we'll work through the night if we have to. Again, if anyone questions us we can say we're getting ready for the legate's visit and hit a few last-minute snags."

"Sounds like a plan," said Rachel. "I'll come and give you a hand."

"We can manage – there's enough of us. You can only get so many people in a trench. Why don't you go back to the hotel and get some sleep?"

"Hey, we're in this together. I'm not going to swan off back to the hotel while you do all the hard work. I'm going to be there with you, every step of the way – even if it's only making cups of coffee to keep you guys going."

The next 24 hours were a frenzy of activity. David rounded up the dig team as soon as they arrived on site and told them about the new plan. There were a few raised eyebrows when he said they had new information about an entrance to the crypt, and the archaeological corner-cutting that would be needed. But such was the level of anticipation about finally reaching their goal, there was little complaint.

There wasn't much for Rachel to do, but she couldn't leave them alone. In between ferrying supplies of baguettes and coffee, she tried to distract the museum staff as much as possible by idly chatting about the upcoming visit of the papal legate.

No-one mentioned the unlocked door to the sacristy, and as far as she could tell, everyone was reacting quite normally. When she couldn't distract them any longer, she started surfing the net, checking up on the history of the

Visigoths. At one point she dozed off in her chair, and woke up with a start some half an hour later feeling guilty, but no-one seemed to have noticed.

Darkness fell and the team carried on working under arc lights, their explanation about having to complete their work before the arrival of the legate being accepted without question. Finally, at about 10pm, David came to find her.

"We're about to break through," he said. "Do you want to come and join us?"

"Do I want to join you? I wouldn't miss this for a million bucks."

Rachel followed David back to the trench and clambered down, ducking under the heavy timbers shoring up the wall of the Secret Room to join David and Guy at the 'coal face' of the dig.

"I reckon we've only got a couple of feet to go," said Guy, giving her a sly wink. "David told me about last night. Shame you didn't have time to look inside."

"Er, yes," said Rachel sheepishly. "It took much longer than expected. Still, at least we found the entrance. We'll just have to hope the papal legate plays ball."

"Some hope," said David. "Still, if nothing else, we've proved the existence of the crypt, which was our official brief. The Church will find it hard to prevent it being opened up to the public with the whole of the world watching."

As Guy started hacking at the last few inches of soil, Rachel raised her eyebrows at David, but he just shrugged. He had obviously decided not to tell Guy the full story at the moment, and while she knew he was trustworthy, she could understand why. The fewer people who knew the truth, the safer for everyone.

"Whoa," said Guy, as he his spade suddenly bit through the last piece of soil and flew into the void behind, clattering down the steps to the crypt. "That must have been quite a big hole you made up there."

"Shh!" said Rachel conspiratorially.

"Sorry!" Guy grabbed David's spade and started enlarging the entrance, pushing the final few inches of spoil onto the steps below. "There she blows," he said, leaning forward and shining his headtorch down the steps. "Quite impressive."

"OK Guy, I'll clean up now – you take a break," said David.

"Oh – OK," said Guy, clearly disappointed.

"That was a bit harsh, wasn't it?" said Rachel, as Guy disappeared.

"I didn't want him charging down there and finding the tomb – or the trapdoor, for that matter," said David.

"Hell, no."

"It's left a pretty big hole," he said, looking up into the Secret Room above. "We'll just have to claim the floor fell in, and blame it on Cholet's backfilling.

Right, let's go and shut that trapdoor. We don't want any incriminating evidence that we've been exploring down there."

He lowered himself onto the staircase, and was joined by Rachel, who could now walk more or less unhindered straight through from the trench. They descended the steps to the door, which they noticed was shut.

"Didn't you leave the door open?" queried David.

"I thought so," said Rachel, unsure of herself. The door pushed open easily, and David continued down the stairway ahead of her – but stopped short as soon as he entered the crypt.

"It's shut!" exclaimed David. "The trapdoor's bloody shut! How the hell did that happen?"

"There's only one way it could possibly have been closed," said Rachel slowly. "Someone knows we were here."

Chapter 17

Two hours' snatched sleep and a hot shower were all they had time for before returning to the dig to meet the papal legate, David attired in his single, slightly crumpled suit, Rachel in a sexy, figure-hugging skirt and a blouse with plenty of décolletage. She might be a feminist, but she knew men's weaknesses and intended to use every weapon in her formidable armoury. They arrived on site at 9am and waited nervously for the cardinal to arrive.

Following complaints from town councillors, Hélène tried to quiz David about why the trench had diverted under the Secret Room, but he played on his bad French and pretended not to understand. Rachel, whose French had become fairly good during her months in the Languedoc, explained they had discovered the hidden steps to the crypt during the final stage of the dig, and diverted the trench to minimise damage and make it easier for the legate to gain access. Hélène clearly wasn't happy, but it was a fait accompli, and with the legate due at any moment, she let the matter drop.

Finally at 11am a small cavalcade of cars drove up the narrow street and stopped outside the churchyard. The cardinal, a tall, burly man in his early 60s, easily identifiable by his red zucchetto, stepped out, accompanied by a young, clean-cut, bespectacled priest, who was obviously his personal assistant. Monsigneur Billard, the Bishop of Carcassonne, whom they had already met, completed the party.

David and Rachel walked over to introduce themselves, and the cardinal's secretary stepped forward. "Mr Tranter? And Miss Spencer? It's a pleasure to meet you," he said in a hard, crisp voice. His English was almost flawless, coloured by a light Italian accent. "Allow me to introduce Cardinal Bertolotti, the most trusted envoy of His Holiness the Pope."

"Your Eminence," said David, bowing slightly and taking the cardinal's outstretched hand. "We are honoured by your presence."

"It is my pleasure," he said, in a heavily accented voice, almost crushing David's hand in a vice-like grip. "This is a big occasion, no? Perhaps we solve this mystery now. Though maybe the town is not happy if no more tourists are coming," he joked. "And Miss Spencer? Enchantée, as they say here in France. You are a lucky man, Mr Tranter."

Rachel blushed deeply and tried hard not to look at David. "Thank you – Your Eminence is too kind."

David took the cardinal to meet the rest of his team, and then introduced the museum staff. "Would you like some coffee, Your Eminence?"

"Coffee? We must solve this mystery, no? It is too exciting for coffee! Let us go and look now at your… how do you say in English? Dig?"

"That's correct, Your Eminence. As you say, this is an exciting moment."

David led the cardinal over to the trench, and noticed a frown cross his face when he saw the trench disappearing under the Secret Room. The man had clearly been doing his homework.

"We had intended to break through into the crypt over there," said David, gesticulating vaguely further up the wall, "but we uncovered the edge of these steps, which clearly provided access to the crypt in earlier times. It was much safer and less intrusive this way. We will, of course, make this good in any way you wish, in consultation with the Church and the town council – though I assume you will want to retain access to the crypt in some way." The cardinal struggled with the explanation and turned to his secretary for a translation.

The cardinal nodded. "Very well," he said gruffly. "It is not what we agreed, but now we are here…" he shrugged.

David glanced at Rachel for help, and she sidled up to the cardinal. "We didn't think it would be very dignified for you, crawling through a hole under the church," she said with a winning smile. "This is much better. And there is less damage to the building, too."

The cardinal seemed mollified by her presence, returning her smile with warmth. "Very well," he said. "Your explanation is 'OK', Miss Spencer…"

"Please, call me Rachel."

"As you wish. Now, you show me the way?"

They all climbed down into the trench, and with Rachel leading and David bringing up the rear, they ducked under the foundations of the Secret Room and emerged onto the stone staircase.

"Thank you," said the cardinal. "And now I make the inspection. You have not entered the crypt, as was agreed?"

"No, Your Eminence. We checked to ensure there was access, of course – there is a door further down, but it's not locked."

The cardinal waited for an interpretation from his secretary. "But you did not go in?" he repeated sternly, at length.

"No, Your Eminence."

The cardinal studied David's face intently for a few moments. "Very well," he said at length, and beckoning to his secretary to go ahead with the torch, he started down the stairs.

The two men were gone for nearly an hour, and when they reappeared the cardinal face was grim.

This time he left the talking to his secretary. "His Eminence cannot allow you to enter the crypt at the moment," he said. "There are some unusual features that we would like Vatican experts to examine. And to be frank, Mr

Tranter, by departing from the agreed plan, you have committed a breach of trust. The graveyard belongs to the council, but we expressly forbade you to dig on church property. Our agreement only allowed you to excavate a small opening in the outer wall of the church, to prove the existence of a crypt. As a result of your actions, we are under no obligation to cooperate further with National Geographic on this matter."

David's face grew thunderous. "Are you saying you are not going to tell anyone what you've found down there?" he asked angrily.

"And what have we found down there, Mr Tranter?" queried the secretary icily. "You seem very agitated – I am sure you have seen many such crypts in your time; what makes this one so special?"

"You know damn well what makes this special! You can't just sit on this…" He broke off as Rachel stepped forward and put her hand on his arm.

"Not now, David," she said quietly. "You're tired, and this is neither the time nor the place. We can use the media to put pressure on the Vatican – having a row with the cardinal isn't going to help matters. In the meantime, we have other fish to fry, don't we?" She gave him a conspiratorial smile.

David relaxed at her touch. "OK," he said ruefully. "I guess you're right."

He turned to the cardinal and bowed slightly. "Please accept my apologies, Your Eminence. We meant no harm – were simply trying to make the inspection easier for you. When we found the steps it just seemed the logical course of action. I should have discussed it with you first, of course, but we were so close to your visit – I didn't want to hold things up."

The cardinal, still visibly angry, searched for the words to reply, but his secretary quickly stepped in. "Your personal apology is accepted, Mr Tranter. I understand your explanation – you have been working hard here for many months. But we cannot condone your actions. I'm afraid it is bound to effect our relationship with National Geographic, at least in the short term. Perhaps we can talk further in a few months' time, when our experts have finished their examinations. As from today, this access will be locked, and we will be installing CCTV cameras on the site." He looked at David meaningfully.

David swallowed his anger as the two men left the scene and returned to their cars. There followed a little flurry of activity as another priest in full clerical attire, looking slightly surreal with a Nikon hanging from his neck, returned to the crypt with the secretary to take some official photographs. Workmen were summoned in a miraculously short period of time, and an hour later the cardinal and his entourage had gone, leaving an industrial-sized padlock and chain on the crypt door.

"Damn," said David, as they sat in the Finds Room later, drowning their sorrows in a bottle of wine. "I know it was all totally predictable, but it's still frustrating. "People have a right to know…"

"And they will, David," said Rachel, putting her hand on his. She couldn't help feeling guilty, having badgered David into their night-time expedition. But she equally knew that had they not done so, they would have learned nothing about the contents of the crypt. There was no way the Vatican was going to release that information, not now, not next year, not ever.

"Let's focus on what we have got." She lowered her voice. "We know about the Magdalene. We know she had a child, paternity unknown. And we have that scroll, which may give us the proof we need to go public. And on a different track, we have the coin from the Visigoth burial chamber…"

David's face blanched.

"What's the matter?" she asked.

"The scroll is still in the camera case!"

They rushed out of the museum and across to the dig cabin. The rest of the team had been sent home for the day, and it was now locked. David fumbled with the keys, and once inside, rushed to pick up the case, still lying on the table where he had left it. He opened it up and gave a sigh of relief.

"Thank God for that," he said. "It's still in one piece – that really would have been a disaster. I'll get this into preservation straight away. It will mean using the Finds Room, but I don't see any alternative. The museum is alarmed, and no-one will have a clue what it is among all the other bits and pieces we've dug up."

Chapter 18

Philippa ran up the stone spiral stairway, her face dancing with delight, and burst into the isolated tower room where Pierre-Roger, dispossessed Lord of Mirepoix, was ensconced with her father Raymond.

"Husband, have you heard the news? The Count of Toulouse is finally packing his bags and going home – the siege is no more!"

She hesitated as she took in the scene in front of her: the two men were standing over the table studying a crude map, but their body language suggested she had broken in on a heated argument.

Pierre-Roger looked up testily, annoyed at the interruption. One glance at her glowing face, however, and his anger melted. They had been wedded these three years past, but she had not shared his bed until her 16th birthday, barely three months before. Now that they were together at last, they were blissfully happy.

At 45, he had felt awkward, though such dynastic alliances were commonplace. His initial doubts and fears about the match had been ill-founded, however, for Philippa's vitality and sparkle – not to mention her raven-haired beauty – had rapidly made her mistress of his heart. And in a country ravaged by war, children had to grow up fast; she had shown evidence of a sharp mind and a wise head to match her physical maturity.

As for Philippa, marrying the dashing Pierre-Roger de Mirepoix, the knight commander of Montségur – famous for his exploits as a warrior in the Cathar cause – was a dream come true. Despite her initial unhappiness at Montségur, when Pierre-Roger had arrived in 1234 to help her father run the militia at the new Cathar capital, she fell head over heels in love with him in the way that only a young girl could. But childhood hero-worship turned into something much deeper over the next few years as Philippa came into womanhood, and his daring raids on the forces of King Louis served only to heighten her feelings for him – a fact not unnoticed by her mother.

Corba saw the budding romance as a way of providing her daughter with protection in dangerous times, notwithstanding Pierre-Roger's sometimes foolhardy exploits. She, too, had misgivings about marriage at such a tender age, but events on the ground were moving rapidly, and she had to act. Now that Philippa's single-minded elder sister, Esclarmonde, had not only taken the Cathar faith but become a parfaite, Corba had been left with no option but to engineer a marriage for Philippa. Parfaits were celibate, and Corba's bloodline must continue. She couldn't afford the risk of Philippa following in her sister's footsteps. Corba had expected some resistance to the suggestion of marriage, given the age difference, but Philippa had been overjoyed at the suggestion.

Now the child-bride was fast becoming a woman of substance.

"Yes, I heard," said Pierre-Roger, smiling. "Though in truth, it was no real siege. They never tried to stop us smuggling supplies into the château. Raymond VII may not be the man his father was, but he still supports the Cathar cause, whatever he has told King Louis."

"So what plot are you hatching now?" asked Philippa, moving over to the table and standing between the two men she loved most in the world. She looked down at the map spread out before them. "Not another sortie, I hope – your leg has barely healed from that crossbow quarrel you took in the raid on Puivert." A puzzled look crossed her face as she continued to stare at the crude cartography. "Why have you drawn a circle around Avignonet? It's half-way to Toulouse."

"I'm sorry, Philippa, but I'm not at liberty to discuss this with you. Too much rests upon the outcome."

"I am your wife, now," she said, flushing with anger at his tone. "And not just in name. I might be carrying your child – I have a right to know if you're putting yourself in needless danger."

"You are with child?" he queried.

"I cannot be sure yet, but I believe so. That gives me a right to know. I am not just your wife – you know my heritage."

"Raymond," said Pierre-Roger, turning to his father-in-law. "Please reason with the girl. The fewer people that know about this, the better."

Raymond gave his daughter a rueful look and smiled. "She has a point. You were warned what you were getting yourself into when you married her – in more ways than one. I know she can be headstrong, but she is mature beyond her years. And you did swear an oath to protect her, and consult her at all times on anything that might affect the safety of her bloodline."

"And so I will! But does that extend to military strategy?"

"You were planning to lead the raid yourself, were you not? As I was saying before she came in, I myself am not happy with the idea."

"You're not seriously thinking of attacking Avignonet?" exclaimed Philippa in disbelief. "Have you completely lost your wits?"

"Mind your manners, wife," said Pierre-Roger, running his hands through his hair in exasperation. "It's not as simple as that. Very well then, I'll tell you. But you must swear on your life not to breathe a word of this to anyone – not even to your mother."

"I swear," said Philippa, steadily holding his gaze. "Now tell me, what is so important about Avignonet that you would risk your life travelling 20 leagues through countryside swarming with the king's men?"

Pierre-Roger took a deep breath. "You mentioned the siege that King Louis forced Raymond to undertake to prove his allegiance, after he refused to help put down Trencavel's uprising."

"Never mind not helping Louis! Raymond should have gone to Trencavel's aid when he returned from Aragon – he is the rightful lord of Carcassonne!" said Philippa angrily. "Trencavel took Limoux and Montréal with just a small band of Catalan mercenaries – imagine how easily Carcassonne would have fallen if Raymond had joined his side. But no, he sat on his hands and did nothing."

"There's a reason for that: it was a question of bad timing. Yes, Raymond should have helped Trencavel. I thought so at the time, and I still think so. But he held back because he had other irons in the fire. This past year Raymond has been secretly building an alliance with King Henry III of England. The king's troops will be landing at Royan within the next fortnight."

"Why are the English getting involved?"

"You should attend to your history lessons more closely," chided Pierre-Roger.

"Don't speak to me as if I'm a child," said Philippa, scowling.

Pierre-Roger bit back his tongue. "Sorry. But you should know that England once owned more of France than the King of France himself. Henry is keen to regain his lands in Normandy, Anjou and Aquitaine, and has every reason to help us keep the Languedoc free – a thorn in the French side."

"And what does all this have to do with the raid you are planning on Avignonet?"

Pierre-Roger hesitated, and Philippa's father gave him a hard look. "I think you should tell her."

"Very well. The Inquisition has moved out of Toulouse, intent on spreading its terror throughout the land All suspected Cathars will be taken in for questioning by the Pope's men, and those that don't recant will be burnt at the stake."

Philippa blanched. "Does the Church not have enough blood on its hands already? When will this ever end?"

"I agree. We must put a stop to it – which brings us to Avignonet. I have received a letter from one of our agents, Raymond d'Alfaro, who happens to be bailiff at the château."

"The bailiff is one of our agents?" interrupted Philippa.

"His mother is the illegitimate half-sister of Count Raymond. As I was saying, he has sent word that the Chief Inquisitors of Toulouse, Etienne de Saint-Thibery and Guillaume-Arnaud, will be arriving at Avignonet in the next few days, along with their assistants and notaries. It is my intention to lead a small band of men in a surprise assault, and end this infamy once and for all. There is no great danger; the bailiff's men will let us into the château undetected."

"You intend to kill the Inquisitors?"

"It is the only way to halt this cancer that eats away at our faith. And by timing the attack to coincide with the arrival of English troops to bolster Raymond's cause, we will together launch an almighty blow for freedom. Freedom from persecution, and freedom from King Louis and his northern lords."

"And you accuse me of not knowing our history? Do you not remember what started this accursed crusade 30 years ago – the killing of the Pope's legate, Pierre de Castelnau, by Count Raymond's father? Have you so easily forgotten the sacking of Béziers that followed, and the massacre of its people – including my grandmother? Does the name De Montfort mean nothing to you now? You should remember – you're old enough."

Pierre-Roger's face flushed at her stinging jibe.

"My fear," interjected her father diplomatically, "is that not enough English troops are being sent to support Raymond. Henry has problems at home – the Scots are threatening to invade, and De Montfort grows stronger by the month."

"De Montfort?" breathed Philippa, wide-eyed with fear. "Surely that devil's spawn cannot still live!"

"Indeed not, thanks be to God. It is his son, of the same name; the Earl of Leicester. He is as different from his father as chalk from cheese. He seeks to curb the king's supremacy and give more power to the barons – there is even talk of a parliament, where ordinary people can make laws themselves."

"A noble aim," said Philippa, surprised. "The seed has fallen far from the tree."

"Indeed, but it does not help our cause. I fear these distractions mean but a token force will arrive, and Raymond's bid to recover his estates will end in disaster. And as you rightly say, Pippa, an attack on the Inquisition will bring swift and fierce retribution. Even Henry, distant though he be from Rome, is still the Pope's man."

"So what do you suggest, father?"

"I fear there is no option but to wait and see how events unfold."

"That sounds like wise counsel, to me," said Philippa, turning back to her husband. "Forgive my hurtful words, my lord. I meant nothing by it. But surely you can see that this way can only lead to bloody vengeance? They will stop at nothing if we take this course."

Pierre-Roger looked at her, grim faced, his lips set straight. "I'm afraid there is nothing more either of you can say to dissuade me. My mind is made up, and I have already given my word to Count Raymond. We need to give our people hope, and warn the Pope that we will not sit idly by while our women and children are sent before the Inquisition. It would be easy for us to sit here in the heights of Montségur, safe from attack, and watch and wait. How would you feel if you were one of our brethren in the towns and villages below, waiting for a knock on the door? No, we must act, and act decisively.

This is our chance to change the course of destiny."

"As you wish, my lord," said Philippa stonily. "But if this is your intent, I must insist that you do not lead the attack yourself. You still carry a wound. I will not allow you to risk your life in this way; not while I carry your child."

Darkness shadowed Pierre-Roger's face, and he gave a mock bow of obeisance. "So be it, my lady. I will accompany my men as far Avignonet, but I will not take part in the final assault."

Chapter 19

Languedoc, May 28, 1242

Moonlight filtered through the dense foliage of Antioch Wood outside Avignonet, glinting off mailcoats and scabbards as the raiders prepared for the final assault. The small band of townsfolk from Gaja-la-Selve, recruited along the way, weighed their hatchets and cudgels in their hands meaningfully, anxious to extract revenge on the murdering churchmen.

A dark figure wrapped in a cloak appeared silently at the edge of the woods, and made his way quickly to where the knights stood waiting with their mounts.

"My lords, my name is Guillaume-Raymond Golairan. I come in the name of Raymond d'Alfaro. He bids me to tell you the way is made clear. The Devil's men are lodged in the keep, and none will stop you. Make it swift and silent, and all will be well."

One of the knights stepped forward and grasped the man by his throat. "You can be sure of this?" he demanded.

"I have put them to bed like my own children. You will find them a-slumber in the chamber to the right of the great hall."

"And the guard?"

"I issued the week's wine ration this evening. You will find no trouble there."

"Then let us waste no time," said the knight. "And you will not join us, my lord?" he said, turning to where Pierre-Roger de Mirepoix was seated on the ground.

"It sticks in my craw, Sir Bernard, but I cannot. I have given my word to Raymond de Péreille."

"It is wise counsel, my lord. You are still weak from your wound, and Montségur has need of you. For my part, since the Inquisition saw fit to condemn me to death in my absence, I welcome the chance to show the Pope that I am still very much alive."

"Then go, and I will be with you in spirit. Bring me an inquisitor's skull – I would use it for a cup."

The knights met no resistance. Sir Bernard de Saint-Martin led the onslaught, battle-axe aloft; swords ripped through slumbering bodies, and cudgels crushed shaven skulls until only bloody pulp remained.

And then they were gone, as swiftly and silently as they had arrived.

Hours passed as Pierre-Roger waited anxiously for the knights to return to the safety of Antioch Wood. He jumped to his feet, wincing with pain, as he saw the small troop of men filter through the shadows.

"Did it go well?"

"Indeed it did, my lord," said Sir Bernard.

"Why then, where is my cup?"

"I fear it is broken," he replied, grinning.

"You should have brought it, anyway. I would have bound it with a circle of gold and drunk from it all my days."

As the knights led their horses up the steep path into Montségur, an excited page boy raced ahead to the tower where Philippa awaited news of the raid.

"They have killed the Inquisitors," he told her excitedly. "All is free!"

"All is dead," she replied, turning her head away, her face wet with tears.

Chapter 20

Father Pietro Agostini of the Society of Jesus hesitated a moment before picking up the phone. He did not like dealing with the 'other side' – especially these American evangelicals. They each regarded the other as heretics, but in this case, the alternative was far worse. They both had a vested interest in maintaining the status quo. Now the sacrilege which he and Cardinal Bertolotti had seen at that confounded church left no alternative.

He lifted the handset and dialled. "Pastor Bob? This is Father Agostini from the Vatican. It's about our little problem at Rennes-le-Château. I'm afraid it's considerably worse than we thought. Despite our best efforts to make the excavations as difficult as possible, they have gained access to the crypt. Naturally we insisted on going in first. It confirms our worst fears – the crypt does indeed contain the tomb of the Magdalene."

"That damned woman…" came back a Texan drawl. "I sometimes wonder what Our Lord was thinking of…"

"That's the least of it," cut in Father Agostini abruptly. "I'm afraid the effigy quite clearly shows her as being pregnant. The implications…"

"Yeah, I get the implications. Who else knows?"

"Cardinal Bertolotti, the official legate sent to investigate by His Holiness."

"Can he be trusted?"

"I think so – for now. He is obviously aware of the damage this could cause."

"No-one else?"

Now it was Agostini's turn to hesitate. "I'm not sure about the archaeologists. They discovered a door to the crypt. We knew the entrance was there – we tried to keep the dig away from it and slow them down as much as possible, but they found the steps at the last moment. Unfortunately, I think they probably did gain access before we got there…"

"Goddamn it, Pietro! You were supposed to stop this happening. Now the whole world is going to know. Can you imagine what this is going to do our faith, Protestant or Catholic? Putting a woman – a whore – at his side as his equal… I mean, have you read her so-called gospel, what's left of it? This is going to put the Gnostics right back on the map. Can you imagine what it's going to open the door to? Our success in the West is built on a God-fearing society. It will undermine the very foundations of civilisation – we'll end up like some goddamn Buddhist country where no-one wants to work and no-one's afraid of anything…"

"Pastor Bob, I don't mean to cast stones, but if your people had been successful in silencing Miss Spencer a few months ago, this might never have happened. As I said in our previous discussion, she is clearly the brains behind this exercise. I understand from my sources that it was her idea to extend the dig at the last minute. We believe she engineered a clandestine visit to the forbidden Secret Room to pinpoint the entrance. As I said, she is intelligent – and dangerous. She and Tranter, the head archaeologist, must be eliminated before they can do more damage."

"My people did a good job in London – it was a fluke she survived. She must be in league with Lucifer himself…"

"Perhaps. Or maybe she's tougher than we give her credit for. This time, we need to get it right."

"There's nothing to stop you doing that. You Jesuits have a pretty damned ruthless reputation."

"Despite what you may see in the movies, Pastor Bob, the Catholic Church cannot go around killing people."

"That's not stopped you in the past. The Inquisition did darned well in that department…"

"Nothing will be served by dredging up ancient history," said Agostini, trying to control his temper. "As we have agreed, the time has come for us to abandon our differences and cooperate in our mutual self-interest. Your contacts in the CIA are much better placed than we are to end this nonsense. They have the tools and the training. America has as much to gain in suppressing this information as the Vatican."

"OK, OK, point taken. I'll make the calls."

"One more thing."

"What now?"

Father Agostini paused. "We have reason to believe the archaeologists have removed evidence from the tomb."

"JE-HOS-A-PHAT! Can't you people do anything right?"

"Our sources believe they recovered a scroll…" went on Agostini hurriedly.

"A scroll? This goes from bad to worse! What does it say?"

"We don't know – that's the whole point," said Agostini, biting back a sarcastic rejoinder. "It may contain information that would lead to even more damaging revelations. The simplest course of action would be to destroy it, but some of the information may have already leaked out. To prevent unwanted surprises, we need to know what the scroll says. Forewarned is forearmed."

"So get your man on the inside to recover it."

"It's not that simple. The parchment is fragile – Tranter is treating it. We must wait until the restoration process is complete; then we can strike. Tell your people to watch and wait."

Chapter 21

Rennes-le-Château, August 1792

Abbé Antoine Bigou stood in front of the dilapidated old church of St Mary Magdalene and contemplated the majestic view. The foothills of the Pyrénées were ranged before him, clad in their pastel greens and mauves and yellows, while beyond, the savage, snow-capped peaks of the Hautes Pyrénées, jutting through the clouds, marked the route he must take to the safety of neighbouring Spain.

Damn those Revolutionaries – damn them to hell. Where they would surely go, he reassured himself. He had been curé of Rennes-le-Château for 18 years, and he would miss this beautiful place; not just because of the dramatic views, of which he never tired, or the villagers, with their strange, archaic customs and unholy symbols over the doors of their houses. Mistrustful at first, they had taken him into their hearts, and he now regarded himself as one of them. There would be tears when they parted, of that he had no doubt.

No, the biggest wrench would be leaving the place where the body of the sacred Madeleine had lain, until its removal at some point in history. His discovery of the crypt, the presence of which he had always suspected, under the Knights' Stone in front of the altar, had led to a moment of spiritual epiphany. The fact that the effigy on her tomb showed her to be obviously pregnant had caused him to rethink his entire religious framework. There could be no doubting who the father had been, and the fact that the Son of God had taken a mortal woman to wife, and had progeny, altered his whole perception of God – at least as far as Jesus, his son, was concerned. The Arians had been right, after all; Jesus was first and foremost a man.

Granted, the Church also alluded to him as the Son of Man, but Christ was supposed to be the nearest thing to God on earth, while he was alive; God-like, omniscient, infallible. Now Bigou knew Jesus had also been a husband and a father, it put a different perspective on things. Jesus had married Mary, lain with her, no doubt on many occasions. He had carnal knowledge. If the Son of Man were able to have sex, sinlessly, then many of the things the Catholic Church had proclaimed over the centuries began to look very shaky. In particular, that priests should remain celibate.

Then there was the other thing… That he would put back where he found it; leave someone else to deal with its legacy. That particular secret would rock the Church to its foundations, he had no doubt. Even those Protestant upstarts wouldn't escape the ramifications if that got out.

Meanwhile, in the few weeks left before he must flee, he must instruct a mason to prepare a new gravestone for the former lady of the manor, Marie de Nègre d'Ables, Marquise d'Hautpoul de Blanchefort. It had been 11 years since she had passed away in 1781, leaving no male heir, though one of her three daughters, Marie-Anne Elisabeth d'Hautpoul de Rennes, still lived in the château.

Bigou had heard Marie de Nègre's confession on her deathbed. She had told him many strange and disturbing things, most of which he had confirmed for himself on opening the crypt, and during subsequent explorations. The crypt, she told him, had been sealed on the express wishes of her husband, François, interred there on his death in 1753, long before Bigou's arrival. François had never recovered from the death of his infant son, Joseph, at the age of just two – the last male heir to the Hautpoul line. Marie, however, a lovely woman – how could she not be? – seemed to have recovered from this blow, and was focused on the welfare of her daughters, particularly Marie-Anne Elisabeth, with whom she had a special bond.

Bigou's discoveries had left him facing a difficult choice. To leave everything for the Revolutionaries to find was inconceivable – the avowed atheists would distort everything to their own ends. But should he conceal everything, leave nothing for future generations to find? Or should he leave clues so that a future curé, a man of learning, might uncover the secrets at a time when Christendom might be better placed to receive them?

He had chosen the latter course, first with a message, discreetly concealed in the side of a wooden pillar under the pulpit, giving simple clues to find the entrance to the crypt. And he had replaced the Knights' Stone upside down, lest the Revolutionaries get too inquisitive.

As for the other… That required a work of greater subterfuge; that was not ready to be revealed for many generations. But at some point, people had a right to know. It altered the whole meaning of Christianity. Perhaps now was a good time to see that mason…

Chapter 22

"I've had the carbon-dating results from Oxford," said David, putting down the phone as Rachel walked into the Finds Room. "As I suspected, those scraps of funeral shroud we found aren't 1st century, they're 10th century – around the time the church was built."

Rachel looked crestfallen. They had been waiting three weeks for the results to come back from Oxford; three weeks of boredom, tidying up the site and cataloguing their finds, alleviated by a few snatched days back in England with her daughter. Emma was happy enough with her grandmother, who adored her, but she couldn't help feeling a bad mother for leaving her so long. She would be glad to see the back of Rennes-le-Château.

"Well, you thought they would probably be medieval. What about the parchment?"

"That's interesting…" said David in a teasing voice.

"Are you holding out on me?"

"Maybe."

"You had better level with me, David Tranter." She walked over and stood in front of him, her arms folded in mock anger.

"Well, from the fragment we sent them it would appear…" he hesitated deliberately.

"What!" shrieked Rachel in frustration.

"…to be 1st century Middle East."

"You're kidding!" she said, giving him a bear hug.

"And there's some more good news." He walked over to the table where the small, yellow parchment scroll lay in its polycarbonate container. "I think this baby is about ready to reveal its secrets."

Rachel went over to where David was standing. "Why does it take so long to treat this stuff?" she asked, as David gently lifted out the ancient parchment scroll with a pair of tweezers.

"Parchment becomes very fragile with age, and because it's made from animal skins, you can't treat it with anything water-based or it turns to mush. I've used a 90 per cent mixture of isopropyl alcohol, with just enough water to rehydrate the skin, no more. Now, if I'm careful, I should be able to open this up without breaking it. Here goes…"

Picking up a pencil, David inserted it into the middle of the tightly bound parchment scroll, gently unrolled it and clipped it flat. "It's in Latin," he murmured in surprise.

"Not what you expected, then?" queried Rachel.

"No. Most parchments of this era – the early Christian period – are either in

Greek or Aramaic, the language of ancient Palestine. Or sometimes in Coptic, if they are Egyptian."

"So what does it say?"

"Latin's not my strong suit, but I'll give it a go. Sue can give us an accurate translation later – she's the languages expert. It starts off with a place name – Alexandria, the capital of Egypt at the time, though Egypt was really just a Roman province by then. But it was home to the biggest Jewish community in the world outside Israel, so it's not totally surprising – some of the earliest versions of the Bible were drafted in Egypt."

David pored over the manuscript for several minutes, scribbling a rough translation onto a notepad, while Rachel fidgeted impatiently. Eventually he looked up at her, a strange expression on his face. "OK. This is roughly what it says. I'll try to put it into 'King James' English so you can get the flavour." He started to read:

"Here lies the body of Mary,
That is called the Magdalene.
Companion of Christ, light to the Light.
As she bore witness,
So shall her daughter,
And her daughter's daughters.
When the time is come
Her truth shall be revealed
For as the Lord hath said
'Seek and ye shall find,
Knock and the door shall be opened unto you'.

For the Lord hath foretold,
There will come a time
When poverty and hunger shall roam the land
And nation shall wage war upon nation
And great terror and bloodshed
Shall be wrought upon the world.
For man hath broken his covenant with God.
The meek shall inherit the earth,
The mighty shall be cast down
And the true kingdom
Shall be raised up.
For as the Lord hath said,
'Beware that no-one lead ye astray,
Saying "Lo here" or "Lo there",
For the Son of Man is within you.

Seek out she who waits
At the grotto where Our Lady is laid to rest
Find her, and she will guide you
Past the Devil's door
And unto the holy sepulchre.
For it is the destiny of her issue
To reveal Christ's truth unto all men."

David and Rachel stood in awed silence.

"Wow," was all Rachel was able to say after a few minutes. "Heavy stuff – it's like something from Revelation."

"It's odd, though, that last section," said David thoughtfully. "It's in different handwriting and ink from the original. Interestingly, the word 'companion', or 'consort' – the Greek word koinonos – is also used about Mary in the gnostic *Gospel of Philip*, a gospel conveniently left out of the New Testament."

"That's the gospel which describes Jesus kissing Mary on the mouth, isn't it?" said Rachel.

"That's right. It would also explain why, in the Garden of Gethsemane after the Resurrection, Jesus told Mary not to 'cling' to him because he was not yet fully resurrected. Traditionally this was interpreted as 'touch', but the Greek word haptomai is much stronger than that – it actually means to cling or hold."

"Surely in first-century Palestine, the code governing the behaviour of women was very rigid – much as in strict Islamic societies today?" queried Rachel. "It would have been unthinkable for a woman to even consider 'clinging' to a man who was not a family member in some way. Doesn't this back what we've found – that Mary and Jesus were, in fact, married, and had a child? And that perhaps that line is still alive today?"

"As I've said, there is no 'fact' at all about that theory, although I'm sure it will make good TV. But with an empty tomb, the proof is missing – other than the scroll, which let's face it, is pretty rambling. But why would Mary's body have been moved? It must have been prompted by something pretty catastrophic."

Rachel started pacing up and down, trying to force her tired brain to make sense of all the disparate facts. Then she spun round and stared at him, her eyes gleaming. "Of course! The Albigensian Crusade! Thousands of Christians – the Cathars – were labelled heretics and murdered on the direct orders of Pope Innocent, right here in the Languedoc in the 13th century. If the Pope's men had found the tomb of a pregnant Mary Magdalene they would certainly have destroyed it. We know so little about the Cathars – maybe they venerated her in some way, and moved her body to a place of safety."

"That's a pretty good working theory," said David.

"It's much more than a working theory," said another male voice.

David and Rachel spun round in surprise. An impeccably dressed man, complete with cravat, stood a few feet away, regarding them with an air of detached amusement. He was in his mid-60s, with greying, well-groomed hair, and a trim figure. "Forgive me," he continued in slightly accented English. "I heard the news about the carbon-dating, and your colleagues said I would find you here. Allow me to introduce myself. My name is Pierre Dubois. I have been studying the mysteries of Rennes-le-Château for many years. I could not resist the opportunity of seeing for myself what it is that you found in the crypt."

Rachel and David looked at each other in stunned silence. They had been so engrossed in the parchment that neither had any idea how long the man had been standing there.

"How on earth do you know about the Oxford results?" asked David in a strangled voice, quickly removing the clips from the parchment and allowing it to curl up again. "I've only just heard myself."

"There are way and means of discovering these things," he replied enigmatically, walking over to join them. "So this is what all the excitement is about. You found it in the Magdalene tomb?"

David's mouth fell open in disbelief. "I don't know what you mean," he said unconvincingly. "We haven't been allowed down into the crypt. It's been sealed by the papal legate."

The man smiled condescendingly. "Come, Monsieur Tranter, you really cannot expect me to believe that. An unlocked door, and your curiosity didn't get the better of you?"

"We agreed not to enter the crypt without the Vatican's permission."

"So you claim to know nothing of Mary's tomb, or the treasures that lie beyond," said Dubois smoothly. "In which case, if you don't mind me asking, where did you acquire this parchment?"

David blanched visibly. "With respect, we need to time to evaluate our findings," he blustered. "We will publish a paper in due course, and it will be covered by National Geographic."

"You assume I am just another amateur treasure hunter," said Dubois. "I cannot blame you. There are hundreds of them climbing all over this place in the summer. But my interest is rather more... how do you say... personal. You see, Marie Dénarnaud was my great-aunt."

Rachel raised her eyebrows and shot a look at David.

"I was born and raised in the village, though now I live in Couiza. Ever since I was a boy, I have devoted myself to finding out more about the mysteries of this place. Perhaps I can help you with your quest."

"Thanks, but I'm not sure that s practical..." started David.

"That's really interesting," interrupted Rachel, seeing a great chance to add a human interest twist to the upcoming docu-drama. "We would be grateful for any help you can give us. But – and I mean no disrespect – how do we know you're who you say you are?"

"I understand your caution, mam'selle. It is very sensible. Perhaps the fact I knew about the carbon-dating might suggest I have some excellent connections. I also have some documents that will prove my authenticity." Dubois opened his briefcase and pulled out a thick file. From it he took a series of ageing yellow documents. "Here," he said, passing them over to Rachel. "Records of the cash Saunière withdrew from the Fritz Dörge bank in Budapest, for what today would be hundreds of thousands of dollars."

"Payments from Emperor Franz Joseph, of the Austro-Hungarian empire? I've heard about that theory," said Rachel.

"It's more than a theory, though it was probably arranged through a close relative, Archduchess Maria Theresa of Austria-Este. She was also the Countess of Chambord, wife of the pretender to the French throne at the time, and we know she gave Saunière an endowment of 3,000 gold francs – the equivalent of five years' salary – soon after he became priest at Rennes-le-Château. These documents show the payments continued long after her death in 1886 – right up to the First World War, in fact."

"Wow, that's impressive," said Rachel, leafing through the papers. "Clearly, as staunch Catholics, they were paying him to keep quiet about this whole affair. This is just the sort of thing we need for the documentary – can I keep these for the time being?"

"You may certainly use them, but I would prefer it if you copied them and returned them to me. One cannot be too careful. Now will you tell me what you found in the crypt? In return, I would be happy to share with you some of my own findings over the years."

"Rachel, I need to talk to you. Now – in private," said David, looking pointedly at Dubois.

"If you must," she said irritatedly. "Will you excuse us a moment, monsieur?"

"Bien sûr, mam'selle."

Rachel followed David out into the yard.

"Well?" she asked impatiently.

"Rachel, listen to me. We don't have a clue who this guy really is. He could be anybody – he could even be a Vatican stooge, for all we know. By all means let's listen to what he has to say, but I think we should be very careful about how much we tell him."

"He seems pretty genuine to me – look at all that paperwork he brought with him."

"Nevertheless, the timing is fishy, to say the least. The guy turns up the moment we get the carbon-dating results, just as we open the scroll. Even allowing for loose talk among the team, that's a pretty big coincidence."

"You're being paranoid..."

"I am not being paranoid, Rachel – I am just saying we've got some great stuff here, let's not hand everything over on a plate to someone who could very well be a spy. And whatever you do, don't tell him what was on that parchment."

"OK, you've got a point, though I still think you're being paranoid…" She held up her hand to silence David's incipient protest. "I'll be careful what I say, particularly when it comes to the parchment. What the hell was that all about, anyway? 'Seek out she who waits, At the grotto where Our Lady was laid to rest' – it's all a bit cloak-and-dagger, isn't it?"

"Totally – and you know how much I hate that stuff. It's probably just some medieval mumbo jumbo. But it's our find, and for now it's all we've got to go on."

Rachel led the way back into the Finds Room, where Dubois was waiting for them patiently.

"Monsieur, we will gladly accept your help, but you must promise to treat any information we give you with the strictest confidence. Would you be prepared to sign a confidentiality agreement and agree that nothing we discuss is made public until after the programme has aired?"

"Mais bien sûr," said Dubois, bowing slightly.

"Now's a good a time as any," said Rachel, going to a filing cabinet and pulling out one of National Geographic's pro-forma non-disclosure agreements. "They have been translated into French, though your English is excellent, monsieur. Would you like to take this away and have it checked?"

"I am happy to trust you, mam'selle," said Dubois, taking out an exquisite Mont Blanc fountain pen and signing the form with a theatrical flourish.

"Now, may I see the parchment?"

"Very well," said David reluctantly, giving Rachel a hard stare. "But please don't touch it – it's still extremely fragile."

Dubois took some spectacles out of his jacket pocket and peered closely at the rolled-up parchment. "Fascinating! Is it possible to open it up again?"

"I'd rather not, just for the moment," said David. "I want to give it another soak, just to be on the safe side."

"Of course, m'sieur – you know best. Would you be so kind as to let me have a translation, once your linguist has done her job?"

"Of course," said Rachel casually. "You mentioned findings of your own – what would they be, exactly?"

The Frenchman smiled enigmatically. "Let us say I know what Saunière found."

"Something relating to the tomb in the crypt, presumably," said David. "Though we know he can't have seen this parchment."

"Indeed not. But he did find something else."

"How do you know?"

"Because what he found was eventually passed on to me, in a manner of speaking. And the discovery is quite, how do you say – earth-shaking."

"If you know this, why haven't you published a book, or gone to French TV?" queried Rachel.

"I did not want to be dismissed as just another crank, mam'selle. And I did not want to damage Marie's reputation further. I knew that sooner or later scientists would carry out a full excavation of the crypt – it was only a matter of time before money talked." Dubois smiled benignly.

"So what was passed down to you?"

"An explanation of the puzzle that has confounded everybody investigating the mystery of Rennes-le-Château. An explanation that shows that not only did Saunière discover the Magdalene tomb, but..." he paused and looked around him melodramatically.

"Yes?" said Rachel, impatiently.

"This you will find hard to believe, mes amis. But it is true. You must promise me you will not reveal it to a soul – not ever, not on TV, not in your research paper. Unless you are given permission."

"What if we find out by some other means?" queried Rachel, reluctant to give up so easily on a potentially great exclusive.

"Believe me, mam'selle, you won't," said Dubois.

"Very well, then. Unless you give us permission," she said, wondering how much money he was angling after.

"It's not about money," said Dubois, reading her mind. "It's about ensuring someone's safety. There are people who would kill to discover the information I am about to tell you. You will understand when you have heard."

Rachel looked shocked, but nodded her assent.

"Very well, then. Mary Magdalene – or at least, her direct descendant – is alive and well today, even as we speak."

Chapter 23

There was stunned silence in the room. Rachel and David stared open-mouthed at Dubois.

"How on earth do you know that Mary Magdalene – or at least her God-knows-how-many-greats granddaughter – is still alive?" asked David, eventually.

"I have met her," said Dubois, without batting an eyelid. "It was many years ago when I was just 11 or 12 years old, but what she told me – and showed me – convinced me she was genuine."

"Where is she?" asked Rachel.

"Here, in the Languedoc – where the first Mary Magdalene made her home all those centuries ago. She lives her life as just another French woman. You wouldn't know her if you passed her in the street."

"What did she show you?" asked David.

"A number of parchments, similar to the one you have here."

"That doesn't prove anything!" said David caustically. "As far as I'm concerned, this could just be a red herring."

"Don't be so quick to dismiss it, David," said Rachel, frowning. "Who knows where it might lead? And these other parchments – aren't you curious as to what they might say?"

"But it's taking us away from Rennes-le-Château," argued David.

"Mon ami, this is Rennes-le-Château – it's what it's all about," said Dubois. "It's not just what Saunière discovered, it's who he met on those long walks in the countryside for which he was famous. It's how he was able to blackmail the Church. I'm afraid he wasn't a very honourable man; selling masses was the least of his sins. If you think the idea of Jesus being married to Mary is controversial now, think what it must have been like in the 19th century – it would have been a sacrilege to the Catholic Church! They would have stopped at nothing to keep the truth from leaking out. Why else would the Archduke of Austria-Hungary have been involved? They were devout Catholics who wanted to protect the established order. The real mystery is why they let Saunière live as long as they did."

"You think..." Rachel's voice trailed off.

"His death was no accident, mam'selle, that much is for certain. It was a critical point in the Great War for the Austrians – they and the Germans were facing certain defeat. Saunière had outlived his usefulness, if you can call it that."

"And now?" queried Rachel. "You say this woman who claims... this latest Magdalene could be in danger?"

"Is in danger. Serious danger. Do you think the Catholic Church is any more ready now for a woman to proclaim herself the direct descendant of Jesus and Mary than it was a century ago? Think of the implications! Catholicism is a male-only hierarchy that justifies its existence on the basis that Jesus was celibate, and entrusted his message only to men – his 12 disciples. It's why only men can be priests, and is the reason for their enforced celibacy."

"Of course," said Rachel. "I hadn't stopped to think about things from that perspective. The issue of women priests is one of the biggest barriers in the move to reunify Rome with the Anglican Church, even as things stand now. Living proof that Mary was not just Jesus's wife, but also his closest disciple, would shatter centuries of complacent male domination."

"And think of theological implications! continued Dubois. "Jesus was – is – God; that is what the Church believes. That Jesus, while on Earth, was both human and divine. What would that have made his children, or their descendants? Demigods? It would give them greater moral authority than the Pope! It would undermine the whole credibility of the Church."

Rachel stood silently for a few moments, struggling to take in the implications of what Dubois had said. "If that's true, it makes you wonder why they didn't pull every string in the book to get this dig stopped," she said finally.

"They did – but as I said, money talks."

"And now the dig has gone ahead, you think they are waiting for a chance to silence her?"

"If they find out where she is. Of course, at first they just wanted to stop the whole thing – but our bull-headed mayor was determined to bring in National Geographic and put Rennes on the tourist trail for the Americans. So then they turned to more devious means – I'm afraid I don't think your 'accident' was an accident at all, mam'selle," he said, turning to Rachel. "Your reputation as an investigative journalist precedes you. They hoped the exercise would not turn up anything conclusive, and without you digging around behind the scenes, as it were, the whole thing would be a five-minute wonder. At worst, another Magdalene tomb to add to the ones in Vézelay and St-Maximin-la-Sainte-Baume. But now you have got this far…"

"They didn't know the full truth about the tomb," observed Rachel.

"I think not, or they would have taken more extreme steps to stop you."

"More extreme than trying to kill me?"

"Why stop at one murder? You must understand, this has been going on for centuries. For these people, the preservation of the Roman Catholic Church exceeds all other considerations. You would have been casualties of war."

"Like the Cathars…"

"That was not war, that was genocide – but yes, in a manner of speaking."

"So what do you suggest we do now?" asked Rachel.

"We need to find Anne-Marie and take her to a place of safety."

"Anne-Marie?"

"The current descendant of the Magdalene."

"And how do we do that?"

"I may be able to help you. As I have said, I met her many years ago – she was middle-aged then; she would be an old woman by now."

"How did you meet her?"

"I used to run errands for Nöel Corbu – the man who befriended Marie Dénarnaud in her later years. He bought the Villa Bethania from her, Saunière's grand house – it was always in her name, not Saunière's. I was inquisitive – always asking questions about my great aunt. One day he said to me, 'Would you like to meet the woman at the centre of all this?' Naturally, I was confused. I said, 'But Aunt Marie is dead.' He said, 'Come with me, and you will understand. Someone else must know the truth besides me. I will not live forever.' To be truthful, I thought he was a little mad.

"He asked if he could trust me, and of course, I said yes. He swore me to secrecy – he told me many lives depended on it – and took me to a village several kilometres from here. He told me he would not take a direct route because he did not want me to remember how to get there. We went into an old cottage, and there she was. I'm afraid I can't remember much more about it."

"Did you ever meet her again?" asked Rachel.

"No, mam'selle. A year or two after our meeting, Corbu was killed in a tragic car accident."

Rachel shuddered.

"Now there's a familiar theme," observed David drily. "So how do we go about meeting this… Anne-Marie, if you don't know where she lives? Is there any other way we can get in touch with her?"

"Not directly, m'sieur. But as you may have discovered for yourselves, Saunière left many clues here at Rennes, both in the church and elsewhere. It may be that if we follow them carefully, they will lead us to her."

"How can clues left more than 100 years ago possibly help us find this woman now?"

"If we are meant to find her, we will."

"Spare us the cryptic mumbo-jumbo," snapped David in exasperation. "I've had quite enough theology for one day."

"I think you're being a little harsh," said Rachel, putting her hand gently on his arm. "Give the guy a break – he's offering to help us. He has met her, after all."

"He met someone who claimed to be her, based on a totally uncorroborated theory. If he's telling the truth."

"Correct me if I'm wrong, monsieur, but I suspect you followed certain clues to discover the tomb of St Marie?" said Dubois, ignoring the slur.

"Yes, but that tomb has been there for 1,000 years."

"Saunière was alive only 100 years ago – is it not possible he left some clues that may still be relevant today?"

"I suppose so," said David irritatedly, still suspicious of his motives.

"Well then, let us look at the evidence before us. What do you have to lose? You cannot go back into the crypt – perhaps we will uncover some more clues."

"Any suggestions as to where we should start?"

"Do you remember I said Saunière made a discovery on those long country walks that caused so much speculation? I believe he met Marie – or at least, her great-grandmother. I do not know whether it was by chance, or whether he found some evidence – but I am convinced he met her. That was why he built La Tour Magdala, at such vast expense – not just to honour La Madeleine, but as a work of homage to her descendants."

"So you're saying La Tour holds the key?" interrupted Rachel.

"Exactement, mam'selle! For instance, did you know there are precisely 22 steps leading from the study to the top of the tower? And 22 holes in the battlements…"

"Crenelations," corrected Rachel.

"Oui! And there are also 22 steps in the glass tower opposite, the Orangerie. And 22 steps – 11 on each side – in the staircases that lead from the garden to the balcony that connects the two towers."

"So what does that prove?" asked David.

"M'sieur, the 22nd of July is the feast day of La Madeleine."

Rachel turned to David, an expression of incredulity on her face. "The inscription over the statue of the Devil inside the church – 'By this sign you will vanquish him' – the extra two letters, making a total of 22. Remember? It all adds up – quite literally."

"So what? Saunière was obsessed with Mary Magdalene – we know that. But that still doesn't put us any nearer finding her alleged – and I stress alleged – descendant."

"David, for God's sake stop being so dismissive. It's a clue. Let's go and see if there any other clues hidden in the tower. We haven't really paid it much attention so far."

"It wasn't in the brief."

"It is now. Let's go look."

"Now?"

"Do you have any better plans?"

The three of them walked over to La Tour Magdala, the strange neo-Gothic tower, complete with its quirky miniature turret in one corner, perched on the edge of the hilltop. It looked like something out of a Victorian romance fantasy – or, perhaps, a Monty Python sketch, thought Rachel whimsically.

A grand stone balcony – known locally as the Belvedere – ran from one side of the tower along the edge of the hill until it met the Orangerie. This tower, a mirror image of La Tour Magdala, had a stone base but a glass superstructure, which Saunière had used as a greenhouse. Below the Belvedere, and half encircled by it, was the garden, now somewhat scrappy and forlorn, but once meticulously maintained to a precise geometric design laid down by the mysterious priest. No-one was quite certain what the pattern was supposed to mean, though some speculated it represented key points in the life of Mary Magdalene. Collectively, the whole area, including the Villa Bethanie, the house he had built for himself, had become known as the Domaine.

"I still don't get it – why the two towers?" asked Rachel as they crossed the garden.

"No-one has really come up with a convincing explanation for that, mam'selle," said Dubois. "Though it is true to say that this whole area – the garden and the two towers – form half of an imaginary chessboard. That is to say, this garden, with its two sides at right angles, is one half of the board. If you were to continue the lines to make up a complete board, the area is exactly 64 times that of La Tour. And, of course, there are 64 squares on a chessboard. Furthermore, the two towers occupy the precise positions of the rooks on a chessboard – La Tour being the black rook, one assumes, and the glass one the white rook.

"When we go inside La Tour, you will note there are 64 squares on the floor. There is symmetry in everything he did."

"What on earth does it all mean?" asked Rachel, bemused.

"I'm afraid, mam'selle, the only person who knows the answer to that was struck down here on January 17, 1917 and died a few days later – on the 22nd, as it happens."

"January 17 seems to be a recurring theme," said Rachel, glancing at David. He shook his head to indicate she shouldn't say any more about the date on the tomb in the crypt.

"Indeed, it is a date that occurs with great regularity in the history of Rennes-le-Château, mam'selle," said Dubois, apparently oblivious to their brief interchange of looks. "Most notably, it is the date on which Marie de Nègre d'Ables died – the date written on that famous tombstone."

"Isn't there something else about January 17? Blue apples, or something bizarre?"

Dubois smiled indulgently. "Oui, for sure. It is said that on that day a ray of light shines through a stained glass window in the church and creates an illusion of blue apples on the wall. It has achieved significance among our treasure-hunter friends because some of the parchments allegedly discovered by Saunière can, it is claimed, be decoded to reveal a hidden message. That message contains a garbled reference to 'blue apples at midday'. But those parchments are almost certainly fakes."

"Well there's a surprise," said David.

Dubois turned abruptly and entered La Tour.

105

Rachel gave David a glare before following Dubois into Saunière's study in the basement of the tower. She had, of course, looked around the tower on many occasions during the course of the dig, but now she examined it with renewed interest. The walls were covered with rich, wooden art nouveau panelling, but it was the floor that held her interest. As Dubois had said, there were 64 squares, each made up of four tiles. The richly patterned tiles were quite remarkable in their detail – a gold cross inside a multi-pointed star, inside what looked like a pale yellow marigold with tendrils trailing down inside. This complex image was contained in a red circle with a black and gold border.

The intersection of each group of four tiles made up another, smaller circular pattern: a blue flower within a white flower within a red circle, and again a black and gold border. Here and there the tiles were damaged where the floor had been dug up by treasure hunters desperate to discover the elusive secrets of Rennes-le-Château.

"This is incredible," said Rachel. "I never really noticed the complexity of the patterns before. They look highly symbolic, but what does it all mean?"

"Again, no-one is sure, mam'selle," said Dubois.

"It reminds me of a Templar floor tile I saw at Templecombe in Somerset," mused David. "I was part of the crew on the Time Team dig at the site of the former Templar lodge there."

"So the Templars crop up again," mused Rachel, studying the tile pattern thoughtfully. "I suppose the cross in the centre must symbolise Jesus. And the star could be the star of David. Or maybe the star that supposedly led the three wise men to the infant Jesus. And perhaps that fuzzy marigold shape is meant to signify a womb – the marigold is supposed to be the flower of the Virgin Mary, and those strange tendrils would fit the womb analogy."

"You have a keen mind," observed Dubois. "I can understand why the Church didn't want you… how do you say… poking around!"

"It's just guesswork, really – with perhaps a little feminine intuition thrown in. And I suppose the smaller, blue flower in the adjacent circles could symbolise the Magdalene. The Christ and the Magdalene theme would certainly fit in with what we have discovered."

"You may well be right, mam'selle."

Rachel moved over to the window and looked down to the fields below. "But why did he build the tower here, right on the edge of the cliff? It must have made it much more difficult to construct. As it is, I've noticed a huge crack in the outside wall where the foundations have moved."

Dubois hesitated briefly. "It's the view, of course," he said awkwardly. "Saunière would spend hours admiring the landscape, either from here or, in the summer, from the belvedere. C'est magnifique, n'est-pas?" he added, gesturing to the stunning vista framed in the window.

Rachel certainly couldn't deny that, with row upon row of dusky hills rising up one behind the other to meet the brooding massif of the distant Hautes Pyrénées. Greens, browns and golds stretched in every direction as far as the eye could see. It was quite breathtaking.

"I can see that he would never tire of this," she admitted. "But still I wonder, why right on the edge like this? Anyway, let's go up to the top and see if we get any more insights "

She started up the staircase, counting as she went. As she reached 11, she found herself in front of an embrasure enclosing a small arched window overlooking the countryside below. "If there are 22 steps here, as you say, it's interesting that the half-way mark stops directly in front of this window,' she remarked. "Is there anything significance?"

"Who knows?" said Dubois evasively.

Rachel gave him a hard stare before moving on up spiral staircase, emerging onto the roof platform exactly 11 more steps later. She grasped hold of the parapet and gazed into the distance, losing herself in the soft outlines of the hills, limned with gold in the soft summer sunlight. What was going on here? What had Saunière been hinting at? Something more than just the tomb of Mary Magdalene – significant though that undoubtedly was. She felt sure there was something more; something she was missing.

She looked across at David and Dubois. David looked angry, and was obviously not happy at with Dubois' involvement. The articulate Dubois, on the other hand, was a picture of certitude – if not smugness.

"Well, I don't suppose there is much to be gained standing here admiring the scenery, stunning though it is," said Rachel. "I think I'll go back to the hotel and do some more research."

"The hotel?" queried David. "Why don't you do it here?"

"It's more relaxing back at the hotel. I can get some peace and quiet, and I'll be out of your hair."

David shrugged and stood up. "OK. I'll get back to work." He turned to Dubois. "Is there a way we can reach you? You've told us about this woman Anne-Marie, but unless you can give some information on how to find her, it's not going to get us very far."

The Frenchman looked uncomfortable. "I have more papers at home – as I say, I have been researching Rennes-le-Château for many years. I will show you tomorrow. Perhaps we will find something to help us in our quest."

"Quest is about the right word," said David. "It's just like some bloody pointless medieval knight's quest to find the Holy Grail."

"Except in this case, David, maybe we really will find the Holy Grail," said Rachel sharply. He said nothing, but his expression spoke volumes. "Right, I'm off. I'll see you tomorrow morning then?" she said to Dubois. "And David, try to lighten up." Turning on her heel, she marched back to the office to collect her things.

As Rachel was driving out of Rennes she hit the brakes outside the village bookshop. She had driven past the shop – a rival to the museum bookshop – every day she had been on site, but after a brief visit when she first arrived, she had never felt inclined to return. Today, for some reason, she felt compelled to stop and take another look.

Browsing the shelves of books devoted to the mysteries of Rennes and its enigmatic priest – of which there were several hundred in various languages – she eventually came to the English section. There was everything from the Da Vinci Code to in-depth academic treatises on the Rennes phenomenon. The problem, as with anything to do with the village, whether it be books or the many websites devoted to the topic, was sorting the wheat from the chaff. There was so much wild, uninformed, speculation – not to mention downright fabrication by people trying to cash in on the Saunière legend – that it was hard to know where to start.

Rachel picked up a few books at random and flicked through the pages, discarding them one by one. Eventually she came to one by a French author, Jean-Luc Robin, entitled *Rennes-le-Château: Saunière's Secret*. Robin, it seemed, had owned the Villa Bethania at one time, and, looking through the chapters, seemed to take a more rational stance than most writers on the subject. On impulse she decided to buy it.

"Bon choix," said the young man behind the counter, giving her a mysterious smile.

Back at the hotel, Rachel made herself a cup of strong tea from the stash of teabags brought over from England and settled down to read. It was a fascinating account not just of Robin's own dealings with Rennes, but the whole history of the Saunière affair. As a journalist, it was intensely satisfying to at last find a writer who didn't simply repeat rumour as fact, like so many others, but examined theories carefully before presenting reasoned conclusions. He made it clear when he was dealing with hearsay, and made a distinction between fact and rumour.

Half-way through the book, she came on a chapter describing Saunière's frequent country walks with Marie Dénarnaud. Robin described how the trips started shortly after the episode in which Saunière dug up half the churchyard looking for something – much to the anger of villagers. Forced to halt his excavations, Saunière would instead set off into the countryside each morning, returning at dusk laden with a basket of rocks, which he used to create the grotto at the front of the churchyard.

Rachel had always assumed the grotto was meant to commemorate Jesus's birth, but it appeared that officially it was a re-creation of the grotto of Our Lady of Lourdes, not far away in the Hautes Pyrénées. The alleged miraculous sighting of the Virgin Mary by 14-year-old peasant girl Bernadette Soubirous had occurred in 1858, just 30 years before Saunière's induction as village priest, and such replicas were not uncommon in the Languedoc.

However, it seemed the stones brought back by Saunière and Marie came from a local cave known as La Grotte du Fournet a mile or so distant. It begged the question as to why they should carry heavy rocks over such a distance simply to create a replica of the Lourdes grotto. Moreover, why did Saunière originally place a bronze statue of Mary Magdalene in the grotto, when Bernadette claimed she had seen the Virgin Mary? To add to the confusion, the statue was later stolen, and replaced in 2003 with a politically correct statue of the Virgin.

What she read next, however, left her open-mouthed in astonishment.

Chapter 24

It was some hours later that David returned to the hotel weary after a day spent cataloguing the team's finds from the trench. Though not important to their overarching mission, they had to be recorded as part of the archaeological process. He was also recording – in a secret file on his laptop – everything he could remember of their journey into the crypt and undercroft, as well as analysing the scores of photographs taken in the process.

"How's it going?" asked Rachel, barely able to contain her excitement.

"Tediously, for the most part," said David.

"You've just made the find of a lifetime and you find it tedious?"

"Oh come on, Rachel, give me a break, I'm tired. Why don't you just tell me what you've been up to this afternoon?"

"Because you'll probably just dismiss it as some wild fantasy."

"That pretty much seems to sum up everything about this place."

"Yes, I know – but just give me a break and accept the possibility that somewhere hidden among all these seemingly bizarre and random clues, the truth is waiting to be found. Anyway, I think I've hit on something. I stopped in that bookshop in the village and found a useful guide to what's actually been going on up there. I think you'd like the guy's style – he focuses only on the facts, and dismisses some of the ideas that have been floating around here as pure fantasy."

"Sounds like a breath of fresh air."

"Exactly. Anyway, he mentions those country walks Dubois referred to. Apparently, Saunière and Marie would regularly disappear in the morning and come back in the evening with a basket full of rocks. He used them to build that artificial grotto at the front of the churchyard, which he told the villagers was a replica of the grotto at Lourdes. Why would the two of them be disappearing, day after day, and hauling a pile of heavy rocks back up the hill? There are plenty of places around the village he could have sourced them."

"I can think of one obvious reason – they were supposed to have a suspiciously close relationship. It would be a good opportunity to get up close and personal without anyone finding out."

"Every day? For weeks on end?"

"He was a 'vigorous' man, from all accounts," said David drily. "The villagers even referred to her as the 'priest's skirt'."

"Sorry, I don't buy it. OK, maybe they did have an intimate relationship – I don't deny that's a strong possibility. But why bring back rocks from so far away? Anyway, I think I know the answer."

"And?"

"The book's author says the grotto they used to visit is known locally as La Grotte du Fournet – dit de la Madeleine."

David raised his eyebrows. "OK, you've got my attention. If Saunière was bringing back rocks from there, that could provide a motive."

"And another thing. Remember what it said on the scroll? 'When the time is come, you must seek out she who waits, at the grotto where Our Lady was laid to rest.' It could be referring to this place!"

"Possibly – though if any artefacts were ever hidden there, they would long since have disappeared. You can bet your bottom dollar the cave has been turned over by treasure hunters, like everything else in this godforsaken place."

"But there is a connection – so let's go and have a look. What have we got to lose?"

"Where exactly is this grotto?"

"Now you've got me. Nothing I've found seems to explain exactly how to find it. I've trawled the internet, and all I can find is a reference to it being above the Couleurs stream."

"Let's get the map and have a look." David grabbed his car keys and returned a few minutes later holding a large-scale map of the area. "Pity these aren't as detailed as the Ordnance Survey maps back home, but it's the best we've got," he said, opening it out on the table. "OK, here's Rennes-le-Château..." he said, poring over the map, "and here... Damn, where is it? Ah, typical – the other side of the fold! Here is the Couleurs, directly south of the village. Looks like the stream runs through some kind of gorge – there's a cliff shown here. Being limestone, however, there are probably scores of caves along there – trying to find the right one could be a nightmare."

Rachel studied the map intently over his shoulder. "David," she said thoughtfully, at length.

"Yes?"

"Where is La Tour Magdala on here?"

David peered closely at the map. "Well, there is Rennes-le-Château... And that, if I'm not mistaken, is La Tour – at the western end of the village; that tiny circle. Look, you can see the ramparts of the Belvedere stretching around to the right of it."

"So it overlooks the gorge, then?"

David looked at her, stunned. "My God, you're absolutely right. Maybe Saunière did build the tower there, to overlook the La Grotte du Fournet. Maybe the cave's Magdalene connection isn't just folklore; maybe he found something significant – something so significant he built the tower so he could watch over it."

"I noticed when we were up there earlier today that there was a gorge in the distance. I obviously didn't realise the significance at the time. As Dubois said, maybe the tower does hold a clue – and not just the number 22. We need to go and have another look tomorrow morning."

"Preferably before Dubois gets there," said David. "I don't trust that guy."

"I think you're being a bit harsh, though I do think he's holding out on us about something. I guess he's not going to lay all his cards out on the table at once, any more than we are. But let's go and have a look before he arrives."

* * * * *

The next morning they got up early, and after a swift coffee and croissant, headed back to Rennes-le-Château. They were waiting impatiently when Hélène, the museum curator, arrived, and Rachel asked her to unlock La Tour for them straight away, before the tourists started flooding through.

"Why such a hurry?" asked Hélène, as she fetched the keys.

"We're working on a theory – there's something we need to check," said Rachel casually.

"Mon dieu – another theory!" laughed Hélène. "What is it?"

"Just a hunch. I'll let you know if it pays off."

"D'accord! Let's open up, then."

They followed Hélène over to La Tour. "Happy hunting," she said, and returned to the museum ticket office, where her first customers were already queuing up.

"Let's crack on before the tourists get here," said David. "Now, let's do this scientifically. First of all, the floor. We know there's a pattern here. Let's have a close look and see if there's anything we've missed – anything the slightest bit out of the ordinary."

They walked slowly up and down the floor, examining every tile closely, but the same pattern appeared to be repeated over and over again, without variation.

"This is hopeless," said Rachel at length. "I'm going to go up to that window in the staircase again. We know it overlooks the gorge – perhaps there's a mark in the stonework or something."

"OK, I'll keep looking down here."

Rachel had barely gone up half a dozen steps when David gave a yell of excitement. "Hey, Rachel, I think I've got something."

She hurried back down the stairs. "Stop!" yelled David. "Look, right at your feet!"

"What?" said Rachel in exasperation.

"That last complete square of tiles – look at the tile in the top right-hand corner, in front of the stairs. Do you notice anything odd about it?"

"No…"

"OK, look at the centre of the square of tiles. Do you see that red quadrant?

All the others are black!"

Rachel looked around the floor. At the centre of each gold cross created by the square of four tiles was a black circle – except in the tile nearest the spiral staircase, where one quarter of the circle, the quadrant nearest the stairs, was blood red.

"You're right, goddamn it!" she exclaimed.

"You see? The victory of science over speculation," said David, smirking.

"All right, smart arse. I'll give you that one. It's pointing up the stairs, so let's see where the trail leads." She skipped up the staircase with David in hot pursuit, then stopped in front of the window at the half-way point and looked out across the valley below. "There's the gorge I noticed last time… But nothing really stands out."

"I can see what appear to be several caves," said David. "And it looks pretty steep, too. We could spend days wandering around there looking for the right one. Are there any markings in the stonework – the sill, perhaps – that might give us a clue?"

They examined the stone surrounds in the minutest detail. "Nothing that I can see," said Rachel reluctantly, after a few minutes. "But if that red marker means anything, the answer must be up here somewhere. Let's carry on up to the roof and have a look from there."

They continued up the staircase until they reached the roof platform where they had admired the view with Dubois the day before. They walked slowly around the platform, examining every nook and cranny, but nothing obvious came to light.

"Same stunning view, same gorge, but nothing to pinpoint the location," said David frustratedly. "That red quadrant must mean something; I just don't get it."

"Let's go and have a cup of coffee and mull it over. Dubois will be here soon – perhaps he'll know."

David snorted. "I've told you – I don't trust that guy. I don't think we'll get anything out of him that he doesn't want to tell us."

"Why shouldn't he want us to know the location of La Grotte du Fournet?"

"I don't know. But if he's been studying this place for years, why didn't he know about that red marker? Most likely he does know about it but decided not to tell us. He's not being open about everything – I'm going to have it out with him when he gets here."

"David, for God's sake don't blow this. He's our only lead – we need him more than he needs us at the moment." She turned to go back down the staircase, then stopped, frozen in her tracks. "David!" she said in a strangled voice. "I've found it!"

The railing at the top of the spiral staircase was in her clear line of sight. It ended with a theatrical flourish; an architectural detail that looked like an apple, though that in itself was not unusual for art nouveau design. But this particular 'apple' lined up perfectly with an arrow-slit window and allowed the eye to fall on the gorge – a specific point in the gorge.

"Look," she said, pointing. "The top of the post at the end of the railings. Follow the line through the window, across to the gorge."

Even from a distance, David could see the dark shape of what appeared to be a cave.

Chapter 25

Rachel and David quickly took some photos to try to get the orientation of the cave, before hurrying back to the museum. "I'm going to ask for directions," said David over his shoulder.

"I'm not sure that's such a good idea," said Rachel. "Word will get around the village…"

David ignored her and went straight to the admission desk. "Hélène! Tell me, do you know where the Grotte du Fournet is?"

"La Grotte? Oui, I know it."

"Is it possible to arrange for us to go there? Perhaps someone could accompany us – I would be happy to pay for his time."

Hélène hesitated. "Perhaps, m'sieur. I will have to ask someone."

"The mayor?"

"Non – someone else."

"When will you see him?"

"Is it urgent?"

"Fairly."

"Then I will try to speak to him at lunchtime, David."

"Thanks, Hélène – I really appreciate it. You don't happen to have any photos of it, do you?"

"Sure, I have one on my computer – here, you can look," she said, turning the monitor round so he could see it. David could see a clear picture of the cave entrance, plus, unusually, two smaller pictures taken at different angles on the right-hand side of the screen.

"Is there any chance of printing that off for me?"

"Perhaps, after lunch. It is quieter – I will have more time," she said, nodding to the queue of people waiting at the caisse.

Rachel grabbed David's arm and frogmarched him into the Finds Room. "Are you crazy? Now everyone is going to know what we're up to."

"You were quite happy to 'tell all' to Dubois. This could save us a lot of time and trouble."

"That was different. He genuinely seemed to have something to offer – he showed us those deposit slips from the bank in Budapest, remember."

"Well, for all Hélène knows, we're just doing a bit of sightseeing now the dig is over. I'll say something to that effect when she gets back from lunch."

The morning seemed to drag, and at 12 o'clock sharp, Hélène closed the museum for the customary two-hour French lunch break. David focused on writing his official report for DRAC, the French archaeological authority, while Rachel took advantage of Hélène's absence to go through the photos on

David's laptop of their illicit excursion into the crypt.

Eventually, after what seemed like an age, Hélène returned. She seemed ill at ease, and a little more distant than usual.

David gave her a few minutes to get settled back at her desk before going over. "Any luck?" he asked.

"Luck?"

"La Grotte du Fournet – did you manage to speak to someone about taking us to see it?"

"Ah – oui."

"And?"

"I'm afraid he does not have time today."

"Tomorrow, then?"

"Or tomorrow. Or the day after, I'm afraid."

"Oh. That's a shame. Never mind – can you print out that picture for me?" Hélène visibly blanched. "Non, c'est n'est pas possible."

"But you said…"

"Non, David!"

"Well, could you at least point it out for us on the map?"

Hélène hesitated, clearly very uncomfortable at refusing such a seemingly harmless request from someone who had become a close colleague.

"You said you knew where it was?" queried David.

"Oui…"

"Then I'll go and get the map." He went out to the car and returned moments later. "Here we go," he said opening out the map. "Here's Rennes-le-Château. So where exactly is La Grotte du Fournet?"

Again, Hélène hesitated. "Un moment – I am not familiar with the map." She hesitantly traced her finger all over the map around Rennes, before unconvincingly settling on a spot close to the road leading up to the village.

"It is here, David. Definitely here," she said, beaming at him.

"Right – thanks," said David tersely, and grabbing the map, marched out of the museum.

"What was all that about?" asked Rachel.

"You tell me!" said David angrily. "You saw where she was pointing on the map! We pass that spot every day – there's nothing there, and she damn well knows it! Someone's got to her – she was quite happy to print off a picture before she went to lunch."

"For God's sake keep your voice down! We're going to be here for a few more weeks yet, and we don't want to alienate her. Obviously someone's given her orders to keep shtum about it. They probably get fed up with treasure hunters traipsing all over the place – you know how much damage they've done. Frankly, it was a daft idea to ask her in the first place – I'm sure Dubois will know."

"Well, just in case he doesn't, let's ask at the bookshop."

They walked the few yards down the hill to the shop where Rachel had bought her book the day before, and went inside. A smattering of tourists were browsing the shelves, and this time an earnest-looking young man was seated at the caisse.

"Let me do the talking," hissed Rachel, then turned on her most alluring, wide-eyed smile. "Bonjour," she said to the man.

"Bonjour, mam'selle," he said, with obvious interest.

"I wonder if you could help us. As you know, we've been working on the dig, and now it's finished we want to do some sightseeing."

"Of course, I have been following the dig with interest! How can I help?"

"I understand Saunière used to visit a place called La Grotte du Fournet – could you point it out on the map for us?"

His face darkened. "I'm afraid not, mam'selle. It is forbidden," he said sternly.

"Forbidden?"

"Yes – La Grotte is on private land. You would be trespassing. It's the treasure-hunters," he added, trying to soften the blow. "They cause so much damage."

"Yes, I know," said Rachel, visibly disappointed. "Thanks, anyway."

They slowly made their way back up to the museum to find Dubois waiting for them.

"Bonjour, mes amis," he said as they approached. "Did you find what you were seeking?"

"No," said Rachel shortly. "We were asking for directions."

"Directions? You should have asked me."

"Well, since you're offering, perhaps you can tell us how to find La Grotte du Fournet, because no-one else around here seems inclined to help us."

"La Grotte du Fournet?" queried Dubois smoothly. "I can explain where it is, but it is hard to find on foot, and it is on private land."

"As everyone has been at great pains to tell us," put in David acidly. "Tell me, if you knew about this place, why didn't you mention it? You said you wanted to help us, yet you failed to mention the grotto, or the fact that La Tour Magdala directly overlooks it. That's quite relevant, don't you think?"

"M'sieur, I understand your frustration, but you must realise the damage that treasure-hunters have caused around here. They will stop at nothing – they have already dug up most of La Grotte, which is a burial site ancien. People here are wary – tourists are one thing, but they do not want their heritage destroyed. If you lived here, perhaps you would feel the same way."

"Yes, I do understand that," said Rachel. "But we're archaeologists – we're not going to dig up anything without permission." She blushed as she realised that Dubois, of all people, would know that was a lie.

He smiled benignly. "Pas de problème. I will take you there later this afternoon, if you wish."

117

"Really?" said Rachel enthusiastically. "That would be fantastic."

"It's my pleasure! But no digging – or you will get me into trouble with the mayor. And in the meantime, can I suggest you put that parchment somewhere safe?" he said, turning to David.

"This place is alarmed, if that's what you mean," said David.

Dubois smiled patiently. "That would not deter the people we are dealing with. Do you have a safe?"

"The museum has a small safe we sometimes use."

"That will do for now, though I suggest that as soon as possible, you place it in a safety deposit box at a bank."

"Well, it's stable now, so I can arrange that, once it's been photographed. We've got a special camera here for copying documents, so I can get that done before we go."

"Very well – there is someone I have to see, in any event. Shall we meet back here at, say, four o'clock?"

When Dubois had left, Rachel turned to David. "I get the impression you don't really believe any of this," she said accusingly.

"I believe we have a first-century parchment, with a fascinating message that will be of great interest to theologians. And I suppose it's theoretically possible that a descendant of Mary Magdalene is alive today who can somehow prove her lineage – assuming Mary did actually marry someone. Beyond that, it's just so much speculation. Uninformed speculation, at that. It's one thing to draw up rational theories, based on facts you have already uncovered. But this… this is just pure Da Vinci Code territory. I mean, we've no proof your road accident was anything other than just an accident. Do you really think the Church would go around plotting to kill people? I'm a scientist, not a New Age investigator."

Rachel rolled her eyes in frustration. "I agree there's no proof of any kind of plot. But that accident was weird – I'm sure that car was waiting, and I certainly heard it accelerate before it hit me. It doesn't hurt to take precautions, does it? Even if the Church doesn't want to get its hands on that parchment, you can be sure plenty of treasure hunters would. You've seen what it's like up here. There's hardly a patch of ground they haven't dug up trying to find the gold they're convinced is buried here somewhere. And from my point of view, if I can find the living relative of the Magdalene, can't you see what a coup that would be? The implications are enormous. Not just for obscure theologians – for everyone. Jesus was married and his offspring are alive today – it would change the world, forever!"

"Even if she's alive, even if we can get DNA proof that her ancestors came from Palestine, that doesn't prove she married Jesus. Look, I realise you've got a documentary to produce, and National Geographic is footing the bill, so I'll go along with this – up to a point. But please don't ask me to suspend my critical judgement."

* * * * *

They grabbed the camera, theodolite, tape-measure, sketchpad and notebook, and after donning their walking boots they met Dubois back at the Range Rover at the appointed hour.

It was a short drive out of the village down some increasingly narrow country lanes, until the road abruptly turned into a gravel track. Dubois urged them to keep going, and after another mile or so of off-road driving, he indicated to pull over. An ill-defined path meandered across the hill from the road, and they set about following it through the maquis, a mixture of dense, evergreen shrubs and small trees and bushes, stunted by a combination of poor soil and scorching heat. Eventually this gave way to much wetter ground, where despite the soaring July temperatures, subterranean springs bubbled up through the limestone and ran down the escarpment to join the Couleurs stream far below. On more than one occasion they had to wade through sizeable streams, and after clambering over a number of rocky outcrops they were soon dripping with perspiration, even though it was, by now, late afternoon.

Eventually they came to the top of a steep cliff – a raw, jagged fault-line descending some 150ft or more into the Couleurs, punctuated by outlying stacks of limestone. In places there was nothing but scree, threatening to send anyone foolhardy enough to venture down there to a certain death. Elsewhere the cliff-face tumbled down in a series of rocky outcrops, allowing dense scrub to cling to the slopes.

"Where now?" gasped Rachel, trying to quell the feelings of vertigo welling up inside her.

"We must follow the cliff for a little way, then there is a path down," said Dubois. "The path is well trodden – it is not as difficult as it may appear. We have done the hard work."

They walked on a little way before Dubois turned off down a stony track that led steeply down the cliff at an angle of at least 45 degrees. The path appeared to have been partially cut into the rock-face, and Rachel tried hard to avoid looking at the precipitous drop that fell away just inches beneath her feet. Eventually the path levelled out, following a natural ledge in the gorge, before disappearing into a small patch of undergrowth and stunted trees. Rachel and David plunged in after Dubois, nearly running into the back of him as he stopped abruptly in front of the entrance to a cave.

"Voilà" he declared dramatically. "La Grotte du Fournet."

Dubois let Rachel lead the way inside, clambering up the muddy slope into the dark, dank chamber beyond. She could scarcely contain her excitement, though once inside, she couldn't help feeling a sense of anti-climax. The cave was nowhere near as large as she had expected. In the foreground was an

119

area of depressed mud, roughly in the shape of a small coffin, around the edges of which a few bunches of flowers had been strewn. Several partially burnt candles were close by: local people clearly still came here to pay their respects. Further back, as the cave roof sloped down to meet the damp ground, there was a shallow pit that might have once have contained another grave.

"So this is it," mused Rachel. "Was this the original resting place of Mary Magdalene – before she was moved to the crypt?"

"Perhaps, mam'selle," said Dubois quietly. Even David seemed sombre.

Rachel knelt down and laid her hands gently on the bare earth where a coffin had obviously once lain, closing her eyes, as if trying to read an unwritten message through the palms of her hands.

A shudder ran through her; an inexplicable frisson of awareness. This had been the grave of the Magdalene, of that she had no doubt. But there was something else here, too; something even deeper and stronger; an immense, benign force: a force as full of love and compassion as the presence in the undercroft had been consumed with hatred and violence.

But there was sadness here, too; a deep, ineffable sadness. She looked up, blinking away the tears. David looked at her, his eyes full of understanding. Whatever it was, despite his beliefs, he felt it, too.

She slowly climbed to her feet. "So what did Saunière find here?" she asked at length. "We know the body was moved to the crypt in the 10th century." Dubois' eyes flickered with interest. "Was he just commemorating this, her first resting place?"

"Possibly," said David. But they both felt that explanation fell short of the truth. "OK," he said after a further pause, "Let's get this place measured up and take some photos before the light starts to go. The sun will be over the top of the cliff in half an hour."

Rachel took the camera and started rattling off some shots, while David used the theodolite to get some precise measurements of the height and depth of the cave. Having exhausted the entrance chamber, Rachel set up the tripod and took some more shots at the back of the cave where the shallow grave was situated. As the flash illuminated the back of the cave she caught a faint carving on the wall. Grabbing the torch, she inspected it more closely.

"David!" she yelled, dashing to the front of the cave where he was packing his equipment, and beckoning. He put down the theodolite and followed her inside.

"It's an ichthus!" she said, pointing to the carving. "Treasure-hunters wouldn't give a damn about that, nor would New Agers. It was only used up to the third century, wasn't it?"

"Until the bumper sticker was invented, at any rate," said David cynically. "But I agree, it looks pretty old – stuck up here in a remote cave, it's possible it does date from that era, though it could have been added later."

"Let's try to piece this together," said Rachel. "Perhaps this was the original burial site of the Magdalene, and they moved her to a more fitting place in the 10th century when they built the church at Rennes-le-Château."

"That's plausible," agreed David.

"Then, for some reason – perhaps because of the crusade against the Cathars – in the 13th century, her body was moved again to another, more secret hiding place. We also know from Dubois…" she turned round to look quizzically at the Frenchman, who had been watching them intently, "that Mary Magdalene's direct descendant is alive today. So it's possible she may know of Mary's final resting place, assuming we can find her. If not, apart from the parchment, we're right out of clues – unless there's anything to be gleaned from the de Blanchefort tombstone."

"Since we're not cryptologists, we may never know the answer to that, I'm afraid," said David. "Come on, it's nearly seven o'clock. Let's start heading back."

Chapter 26

They gave themselves a lie-in the next morning before heading up to the village. As the Range Rover threaded its way through the narrow main street of Rennes-le-Château and pulled up outside the museum, they immediately realised something was wrong – not just because of the police car parked outside, but the throng of people milling around outside the building.

David hit the brakes and jumped out of the car door. "Qu'est-ce qui se passe?" he asked, grabbing the shoulder of a gendarme. The officer turned and looked pointedly at David's arm on his uniform. "Pardon, monsieur," said David, hurriedly removing his hand. "Je travail ici – je suis le chef responsable pour les excavations archaeologiques. Qu'est-ce qui ce passe ici, si vous plaît?"

"You are David Tranter?" the gendarme replied in fair English. David nodded.

"There has been an incident, m'sieur – it seems that during the night someone broke into the museum."

Rachel stared at David in disbelief. "Was anything taken?" she asked.

"At this stage we cannot be sure, mam'selle. But perhaps you can help us."

"Yes – of course. Can we go in?"

"Please; follow me."

They made their way through the throng of bystanders, including, Rachel noted, at least one TV crew. Rennes-le-Château was once more living up to its reputation of making headlines. As they went into the museum, Rachel could initially see nothing out of place, other than a broken window – clearly the intruder's route into the building. But as they entered the Finds Room, a cold shiver ran through her body. She stood there speechless, hands clutched to her face, staring at the chaos before her – artefacts swept onto the floor, filing cabinets hanging open. The hermetically-sealed box containing the manuscript was nowhere to be seen.

She swung round to face David. "The manuscript – did you give it to Hélène to put in the safe?"

"Yes – of course I did," he protested angrily. He turned to the gendarme. "Inspector, is the safe OK? Le coffre-fort – c'est bon?"

"Du musée?" The gendarme turned and walked back into museum, where the safe stood behind the counter, its door hanging open. "I'm afraid not, m'sieur."

"Christ!" exclaimed Rachel, rushing over to look inside. A petty cash tin containing the previous day's museum takings was untouched, but of the manuscript there was no sign.

"Fucking hell!" she swore. "That was our star exhibit – even if we'd found nothing else, that would have made the programme a real show-stopper. It was our only hard evidence. Now what do we have?"

"For God's sake calm down, Rachel. I'd already emailed the parchment text to Sue for translation. And there are the photos…"

"Oh, brilliant – they will look really good on TV. And as you yourself have said, photos can easily be faked."

"The Visigoth coin – is that still there?"

"Where was it?"

"I stashed it at the back under those papers."

Rachel rummaged around in the safe. "Nothing!" she exclaimed angrily. "This is a disaster."

"Well I put them both in the safe – what more could I do?"

The gendarme coughed politely, and they turned in his direction. "I take it, then, that something of value has been taken?"

"Indeed," said David. "We found a parchment…" He winced as Rachel slipped her hand behind his back and pinched him, hard.

"An old scrap of paper – nothing of any value," said Rachel, hurriedly. "At least not to a thief. But it was important to our research."

"You discovered this… comment dire en anglais… on your dig?"

"Yes."

"How old was this… piece of paper?"

"We're not sure, really. We're still waiting for the dating results," she lied smoothly.

"Still, any artefact is worth something to someone – especially if it has something to do with this place," observed the gendarme, gesturing with his hands, a bemused expression on his face. "It seems strange that the thief did not take the euros – or these other objets…" he gestured to the artefacts strewn across the floor in the next room. "Is it possible he was looking for this… paper?"

"I suppose it's possible," said Rachel. "Though I can't think why."

The gendarme gave her a long, hard stare. "And you, mam'selle, what is your role here? Do you work on this dig?"

"In a manner of speaking…" The gendarme's stare turned into a frown. "I work for National Geographic," she said hurriedly. "The American TV station…"

"We are not peasants, mam'selle. We have National Geographic here in France, too."

"Of course, I didn't mean…"

"So what is National Geographic doing here?" interrupted the gendarme.

"You are filming the dig?"

"Yes," said Rachel brightly, happy to leave it at that. Telling him they were paying for the dig could open up a whole new can of worms.

"Very well." He turned to David. "M'sieur, I would like a complete list of everything that has been taken as soon as possible."

"Of course. Though given this mess that might take a little while."

"Please give it to me as soon as you can." The gendarme turned and walked away.

"Now what!" said Rachel furiously, turning on David. "This is a complete catastrophe!"

"I wouldn't mind asking Monsieur Dubois if he knows anything about this," he replied tersely.

"Why the hell would Dubois be involved?"

"He was the one who suggested we put the scroll in the safe yesterday – that there was a security risk."

"Precisely! If he had wanted to steal it, he wouldn't have made the job harder for himself!"

"Or it could be an elaborate double-bluff – to make it look as if he couldn't possibly be involved. The timing is a little suspicious, don't you think?"

"No I don't – but I do think you're getting paranoid again."

"Really? There's something not entirely straight about that guy. I've a good mind to mention it to the gendarme."

"Look, there's nothing to be gained by making an enemy of Dubois. Whatever his motives, he may still be able to help us."

"Well, the archaeology is my responsibility, and I've got to go and help the police right now," said David, still seething. "So either way, I'm going to be tied up here with paperwork for the next couple of days. Perhaps while I'm doing that you can figure out where we are supposed to go to from here." With that, he headed off to the Finds Room.

Rachel trudged dejectedly after him. She offered to help out with the gendarmerie, but David was insistent on handling everything himself. Although she had overall responsibility for the project as far as National Geographic was concerned, when it came to the dig itself, David was very much in control – it was his professional licence on the block, and there was no point alienating him further by stepping on his toes. After helping to clear up some of the debris, she headed over to the cabin to escape the mêlée and think. She would have preferred to go back to the hotel and do some research, but she didn't want David to think she was deserting him – whatever his protestations.

She fired up her laptop and checked her mail. Thank God – David had copied her in on the email to Sue; she wasn't in the mood for explanations to head-office staff about losing their star exhibit. She looked again at the parchment translation. The first part appeared to be a vague, rambling prophesy. She read down to the last six lines of text, separated from the rest, and clearly written in a different hand. Was there anything more here to go on?

'When the time is come, seek out she who is called Mary, at the grotto where Our Lady was laid to rest.'

Well, they had found the grotto – she was fairly sure of that. But 'seek out Mary'? Was that referring to the Magdalene's descendant? The lines seemed to make a distinction between 'Mary' and 'Our Lady'. But how, and where, was one supposed to meet her? Was there a hint in that cryptic 'When the time is come'? Yet it could mean anything, particularly since it had been written hundreds of years earlier. They could hardly camp out there on the off-chance she might turn up one day in the not too distant future.

Rachel sat at the battered aluminium desk, covered with spots of mud and odd shards of pottery and buried her head in her hands. The whole project was turning into a disaster. They had lost their key artefact, and the crypt had been sealed, perhaps indefinitely – with only photos to show the tomb of Mary Magdalene had ever existed.

She looked up and glared out of the window, drumming her fingers on the desk in frustration. Then she froze as her eyes alighted on Saunière's quixotic La Tour Magdala. Of course! The answer was quite literally staring her in the face.

Chapter 27

Montségur, Christmas 1243

Pierre-Roger de Mirepoix stood on the battlements of Montségur as the first grey light of a cold winter's dawn broke through the blackness, gazing down at the armies encamped 500 feet below. From the vertiginous heights of the limestone pillar that rose dramatically from the valley floor, they looked as if they could be brushed away like a swarm of insects, but Pierre-Roger knew they were all too real.

Some 7,000 troops flying the colours of King Louis had pitched their tents in the valley nestled at the foot of the pog, even though their numbers had been decimated by the worst winter in memory. The snow had arrived in late November, and in the weeks that followed, blizzard after blizzard had howled through the valleys like icy demons, cutting through wool and leather jerkins like a surgeon's knife, chilling to the bone.

Those within the walls of Montségur had enjoyed more shelter than the royalist soldiers below, but thrust high into the icy wind, the isolated outcrop was exposed to the worst of the freakish elements. On one occasion the wind had been so violent it lifted a man-at-arms bodily off the battlements and dashed him to the ground far below.

Still, it mattered little that hundreds of the king's troops had died, thought Pierre-Roger, wryly. With the number of trained men-at-arms in the châteaux numbering little more than 100, just a fraction of the force gathered below could rout them if they dared descend from their mountain-top retreat. Their only hope was to sit it out, and hope that smuggled supplies of food and cloth continued to find their way through.

Retribution for his attack on the Inquisition at Avignonet may not have been swift, but when the royal army arrived more or less a year to the day after the assault, it had done so in overwhelming force. This was no token siege, as two years before, but a statement of intent: the last remaining Cathar stronghold would be destroyed, stone by stone if necessary.

As his father-in-law Raymond had feared, the English army that landed at Royan was but a token force, and Raymond VII and his allies had been easily defeated at the battle of Taillebourg two months later. Raymond sued for peace, but was excommunicated by the Pope. The insurrection fizzled out, and it had only been a matter of time before the Crusaders arrived at Montségur. A thousand men had seemed plenty at first, but as the challenge of cutting off the castle's supply lines through the myriad mountain paths became clear, the commander, Hugues des Arcis, had called up reinforcements. Now, though some supplies trickled through thanks to the bravery of Cathar sympathisers, there was no escape for the castle's 500 besieged inhabitants.

Pierre-Roger's wife had been proven right, and although the savage rift of the first few days after Avignonet had largely healed, there was still a lingering hurt between them, despite the birth of their first baby, Mariette. He bitterly regretted his rash decision to back Count Raymond of Toulouse, but regrets would not turn back time. Now he could only wait, and hope for a miracle.

A sudden movement far below on Tower Rock caught his eye, and he focused his gaze more closely on the stone fortification that he had ordered built on the massive outcrop. Although the lowest point of the small hilltop plateau, its cliffs still plunged vertically nearly 350 feet to the valley below, and some had questioned the necessity of such a move when resources were scarce. But for all his faults, Pierre-Roger was a brilliant and capable military commander, and he had no intention of leaving his defences vulnerable.

What, then, was going on? A clammy hand grabbed his heart as he saw a lithe figure in a black jerkin scramble over the top of the cliff-face 500 feet to the east of his vantage point, closely followed by another, and yet another. Desperately he shouted a warning, but his voice was lost in the icy north-east wind. Within minutes the small band of mercenaries had quickly and efficiently slit the throats of the few defending foot-soldiers. His greatest fear had come to pass: the Crusaders finally had a foothold on the pog.

Chapter 28

Rachel ran to the Finds Room to discover David in earnest conversation with the gendarme. Hardly able to contain herself, she went back outside and paced up and down in front of the church, watched curiously by the tourists streaming past. Every so often she would look through the door, but he was still busy, either talking to the gendarme or Hélène, or checking that nothing else had been taken.

After a while she returned to the cabin and tried to distract herself by surfing the net. Finally, at noon, the gendarme disappeared for lunch and David emerged into the searing heat of the yard looking weary and dishevelled.

"David…" she said, in the most submissive tone she could muster.

"Yes?" he said irritably.

"I think I've cracked it."

"What, for God's sake?"

Rachel bit back her natural response, and continued, sotto voce. "The message on the parchment. You know – 'seek out she who waits at the grotto where Our Lady was laid to rest.'"

"What about it?"

Rachel looked anxiously over her shoulder. There were several people within earshot. "Come to the cabin," she said.

"Well?" he asked as they walked inside. "I've still got a huge amount of work to do for the gendarmerie, you know."

"I know – I did offer to help. Anyway, just hear me out. Dubois has told us the descendant of Mary is still alive…"

"If you can believe him."

Rachel ignored his scepticism. "Well, I was sitting here while we were talking to the gendarme. I was feeling really frustrated about not understanding the message… and then I looked across the yard, and there it was, staring me in the face…"

"What on earth are you rambling on about? Have you been hitting the vino already?"

"No!" she said, laughing. "Look, I'm talking about La Tour Magdala. Remember what Dubois mentioned about the significance of the 22 steps, and St Mary Magdalene's feast day – July 22nd?"

"Yes," said David slowly.

"Well I'm pretty damn sure that's the answer! I think we should 'seek out she who waits' on Mary's feast day – July 22nd! It would make sense, wouldn't it? Maybe that was how Saunière met her, on those long walks in the country."

"Bit of a coincidence, don't you think?"

"Maybe it wasn't an accident; if the grotto was known locally as being associated with Mary Magdalene, maybe he went there on her feast day to pray. I believe it's normal for a priest to pray to a saint on their allotted day." She held her hand to silence him. "There's more. After I realised the significance of the number 22 in La Tour Magdala, I thought I would quickly Google the number 22 and see what came up. You'll never guess what…"

"Enlighten me," said David.

"It seems the number 22 was of particular significance to the Templars."

"Please God, not the Templars again…"

"Just bear with me, David. In one of the first tellings of the Grail legend, The Young Titurel, written in the 13th century, the Grail temple is described as a 'domed structure, surrounded by 22 radial chapels or arched recesses'. The author, Albrecht, devotes more than 100 lines to it. We know the Templars had a big presence here in southern France. The suggestion is that the troubadours, the wandering minstrels who played in the Cathar courts in the 12th century, were referring to the Templars when they told their stories about the Grail knights. We know the Cathars venerated Mary Magdalene. The Templars were supposedly devoted to the Virgin Mary. But what if their devotion was, in fact, to the Magdalene? Wouldn't that go a long way to explaining their extraordinary empathy with the Cathars?"

"I suppose it's plausible – assuming you buy the whole story…"

"David, what's got into you? You saw the tomb with your own eyes!"

"I don't doubt it's highly plausible that Mary came to France and that it's her tomb in there. But it's a big leap from that to say that the bloodline of Mary and Jesus has continued to this day, and that their direct descendant is living nearby – and is able to prove her lineage."

Rachel sighed. "I guess it does sound a little far-fetched. But as I've said before, what have we got to lose by checking it out? We've got to explore every possible lead – anything that will add some weight to the documentary. And July 22nd happens to be next Wednesday. Humour me! If nothing else, it will be good to go for a walk and get away from this place for a few hours."

"Well, as you say, we've got nothing to lose. Just don't get your hopes up."

"Aren't you going to ask me what time we need to be there?"

"I assumed you were just planning to hang around all day."

"Not necessarily. There's another number linked to this place that keeps recurring: 17. Dubois mentioned it. Maybe it's the 17th hour of the day."

"I don't think they had 24-hour clocks back then."

Rachel gave him a withering look. "They could still count the hours in a day – that way there's no room for ambiguity."

* * * * *

For Rachel, the next few days seemed to crawl by. David finally gave in and let her help out with the aftermath of the break-in, and much of the time was spent tediously putting together a report for the police and the mayor – who, having discovered that some kind of parchment had been stolen, demanded to know exactly what it contained.

Since he had given them permission to dig in the churchyard, they went to great lengths to mollify him, going to see him in person as well as submitting an official report. They assured him the artefact had come from an old grave uncovered by the dig – probably one of the many that Saunière had disturbed in his search for the crypt – and had been of no great significance in the overall scheme of things.

The mayor also demanded to know when the trench was going to be backfilled and the churchyard returned to normal, and David had to agree that if they didn't hear from the Vatican by the end of September, the crew would return to restore the site.

David took the risk of suggesting that the entrance through the Secret Room be left open for future investigations, and, somewhat to his surprise, the mayor agreed it would make sense – but said this fell within the Vatican's jurisdiction, not his own.

Dubois heard about the theft on the grapevine and put in an appearance on a couple of occasions to offer his help. He was also anxious to know whether the parchment had yet been translated. David stalled him, saying it was written in Aramaic, and they had been forced to refer it to a specialist academic – he didn't think Dubois believed him, but he didn't really care.

Finally, early on the morning of July 22nd, Rachel and David set off for the grotto, deciding to spend most of the day there in case Rachel's theory on the timing was wrong. Rachel had wanted to invite Dubois along, but David would have none of it.

"I don't trust him – and neither should you. If a descendant of the Magdalene really is still alive, and Dubois is in league with the Vatican, we would be leading him straight to her."

Rachel reluctantly agreed to err on the side of caution. They retraced the route they had taken with Dubois and arrived at the cave by nine o'clock. Not wanting to waste their time, David made a further examination of the cave, searching the walls for further markings, and sifting through the thick layer of loose sand on the ground for anything that might have been missed. However, after trawling through the debris for an hour or so and finding nothing, he gave up and went outside to explore the cliff for other caves nearby.

The hours dragged. Rachel tried to read a book, but found it impossible to concentrate. Eventually, at around three o'clock, she heard a scrabbling sound outside the cave. She looked up at the entrance, startled, as a female figure appeared outlined against the bright sky beyond. It was Hélène from the museum.

Rachel jumped to her feet, startled. "Hélène!" she exclaimed. "What on earth are you doing here?"

"I might very well ask you the same question," she replied curtly. "You were told this was private property."

Rachel paused a moment before answering. She owed Hélène an explanation – as curator of the Rennes museum, she had shown them a considerable degree of trust over the past few months.

"I found out on the grapevine that according to local tradition, the Grotte du Fournet was where Mary Magdalene was buried. We know, of course, about the legend that she came to France after the death of Christ. And since it is St Mary Magdalene's Day today, we thought we would come and pay our respects."

Hélène studied her face carefully. "How very thoughtful," she said icily. "You didn't have any trouble finding it, then?"

"It certainly wasn't where you showed us on the map, Hélène," said Rachel. "But I guess you had your reasons."

"Indeed," said Hélène. "The landowner is a friend of mine. I'm afraid he doesn't like uninvited guests. We have had enough trouble with treasure-hunters desecrating this place."

"We're not treasure hunters, Hélène, as well you know."

"No, but you came here before, didn't you? Did Dubois show you the way?"

"Yes, we did. Is there anything wrong with that? He's a local historian, and he's related to Marie Dénarnaud, isn't he?"

Hélène snorted with derision. "Is that what he's been telling you?"

"Do you know something we don't?"

"Plenty, but now is not the time. I'm sorry, but I must ask you to leave."

"Why?"

"As I have said, you are trespassing."

"Well, I can't go until David gets back."

'Where is he?"

"He's gone off exploring, looking for other caves – you know what men are like," said Rachel coolly.

"And you? You are not exploring?"

"No, just soaking up the atmosphere. Look, Hélène, I understand your concern, but we're not doing any harm. I'll wait until David gets back, if it's all the same with you. I can't remember the way back to the car, anyway," she lied. "I've got a terrible sense of direction."

Hélène looked nonplussed, unsure of what to do. "Very well," she said eventually. "You may wait here until David returns, but then you must leave."

An hour passed in awkward silence, broken only by the occasional snatch of forced conversation. Just before four o'clock there was a scrabbling sound outside and David appeared in the cave entrance, bathed in sweat.

"Hélène!" he exclaimed. "What are you…"

"We've been through this already, David," said Rachel, jumping to her feet. "It turns out Hélène is a friend of the owner, and she is not desperately happy about us being here. She says we are trespassing and has asked us to leave."

"So what's the big deal?" he said, giving Hélène a hard stare. "You should know we can be trusted."

"Oh, really? This coming from someone who broke into the crypt?"

David started to protest, but Hélène raised her hand to stop him. "Don't try to deny it," she said angrily. "I know all about your little midnight expedition – and what you found down there."

He shrugged; the game was clearly up. "OK, so we went into the crypt. It's no big deal, unless you're working for the Vatican. Don't you think people have a right to know what's down there?"

"That is not for you or me to decide," retorted Hélène. "Now, please – go!" she ordered, pointing to the cave entrance.

"We'll go when we're good and ready, and not before," said Rachel, as she saw David hesitating. "You don't own this place. For all we know, you could have your own reason for wanting to be here."

"And what would that be?" said Hélène, her eyes flashing dangerously.

Rachel fell silent. There was a moment's pause, then in a swift movement, Hélène reached into her bag and pulled out a pistol. "Now perhaps you will go," she said.

Chapter 29

The floor shuddered as a stone ball from a trebuchet cannoned into the castle's curtain wall, and lumps of mortar rained down from the ceiling.

Pierre-Roger raised his hands to Philippa in a quizzical gesture. "What more evidence do you need? Scarcely an hour passes without the king's war machines bringing down destruction upon us. You know I am not a man who would idly contemplate defeat, but it is only a matter of time before Montségur is captured. Now they have advanced from Tower Rock to the Barbican and assembled their siege engines, we cannot survive for long. Our supply lines are cut. You must escape while there is still the chance to smuggle you out."

"I will not leave you," said Philippa, her eyes blazing defiantly.

"In God's name, why not? It was I who brought this destruction upon us; you warned of the consequences but I would not listen. You are rightfully angry, yet you refuse to go."

"Because I love you, husband," she said quietly. ""What is past is past, and cannot be undone. You are the father of my child. My place is here at your side."

Pierre-Roger sighed in exasperation and turned to her mother, Corba. "My lady, please, will you insist that she leaves Montségur? Your bloodline is at risk – you must see the inevitability of our situation. There is no way, militarily, that we can avoid defeat."

"Believe me, her father and I have both tried," she said wearily. "But when her mind is made up, there is no changing it."

Pierre-Roger turned away, struggling to get his temper under control, pacing around the small tower room like a caged animal.

"Bishop Marty," he said at last, turning to a man in a simple grey cassock, "you of all people must understand the importance of this. I seek not just to protect my wife and child, but the future of Christendom. You are now the leader of our faith; surely you can persuade my stubborn wife?"

The bishop smiled wanly. "I wish that I could, my lord, but you must know I have no sway over either Lady Corba de Péreille or her daughter. If Bishop Benoît were still with us, God rest his soul, he might have been able to intercede, for he was like a second father to the girl. But I have little influence; this goes beyond the Cathar faith. By all normal conventions, as your wife, Lady Philippa should obey you; but by virtue of her heritage, she has the right to make such decisions herself. Were she without child, her mother could insist that she goes, but now she has a daughter, the final decision rests with her alone. I will say one thing, however, my Lord: it is vital that we remove from here our sacred writings. They must be preserved for future generations – we cannot allow them to be taken by the Inquisition and used against us. That is especially true of the gospel that Lady Corba carries with her; I have discussed this with her, and we are both agreed it must be taken to a place of safety."

"Well then, so be it," said Pierre-Roger, resignedly. "Make plans to take the scrolls from here. I know of a place where they will be safe, but let no word of it be mentioned outside this room, save to the man to whom you entrust this mission. There is a place deep beneath Rhédae known only to a few of our number – an ancient burial chamber within the hill itself. I have used it as a refuge on more than one occasion when fleeing the king's men."

"Rhédae? But that is where the Madeleine was interred before her body was moved at the start of this vile crusade. Is that wise, when the town is under royal control?" queried Corba.

"Where better to hide it than right under their noses? In any case, since the armistice that followed the Treaty of Meaux it has become a backwater, and many Cathars have returned incognito. As I have said, only a few trusted men know of the entrance to the cave, on the hillside below the town. It is impossible to find unless you know the way. Now, Bishop Marty, and you, my Lady Corba, talk to my seneschal about finding some reliable men to undertake the mission. In the meantime, I will plan a counter-attack on the siege engines to give them some cover."

He paused and looked over at Philippa, a grave expression on his face. "As for you, my wife, I appreciate your love, loyalty and forgiveness, but I will not halt in my efforts to persuade you to leave."

Philippa smiled and bowed her head. "You may try all you wish, my lord, but I think we both know who will win that particular argument."

Three days later, shortly before dusk, a defiant counter-attack was launched on the enemy position at Tower Rock. During the fierce fighting, two of the most trusted Cathar faithful, Matheus and Peter Bonnet, slipped out of Montségur with their precious cargo, and taking a secret mountain path, disappeared into the hills beyond.

Chapter 30

"What the hell…" said Rachel, dumbfounded, staring at the gun in Hélène's hand. "Who are you really working for?"

"That's none of your business," said Hélène. "Now get out of here before I do something we will both regret."

Rachel looked across at David, who was still standing near the cave entrance, looking on in disbelief. "I think you're bluffing," she said quietly. "Do you really want to stand trial for murder? You don't strike me as the type."

Hélène eyed them both warily, weighing up the situation. "No, I won't kill you, but I'm not afraid to draw blood. David, get over there with Rachel," she said, backing up against the cave wall. "Move – now!"

He hesitated, and a bullet spat into the floor and pinged against the cave walls as it ricocheted around the small chamber.

"Jesus, Hélène – careful what you're doing with that thing," said Rachel, shocked and deafened by the noise of the gunshot in the confined space.

"David, move over to Rachel or the next one goes in your leg," said Hélène. "Please don't think I'm bluffing."

Confused and shaken by the gunshot, David edged over to where Rachel was standing. "Now sit down – both of you," demanded Hélène. "OK, now we wait," she said, as they shakily complied with her order.

"For what?" said Rachel sarcastically, fighting the panic that was threatening to overwhelm her.

Hélène studied her face, trying to gauge how much she knew. "Until I am ready to go," she replied darkly.

The next hour tested Rachel's patience to breaking point. Had all their painstaking work, all their hours of research, come to nothing? And what was Hélène's role in all this? To order them out, as a friend of the landowner, was one thing – but to pull a gun on them? That put her in a different category altogether – a very dangerous category. Was she operating on behalf of the Vatican, or some other interested party?

Five o'clock came and went, and Rachel began to wonder if the whole thing was an elaborate charade. She looked across at David and grimaced, while he just shrugged his shoulders.

Even Hélène started looking anxiously at her watch, then stood up and started pacing up and down, all the while keeping her gun trained on Rachel and David.

"Who are you waiting for?" asked Rachel once more, prodding for a reaction.

"As if you don't know!" snapped Hélène.

Moments later the sound of footsteps on the steep path outside echoed into the cave. "Now, silence – if you make a sound, you will pay for it," hissed Hélène.

The footsteps grew closer until they were just outside the entrance. Rachel's heart raced. If this really were a descendant of the Magdalene, then a huge weight rested on her shoulders. She could hold the key to the future of Christianity; a figure perhaps second in importance only to Jesus himself. Could she allow a bunch of scheming diehards to bring to an end a line dating back two millennia; a direct bloodline to Christ?

"Gardez-vous – elle a un pistolet!" screamed Rachel at the top of her voice, throwing herself across the cave to avoid a gunshot.

Hélène covered her with the pistol before turning back to the cave entrance. "Ne vous inquiétez pas – c'est moi, Hélène," she shouted. "I have some treasure-hunters here."

After a few seconds, a slim teenage girl appeared hesitantly at the cave entrance, her eyes anxiously peering into the gloom.

"C'est vous, Hélène?" she called, trying to keep her body behind a rock.

"Oui, c'est moi, Angeline!" replied Hélène, dropping the gun to her side and walking towards the entrance.

Rachel seized the moment and threw herself at Hélène, grabbing her legs in a rugby tackle and bringing her crashing to the ground.

The girl fled, and Rachel picked herself up and dashed after her. "It's OK, Angeline!" she shouted at the girl's rapidly receding figure. "We have been working on the dig at Rennes – we are not dangerous! We only want to talk…" The last words were uttered in desperation as the girl scrambled her way back up the steep path.

The teenager paused at the American accent. "We need to talk to the Madeleine – c'est très important!" said Rachel. "That's why we came here today. We must talk to her; her safety is at risk."

The girl paused, mid-flight. "You know of the Madeleine?" she said hesitantly.

"Yes!" Rachel looked over her shoulder at Hélène, who was standing watching her, a curious expression on her face. She decided to throw caution to the wind. "We found a hidden message in the dig at Rennes. The Madeleine is in grave danger."

The girl slowly made her way down the path once more. Rachel could see she was trembling. "Please don't be afraid – we want to help," she called.

Angeline slowly edged into view. Underneath her long, dark hair, her dusty face was streaked with tears. "You are English?" queried Angeline, in a strong Occitan accent.

"American," corrected Rachel. "But I was brought up in England."

"What is going on, Hélène?" asked the girl, looking from Rachel to David, and then back to Hélène, still standing behind them, her gun no longer in sight.

"They are uninvited guests," said Hélène. "I do not trust them. They work for American TV – they will expose the Madeleine to great danger."

"We need to talk to the Madeleine, for her own safety," said Rachel quickly. "It's true we work for National Geographic. But we give you our word we will say nothing about the Madeleine that she does not want us to say. And under no circumstances will we reveal her identity or location."

"How do I know I can trust you?" asked Angeline.

"We found a scroll in the tomb of the Madeleine in the crypt at Rennes," said Rachel.

Angeline gasped.

"The scroll has a message: it says, 'When the time is come, seek out she who waits at the grotto where Our Lady was laid to rest, for it is the destiny of her issue to reveal Christ's truth unto all men. Find her, and she will guide you to the light.' And so we have come here. Tell me, Angeline – are you the Madeleine?"

"Mois?" said the girl, startled, before bursting out laughing. "Non, she is my grandmother's sister. She is too old to come herself, and anyway the risk is too great with les trésor-chasseurs everywhere. But no-one cares about a girl like me."

Hélène moved forwards and confronted Rachel. "Is what you say true – did the scroll really come from the tomb of la Madeleine?"

"It did."

"And you have a copy?"

"Yes, we managed to open the scroll before it was stolen."

"This changes everything." Hélène turned to Angeline and spoke to her rapidly in Occitan, the language of the Languedoc. "I have explained what happened here," said Hélène. "Frankly your presence here is not welcome, but it seems you may have information that is vital to our cause – information that has been lost for centuries."

"Lost when the body was moved, perhaps?" put in David, who had been hanging back for fear of adding to the confusion and scaring Angeline further.

"Oui."

"Where was the body moved to?"

"Do you think if I knew I would tell you? But I do not know. No-one knows, not even la Madeleine. The body was moved in great haste during the crusade against the Cathars." David shot a meaningful glance at Rachel. "Since then the knowledge has been lost. We knew of the scroll, but not where it had been hidden. To think it was still in the tomb!"

"You say, 'We knew'... Who is 'We'?" asked David. "Who are you working for? And what is 'the cause'?"

"We work for no-one, except the love of Jesus Christ and la Madeleine," said Hélène indignantly. "For those few of us who know, it is our duty to protect la Madeleine."

"From whom – the Vatican?"

"Among others – they are not the only ones seeking to kill the bearer of Christ's true message."

"You keep calling her 'la Madeleine'. Isn't that the name given to the original Mary Magdalene?"

"Every direct descendant of Marie de la Madeleine is known simply as 'la Madeleine'," said Hélène.

"All of them?" queried Rachel.

"There is only one in each generation. Each Madeleine chooses one of her daughters to be her successor – usually the eldest, but there have been exceptions. When the mother dies, her daughter becomes la Madeleine."

"Going only through the female side makes for a vulnerable bloodline," said David.

"Indeed. But la Madeleine enjoys God's protection – with our help," she added pointedly.

"Are you related to her?"

"By marriage, through the family of la Madeleine's husband. He passed away two years ago. So now, enough questions. What is in the scroll?"

"We would like to meet la Madeleine," said Rachel cautiously. She didn't want to antagonise Hélène any further, but she wasn't about to give up that information lightly. "We give you our word that if she doesn't want us to mention her existence, we won't. All we seek is further proof that Jesus and Mary were married, and had a child. As you know, the Vatican has banned us from entering the crypt – officially!" She smiled at Hélène, trying to lighten the moment.

Hélène turned once more to Angeline and spoke again in Occitan, before turning back to Rachel.

"Very well, it is agreed. We will take you to see la Madeleine, but you must bring a translation of the scroll. Just the two of you – no-one else, especially not Dubois. Do not even discuss this with him – ever. And no cameras, no hidden microphones or tape recorders."

"You've got a deal," said Rachel. "But we go today."

Chapter 31

Montségur, February 27, 1244

S now had given way to cold, hard, driving rain, and the raw wind still carried enough force to cut through sodden clothing and chill to the bone. Matheus Bonnet stole past the weary enemy sentries and arrived back at the postern gate of Montségur to give the pre-arranged signal. The gate opened quickly, and the exhausted Bonnet was dragged inside and half-carried to the keep. He stood swaying, cold and bedraggled, in front of a furious Pierre-Roger de Mirepoix.

"You say the mission was successful, yet you fear for the safety of the relics? What kind of nonsense is this, man? Did you hide them in the burial chamber, as discussed?"

"Yes, my lord," he muttered. "But my brother was captured shortly afterwards. I barely escaped with my life. There are informers everywhere. Many believe we have great treasure hoarded here at Montségur, and rich rewards are being offered for information that leads to its seizure. I fear they may torture him."

"But that is absurd! They must know we Cathars abhor the pleasures of the flesh."

"The Pope's men do not believe that. Their own priests and bishops are so wealthy and corrupt they cannot accept that we have different values. They do not understand our faith."

"They do not want to understand," said Pierre-Roger, moodily. He looked Bonnet up and down, taking in his emaciated appearance and torn, wet clothes. "Oh sit down, man – here, in front of the fire, and have a pitcher of mulled wine. I need time to think."

At dawn's first light, the plaintive sound of a trumpet rang out from the ramparts of Montségur. Raymond de Péreille's standard, which had flown so bravely over the château throughout the siege, was reverently lowered to half-mast.

Raymond, together with Roger-Pierre de Mirepoix, stood exposed on the battlements and shouted to the Crusaders that they wished to parley.

The huge main gates of the château slowly creaked open for the first time in a year, and two heralds emerged bearing the white flag of truce.

Chapter 32

The journey took the best part of an hour, passing through some of the most spectacular countryside Rachel had seen during her time in the Languedoc. The road twisted and turned its way through gaunt limestone hills and steep, winding river valleys, occasionally passing through dense tracts of forest before re-emerging amongst mountain pastures.

At one point the road made a tortuous diversion around the base of a brooding mountain, which Hélène informed them was called Le Pech de Bugarach. "Some people say Bugarach inspired Steven Spielberg's film Close Encounters of The Third Kind," she told them, a smile playing on her lips.

"You're kidding!" said Rachel, half in disbelief.

"That's what they claim. Apparently the shape of the mountain inspired him to re-create something similar in the film. And then in 2012, thousands of people climbed to the top of Bugarach because they believe the world was about to end, and that UFOs would rescue them when the planet perished."

"Some people will believe anything," muttered David.

Eventually a small village came into view, perched on top of a hill rising from the valley floor, its ancient, yellowing stones mirroring the golden, late-afternoon sunlight. The jagged remains of a château rose up from one side of the hill like the stump of a decaying tooth.

"So this is Camps-sur-Agly," said Rachel. "It looks like a miniature version of Rennes-le-Château."

"It has a similar history, too. During the Albigensian Crusade, several leading faydits – Cathar nobles dispossessed of their land – were given shelter here, and it was used as a base by one of the leading Cathar rebels. I suppose today they would be called freedom fighters. Curiously, his name was Béranger, too, though the spelling was slightly different; Béranger de Cucunhan, though I think his calling was rather more noble than Monsieur Saunière's."

They drove into the village and parked outside the church. "There aren't more than 60 people living in the village today," said Hélène sadly, as they walked down the quaint little street. "Most of the houses are now just holiday homes."

They came to an ancient Romanesque church, and Hélène paused, turning to Rachel. "Would you like to have a quick look inside? I think you might find it enlightening."

The door was stiff and heavy, but opened slowly to reveal an almost pitch-black interior. The only light came from a stunning circular stained-glass window high up in the curved wall of the apse. They walked in, leaving the door open behind them to admit some light to the stygian gloom.

The window was a breathtaking kaleidoscope of colour; deep, rich blues and reds interspersed with luminous yellows and azures. Around the circumference ran a ring of fleur-de-lys in a geometric pattern, while a concentric band inside contained symbols of what appeared to be a flowering plant with a blob of red at its roots. At the centre of the whole window was an image of the head and shoulders of a woman in blue, surmounted by a brilliant gold halo.

"That window is just astonishing," breathed Rachel.

"It is magnificent," agreed Hélène. "13th century, we think."

"That's around the time of the Cathars... But they didn't have churches as such, did they?"

"No, but some of their beliefs crossed over into local church architecture, much as many old English churches contain pagan motifs like the Green Man."

"Is that the Virgin Mary portrayed in the window?" queried David.

"Officially," said Hélène.

"But the white shape in front of her chest doesn't look like a baby – it's too small. It's more like a hand," said Rachel.

"Ambiguous, isn't it?"

"But why would they portray Mary without the baby Jesus?"

"Perhaps it is not the Virgin you are looking at," said Hélène.

"The Magdalene?"

"What do you think?"

"Do those plants have any particular significance?" asked David.

"There are various legends in Europe about plants springing up where the Saviour's blood has fallen. It is also thought to symbolise rebirth. Of course, there may be another explanation."

"Such as?"

"A holy bloodline," said Hélène.

David snorted.

"You may laugh, David, but do not judge until you have met Anne-Marie," said Hélène, sharply.

They went back outside, squinting as their eyes adjusted to the bright sunlight, and followed Hélène down the winding village street, past more ancient yellow-stoned houses – the over-restored gîtes with their ugly plastic windows outnumbering the more careworn homes belonging to local inhabitants. They turned off up a side lane that wound its way towards the outskirts of the village, and stopped in front of a tumbledown cottage that had clearly seen better days.

Angeline pushed aside the gate, hanging awkwardly on rusty hinges, and ran up to the door, disappearing inside. There was a long delay before eventually the door opened again and the smiling face of an elderly woman could be seen, hugging the slim figure of Angeline. She beckoned them to follow, and disappeared inside once more.

As they stooped beneath the low stone lintel and went inside, it was like stepping back in time – ancient flagstone floors, lime plaster crumbling from the walls, a stone sink with a solitary cold water tap above it. An ancient black cast-iron range cooker occupied most of one wall of the tiny room, brightly-glowing coals visible through the partially open fire door. Despite – or perhaps because of – its age and timeless appearance, the cottage felt homely and welcoming.

The old woman looked at Rachel and smiled, nodding her head shyly in greeting. "Allow me to introduce you," said Hélène. "This is Madame Anne-Marie de Blanchefort. The direct descendant of Mary Magdalene."

The two of them shook the old lady's hand, then stepped back, unsure of what to say next. What could you say, thought Rachel? They were supposedly in the presence of the descendant of the bride of Christ, yet it felt very ordinary – if slightly surreal. She looked again at the tiny woman, half-hoping to sense some spiritual presence, but all she could see was the careworn face of an elderly French woman, albeit with a twinkle in her eyes, dressed in the traditional black garb once so typical of southern France.

Anne-Marie ushered them to the scrubbed pine kitchen table, and they sat down. She murmured a few words to Hélène, who asked if they would like some stew.

"Oui, merci, madame," said Rachel politely, addressing her directly. The old lady made her way over to the range where a large pot was gently simmering and ladled out two large bowlfuls which she placed in front of Rachel and David.

"Do eat up," said Hélène. "I'm afraid she doesn't speak much English, and her French is more Occitan than anything else. Let me talk to her while you're eating, and I will try to find the answers to some of the questions I know you want to ask."

"Wow, this is good," said Rachel as she tucked into the steaming bowl of stew, while Hélène and Anne-Marie talked quietly. "What do you think it is?"

"It's fantastic," agreed David. "Tastes like rabbit to me."

Rachel gave him a filthy look and stared at the bowl in distaste. She leaned forward to whisper. "Putting aside that you're an ass, did you pick up on the name when Hélène introduced her?"

"De Blanchefort? I could hardly fail to given that riddle on the gravestone is at the heart of the whole Rennes mystery."

"Do you think there's a connection – or is Hélène trying to lead us a merry dance?"

"There are probably distant relatives of the original de Blancheforts still living around these parts, so it's plausible," said David thoughtfully. "On the other hand, if, as you suggest, Hélène were trying to misdirect us, it would be a clever way of doing it. I think the jury's out on that one until we get some more evidence. I have to say, though, she doesn't look much like the descendant of Christ," he added, through a mouthful of food.

"Actually, I'm inclined to agree," said Rachel, dipping absent-mindedly into her stew again. "But then again, what were we supposed to expect? A flash of lightning? Some kind of divine revelation? I don't know... I'm beginning to see your point. How can we ever know, for certain? And even if we could somehow be sure, how could we convince viewers? Hélène's made it clear we can't do anything that might identify her."

"Well I'm not expecting much, but we've come this far, so let's hear what she's got to say," said David. "If nothing else, she's a lovely old girl, and she makes a mean rabbit stew. I can think of worse ways to spend the evening. I just love this cottage – it's so rustic and unspoilt."

"You'd probably live in a ruined castle if you had the chance," laughed Rachel.

"Too right!"

After they had finished their food the old lady shuffled over and sat down with them. Rachel looked up into her eyes, beyond the warm, kindly smile, and a frisson ran through her body. There was a light in those eyes she hadn't noticed before; an ancient, ineffable light that came from far beyond her own soul. It drew her in and bathed her in its golden warmth, her anxieties evaporating like so much summer mist. She was floating again, in time and space, just as she had done after the accident. A face was solidifying before her; the face of a different woman...

"Rachel?"

She jumped, startled out of her reverie. "Sorry, Hélène. I was miles away."

"That's quite all right. She often has that effect on people!" She smiled enigmatically. "It seems Anne-Marie has heard of your excavations at Rennes, so she was not completely surprised to see us here. Please forgive what happened at the cave – you must understand we are sworn to protect Anne-Marie and her granddaughter."

"Granddaughter?"

"Oui – Marianne. She lives and works in Paris."

"And Marianne's mother?"

"She died in a car accident when Marianne was quite young, and the child was taken to a place of safety."

"An accident?" asked Rachel, glancing at David.

"I share your doubts," said Hélène. "Anne-Marie and her forebears have lived their lives in secret because of threats from the Church. During the last century, between the two wars, there was so much upheaval that everything was quiet. But after the last war, when people took an interest in Rennes once more, the Vatican sent a legate to investigate the rumours. It was to protect Anne-Marie that there has been so much – how do you call it... disinformation?

about Rennes. The fake parchments were all part of an attempt to put the Vatican off the trail by spreading wild and exotic rumours. A little like you Americans with the UFOs at Roswell," she added mischievously.

"The parchments were definitely fakes, then?"

"Yes, the parchments allegedly found by Saunière in the pillar of the old altar at Rennes – Les Dossier Secrets, as they became known – are certainly not genuine. Firstly, that rumour only emerged in the 1960s, and secondly, on a practical note, the parchments would not even have fitted in the pillar! The column is on display in the museum, and you can clearly see there is only a very small cavity in the top.

"Philippe de Chérisey, the author of the fakes, had been introduced to Anne-Marie by Noël Corbu, who, if you remember, bought Saunière's estate from Marie Dénarnaud. The complex codes he used in the parchments were all part of an elaborate ruse to confuse people – he even managed to place the documents in the Bibliothèque Nationale in Paris. The parchments were mentioned in a book about Saunière soon afterwards as if they were fact, and since then treasure-hunters all over the world have been poring over them, trying to decipher clues to the gold they believe is hidden somewhere in Rennes.

"It all worked rather well – until, of course, the authors of *Holy Blood, Holy Grail* came up with the idea of a holy bloodline, and de Chérisey's friend Pierre Plantard, a vain self-publicist, saw the chance to draw attention to himself by backing the claim. It was he who invented the Priory of Sion, a secret society with grandiose claims of guarding a holy bloodline, whose membership, he claimed, had included the likes of Isaac Newton and Leonardo Da Vinci. Then, of course, the Vatican took a renewed interest."

"Does the Vatican know about Anne-Marie and Marianne?" asked David.

"Not as far as we know. But they know that Rennes-le-Château holds a vital clue. And as I have said, they will stop at nothing to prevent the truth being known."

"What proof is there that Anne-Marie really is a descendant of Mary Magdalene?" asked David.

Rachel glared at him.

"It is a fair question," said Hélène. "She has information that will lead you to the truth. Only she and Marianne know this."

A shiver ran down Rachel's spine. "What is it, this truth?"

"It is Mary Magdalene's account of her time with the Lord."

"A lost gospel?"

"If you like."

"Is it the complete version of the Gospel of Mary, the gnostic text?" asked David.

"No, not the *Gospel of Mary*, which was written long after her death, but a much earlier text, written by the Magdalene herself."

"Written by Mary?" said David in astonishment.

"Why the surprise – because she was a woman? Remember, she was an educated woman from a wealthy family – far more sophisticated than most of Jesus's other disciples. Peter was a simple fisherman, yet scholars are happy to accept him as the source of Mark's gospel. Mary was not just a disciple, but an apostle. Even the early Catholic Church called her *apostola apostolorum* – apostle to the apostles."

"That's a little ironic, considering their attitude to women priests," said Rachel. "Even the Church of England is divided over the issue of women bishops. The theological argument that all Jesus's chief disciples were men just doesn't hold water."

"Indeed. I suspect that deep down they really just want to keep the Church as a cosy all-male institution, don't you think?" said Hélène.

"Forgive me for interrupting your cosy feminist love-in, but I think we should reserve judgement on the authorship of this gospel until it's been studied by academic experts," said David. "And of course, there's the small matter of finding it. You say Anne-Marie has access to this gospel?"

Hélène hesitated. "Let us say she has information about where it may be found. But she is too old to go with you herself. I'm afraid you will have to rely on your own resources."

"And Marianne?" asked Rachel. "Is she in a position to help us?"

"I know she would like to, very much," replied Hélène. "But it is much too dangerous for her to be seen with you. No-one knows who she is. We must guard her secret, at all costs."

David's phone broke into a distorted snatch of AC/DC's *Highway to Hell*. "Excuse me, madame," he said to Anne-Marie in embarrassment, taking the call. "Yes, this is David Tranter. Hello, Inspector. You have some information about the burglary? Of course we can come back. Thank you. We'll be at the museum in an hour."

David turned to Rachel and Hélène. "It's Inspector Aubuchon from the gendarmerie. He has some important information about the missing parchment."

Hélène's hand flew to her mouth. "Mon dieu! He knows about the parchment?"

David coloured. "He knows about a parchment. He doesn't know its real significance. Anyway, he says he has a lead, and would like to meet us back at the museum as soon as possible."

"But there are loads of questions I want to ask yet," protested Rachel.

"Don't worry, I'm as fascinated as you are, but it can wait until tomorrow. Excusez-moi, Hélène – madame," he added, turning to Anne-Marie. She smiled and nodded her head.

"Goodbye, madame," said Rachel, moving over to the old woman and, on impulse, giving her a quick hug. As she held her, she felt an infinity of love and compassion flowing through her. She gave her a quick kiss on each cheek, and turned away, tears starting in her eyes.

"Let's make tracks," said David quickly. "Hélène, do you or Angeline want a lift anywhere?"

"Angeline lives here in the village. I will stay with Anne-Marie and talk things through – I'll phone you in the morning to arrange another meeting."

Chapter 33

Montségur, February 28, 1244

"Y ou call these terms reasonable?" exploded Corba. "That all Cathars refusing to recant their faith will be burnt at the stake?"

"My dearest, what does it matter if they merely say they recant their beliefs? God will know what is in their hearts, and he will understand what has driven them to this. They can all still partake of the sacrament before they leave the château. The Crusaders are as weary of this siege as we are; it has been a cruel winter. All knights and soldiers will be allowed to leave with their possessions; the common people will be forgiven past crimes – even those who killed the inquisitors at Avignonet will receive a full pardon."

"Providing we confess our sins to the Inquisition! And everyone knows what means they use to extract the information they seek."

"They have given us their word they will not use torture to extract confessions."

"Do you seriously expect me to believe that? In any event, you know none of the parfaits would consider recanting their faith. They are more concerned with their souls than they are with the fate of this world. Do you wish to see Esclarmonde die in the pyre?"

Raymond winced at the reminder of his elder daughter's status as a parfaite. "I will talk to her," he said in an unsteady voice. "She will see reason. Failure to surrender would mean certain death for everyone at Montségur, whether by the sword or starvation. You know that."

"Well, my lord, be warned: should Esclarmonde elect to die rather than recant her faith, she will not enter the flames alone. I will be at her side."

The blood drained from Raymond's face. "You cannot…"

"I can, and I will."

"This is not your fight."

"It is my daughter's fight, and so it is mine. You cannot blame her for taking up the Cathar cause, given the persecutions of this accursed crusade. And in truth, I am tired of running."

Raymond bowed his head in defeat, and his body started to tremble; to those watching it was as if he aged 10 years in the space of a few, brief moments. He ran his tongue nervously over his lips. "And Pippa?"

"She was always your favourite, wasn't she? I have managed to get her to see sense, and she will recant, if necessary, as will Pierre-Roger. She has little Mariette to consider, and she understands the need to protect the Madeleine's legacy."

"She may not need to recant," said Raymond, quietly.

"What do you mean?"

"I told you the grim news about the Bonnet brothers' expedition, and the threat posed to the gospel. I have been discussing the matter with Pierre-Roger, and we are agreed that we should send another party to recover the relics and find a safer hiding place. If you approve, we will send Pippa and Mariette with them."

"But how? We have just agreed terms of surrender."

"We have negotiated a period of two weeks' grace in which people will have time to examine their souls before deciding whether to recant. The delay will give us time to organise one final escape. It will also give you the chance to change your mind." His voice softened. "Give me your word you will think on it, Corba."

"Only if Esclarmonde has a change of heart. I will talk to her again; I have no wish to see her die; but if she chooses to do so, she will not die alone."

Chapter 34

More than 200 Cathar faithful walked slowly down the tortuous path on the west face of Montségur, escorted by the soldiers of King Louis IX. Among their number were foot soldiers, squires, merchants and a baker. Ordinary people, prepared to die for the right to practise their faith. Leading the procession, head held high, wearing a simple white shift, was Corba de Péreille, accompanied by her daughter, Esclarmonde.

They were herded like cattle into a wooden pen piled high with pitch-soaked firewood. The Catholic Archbishop of Narbonne lowered his sceptre, and blazing torches were tossed into the enclosure.

The Pope's men had done their job well. Corba clasped Esclarmonde tightly as the flames eagerly took hold, lapping hungrily at the victims' scant clothing, searing flesh, sinew and bone; the acrid black smoke scorching their lungs.

Another signal, and a monotonous chanting rose above the screams as the assembled monks and priests sang psalms to drown out the sound of slaughter.

Raymond de Péreille could do nothing but watch and weep as the sickly-sweet smell of burning human flesh rose on the breeze to the battlements high above. A broken man, he would not see out the year.

Chapter 35

David and Rachel pulled up outside the museum expecting to see a police car waiting for them, but the place looked strangely deserted.

"That's odd," said David. "This is where the inspector wanted to meet us."

Rachel started to get out of the car, but her bag snagged on the gearstick, spilling its contents over the floor. "Goddamn it!" she exclaimed angrily, climbing back in to pick up the debris.

David got out and looked around for signs of police activity, but there was no-one in sight and he bent down to talk to Rachel through the open door. As he did so a shot rang out, ricocheting off a nearby wall.

"Jesus!" he exclaimed, scrambling back into the car. Executing the fastest three-point turn he had ever made in the huge Range Rover, he drove back down through the village at break-neck pace, scattering a group of children who appeared from nowhere as he rounded a corner.

"For God's sake, David! You nearly killed those kids!"

"You didn't hear the shot?"

"Yes, I heard a shot – I assumed it was a local hunter."

"I was the prey. That shot was meant for me – I felt the wind as the bullet passed my head. If I hadn't bent down to talk to you, I'd be dead right now."

"Christ!" The blood drained from Rachel's face. "First me, now you. Someone seriously doesn't want us to take this any further."

"You don't say," said David sarcastically, flooring the accelerator as he left the winding road to the village and hit open countryside. "You'd better hold on – I'm going to take the dirt track."

The Range Rover sped down an increasingly narrow lane until the tarmac ended abruptly, and the vehicle jumped and lurched over the unmade road.

"For heaven's sake, David, slow down or you'll save them the job of killing us," gasped Rachel, clinging on to the roof strap.

David glanced in his mirror, and seeing no sign of pursuit, eased off the accelerator. "Well that was a clever ruse, and we walked right into it," he muttered, his hands trembling as the adrenalin rush eased off.

"What do we do now?"

"Good question. We certainly can't go back to the chambre d'hôte – everyone knows where we're based. I'm going to make for Carcassonne – we'll blend in with all the English and American tourists. We'll dump the car, book into the first half-decent hotel we find, and hire a car in the morning. This Range Rover is way too conspicuous with its British plates. Apart from making an easy target to follow, for all we know they could plant a bomb under it overnight."

David drove hard and fast down the twisty main road towards Carcassonne, but not so manically as to attract attention. Eventually the road straightened and widened as they hit the plain, and soon they were on the outskirts of the ancient medieval town. Heading straight into the centre, they left the Range Rover in a municipal car park, put a week's ticket on it, then cut through a maze of side streets on foot until they found a small, smartly painted family hotel. "The Astoria – good name for a hotel," he observed. "Not quite the Waldorf, but it will do for us. Let's hole up here and have a council of war."

The school holidays had not yet started, but the tourist season was well under way. "I'm afraid we only have one room left, m'sieur. Luckily for you and your wife it is a double," said the concierge, beaming.

Rachel blushed violently. "Thank you very much – that will do nicely," quipped David as he gave his credit card details and signed the register, grinning at her obvious embarrassment. "Come on, sweetheart." As they moved away from the desk, Rachel started to protest, but he grabbed her hand and dragged her up the stairs.

"You have no bags, m'sieur?" called the concierge.

"We'll get them later, thanks."

"If you think for one minute we're going to share the same bed, you've got another think coming," said Rachel, pulling her hand away as they disappeared from sight.

"If you want to sleep on the floor, that's fine by me. As a card-carrying feminist, I'm sure you wouldn't have it any other way."

Rachel glared at him as he fumbled with the key. "OK," she said as they went into the room. "We'll both sleep on the bed. But you'd better make damn sure you stick to your side."

"Your wish is my command," said David.

"And you can wipe that schoolboy smirk off your face, too."

David burst out laughing, and after a few moments, Rachel joined in. They collapsed on the bed in exhaustion, and within a few moments they were both asleep.

Chapter 36

Languedoc, April 1244

Philippa de Mirepoix crouched low in the sweetly scented sagebrush on the rocky hillside below the Château de Blanchefort, her hand clasped over Mariette's mouth to prevent her from crying. She had come too far to fail now. She waited, heart in mouth, clutching the precious jar tightly, as the troop of soldiers rode by.

Her journey had been fraught with danger. Lowered in a basket 300 feet down the cliff at Montségur under cover of darkness, with Matheus Bonnet at her side, she had made good progress to Rennes-le-Château, the two of them posing as husband and wife and staying at remote farmsteads. Little Mariette had provided good cover, with no-one suspecting their story.

Once at Rennes, at the dead of night, Matheus had led her through the network of caves below the town deep into the heart of the hillside, until they finally reached the Visigoth burial chamber. They retrieved the gospel, leaving in its place just a few pages of a Latin copy revealing nothing contentious. Then at Philippa's insistence, and despite his misgivings, Matheus led her on to the crypt below the Church of St Mary Magdalene. She wanted to see the tomb of the Blessed Mary with her own eyes for what would probably be the only time in her life.

They had already visited the cave nearby where she had originally been buried – a place known only to her family. It had been a poignant moment. But on seeing the ornate tomb of the pregnant Mary, Philippa collapsed sobbing, overcome with emotion. A year's brutal siege, through the worst winter imaginable, culminating in the death of her mother and sister. And now this. Confirmation, if she had needed it, of her own link to the bloodline of Mary and the Christ.

She had bade Matheus open the lid a fraction; it was heavy, but it shifted just enough for her to see inside, by the light of the lantern. She knew the body had been moved, but she had to see for herself. And, of course, the tomb had been empty. But there, half-hidden in the corner under some torn scraps of funeral shroud, was a small jar.

Squeezing her slim arm through the narrow gap, she gently retrieved the jar, and curiosity getting the better of her, removed the stopper. Inside was a small, tightly bound scroll. Prising it from the neck using the pin of her brooch, she gently unrolled it, her eyes opening wide with astonishment as she read the Latin text. Quickly putting the scroll back into the jar, she dropped it into her pocket and they made good their escape.

The small detachment of royal troops disappeared slowly round a bend in the track towards Rennes-les-Bains, and Philippa breathed a sigh of relief. She glanced at Matheus, and they continued forward up the steep flank of the hill towards the château high above. The path twisted and turned tortuously towards the summit, where the Templar watchtower stood guarding the approaches to Mount Cardou.

As they approached the defensive outer perimeter, their way was blocked by two men at arms who barred their way, their swords a cross of steel.

"Who seeks entry?" asked one, sharply.

"My name is Lady Philippa de Lanta, and I wish to see the seigneur," she said boldly.

The two men glanced at each other briefly, then at the toddler clinging to her waist. A woman visiting the remote Templar outpost was unheard of... "My lady, I would that I could be of service to you, but no-one outside the order may enter this building."

"I thought you offered succour to refugees and pilgrims?"

"Indeed, good lady, and we will gladly escort you to a place of safety, but..."

Philippa held up her hand to silence them, then stopped to twist a silver ring off her finger. "Will this satisfy you?" she said angrily.

One of the sentries stepped forward to look at the heavy silver band, and bowed deeply to her. "My lady, I am yours to command," he said humbly.

"I repeat, I wish to see the seigneur. In private."

"Very well, my lady. If you would follow me to the keep, I will bring you some bread and wine while I speak with my lord."

Barely half an hour later, Philippa was ushered into the chamber where Sir Guillaume de Sonnac, a tall, gaunt man, with short grizzled hair and a battle-scarred face, stood waiting.

He studied the attractive, dark-haired young woman standing before him. Though her clothing was tattered, she had a courtly bearing and an air of authority about her. Her deep, brown eyes showed a depth of mind and spirit beyond her years.

"My lady," he said, bowing deeply. "It is an honour to make your acquaintance – forgive the humble hospitality I am able to offer you. This is a military fort, and there is little room for luxuries."

"My lord," she replied politely, "after 10 months under siege at Montségur, this has one luxury I find very sweet: freedom."

The knight gave a sharp intake of breath at her statement. "My lady, that is a brave thing to say at this time. Perhaps too brave."

"We are among friends, are we not?"

"Indeed, my lady, but it would be wise to keep that information between us. The king has spies in every quarter."

"I appreciate your advice, my lord. I have been careful – indeed, I must confess to using a little subterfuge with your guards by using my mother's maiden name, which is not, I think, well known in these parts. My married name is Lady Philippa de Mirepoix. I am wife to Pierre-Roger de Mirepoix, and daughter of Lady Corba de Péreille, who perished with my sister in the slaughter at Montségur." A tear pricked her eye, and she brushed it away angrily.

Sir Guillaume moved quickly to her side, and taking her hand, bowed gently before her. "My lady, please accept my deepest condolences. It was the work of the Devil himself. It shames me that our Order has the blessing of a Church that commits such atrocities in the name of God."

"Thank you, Sir Guillaume. Your words are reassuring; I know that you did much to protect the Cathars. I know also that the Templars have made it their sacred duty to protect the legacy of our lady, the Madeleine, here in France."

Sir Guillaume showed no reaction, so she continued. "Know, then, that I am the direct descendant, through my mother's line, of Mary Magdalene, bride of Christ, apostle to the apostles."

Sir Guillaume gazed in awe for a moment, then in a swift movement, dropped to his knees before her. "My lady," he said in a choked voice, "I have long dreamt of this moment. I can now die at peace with my soul."

Philippa laid her hand on his grizzled head. "Arise, Sir Guillaume, and be at peace. Let there be no more talk of death; there has been a surfeit of that of late."

"Indeed, of course – I am sorry…"

She put a finger to his lips. "You have nothing to apologise for," she said smiling. "Come, stand, my lord knight – the Templars have given us much help since your order was founded. However, there is one more thing I would ask of you."

"Name it, my lady, and it shall be done."

"It is a task of the highest importance that I seek to entrust to you. It involves a holy relic which the Church, were it to discover its true nature, would do all it could to destroy."

"Why would the Church seek to destroy a holy relic, my lady?"

"Because the relic is a sacred gospel written by the Madeleine when she fled here from Palestine, and its contents would undermine many of the Church's teachings. The time is not yet right for it to be revealed. I would like you to hide it in the most secret place you know. One day, the world shall know its true glory."

"I am honoured that you would entrust me with such a task, my lady."

"It is rumoured that you brought back sacred relics from the Crusades to the Holy Land, and that they are hidden close by – perhaps kept safe with the body of Our Lady, which I know you helped to move at the start of these troubles. Would that be a suitable hiding place?"

154

"You are well informed," said Sir Guillaume, with a wry smile. "Do you know the nature of those relics?"

"I have an idea, but I wish to hear no more. Should the Inquisition find me, the least I know, the better."

"Let us pray that never comes to pass."

"Indeed."

"My lady, may I ask where you intend to travel next? I fear for your safety, travelling alone with your baby, and just a manservant for protection – I must insist you allow me to provide you with an escort."

"I appreciate the gesture, Sir Guillaume, but Matheus and I will be safer travelling incognito, under the pretence that we are man and wife – there are many such refugees on the move at the moment, as I am sure you must know. I have decided to travel to Piedmont, in northern Italy, where many Cathars and others the Church deems heretics have fled to avoid persecution."

"They may be further from Rome in doctrine but they are closer to Rome by geography."

"Perhaps, but that is a risk we must take – we cannot stay here in France. We will maintain a disguise, and not divulge our heritage. And of course, we have the ring," she said, smiling.

She reached into her purse and withdrew a cylindrical container. "Please, take this, and guard it well."

"With my life, my lady."

"And now I must ask one more small thing. Do you have a pen and ink?"

"Why of course," said Sir Guillaume, gesturing to the desk and retrieving a quill from the drawer.

"Thank you. Now, if you would give us shelter for the night, and provisions on the morrow, there is one last thing I must do before I leave for Piedmont."

* * * * *

"Have you completely lost your reason, Lady Philippa?" protested Matheus furiously. "It would be madness to risk everything and return to Rennes. Have we not just removed the gospel from there to a place of safety?"

"Indeed, Matheus. But we know not where the Templars will hide it, nor do I wish to know. We must leave a clue so that those seeking the truth in years to come will know where to look."

"Ay, and so will the Inquisitors!"

"No, I have made the wording opaque, so that only the right person will be guided to discover the truth. Even then, it will not lead them there directly, but merely to a place where someone can watch and wait at the appointed hour."

"The plan still grieves me – the prophecy of Our Lady is sacred…"

"Indeed, that is why one day it must be found. I will go on my own,

Matheus, if you will not come with me…"

"You will go nowhere on your own, my lady! I think not for my safety, but yours – and Mariette's. Your mother warned me…" He broke off, scowling, as Philippa threw back her head and laughed.

"She was right, too, Matheus – you should have listened! Oh, how I miss her…" She shook her head to clear the darkness that threatened to engulf her once more. "Well, you make a fair point. If it were just my life, nothing would deter me from going, but I have a duty not just to Mariette but to our lineage. I will stay with her at the farmstead near Rennes where we lodged before – the goodwife was quite taken with the little one, I'm sure she won't mind. Now, will you do my bidding?"

"You have no need to ask that, my lady."

Once more under cover of darkness, Matheus made his way back through the undercroft to the crypt at Rennes-le-Château. He paused and prayed for a moment before the tomb, then took the jar from his pocket.

He froze as the sound of voices broke the oppressive silence, quickly dousing the lantern as footsteps rang out on the cold stone steps leading down to the crypt from the church above.

Feverishly, he pushed the jar through the narrow opening of the tomb, cursing as he heard it break. Throwing himself bodily against the lid, he closed it as far as he could before fleeing down the passageway whence he had come.

Chapter 37

David reached into his pocket and answered his phone for the third time in the past hour. Why couldn't the team function without him? Officially they were following a lead at the Inquisition records in Toulouse, but he suspected they thought he and Rachel were having a fling. He looked across fondly to where Rachel was lying asleep, the sheet barely covering her naked breasts, her tousled hair spilling over her face. It wasn't how they had planned it, but the guys weren't far wrong.

"Hello," he said shortly.

"Is that David Tranter?" came a woman's voice. "The archaeologist working at Rennes-le-Château?"

"Yes – who is it, please?"

"My name is Marianne. We've never met, but you know my mother, Anne-Marie de Blanchefort." The speaker sounded distressed.

David gave a start. "The lady who lives in Camps-sur-Agly?"

"Exactement."

"How can I help you, mam'selle?"

"Please, call me Marianne. I was hoping we could meet – something terrible has happened, and there are things that must be explained to you. And, to be candid, Monsieur Tranter, I need your help."

"We would very much like to meet you, Marianne. But I'm afraid it's a little difficult at the moment…" he hesitated, uncertain of how much to say. She sounded genuine, but after what had happened the previous day, he couldn't trust anyone. They needed time to come up with a plan of action. "We had some things stolen from the dig a few days ago, and we are still tied up dealing with the police," he said unconvincingly.

There was a pause at the other end of the line. "Marianne?" prompted David.

"It is as I feared," the woman replied, her voice thick with emotion. "This is dangerous, very dangerous – for all of us. My mother, whom you saw yesterday, has been found dead at her home. Officially she had an embolism. Unofficially…" her voice trailed off as her emotions overwhelmed her. "Unofficially, they killed her. Just as they have killed everyone they see as a threat, for century upon century."

David stood rigidly in shock, the phone clamped to his head.

"Monsieur? Are you there?"

"Yes, mam'selle. I'm so very sorry to hear about your mother's death – it's a terrible shock. She was a wonderful lady. But what makes you think she was killed? I find it hard to believe."

"How can you not believe it, monsieur, after what happened to your girlfriend? And I think maybe there is something else you are not telling me..."

"Actually she's not my girlfriend, we're work colleagues. Look, I'm very sorry for your loss, but as I say, we've got one heck of a mess to sort out and I don't see how we can meet at the moment. Perhaps I can get back to you in a few days..."

David jumped back startled as Rachel, woken by the phone, leapt at him from the bed and prised the phone from his fingers. She had seen the shock on David's face as he took in the news, and disbelief flooded through her at his dismissive response.

"Marianne? This is Rachel Spencer. I work for National Geographic. I'm devastated to hear of your mother's death. Of course we can help. Your mother was an amazing woman – I can't believe she's gone..." Rachel paused, fighting back the tears. "Are you coming down from Paris to sort things out?" she asked finally, in a choked voice.

"I so much want to come, to see maman one last time, but they tell me it is far too dangerous – I will be the next victim. And with me will die the Magdalenic line... I have no children of my own."

"What will you do?"

"I have some friends who will hide me until it is safe; I cannot say where. Rachel, I need your help, not for myself but for the message I carry. I must go now; I will call back later."

"Of course – look take my number and call me next time; David is preoccupied right now, but we really want to help."

She gave the number, and the line clicked dead. Rachel slowly lowered the phone, looking at the instrument in disbelief as if it somehow had the power to warp the truth. She limply put the phone in David's proffered hand, still fighting back the tears. As she put her hands up to her face, David tried to put his arm around her shoulder, but she shook it away.

"Don't you dare!" she spat angrily.

"After what happened yesterday, I wasn't sure how much to trust her. I was only trying to be practical..."

"Practical? An old woman has been killed – a woman who may have a direct bearing on our research here, not to mention the attacks on both our lives – and you want to be 'practical'? You're no Indiana Jones, are you? You've certainly nailed your colours to the mast. Or should I say bedpost – I note I'm not your girlfriend. So what the hell was last night about," she said savagely, gesturing to the rumpled bed. "A one-night stand for Mr Commitment Phobic?"

"So that's what this is all about..."

"No, it's not what this all about, you self-righteous prig. After yesterday I thought that maybe, just maybe, there was some spark of decency there

– a real man willing to put himself out on a limb and take risks for people if the need arose." She snorted in disgust. "You'll sure as hell never be my knight in shining armour. From now on our relationship will be on a purely professional footing."

Rachel stormed into the bathroom, fighting back the tears. She had allowed David to 'get' to her, emotionally; not any more. It made her too vulnerable. She couldn't afford that.

The next 24 hours seemed to drag. The tension in the air between herself and David was palpable. She knew David had good reason to be guarded when receiving the call, but the emphatic way he had declared 'she's not my girlfriend' stung. There was no going back now, however. They were in it together, for better or worse. She couldn't just walk out and fly back to the States – she had a contract to complete, and both their lives were at risk. They had started out on this road together, and one way or another, together they would reach journey's end.

It was late afternoon when David received another call that lasted just a few minutes.

"I take it that was Marianne?" asked Rachel when he was off the phone.

"Yes."

"Thank God – I've been worrying myself silly that something might happen to her. When are we going to meet?"

"Tomorrow morning at ten. We don't know where, yet. She is going to call us at the last minute, for obvious reasons."

"You believe her then?"

"That her life is in danger? Yes, after what happened to us, and the death of her mother. I'm still not signing up to the idea about the Magdalenic lineage, not until we have more substantial evidence. But clearly someone is out to put a stop to this." He hesitated before plunging on. "Look, I'm sorry about what I said. I didn't mean to sound dismissive – I just thought it best to keep it to ourselves for the moment, to avoid complications."

"Complications!" snapped Rachel, a surge of rage boiling up inside her. How could he be so dismissive? It reinforced all her prejudices – and all the damage she had suffered over the years. Baggage she thought she had got rid of, but here it was, back with a vengeance.

Chapter 38

Pastor Bob smiled smugly as he sat in his state-of-the-art recording studio, watching the video of his TV broadcast. Not without reason was he one of America's most successful – not to mention wealthiest – televangelists. America was the most God-fearing country in the Western world, and he had those folk right where he wanted them –in the palm of his hand.

It was hard not to make money when more than 90 per cent of Americans believed in God, 75 per cent believed in hell, and more than half the country believed in the Rapture – that Christ would take them up into heaven before the end of the world. Which was coming soon, of that he was damned sure. At least, that's what he told the faithful. There was nothing like the fear of everlasting hellfire and damnation to make people put their hands in their pockets.

Only in America, he thought wryly to himself, could you turn religion into a business. And what a business! Telling folk that God was happy for them to get stinking rich was a surefire money-earner. Give and you will receive, the Scriptures said. And the more you give, the more you'll get back. What better way to part them from their hard-earned greenbacks. Hell, save that namby-pamby spiritual stuff for the hippies. This was about enjoying the here and now. All you had to do was believe – and give. Generously. And preferably to Pastor Bob.

The recording continued, Pastor Bob's voice building to a powerful, hypnotic crescendo: "And so I say to you now, give generously to my ministry of salvation, give to bring the Word of the Lord to those who it has passed by, give to bring yourself untold wealth and happiness. God wants you to be rich. The Lord tells us, right there in Proverbs 15, verse 6: 'In the house of the righteous there is much treasure.'

"Prosperity comes when we start to believe in God's Law of Abundance. God cares about you. He cares about your bills. He cares about getting your kids through college. He will bring you money – more money than you know what to do with. Haven't you always wanted that Jag-yoo-ar? You can have it! Haven't you always wanted that nice house with a white picket fence? You can have it!

"Don't listen to those whining liberals who tell you it's better to be poor! They sure ain't poor – they're hypocrites, every last one of them. You go ask someone who's homeless if it's good to be poor! You go ask them if they want to be rich! Remember, nowhere in the Bible does it say God wants you to be poor. All you have to do is believe and give, and for every cent you give you will get back 100-fold."

The triumphal credits began to roll and Pastor Bob heaved his bulk out of his electrically-controlled leather armchair and padded across the room to the huge glass doors that afforded a magnificent view across his 1,000-acre ranch. A man needed to be comfortable to come up with new ways of saving those lost sheep out there, though he sure as hell didn't want them to get too close – an electrified fence made sure of that. Who knows what psycho might try to take a pot-shot at him. And then there were those goddamn reporters, always trying to sneak in and ask awkward questions about how he spent his money. As if there were something wrong in having a private jet. Darn it, if a corporate CEO could have one, why shouldn't Jesus's right-hand man enjoy the same privilege? How could he meet and greet the faithful without it?

Pastor Bob crossed through to the study, the nerve-centre of his business, where he controlled the investments made with his $100m gross annual earnings. This morning he had another matter to deal with, however. Something that had been eating away at his sense of wellbeing. And a matter of growing concern, after another phone call from that mincing little Italian papist. Still, sometimes you had to sup with the Devil, and while he may condemn them from his pulpit, on this they had common ground.

He picked up the phone and hit speed-dial. "Delaney, it's me. Have you made any progress with that little matter we spoke of? You took care of that interfering old biddy? Good. And the other two?" There was a pause, and as the voice continued, Pastor Bob went puce with rage. "Your guy missed the shot?" he yelled at the receiver. "And he served in the Marine Corps? No wonder this country's going to the Devil. Goddamn it man, do you have any idea how important this is? I told you what it would mean if this got out. Those two have got to be stopped…"

He paused as an anxious voice sought to reassure him. "I don't care if they have 'slipped off the radar', Delaney – you'd better find them again, and pronto. You sure as hell had better get this mess sorted, or you'll find yourself working out of the Alaska office pretty darn soon. Keep your focus on that damned village – they'll be back, you mark my words. They've got unfinished business there. And next time, your man had better not fucking miss."

Chapter 39

Vanni di Niccolo di Ser Vanni paced the light, airy room of his house in Florence's Via Ghibellinia as vigorously as his ageing bones would allow, wincing periodically as a spasm of pain juddered through his injured hip. He paused, breath rattling in his throat.

"Must you always be so accursedly stubborn, Caterina?" the ageing banker said at length. "I may not be long for this world, and I must needs make provision for you and your mother. She has agreed to this. Since the followers of Waldo chose to spread from their Piedmont valleys and start converting the Pope's flock it has become increasingly dangerous in these parts. It will not be long before His Holiness takes action against them, and that makes you extremely vulnerable. I have a duty to protect you."

The pretty, dark-haired 16-year-old stared at him defiantly. "Like the Cathars before them, the Waldensians are true followers of Christ's teachings – unlike the Church of Rome. They teach the word of God as Jesus intended, not the corrupt, self-serving lies spread by the priests. Thanks to the intercession of my ancestor, Lady Philippa de Mirepoix, by God's grace all men and women will, in time, be free from this heresy that the Pope is God's appointed on earth, that we must only believe what we are told by his priests, and not be free to read and understand the Holy Bible for ourselves."

"Hush Caterina, that talk will have you burned for a heretic."

"Nonetheless, the time is also coming when the minds of men and women will be set free, and I must play my part in that, whatever it may be."

"Your safety is all that matters," sighed Ser Vanni. "Surely you must understand that. And surely, too, you must understand that since I married your mother after your father's death, I have an obligation to protect and care for you. You know, Caterina, that I love you as if you were my own flesh and blood. It grieves me to see you so distressed, but there is a greater good to be served here."

"And you think assigning me in your last will and testament to your friend Ser Piero, as if I were some portion of your chattel, is fitting for a daughter of the Madeleine?"

"Until you come of age, my will must prevail. That is my decision, and it is final. Unless you marry, and then, of course, your husband will control your future. Assuming you can find a man to take you – you are become so headstrong it is hard to see anyone willing to bear that burden. You will be placed under Ser Piero's guardianship, under the guise of a maidservant;

you will serve as his housekeeper until you come of age. Ser Piero is a good man, and a good friend. Your mother and I are agreed that it will be safer for you living in the country than here, in Florence, under the eagle eye of the Medicis – it won't be long before one of them bribes their way to the Holy See, you mark my words. You need a man of position to protect you. And that's an end to it," he added, as she opened her mouth to protest once more.

He smiled to himself as Caterina stormed off. He had to admit there was an ulterior motive to the somewhat unusual arrangement he proposed. He took his duties as her protector seriously, and in his mind there was no question that she needed a strong husband. He would need to be of great intellect, or with her razor-sharp mind she would not respect him, but he would also need to be handsome and charming – for in that regard, Caterina was no different to any other girl her age.

The likeable Ser Piero Da Vinci had undertaken some complex legal work for Ser Vanni which he had accomplished with flair and intelligence, and over the course of several months the younger man had become a firm friend. In truth, he had almost come to regard him as the son God had never granted him. Ser Piero was the perfect match for Caterina: a rapidly maturing young man some 15 years older – mature enough to handle her headstrong ways, and with a glittering career ahead. And he undoubtedly had the looks and charisma to win her heart, of that he had no doubt.

All he had to do was throw them together and let nature take its course…

Barely two summers passed before the ague took Ser Vanni, though he had yet to reach 60 years, and the notary assigned to execute the will – Ser Filippo di Cristofano – went to some lengths to ensure that his wishes for the comfort of Caterina and her mother, Agnola were followed closely.

As prescribed in his will, much of Ser Vanni's wealth was left to the monks of San Girolamo da Fiesole, though the Abbot knew something of his widow's connections to the Waldensians and refused to accept the legacy. The Archbishop of Florence had no such misgivings, however.

Ser Vanni's house in Via Ghibellinia was assigned to Ser Piero da Vinci, with the proviso that Agnola be allowed to remain in the house until her death. Caterina, however, would earn her keep by running Ser Piero's family home in the village of Vinci, a day's ride from the political machinations of Florence.

What Ser Vanni could not have known was that in the months leading to his death, as he lay weak and feeble on his sickbed, Da Vinci had agreed a dynastic alliance with one of his closest legal rivals in Florence, Ser Piero di Carlo del Viva, who saw the younger man's business potential – and had arranged Da Vinci's betrothal to his teenage daughter Albiera.

Chapter 40

Saturday morning found Rachel and David waiting impatiently in their hotel room for another call. Rachel's phone rang out a shrill pop tune, and since she was in the bathroom, David snatched it up. "It's your daughter," he said, as Rachel emerged. "Try to keep it brief."

Rachel took the phone and turned her back on David. "Hi sweetheart – thanks for calling. I'm in a hotel in Toulouse at the moment. No, everything's OK; we're just doing some research here." She hated lying to her daughter, but she knew mobile phone calls could be intercepted.

David grew more animated as the minutes passed, and he gesticulated to her frantically. "You gave her your number," he hissed.

Rachel glared at him. "OK darling, well I'd better go – we're expecting another call. I promise I'll be home to see you soon… I know I said that a couple of weeks ago, but it's been really frantic out here. Daddy's looking after you OK, isn't he? Good. OK, I promise I'll be home soon. Bye sweetheart."

When the call finally came, it was on David's phone. It was brief and to the point.

"This time she handed me straight over to a guy who claims to be protecting her," said David, in response to Rachel's interrogatory look. "He told me to drive to a rendezvous, where we'll get further directions."

Rachel raised her eyebrows. "Well, I guess she needs protecting. I'm glad she's not on her own."

They left the hotel immediately and made their way to the car they had picked up from a hire company the previous afternoon.

"So where are we going?" asked Rachel as they climbed into the Renault.

"I'm not sure, exactly. All I know is we're heading for Bugarach, to start with."

"That's on the way to Camps-sur-Agly, isn't it?"

"Yes – though I doubt we'll be going there again, after what's happened. We'll get further directions when we arrive at the rendezvous."

They sped south out of Carcassonne towards Couiza, where they turned off down a tiny lane that led into the hills.

"We do want to get there in one piece," Rachel said through gritted teeth, as the car screeched round a series of blind, tortuous bends. "This is a Clio, not a Range Rover – if we hit something at this speed, we're dead."

"Timing is critical. If we don't contact them within the hour, it's all off until tomorrow. I know it's all rather cloak-and-dagger, but the guy was adamant. He says his role now is to protect Marianne at all cost."

Rachel kept her silence until, a few kilometres up the road, they skidded around a hairpin bend on two wheels. David lost control and the car spun sideways off the road, narrowly missing a tree before ending up facing the way they had come.

"DAVID!" she bellowed in anger, which, combined with a withering look, was enough to make him drive more soberly – at least until they reached a bigger road. From there it was a simple, if still scarily fast, journey through the winding valley to the pretty village of Bugarach, nestled below the brooding massif of Le Pech de Bugarach

David pulled off the road when he reached the village recycling centre, pulled out his phone, scrolled to the 'Recent Calls' list and punched the last number.

"Pierre? David here. We're at…" he paused, grimacing as he was interrupted. "Of course, I understand. OK, where do we go now? Right, see you soon."

He put the car in gear and set off again, this time at a more sedate pace, before turning down a tiny lane. The road took them down a seemingly impossible route between the steep flanks of Le Pech de Bugarach and a neighbouring peak, picking its way along the side of a stream as it twisted and turned along the steeply wooded bank of the ravine.

"Hey, is that where we're headed for?" queried Rachel, after a while, catching a glimpse of a beautiful white château through the trees. "Now that's what I call impressive!"

"That must be it," said David, turning off down a gravel drive. "And you're right, it is pretty spectacular."

The building in question was a large manor house, originally quite old, but heavily restored with mock battlements and other neo-Gothic flourishes. As they pulled into the courtyard, two burly men in combat fatigues, both armed with pistols, appeared from a stable block. One stood back, pointing his gun at the car, while the other came up to the driver's door.

"Monsieur Tranter?" he asked in a heavy Occitan accent as David wound down the window.

"Oui – and Mademoiselle Spencer."

"The password?"

"Fleur-de-lys."

"Get out of the car, and leave the keys in the ignition, s'il vous plaît."

David and Rachel slowly climbed out of the vehicle, while the second man edged closer. They could see he was holding a pair of handcuffs.

"D'accord. Now turn to face the car and put your hands together behind your backs."

They did as they were bidden and the two men moved swiftly behind them, snapping the handcuffs in place on both their wrists so they were locked together, before patting them down to check for weapons.

"Is this really necessary?" asked Rachel.

"Mam'selle, we do this only to protect our lady. Please accept my apologies, but we have met neither of you before."

Rachel reluctantly acquiesced, and they were politely but firmly escorted by the arm through a side-door in the château. Once inside, they were led down a long, dusty flagstone corridor, up a stone spiral staircase, then along another, more modern corridor with wood-panelled walls and a carpeted floor. Here they paused outside a pair of ornately carved oak doors.

The man who had interrogated them knocked briefly before opening the doors and ushering the pair inside. They entered a spacious, airy room, with large sash windows flanked by ornate panelled shutters overlooking the courtyard below. Two people sat at a heavy mahogany table in earnest conversation, although they stood as their guests entered.

One was an older man, perhaps in his late sixties, impeccably dressed in a light grey suit, and wearing a crimson cravat. The other was a slim, attractive, olive-skinned young woman in her late twenties, wearing a simple pencil skirt and white blouse, her dark hair tied back in a pony tail.

"Please, forgive our manners," said the old gentleman in impeccable English, stepping forward to greet them, "but we must proceed with the greatest caution." He turned to a laptop computer on the table where they had been sitting. "Are these our friends?" he asked.

"Oui, that is them," came the response in a voice they both recognised. From where they stood, Rachel could clearly distinguish Hélène's face on the webcam window.

"Then we have nothing to fear," said the old man. "Merci, Hélène. We will be in touch again shortly." The webcam window went blank. He turned to his guests. "The marvels of modern technology, my friends! Who would have thought it." He spoke briefly to their guards, who unshackled them before abruptly leaving the room, shutting the doors behind them. Rachel had no doubt they were waiting outside.

"It would have been easier if Hélène had been able to join us in person, but she spent too much time with Ann-Marie. She would most certainly have been followed here. And you must forgive me, I forget my manners once more. Please allow me to introduce myself – I am Gilles Lacoste, le Comte de Puylaurent."

Rachel gave a start at hearing the name of one of the faydits, the dispossessed Cathar aristocracy. Was their line still alive to this day?

"And this delightful young lady is my ward, Marianne. Of whom I think you know."

Marianne stepped forward, smiling. "I am so pleased to meet you both at last. Hélène has told me so much about you and your work."

"It's wonderful to meet you too," said Rachel. "We were so very sorry to hear about your grandmother. She was a wonderful lady."

"Oui. It is very sad," said Marianne, her eyes clouding for a moment.

"Marianne," said David, stepping forward and offering his hand.

"You English are so formal," laughed Marianne, leaning forward and kissing him on both cheeks. "So," she continued, "we have much to discuss. Shall we sit down?" She gestured to the table, while Gilles moved over to the wall and rang an ancient iron bell-pull. A few minutes later, a side-door opened and an immaculately dressed waiter appeared, pushing a trolley laden with hors d'oeuvres and a large cafetière of fresh coffee.

"So, where do we start?" said Rachel.

"It is difficult. There is so much to discuss," said Marianne. "First you deserve an explanation for your reception here today. I think you know, now, that we have dangerous enemies – professional killers – and because of what you have found, you are very much on their 'hit list'."

"I think we've already figured that out," said David ruefully. "I didn't have the chance to explain on the phone, but I was shot at two days ago in Rennes-le-Château, outside the museum. I quite literally felt the bullet part my hair. In that context, it's clear Rachel's road accident was a deliberate attempt on her life, though I have to admit I was sceptical at first."

"We heard about the incident at Rennes," said Marianne.

"You knew?"

"We have enemies, but we also have many friends."

"So cutting to the chase – and I mean no offence – if you have so many friends, why do you need our help?"

"No, it's a fair question," said Marianne, seeing Rachel frown. "Put simply, you have the expertise to help us find what has been lost. And you have the ability to put that on, how do you say, 'prime-time TV'? We need to get the message out there. Once the truth is known, all our lives will be safer – they cannot touch us with the world watching. But more importantly, people have a right to know the truth about Our Lord's message."

"You mean the Lost Gospel that Hélène told us about?" put in Rachel.

"Absolutely! It is Mary's own testimony, and reveals not just that she was Christ's wife, but also his most important and enlightened disciple. In the *Pistis Sophia*, one of the gospels conveniently left out of the New Testament, Jesus says to her, 'Thou art she whose heart is more directed to the Kingdom of Heaven than all thy brothers'. This much I know: the gospel contains knowledge that will transform Christianity. It was written here in the Languedoc, where Mary fled after Christ's crucifixion, and the Magdalenic line has been kept alive here over the centuries. I am her direct descendant."

She looked unblinkingly at David. There was something about her calm, hazel eyes and serene expression that suggested she might be speaking the truth – either that or she was completely deluded.

"The gospel is one of the earliest sources of information about Jesus and his work. It predates *Matthew, Luke* and *John*, and probably even *Mark*, the earliest gospel in the Bible we have today. It explains many things that the early Roman Catholic Church chose not to share with its followers when it decided what to include and what to exclude from the Bible."

Marianne took a sip of coffee before continuing. "It's vital you understand just how important this gospel is, and for that you need to know the context. Most people think the New Testament has always consisted of the 27 books it is today. Some have a vague idea that the early Church played a role in collating them – few realise just how much power those early bishops wielded, or how they colluded to leave out gospels they deemed to be unsuitable. In fact, many more gospels were excluded than included in the final version.

"In fact, the New Testament as we know it today was largely put together by just three men in the third and fourth centuries: Origen, Eusebius and Athanasius.

Origen was based in Caesarea, a town in what is now modern Israel, which by the late third century had become a major seat of Christian learning. He was a scholar who travelled widely, and he compiled a list of Christian works which he considered 'inspired'. Later, Eusebius, also based in Caesarea, drew on Origen's work to compile his own list of what he considered suitable works – it was he who chose to leave out the so-called gnostic gospels such as those of Thomas and Mary, though he did not go so far as to call them heretical. Interestingly, Eusebius also considered the book of *Revelation* unsuitable."

Marianne paused and gave a wry smile. "It's ironic that so-called evangelical preachers cite *Revelation* front and centre in their sermons – yet they also teach that the Bible is, word for word, the word of God, because the men who put it together were 'divinely inspired'. On that basis they should remove *Revelation* from their Bibles!

"Anyway, it wasn't until Athanasius of Alexandria came along that the New Testament really took shape. He went through the list drawn up by Eusebius and edited it according to his own extremely dogmatic beliefs – it was he who reinstated Revelation. In his famous Easter Letter of AD 367, Athanasius produced a list of 27 books that he declared to be the only ones that should be given credence by the Church, and they are exactly the same texts as in the modern New Testament.

"But there's more you should know about Athanasius: he is on record as being a violent man who thought nothing of using beatings, kidnapping and imprisonment to silence his critics – fellow Christians, such as the followers of Arius, who happened to have differing beliefs. The Arians just didn't 'buy it' that Jesus was actually God while he was alive on Earth, but rather sent from God to show us that by following his example of love, compassion and forgiveness, we all have the potential to become the sons and daughters of God.

"At one point, the Arian belief dominated Christian thought, and Arians outnumbered those who believed that Jesus was God incarnate. But Athanasius was having none of it. He waged such a powerful campaign of intimidation and propaganda that his arguments won the day – he justified his behaviour by saying he was 'saving all future Christians from hell'. It gets worse: Athanasius was cited as the inspiration for the Inquisition against the Cathars set up by Pope Gregory IX in 1231 – which went on to spread fear and torture throughout the world against anyone who dared disagree with Rome's teachings.

"So the New Testament as you know it today was compiled by the man whose brutal behaviour inspired the Inquisition!" Marianne paused, her soft, dark eyes hardening. "I am sorry – it makes me angry at how the word of Our Lord has been manipulated over the centuries."

"There's no need to apologise – I completely agree with you," said Rachel. "So basically what you're saying is that Mary's role as Christ's foremost disciple was edited out of the Bible, together with the teachings she gained first-hand from Jesus. It's like something out of Orwell's 1984: it's as if she were made a 'non-person'; deliberately written out of history, as far as they were able."

"Exactement! In the Gnostic gospel *Pistis Sophia* alone, her name is mentioned 150 times. Compare that with just 13 times across all four gospels in the New Testament and you have an idea how much of a political exercise the New Testament really is."

"Look, I mean no disrespect, but can we save the history lesson for later?" said David, interrupting "You seem genuine, Marianne, as did your grandmother. But all I have heard so far is conjecture – that and a few rambling verses on a parchment found in Mary's tomb. Forgive me for being blunt, but before we go off on a treasure hunt we need some more evidence."

Chapter 41

Tuscany, northern Italy, August 1451

Cliché or not, it was love at first sight when Da Vinci set eyes on Caterina. Her smooth olive skin, her flowing mane of dark curls, her lissom body – they would be enough to enchant any mortal man. Her fierce intelligence, too, though it might have deterred some suitors, was exciting and enthralling. But it was those mysterious dark brown eyes that truly held him captive, and in which he often found himself lost.

As for Caterina… well, Ser Piero was surprisingly handsome and athletic, with a sparkle in his eye that brought feelings she had never known before. Quite dashing, if truth be told. A little old, perhaps, at 36, but certainly a more attractive proposition than many of the men she might have found herself paired off with in an arranged marriage.

Caterina went about her household chores with more good grace than she had intended, and as Ser Vanni had hoped, embarrassed glances soon turned to ardent stares. And as their relationship became less formal, so the feelings intensified.

Finally, one sultry summer's evening as they lay in the orange grove at the old stone villa in Vinci, watching the sun set over the gentle folds of the bronzed Tuscan countryside, listening to the cicadas' endless song, Ser Piero found the courage to kiss Caterina, and found it eagerly returned.

From their first coupling their relationship assumed an intensity that neither had expected, and for a few months they led an idyllic existence.

As with all clandestine lovers who assume no-one else is privy to their trysts, they continued their liaisons cloaked in a blind passion that soon became the talk of the goodwives of Vinci. It wasn't long before word reached the ears of Da Vinci's potential new business partner Del Viva, and one afternoon he took Da Vinci to task over lunch at an inn near his practice in Florence.

"Do you still have honourable intentions toward my daughter Albiera," he queried, as they finished their pots of ale.

Da Vinci reddened and paused while he drained the dregs of his beer. "That was my intention," he said, hesitantly.

"Was?"

"In truth, she is but 16."

"A marriageable age – you find her comely, do you not?"

"She is most certainly attractive, but she is very young. And while I made the pledge to marry with every good intention, I have to confess I have found my heart drawn to another."

"You are referring, I assume, to your maidservant?"

Da Vinci's face turned scarlet. "You know, then? I don't deny it. But while she is my housekeeper, it is really more of a guardianship – an informal arrangement requested by her stepfather."

"A guardianship?" Del Viva's eyebrows shot up. "And what kind of relationship do you have with your ward?" he asked pointedly.

"Sir!" protested Da Vinci. "I am not her guardian in law; rather she was entrusted to my care. It was agreed that in return for taking her in and looking after her needs, she would keep house for me until she is old enough to marry."

"Well she is certainly looking after your needs, if the goodwives of Vinci are to be believed."

"I cannot comment on market gossip, sir. I do not deny we are close; it is for that reason I wish to wed her. Of course, I very much regret having to break my betrothal to your daughter, but I must follow my heart. I have to confess that we are very much in love."

"Love – pha! I was in love when I was 16, but I soon learned the error of my ways. Love is for youthful trysts – the stuff of poetry and plays, not something that should concern men of status. We have the potential to form a great practice, you and I, perhaps with a couple of other fellows I know. Would you throw it all away for a few nights of passion? It fades soon enough, let me tell you. Look, I am a man of the world – better to sow your wild oats now than once you are wed. Albiera will make you a good wife, and I am willing to put this behind us."

"As I have said, I must follow my heart…"

"Da Vinci, I urge you to think on this very carefully," said Del Viva coldly, dropping his air of bonhomie. "It will not go well for you if you if you pursue this course. By breaking your betrothal you will be dishonouring both my daughter and my family name. And by continuing to have an intimate relationship with a young woman entrusted to your care, you put your legal career at risk."

"I repeat, I am not her legal guardian…"

"If she was entrusted to you in Ser Vanni's will, then, as you should know, whether you were explicitly declared her guardian or not, you have a moral and legal obligation to care for her. And that does not include bedding her!"

"Sir!"

Del Vivo held up his hand to silence his protests. "How old is she?"

"Twenty, sir."

"A wardship does not expire until a woman is 25, or she is married – you of all people should know that. And you cannot marry your own ward without special dispensation from the republic's ruling council – and you know who controls that. Do you have the money to grease the palms of the Medicis? I think not. You must not pursue this liaison further if you wish to keep your licence. Unless you wish to wait five years, of course. But I should warn you that I have eyes and ears in Vinci, and if I hear of any malpractice, the authorities shall know of it."

Da Vinci glared at him with hatred.

"Come, my friend – I have no wish to harm you," said Del Viva, resuming his earlier tone. "I am merely trying to save you from yourself. I know a young man's blood can run hot – and a young woman's, too, for all that. Do not jeopardise your career for this infatuation; for that's all it is. You are doing her no service if you sully her good name. Watch over her, as you were bidden, and find her a husband as soon as you are able."

* * * * *

"You would give me up for that milksap?" exploded Caterina. "Does our relationship mean nothing to you? Have you bedded me for sport?"

"You cannot believe that of me, Caterina – I love you more than life itself. But what am I to do? He has me in a double bind. If I insist on continuing this relationship with you I shall be disbarred. Under law – at least, as Del Vivo interprets it – I will not be free to marry you until you are 25. There is no logical solution."

"What if I were to tell you I am with-child? Would that make a difference to your logic?" she said stingingly.

"With-child? I cannot believe it!"

"You think babies are delivered by storks, perhaps?"

"My love, I had no idea…" Da Vinci paced up and down the room nervously. "What am I to do? If I lose my career, I am nothing…"

"If that is your response then I will save you the worry. You may consider our relationship at an end," said Caterina savagely, her dark eyes blazing with fury.

Chapter 42

Marianne smiled patiently. "You have every right to demand evidence, David," she said. "Unfortunately what evidence there was has been largely destroyed over centuries. The gospel disappeared during the crusade against the Cathars. Other evidence, which may have been in Mary's tomb at Rennes-le-Château, was destroyed by Marie Dénarnaud while Saunière lay dying. There are many accounts from villagers of Marie burning papers outside his bedroom window, so he could see his wishes were being carried out. However, some evidence may already have been passed on to one of his confidantes, such as his fellow priests Abbé Gelis in Coustaussa, or Abbé Boudet in Rennes-les-Bains. As you probably know, Gelis was mysteriously murdered ten years after Saunière took up his post at Rennes-le-Château; Boudet passed away in 1915, just two years before Saunière's death. Boudet may, in turn, have passed information on to his successor at Rennes, Rescanières – who was also mysteriously murdered shortly after he took up the post."

"Another murder in the Rennes saga?" queried Rachel incredulously. "I hadn't heard about Rescanières."

"Indeed – and there are others. In 1967 a briefcase of papers relating to Rennes-le-Château belonging to a collector was being taken by a courier named Fakhar ul Islam to an agent in what was then West Germany. He was refused entry at the border, and returned to Paris. His body was later found on the railway tracks at Melun, near Paris. Needless to say, the briefcase was missing."

"So are you basically saying we have nothing to go on?" queried David incredulously.

"Our best hope is the gospel," said Marianne. "After Mary Magdalene's death, the manuscript was carefully guarded by a small group of followers who later became part of the Cathar movement. As a result, some of its teachings became part of the Cathar faith – we know the Cathars believed that Jesus and Mary were married. However, in the 13th century, the Pope's crusade proved disastrous for the Magdalene legacy. The Madeleine at the time was caught up in the slaughter of the so-called heretics, and she was with them during their last stand at the isolated mountain fortress of Montségur. Thankfully, however, her daughter was smuggled out shortly before the end of the nine-month siege."

"And I'll bet she took the gospel with her," said Rachel.

"We believe so," said Marianne, "though much has been lost in the mists of time. Her escape from Montségur carrying a great treasure became part of local folklore – though no-one knew her identity or the true nature of the treasure. Some think this was the start of the Grail legend that spread throughout Europe. Indeed, one of the earliest Grail stories, Parzival, written by Wolfram von Eschenbach, also in the 13th century, calls the Grail castle 'Monsalvat', which, like Montségur, means 'secure mountain'."

"A coincidence?" queried David.

"Possibly," said Marianne. "You are a hard one to convince! How about this: when the Cathars at Montségur finally surrendered, they were given the chance to live by renouncing their faith. More than 200 refused to do so, and were burned alive in a pyre at the foot of the mountain. That must have taken a huge amount of faith – not to mention courage. It is known that shortly before their surrender, a number of the faithful had been given the consolamentum perfecti – the Cathar sacrament, similar to Holy Communion. Now, if that had been administered by the Madeleine, a direct descendant of Our Lord, and she had vowed to accompany them into the flames, would that have been worth dying for?"

David and Rachel fell silent. They had, of course, heard of the siege of Montségur, but the atrocity still had the power to chill the blood.

"However, the escape of the Madeleine's daughter was not the end of it," continued Marianne. "She fled in disguise to Rennes-le-Château, a sacred place to the Cathars – for reasons you now understand. Although the town had fallen to the crusaders some years earlier, it had become a focus for Cathar sympathisers, many of whom took refuge there. We believe – we hope – the gospel was hidden somewhere in the crypt or undercroft."

"That God-forsaken place." muttered Rachel, blushing violently as she realised her admission.

Marianne gave a knowing smile. "You thought, perhaps, we did not know of your little expedition?" she said, amused.

"Well, I knew you had found out about our discovery of the crypt, obviously, but not the other… it was the only way out – we were trapped. But how do you know the gospel wasn't hidden in Mary's tomb and moved by whoever took her body?"

"It's possible," admitted Marianne. "Mary's remains were removed from Rennes at the start of the crusade in 1209, and the gospel was smuggled out of Montségur in 1244. The undercroft would have been the obvious place to hide it – particularly, it seems, since it had a reputation as a place of great evil. God-fearing Catholics would not want to go in there."

Rachel gave an involuntary shudder. "I hated that place. There was a profoundly evil presence there – a hideous strength. Even David felt something, didn't you?"

"I have to admit it wasn't very pleasant down there, though since I don't believe in God or the Devil, I don't know that I could call it 'evil'. I think it was finding those Visigoth tombs that made it seem so malevolent – that, and the fact we know the Visigoths practised human sacrifices."

Marianne blanched. "Human sacrifices?"

"Before they converted to Christianity – long before the church was built. I have to say, I'm surprised the gold was still there."

"Talking of gold, did you resist the temptation?" she asked, her eyes sparkling with amusement.

"I haven't pocketed any, if that's what you mean," laughed David. "We removed one coin for analysis, but unfortunately it was taken when the museum was ransacked."

"I'm not sorry to see the back of that particular artefact," said Rachel, shivering. "You nearly fell to your death a few minutes later."

"Yes, but I'm still here – it was just a coincidence. Anyway, I mean no disrespect, Marianne, but so far there have been lots of 'ifs' and 'ands' and 'maybes' with regards to this gospel. Can I ask you a blunt question: do you have even a rough idea where it's hidden?"

Marianne hesitated.

"You're kidding me! You don't know, do you?"

"You must understand we are talking of an event that occurred more than 700 years ago, during very turbulent times. First the persecution of the Cathars, then the arrest of the Templars and the seizure of their property."

"What do the Templars have to do with it?" asked David, sceptically.

"Their order was secretly dedicated to the Madeleine and helped to protect the bloodline. They may have played a part in helping the woman who escaped, but if they knew the whereabouts of the gospel, that information has long since been lost."

"Is it possible Saunière found the gospel?"

"It is possible," said Marianne. "But unlikely, I think. He would not have known it was there – we know he found the tomb of Mary Magdalene, and he may have found some gold in the undercroft, but there would be nothing to make him look further."

"Unless the Madeleine who was alive at the time told him so. Is it possible he met her, just as we did?"

"Indeed, they met at the grotto. That much was passed down directly to grandmère. It was the reason why he and Marie spent weeks bringing all those rocks back to the church, to create a replica of the grotto. But I'm afraid the knowledge of where the gospel was hidden had already been lost."

"Marianne, I mean no disrespect, but this really does sound like a wild goose chase," said David. "Have you seen the size of the undercroft?"

Marianne stared at the ceiling.

"You haven't been down there?"

"No, Monsieur Tranter, I have not. It was considered too dangerous – I am not completely in control of my own destiny. There is too much at stake."

"So just who are these guys protecting you?" he said angrily, glancing at the man who called himself le Comte, who had been silent throughout the proceedings.

"Monsieur le Comte is – or was, up until the age of 21, my legal guardian. He is like a father to me. Alas, my natural father died many years ago."

"But you have hinted at others – and I don't just mean Hélène, or those gorillas out there," he said, nodding at the doors through which they had been frogmarched.

Marianne paused and glanced at le Comte, who nodded his head slightly.

"Very well. I must have your word that this will go no further," she said, glancing at them both. They nodded their agreement. "I am being protected by the Rosicrucian Order."

Rachel gasped and David's eyebrows shot up. "They have something of a dodgy reputation, don't they?" he said.

" 'Dodgy'?" repeated Marianne smiling, pronouncing the English word slowly. "I don't know this word, but I think I understand you. The Rosicrucians are not not some strange cult. They belong to an ancient order, founded on Christianity, which seeks to bring people to the spiritual enlightenment talked of by Jesus. I and my forebears have been protected by them for many centuries. It is true they have a reputation for secrecy, but that has helped them to guard us. We are their secret; us and the knowledge we possess."

"What knowledge is that?" asked David.

Marianne hesitated. "The Madeleine who died at Montségur was the last who knew the place to which Our Lady's body was moved at the start of the crusade."

David gave a sharp intake of breath. "That would be a spectacular find. There must be more, though. You talk of ancient secrets…"

"Now is not the time to reveal that," interrupted Marianne, kindly but firmly. "First, we must find the gospel. Will you help me in this sacred quest?"

"Of course we will," said Rachel. "How could we not?"

"And you, Mr Tranter? You are the archaeologist. We need your skills."

"How could an Englishman fail to help a damsel in distress? And, to be blunt, from an archaeological perspective, the Lost Gospel would be the find of a lifetime. So yes, of course I will. Despite my misgivings."

"I thank you, both. I leave it to you as to how you wish to proceed. I'm sure you will want to carry out more research, and here at the château we have one of the largest collections of books on the history and legends of the Languedoc, covering Rennes-le-Château, the Cathars, the Templars and many similar subjects. And, of course, there is Google. Though I'm sure I don't need to warn you about some of the crazy stuff out their on this topic," she added, with a twinkle in her eye. Now, let me show you to your rooms."

"We didn't bring any bags," said Rachel. "We didn't expect to be staying."

"My laptop and camera are in the car, because I didn't want to leave them at the hotel. But I've no spare clothes, either," added David.

"No matter. Rachel can borrow some of my clothes – I think we're about the same size. It is safer not to return to your hotel for the moment, I think. David, if you jot down your sizes, Gilles will arrange for some clothes to be left in your room. I will make sure your camera and laptop are brought up from the car, too."

Marianne led them out of the drawing room, past the guards who had escorted them into the building, and along the corridor to what was obviously the grand staircase, a sweeping symphony of marble and gilded wrought iron encircled by a magnificent balcony overlooking the main entrance hall below. They followed her up the stairs, marvelling at the black and gold Corinthian columns that studded the balcony, supporting an ornately painted ceiling above the stairwell.

Marianne glanced back smiling as they stared around them at the stunning architecture. "It's quite breathtaking, isn't it? The château was built in the 14th century, after the original château of Peyrepertuse was abandoned, but it was extensively remodelled in the 17th and 18th centuries."

"It's a hidden gem," said David, craning his neck to admire the ceiling's intricate detailing.

"Yes, though it can grow wearisome. Sometimes I just long for an ordinary home," she said, a wistful look on her face.

"You're kidding me, right?" said Rachel.

"I know it sounds ungrateful, but I often wish I could have an ordinary life. Find someone I love, have children, a career. Yes, I know one day I will marry – I must marry, and bear children – but will it be for love? For me, finding the right father to continue the Magdalenic line is more important than my own feelings. I must put my responsibilities first, and it can be a heavy burden."

She turned and continued up the stairs. "I'm sorry," she said, as they reached the balcony. "I have been feeling a little down since grandmère died. You must forgive me."

"Hey, don't worry," said David tenderly. "We completely understand – it must have come as a terrible shock."

Marianne led them down a long corridor, pausing after a short distance outside a large panelled door. "Rachel, this is your room." She opened the door to reveal a sumptuously decorated room replete with tapestries, a four-poster bed, two massive oak wardrobes and a writing desk.

"Jeez – this is bigger than my apartment," gasped Rachel.

"Well, you could certainly use all that wardrobe space," said David. "I'm sure it won't take you long to acquire a new collection."

Marianne smiled. "And David, you're in the room opposite, to make it easier should you need to discuss your research." She opened the door on a slightly more spartan, but equally spacious oak-panelled room. "Now, why don't I show you both the library?"

Marianne led the way back to the grand balcony, walked around to the next quadrant and along another equally imposing corridor before pausing in front of a large pair of doors. "The library," she announced, throwing them open and allowing Rachel and David to go ahead of her.

They gasped as they entered a long gallery, with rows of identical, ornately-carved oak bookcases jutting out at right-angles along both sides of the 80-foot room. A series of circular windows just below the ceiling on either side allowed light to flood down into the book-wells below, while two large globes mounted in wooden cradles completed the tableau.

They wandered down the central corridor between the two stands of bookcases, staring at the ancient volumes with their hand-tooled leather covers, and inhaling the deep, slightly musty smell of old books.

"Some of the oldest manuscripts date back to medieval times," said Marianne. "The counts of Peyrepertuse were assiduous collectors, and in the early 18th century this library was created to house their acquisitions. The bays are arranged in date order, with the century carved on the end of each case, then alphabetically within the cases themselves. The newer books are at the far end of the room." They followed her down the long aisle to the final two bays, which were given over to more recent volumes, many with dust-jackets.

"Hopefully you will find what you need here – this side of the right-hand bay is almost exclusively devoted to Rennes-le-Château, together with the Magdalene legends of the region. I'm afraid they are mostly in French – I hope that's not a problem – but there are some English-language books, as well."

"Having been here for six months we can probably manage the French ones – I can read it better than I speak it," said David apologetically. "Thank goodness you speak such good English."

"I spent a year at Oxford after finishing my studies at the Sorbonne," said Marianne. "And don't tell the Academie Française, but let's be honest, English is the language of the internet – at least, from a research point of view. Anyway, David, can we leave you here while we go off and have a girlie half-hour choosing come clothes?"

"No problem," said David. "Though I suspect it may be more than half an hour," he added, smirking.

Marianne chuckled. "You might just be right. Come on, Rachel, let's see what we can find."

Chapter 43

Rachel returned to the library an hour later dressed in a stunning, figure-hugging, sleeveless cream Dior dress, loosely tied with a rope belt.

"Wow," he said.

"Wow indeed. Pity I don't get to keep it – there's no way I could afford one of these on my salary. So what have you come up with?"

"Give me a break – I've only been doing this for an hour, while you've been gallivanting around with Marianne. As she said, there are tons of books on Rennes here – I've put some on the table that look interesting, if you want to start browsing through them. I'm going to skim through some of these archaeological journals on the area."

The pile of books David had sorted through included several self-published booklets from authors putting forward their own theories on Rennes, some flat-out wacky, others more considered.

She leafed her way through them, creating two new piles – one worthy of further reading, the other to be discarded.

"You know, there's something important that keeps cropping up in these that we've been guilty of neglecting," said Rachel, pausing.

"What's that?"

"The tombstone of Marie de Blanchefort, with that weird inscription. Saunière chiselled it off, so it must have had some significance. Thankfully it had already been recorded in a local archaeological review. Here it is again, in this booklet."

David came over and looked down at the familiar inscription:

CT GIT NOBLe M
ARIE DE NEGRe
DARLES DAME
DHAUPOUL De
BLANCHEFORT
AGEE DE SOIX
ANTE SEpT ANS
DECEDEE LE
XVII JANVIER
MDCOLXXXI
REQUIES CATIN
PACE

"It has to be some kind of code, the way the words are misspelt and broken," said Rachel. "Not to mention the random use of lower-case letters."

"I agree," said David. "It's about the only inscription we know to be genuine. Most, if not all, the parchments are fakes – disinformation, if you believe Hélène's story, and it certainly makes sense. But this… this is genuine, no question. Matter of fact, I've just come across a reference to it… Here we are, the Bulletin de la Société d'Études Scientifiques de l'Aude, volume XVII – 1906."

"There are also references here to another, horizontal stone that was allegedly part of the original tomb," said Rachel.

"With the emphasis on the word 'allegedly'," said David. "Its existence has never been proven, so I would tend to discount it. It's not mentioned in this survey. I think it's a fake, just like the 'official' decoding of the Marie de Negre inscription – the so-called 'Blue Apples' clue."

"Dubois mentioned something about that. Sounded pretty weird to me."

"Totally weird – a classic example of some of the wacky theories about this place. Philippe de Cherisey – who admitted faking the Saunière parchments – also came up with a bizarre decoding of the tombstone. In fact, he claimed the inscription was the key for decoding one of those parchments – it had experts scratching their heads for years." He rummaged through the piles of books and pulled out a slim volume. "Here we are," he said, flipping through the pages. "This is what he came up with, allegedly using a complex decoding technique known as the Knight's Tour:

BERGERE PAS DE TENTATION QUE POUSSIN TENIERS GARDENT LA CLEF PAX DCLXXXI PAR LA CROIX ET CE CHEVAL DE DIEU J'ACHEVE CE DAEMON DE GARDIEN A MIDI POMMES BLEUES

"In English?" queried Rachel.

"It translates roughly as:

SHEPHERDESS NO TEMPTATION THAT POUSSIN, TENIERS HOLD THE KEY PEACE 681 BY THE CROSS AND THIS HORSE OF GOD I FINISH OFF THIS DEMON GUARDIAN, AT MIDDAY BLUE APPLES

"That's just gobbledygook."

"Quite. But despite its nonsensical content, treasure-hunters still turn up at Rennes on January 17 when an anomaly of the light passing through the church's stained-glass windows makes smudgy blue blobs appear on the wall inside. Actually, they're not just blue – they are all the colours of the rainbow; I know, I was there setting up the dig in January and couldn't resist taking a look. And then there was all the furore about Poussin and Teniers, and whether they were part of some elaborate conspiracy over the centuries."

"Of course – that Poussin painting *Shepherds of Arcadia*, with the tomb bearing the phrase Et in Arcadia Ego. I've heard there used to be a tomb resembling it on the road to Arques," said Rachel.

"That's right – it dated from the 1920s. The owner got so fed up with treasure-hunters crawling all over the place he blew it up with dynamite. A complete red herring. If there is a connection between Poussin and the Magdalene, it's not that."

"You keep saying 'the Magdalene', without making any reference to Marianne. You're still sceptical, aren't you?"

"Sceptical? Yes, that what you guys pay me for – a scientific approach to history, not giant leaps of faith, if you'll forgive the pun. Marianne is self-evidently a very intelligent young woman who genuinely believes in her cause; someone whose lineage could quite possible be traced back to the Cathars, if you tried hard enough. But does that make her a direct descendant of Mary Magdalene? The jury's still out, as far as I'm concerned."

"So no-one has really decoded the inscription on the genuine tombstone, then," said Rachel.

"Not as far as I'm aware. Most of the world's top cryptographers live in the States, and I'm guessing few of them speak French. They've probably never even heard of Rennes-le-Château – few people in England know anything about it, and we live next door."

"Why don't we take a look at the code? I mean, this cypher wasn't put together by a Nazi Enigma machine. As I understand it, the tombstone was made in 1781 on the orders of Abbé Bigou, one of Saunière's predecessors, shortly before fleeing to Spain from the terrors of the French Revolution. From what I've picked up, a lot of people think it was Bigou who first discovered the secret of Rennes, and deliberately left clues that Saunière duly discovered a century later. One thing's for sure – all those misspellings aren't just the work of some illiterate stonemason."

"Well, I suppose it's worth a try – though I think we're clutching at straws. OK, let's list all the apparent discrepancies in the inscription. First of all the 'T' in CT. CI GIT means 'here lies', as in 'here lies the body', but for some reason the 'I' has been changed to a 'T'. Then, on the same line, the 'e' of NOBLE has been made lower case. Immediately after that, the name 'MARIE' has been split, with the M on the first line, and the rest of the word on the next. And so it goes on."

They noted down the anomalies as they worked their way down the inscription. "There's an odd one there in the date," David noted. "It should be MDCCLXXXI for 1781, but the second 'C' has become an 'O' – and there is no zero in Roman numerals."

"The next one is even odder," said Rachel. That final phrase, 'REQUIESCAT IN PACE' – which I do know is Latin for 'Rest in peace' – has been written 'REQUIES CATIN PACE'. Now it so happens that a few weeks ago I was in

181

the bar at Rennes-les-Bains when a woman stormed in and accused one of the other locals of having an affair with her husband. It got pretty damned heated and at one point she screamed out 'Catin!' at the top of her voice, following which a fight ensued. I discreetly asked the barman, who happens to fancy me, what she said. You'll never guess."

"He fancies anything in a skirt. But do go on."

"He said she called her a whore. And what was Mary Magdalene known as to the Catholic Church, from the 6th century right up until the Vatican cleared her name in 1969? The penitent whore! Even to this day, most of the people you talk to still think she was a prostitute – that's certainly how Bigou and Saunière would have known her."

"You might be on to something. What other reason could there be for including that word, even as a misspelling, on the tombstone of a noblewoman – the lady of the manor, no less? Bigou would have had the mason strung up and had a new headstone made, in the unlikely event it was a pure accident."

"Which takes us back to the third line," said Rachel excitedly. "We were trying to figure out the D'ARLES connection when her title was actually Marie de Nègre d'Ables. But isn't Arles near Saintes-Maries-de-la-Mer, the little seaside town where Mary Magdalene is said to have come ashore? Is Bigou trying to make us see a connection here?"

David grabbed a French road atlas he had put out on the table. "Right again, Ms Spencer!" His eyes held hers momentarily as he crossed the room to show her the map. "Look, it's just a few miles up the road. Back in the 1700s, Saintes-Maries would have just been a tiny fishing village; referencing Arles makes a lot more sense. It's also easy to disguise as a misspelling. So we have an apparent reference to the 'whore of Arles'. Maybe the coding isn't so cryptic as people think. Let's face it, most people couldn't read and write in the 18th century, only the nobility, the clergy, and a small section of the middle class – merchants, clerks and so on. Bigou was probably banking on one of his successors deciphering the clues."

Rachel paused to rummage through the pile of books until she found a tourist guide of the area. "Hey, listen to this: 'According to legend, during the persecution of Christians after the crucifixion, Lazarus, his sisters Mary Magdalene and Martha; Mary Salome, mother of the apostles John and James; and Mary Jacobe fled Egypt in a small boat. They eventually came ashore in the south of France at a village that is now called Saintes-Maries-de-la-Mer. The town is a pilgrimage destination for gypsies, who gather on May 24 every year for a religious festival in honour of Saint Sarah, a dark-skinned girl who is said to have been the Egyptian servant of one the three Marys. Another version of the legend has the three saints being deliberately cast adrift in a rudderless boat with Joseph of Arimathea, rather than Lazarus.'"

She paused and looked at David. "Hey, do you know what I'm thinking?"

"Go on."

"We are looking at the tombstone of Marie de Nègre d'Ables… Doesn't that mean 'Black Mary'?"

"That would be a literal translation."

"Doesn't that strike you as odd?"

"I agree it's unusual, though having said that, there are a significant number of Black Madonnas in southern France, which no-one has really explained." He paused. "We need the internet on this one. I'll go and grab my laptop – I assume it's been left in my room, as Marianne promised."

"I heard her tell one of our minders to go and fetch it," said Rachel.

"OK, I'll be right back. Don't go away."

David returned a short while later clutching his MacBook and fired it up. "OK, let's Google Marie de Blanchefort and see what we come up with. Hmm… quite a lot, is the answer."

He started clicking through the links on the page until he found one that explained something about the family history. "Right, I'm translating from the French, so you'll have to bear with me. 'In November 1732, at the age of 44, François d'Hautpoul married a young orphan girl of 19, Marie de Nègre d'Ables (1714-1781), the last representative of that branch of her family. François d'Hautpoul reinstated the lapsed title of Marquis of Blanchefort, brought to him by the marriage to his wife Marie, Lady of Niort, and Roquefeuil Blanchefort.'"

"That's interesting," said Rachel.

"What, specifically?"

"That she was an orphan. And that the 'de Nègre' and the Blanchefort title came from her side of the family."

"I guess," said David doubtfully. "What else have we got? Hang on, there's a photo on this website of the family coat of arms on her marriage bed – believed to still be in the château at Rennes…" He paused, slack-jawed, the colour draining from his face.

"What is it?" said Rachel, peering at the screen.

"Look at her coat of arms – the shield on the left; the one on the right is her husband's Hautpoul crest."

"My God! It's a pentagram – the Star of David. I knew it, I just knew it! This proves everything Anne-Marie and Marianne told us…"

"Proves is a strong word…"

"Oh for God's sake, David, stop being such a bloody sceptic. Sometimes the truth is in plain sight! You're always banging on about being a scientist – what about Occam's Razor? The simplest explanation is often the most likely one."

"I was going to say, before you went off on the rampage, that this definitely shifts the balance of probability. For now I'm happy to go with Occam on this one. This has to signify a Jewish bloodline – what else could it be? And who knows, maybe there is something in the 'de Nègre' thing. I've heard one theory that Mary Magdalene may have actually been Egyptian. Anyway, let's go back to the Blanchefort inscription and see what we can come up with. First of all, let's take the words 'DARLES' and 'CATIN' out of the mix, since they have already been deciphered. What does that leave? By my reckoning, the letters t,e,m,e,e,a,n,t,e,p,o. What French words could that be re-arranged into?"

"What we need is an anagram solver," said Rachel. "You're good at crosswords, aren't you?"

"Not French ones! But you could be on to something there. I wonder if there's a French website that solves anagrams for you? It's a long shot, but worth a try… Hang on a minute, here we go – let's see what we come up with…"

Rachel moved across and peered over his shoulder. "There are a few possibilities there… met, epee, notat… Could that mean anything?"

"Literally 'He should note the sign of the sword'."

"Hey, that's interesting. I mean, it makes sense, after a fashion. Obviously we need some kind of context."

"Of course, what we don't know is whether this clue – assuming it is a clue – relates to the tomb of Mary Magdalene, which we already know about, or the Lost Gospel."

"You're right," said Rachel, crestfallen. "I was getting carried away there for a moment."

"Still, it could be referring to the gospel," said David. "After all, we can be pretty sure Saunière discovered the crypt, complete with Mary's tomb, quite early on in the process. If you remember from your spiel on the TV trailer, that first parchment that he found in the wooden pillar under the pulpit led him straight to the slab in front of the altar, which the local workmen removed to reveal a tomb. At which point he chucked everyone out and hired outside help. That slab had been turned upside down – the reverse side, which would originally been uppermost, had been carved with a Carolingian bas-relief dating from the 9th century, showing two knights on horseback. Clearly, the stone originally marked the entrance to the crypt, and had been turned over to throw people off the trail – almost certainly by Bigou, before fleeing to Spain, so that the Revolutionaries wouldn't find it. If the clue to the crypt was hidden in the first parchment – which no-one has ever seen since – then why go to all the time and trouble to create that cryptic headstone for Marie de Blanchefort? Just as a back-up to the parchment? It seems unlikely. I think Saunière thought it unlikely, too, because he kept on digging the place up."

"So you think there's a chance it might lead us to the gospel?" asked Rachel.

"It's worth a shot. Marianne told us she thought it was hidden somewhere in the undercroft. And we know there are Visigoth tombs down there – they would be an obvious hiding place. I think we only have one option – to go back and check it out."

Rachel shuddered. "God no! I couldn't face going back into that place."

"Then I'll go with Guy. He's 'in' on everything – well, almost everything."

Rachel frowned. She wasn't going to be beaten by this thing. "No. Guy knows too much already – after what's happened we need to keep a lid on the number of people involved. If we have to go down there again, I'm coming with you."

"You don't have to…"

"No arguments!"

"That's more like the bossy cow I know," laughed David, jumping out of the way as she tried to punch him.

"I think you make a very happy couple."

They both spun round to see Marianne standing a few feet away, an amused expression on her face. Rachel blushed violently.

"So how are you getting on?"

"Marianne!" exclaimed Rachel. "You made me jump. We think we've made progress deciphering the Blanchefort tombstone."

"Really?" said Marianne. "I'm impressed. That has eluded people for more than two centuries. Why don't you tell us about it over dinner? I had just come to say that we plan to eat at 7pm, if that suits you."

"That would be wonderful," said David. "It's very kind of you."

"What kind of hosts would we be if we didn't share our food with you?" laughed Marianne. "I'll see you later, then. Follow the main staircase down to the next floor and turn left. You'll find the dining room about half-way along."

Chapter 44

Rachel and David joined Marianne and Gilles for dinner that evening in the sumptuous oak-panelled dining hall to find Marianne wearing a stunning powder-blue evening gown that flowed like liquid velvet down her slight figure. But it wasn't the gown that caught Rachel's attention. A delicate gold disc emblazoned with a four-pointed crown hung from a fine chain around her neck.

"The necklace!" she gasped, unable to believe her own eyes.

"This?" said Marianne smiling, lifting the pendant.

"It's the crown necklace Mary's wearing in *The Last Supper!*" gasped Rachel. "Look, David – it's exactly the same motif. Now, does that convince you!"

"So is there a link to Da Vinci?" asked David. "Or is it just pure coincidence? A crown is a pretty common icon, after all…"

"Oh there's a link, David," interrupted Marianne. "So much of my story revolves around the Cathars, and this is no different. The last Cathar parfait in the Languedoc, Guillaume Bélibaste, was executed in 1321, and the faith became more or less extinct locally, thanks to the torturers of the Inquisition. But the legacy of the Cathars, and France's other so-called heretics at the time, the Waldensians, lived on elsewhere – especially in northern Italy, where many fled to escape the horrors of the crusade.

"Leonardo Da Vinci was born to a woman whom we know simply as Caterina, at a house in Anchiano, near Vinci in Tuscany. Caterina was a Madeleine; the direct descendant of Philippa de Mirepoix. After fleeing Montségur while under siege, she and her child made their way to join other fleeing Cathars in Piedmont. There the refugees became part of the Waldensian movement – the first ever Protestant sect. Though their beliefs differed from the Cathars, they also rejected papal authority and the corruption endemic in the Catholic Church at the time.

"You must understand that at this time the Church held its flock in a vice-like grip; even those who could read were not allowed to study the Bible for themselves; only the priest was allowed to do that. Your English king Henry VIII was the first monarch to place a Bible in every church for everyone to read. If someone challenged the authority of the Church, they could be excommunicated – that meant when they died they would not go to heaven, but be condemned to an eternity in Hell; or so they believed. All this on the say-so of the Pope.

"Anyway, I digress. Da Vinci's father, Ser Piero da Vinci, had met and fallen in love with Caterina, but was already betrothed to a young girl who was the daughter of a fellow notary in Florence. We can only guess what happened, but it may be some pressure was put on him to fulfil his pledge to marry this girl.

"Nature, however, had already taken its course, and Caterina was with child. Unable to be with Ser Piero, she ended up marrying a local man by the name of Acchattabriga. It is commonly thought that his name – more of a pseudonym, really – suggests he was an outlaw, but in fact this was only because he had been outlawed and dispossessed of his lands by the Church for holding heretical beliefs. He was, in short, a Waldensian.

"Although Da Vinci only stayed with his mother until he was five years old, when he went to live with his father, he never forgot her and paid her frequent visits. She told him of his heritage and his true bloodline. Later, he would paint a portrait of her, which he took with him everywhere during the course of his life. We know it today as the Mona Lisa."

"You're kidding!" exclaimed Rachel.

"Indeed not. Leonardo even had it with him on his deathbed at Tours in France, where he had gone to serve the king, Francis 1, in 1519. That's why the *Mona Lisa* now hangs in the Louvre in Paris, and not in Rome. It was one of only a handful of paintings he kept."

"Perhaps that explains the enigmatic smile," said Rachel. "He was painting his own mother! She must have been so proud of him. No wonder he was one of the world's greatest geniuses and visionaries if he carried Christ's bloodline. So Da Vinci wasn't simply one of the shadowy figures in this fictitious Priory of Sion, guarding some secret about a holy bloodline – he was actually part of that bloodline."

"Exactement. And he stayed in touch with his mother – although she had other children with Acchattabriga, she later moved to Milan to be close to Leonardo."

"So he knew the whole story?"

"Oui. That's why, in many of Da Vinci's religious works, we see those mysterious symbols, particularly the finger pointing to the heavens: he was making a cryptic reference to his own bloodline, and that he knew the real truth – a truth that made a mockery of the Pope."

"Could that finger gesture have been intended as an insult to the Pope, and the Catholic Church?"

"With Leonardo, it's highly possible," laughed Marianne.

"Oh come on Rachel, you don't seriously believe all this, do you?" said David. "Where's the proof?"

"Would it surprise you to know, David, that scientists have recently proven that Da Vinci was of Middle Eastern descent?" said Marianne.

"OK, that's interesting."

"Yes – Italian researchers have analysed fingerprints of Leonardo on his work, and they show a distinctive whorl pattern dominant in the Middle East."

"It doesn't prove anything, though."

"No, but it adds to the evidence, doesn't it?" said Rachel. "And, of course, it explains the necklace!"

"Indeed," said Marianne.

"How long has it been in your family?"

"For centuries. Grandmère gave it to me when I was 21 as a coming-of-age present. It has been held by every Madeleine at some stage in her life, and passed down from mother to daughter. It was, indeed, around the neck of the Madeleine at the last supper Christ held with his disciples."

She paused and looked at David, seeing the doubt on his face. "Perhaps I owe you an explanation," she said at length. "You have every right to be sceptical, and if you are both to help me in this quest, and put your lives in further danger, you have a right to know the truth."

Rachel glanced at David with raised eyebrows. This was intriguing.

"The first Madeleine, my many-times-great grandmother, was indeed the bride of Jesus. It was their wedding, at Cana, that John's gospel records as the scene of Christ's first miracle. Why else would Jesus's mother have come to him to say the master of ceremonies had complained they were running out of wine? If he had been but a guest, it would have been nothing to do with him – indeed, they would have tried to hide it.

"But the marriage of Jesus and Mary Magdalene was much more than that. As you have hinted, Rachel, it was a dynastic alliance between the two greatest tribes of Israel – Judah and Benjamin. For Jesus was of King David's line, and he was from Judah; while Mary was a Benjamite, the tribe of the first king of Israel, Saul, and his son, Jonathan. That is why Mary anointed her husband with oil – it was a ceremonial act to sanctify a royal wedding, if you will, and by custom something only his bride could perform."

Marianne paused. "I am not suggesting this was a revolutionary act. Christ had no desire to become involved in Jewish politics, or challenge the authority of the Roman empire. His comment, 'Render unto Caesar that which is Caesar's' makes that clear. But the marriage was still highly symbolic. Let's not forget – though many Christians do – that Jesus was Jewish, and practised the Jewish faith. But he felt it had lost touch with its original purpose and needed a new sense of spiritual direction. This is what he was preaching: a new version of the Torah based on love and forgiveness, rather than fear and punishment. By uniting the two houses of Judah and Benjamin, he was giving his new sect, as we would call it today, a formidable power-base.

"Mary was the sister of Martha, and brother of Lazarus, and they lived with their father, Simon the Pharisee. There's another anomaly in branding Mary a sinner – for would a Pharisee, infamous for a strict code of behaviour and 'holier than thou' attitude, have allowed a strange 'woman of the city' to come into his house and anoint Our Lord with oil? Matthew devotes a whole chapter to Jesus berating the Pharisees for their hypocritical behaviour. He says, 'Woe to you Pharisees, you hypocrites! You clean the outside of the cup and dish, but inside they are full of greed and self-indulgence.' Yet Christ sits and eats with a Pharisee – because he was his father-in-law!

"After Christ's crucifixion, Christians were widely persecuted, not just by the Romans, but by their fellow Jews, too. Simon and his family, including Mary Magdalene and her sister Martha, were arrested and exiled to Gaul – a fact recorded in the Jewish Talmud, though the father's name was given as Nicodemus, not Simon. Since Jesus had another close follower called Nicodemus, their names may have been mixed up."

"Gaul seems an unlikely place to send someone."

"Why?" said Marianne. "Is it any different to you Brits sending convicts to Australia, on the other side of the world, in the 19th century? Gaul was part of the Roman Empire, on the other side of the Mediterranean – a little closer than the South Pacific!"

Rachel smiled at David. "I suppose if they had wanted to send them somewhere really barbaric they could have been exiled to Britain," she said smugly.

Marianne laughed. "Oh, our cousins across the Channel are not so bad, really! But you are right. France was not considered remote. Even the puppet Jewish king, Herod Antipas, was exiled to Gaul by Caligula for allegedly conspiring against him."

"Herod Antipas was exiled to Gaul? I wasn't aware," said David.

"Mais oui! I am surprised you didn't know that, Monsieur Tranter!" teased Marianne.

David held up his hands in submission. "Guilty as charged. So tell me, is there anything else we should know?"

"Well, Dan Brown was not completely wrong. Although the early Madeleines lived in obscurity during the early centuries after Christ's death, Europe became a much more dangerous place with the First Crusade in 1096, when thousands of knights journeyed to Jerusalem to retake the city from the Muslims. After the capture of Jerusalem in 1099 by Count Raymond IV of Toulouse, many pilgrims journeyed to the Holy Land, but were often robbed and killed. As a result, French knight Hugues de Payens asked the new king of Jerusalem, Baldwin II, for permission to establish a religious order to protect pilgrims. Permission was duly granted, and Baldwin gave the new order quarters in the Al-Aqsa mosque on the Temple Mount, adjacent to the Dome of the Rock, built over the ancient Temple of Solomon.

"The Knights Templar, as they became known, carried out extensive excavations beneath the Temple Mount – archaeologists have found a whole network of tunnels, together with the remains of swords and lances, but due to Arab sensitivities, the tunnels have not been fully explored. What, precisely, the Templars discovered is not known, though there has been much speculation – some believe they found the Ark of the Covenant, others the Holy Grail

189

or the Lance of Longinus that pierced Jesus's side. Suffice it to say that on their return to Europe, they found… how do you say?… an empathy with the Cathars, who came to prominence at just this time, and the Templars took no part in the Pope's genocide. It's also interesting that Alfonso, the grandson of Raymond IV, having travelled to the Holy Land himself, supported the Cathars – and two generations later, Raymond VI of Toulouse was at the heart of resistance to the Pope's crusade against the Cathars. Were they, too, privy to some secret knowledge?"

She paused as a side door opened and a servant brought in a trolley laden with food, and started placing dishes on the table.

"You said the Templars helped to protect the Madeleine?" queried Rachel.

Marianne removed a large silver ring from her finger. "I wore this especially for the occasion," she said, passing it to her.

"A Templar ring!" exclaimed Rachel, the emblem of two knights mounted on a single horse clearly visible.

She passed it to David, who traced the words inscribed around the edge, heavily worn but still just legible: sigillum militum xpisti. "'The seal of the army of Christ'," he said slowly. "I have to say, it looks too old to be a reproduction. How did you get this?"

"Like the necklace, it has been in my family for generations. It was given to one of my ancestors during the crusade to warn anyone who sought her harm that she was under the Templar protection. Some believe this is how the legend of the Holy Grail first started, although the 'grail' in question was not a sacred cup, or any other earthly treasure, but the womb of the Madeleine and her successors, which carried the children of Our Lord. The Knights Templar have always been closely linked to the Grail legend. The first known Grail story, *Le Conte du Graal*, was written by Chrétien de Troyes in 1180, and it was at the Council of Troyes in 1129 that the Templar order was officially sanctioned by the Church."

"So… you are the Holy Grail?" asked Rachel, staring at Marianne in awe.

Marianne laughed. "I have never really thought of it quite like that, but I suppose, yes, I am, though it sounds a little pretentious. I am just an ordinary woman who happens to carry the bloodline of Jesus."

"The bloodline of Jesus? I don't see how that can possibly make you 'ordinary'."

"'Ordinary' in the sense that I am a human being, just like you and David. It is the message I carry that is important; the message for which many of my ancestors have sacrificed their lives. But without evidence, as David would say, there is no proof. And he is right. That is why I need your help. Now let's eat before the food spoils, and then you can tell me what you have discovered about the Blanchefort tombstone."

As the meal progressed, Rachel and David explained their attempt to decode the cryptic inscription.

"So you see," said Rachel at length, "it's not exactly bullet-proof, but it is at least a working hypothesis."

"Well, it sounds like a good enough place to start," said Gilles. "These treasure-hunters always want to complicate things. They have come up with any number of theories, each more unlikely than the last. Maybe they are missing the obvious."

"Indeed," added Marianne. "And this is where the information about the Templars may be of use to you. For as well as helping to protect the Madeleine, we think they helped her to hide the Lost Gospel – together with another secret treasure."

"Another treasure?" queried David. "I've just got used to the idea there's a Lost Gospel out there somewhere. There is something else besides?"

"Oui."

"Do you have any idea what it is?"

Marianne hesitated. "There are legends…" She bit her lip and glanced at Gilles, then fell silent for a while. "I am sorry, David, I cannot say more. I am not willing to repeat things that may be merely the result of centuries of gossip. What lies at the heart of this is too precious for idle speculation. If we find something that leads us in a certain direction, then so be it. But until then, let us be satisfied with the gospel, and the truths I know it will bring to Christendom."

Everyone at the table fell silent.

"Forgive me for being practical, but let's get down to brass tacks," said David at length. "The question is, how do we proceed from here? You've told us, Marianne, that the gospel is believed to be in the undercroft; the Visigoth burial chamber beneath the crypt itself. Since Rachel and I have both been there, I can tell you that it's a large natural underground cavern, containing what appear to be several tombs. As an archaeologist, I cannot agree to simply going in and ransacking the place, however important the 'find' we are looking for. However, I accept that under the circumstances, we would never get permission from the authorities to carry out an official dig – we would be obstructed at every turn. It could take years to get a government permit – not to mention permission from the landowner."

"We would most definitely not want you to 'ransack' the place, as you put it," said Gilles gravely.

"Surely it wouldn't hurt to open up the tombs and carefully sift through the contents?" put in Rachel.

"Absolutely not – who knows what evidence you might be destroying in the process? Archaeology is an exact science: as far as tombs are concerned, it is not just about the contents, but about noting the order in which items are laid out – and, of course, an analysis of any debris. What might appear insignificant to you – perhaps a few fragments of cloth – might actually help to date the whole tomb. Only if we find a specific clue on a tomb would I

191

agree to open it. And then we would only remove an item if there were an obvious connection."

"So be it," murmured Marianne, nodding her head in assent.

"Then that leaves us with only one option," continued David. "We have a clue – a somewhat flimsy clue, but a clue nonetheless. We must go back and search the cave for something that fits in with that phrase from the tombstone; 'He should note where the sword is put'. It might be something else, but a tomb sounds like the most likely option."

"How do you propose to get into the place?" questioned Gilles.

"The same way we got out. The cave is obviously part of an old underground river system – we followed a passage out of the burial chamber and eventually came out on the hillside below Rennes-le-Château. That means we can get back in undetected – hopefully."

"And what will you need?"

"I left all my equipment back at the dig site, and for obvious reasons I have no intention of going back there. So, we will need folding shovels, a couple of small bricklayers' trowels, and some small paintbrushes for cleaning artefacts. We will also need a portable arc light and some head-torches – preferably LED. Oh, and some climbing ropes and pitons – there's a nasty vertical shaft we need to get past. Not to mention a couple of decent rucksacks."

"When are you thinking of going?" asked Gilles.

"As quickly as possible," said David. "The sooner this is all out in the open, the sooner we can get on with our lives. Since we will obviously have to arrive at Rennes under cover of darkness to avoid the risk of us being seen, I suggest tomorrow night – assuming you can get the equipment together in time."

"That will not be a problem," said the Count.

"Tomorrow night it is, then," said David.

Chapter 45

It was well past midnight as the ageing Renault van wound its way slowly up the steep hill to Rennes-le-Château, its ancient springs squeaking in protest at every bump and twist in the road. The Count had insisted they use the battered old vehicle, normally used for maintenance around the estate, to avoid attracting unwanted attention.

"God help me," said David as he crashed through the gears. "I never want to drive one of these things again."

"Well, at least you can't do it much damage," said Rachel brightly. "And you really do look the part with that beret."

David scowled at her. "I hope they make it in one piece," he said, nodding to the back of the van where two of the Count's bodyguards were bouncing around like sacks of potatoes. "I wouldn't want to do this without someone watching our backs. Here we are," he added, as he pulled off the road below an outcrop of rock. "I'm pretty sure this is where we came out."

David got out of the car and opened the rear doors. Marcel and Pierre climbed out stiffly as David reached in and pulled out the rucksacks containing their lighting and excavating gear, each with a coil of climbing rope attached to the side.

"Follow us to the entrance so you know exactly where it is, then move the vehicle down the road, Marcel," whispered David in broken French. "When you get back, make sure you wait just inside the cave so you can't be seen. Pierre, as agreed, you come with us."

Marcel, a thin, wiry man with thinning black hair combed over his bald head, nodded his assent. Pierre, a hulking brute who had played rugby for Toulouse in his youth, merely grunted. The four of them started climbing the steep hillside towards the cave, winding their way between outcrops of rock and dense patches of maquis, the evergreen scrub that covered the slopes where the oak and sweet chestnut could not gain a foothold. It took barely 10 minutes to reach the entrance, but they were all out of breath by the time they arrived at the jagged limestone outcrop, where the action of rain and ice had, over the millennia, splintered the exposed rock into a series of deep fissures. They felt their way along, trying to avoid using their torches, until Rachel found a deep crevice that disappeared into an inky blackness.

She crawled up it a little way on her hands and knees to confirm she had found the right spot. "Here we are," she said quietly.

David nodded to Marcel. The Frenchman nodded back, then turned and retraced his steps to the van.

"OK, it's just us and Pierre now," said David, sotto voce, retrieving the head-torches from his rucksack and handing one to Rachel. "Let me go first – no arguments," he added, as she opened her mouth to speak. "Pierre – you bring up the rear."

Rachel, for once, was happy for David to take the lead. It was an eerie, moonless night and she had a strange sense of foreboding. "Just watch out for the pothole," she warned.

David had no intention of missing that particular pitfall, studying the ground ahead intently as he led the way along the tortuous passageway, the walls worn smooth by the action of an ancient underground river. Eventually his torch picked out the 'chimney' in the floor ahead. "This time we'll be a little more careful," he said, hammering a piton into a crevice in the rock and tying one of the lines to it, before attaching a second line to his harness. "We'll rope ourselves together – I'll go first and anchor the fixed line on the far side of the obstruction; Pierre, you back up round the corner and hold me in case I slip."

"Is Pierre going to make it past that rock-fall, when we're done? He's pretty massive."

"The same thought crossed my mind – I don't remember the gap looking that small. I hope he can make it – if we run into any trouble, he's the kind of guy I want at my back. If it's a no-go, we'll have to tell him to swap places with Marcel."

David reached the far side safely, and anchored the fixed line, leaving it hanging at roughly waist-height alongside the narrow ledge they had just traversed. He threw back the climbing line, which Rachel attached to her harness before venturing across nervously, holding the other rope with one hand, but completed the journey without mishap. Pierre seemed completely unruffled by the whole process, despite having to squeeze his bulk through the tight gap between the rock-fall and the cave roof.

"De rien – it's nothing," he said, shrugging his shoulders in typical Gallic fashion, when Rachel asked if he was OK. "In rugby, you can have five guys my size on top of you."

Rachel shuddered at the thought.

"Right, let's get a move on," said David.

They continued their way along the tortuous passage as it wound its way up steeply through the hillside, the smooth, wet limestone glistening in the reflected light from their head-torches. Then the tunnel suddenly opened out, and they were standing at the entrance to the burial place of the Visigoth kings. The altar stood before them, the goat's skull leering at them across the shadowy chamber. Drawn to it inexorably, they walked across to the ancient stone monolith.

As they approached the altar Rachel froze, pointing at the slab in horror. "Blood," she whispered, barely able to speak. "Fresh blood."

David moved across to her side, and his face blanched. "That's no accident,"

194

he said grimly. "I don't like what's going on here – the sooner we're out of this place, the better. Let's get on with it – I'll rig up the arc light, then you work your way round the far side of the cavern, and I'll look after this side. Examine the outside of every tomb, and the cave walls, but don't disturb anything. We need to crack on, too – we've probably got no more than an hour with that arc-light before the battery dies. After that, we're back to our torches. Pierre – just stay close and keep your eyes and ears open."

They slowly made their way along the sides of the chamber. The sarcophagi themselves were fairly crude; little more than hollowed out limestone slabs. The lids bore a series of markings in an unknown script, running around the edge, but the walls of the chamber were completely bare. They examined every niche and fissure, but there was nothing to be seen; nothing remotely resembling a clue that might reveal the gospel's whereabouts.

"Surely it's OK to look inside the tombs?" asked Rachel, as they met up back at the altar.

"We can try moving the lids, though I don't know if we'll have much success," said David. "They're solid stone – they must weigh a couple of hundredweight each. But I'm not about to start rummaging through the contents. If nothing relevant is visible, then we move on. Let's start with the tomb Saunière found – assuming it was him, and not whoever else has been down here lately."

They went over to the broken tomb and shone their torches inside. "Hell! Someone's been at this," said David.

"What's up?"

"All the remaining coins have gone – I only removed one for identification. Now there's nothing left."

"Seriously?"

"Unfortunately, yes. Whoever uses this place obviously knows we've been down here and didn't want to risk losing them to a museum. OK, let's see if we can shift this lid."

They both heaved as hard as they could on the broken side of the sarcophagus lid, but to no avail. As David had predicted, the slabs were far too heavy. "Now we know why this one's been broken into with a hammer and chisel," he said.

"So now what? All this struggle to get in here – and for nothing."

"Please don't ask me to smash my way into an archaeological treasure trove like this," said David.

"I'm not asking you to do that. I wouldn't do it myself. I'm just bloody frustrated," she snapped, taking off her rucksack and flinging it to the ground next to the altar. She slumped down beside it and buried her head in her hands.

After a few moments she brushed her hair out of her eyes and looked up. The answer was right in front of her. She knew instantly, as if she had known all her life, that this was what they were searching for. Spellbound, she traced her finger around the dusty sign carved into the side of the altar. It was, she knew, a Templar symbol: the cross of Christ within a crown. Except that on this occasion, the crown was pierced by a sword, not a cross. And the crown was the same, four-pointed crown worn by Marianne and the Madeleine.

"David," she said thickly, struggling to find her voice. "I've found it."

"What?" he said, looking up from where he, too, was squatting on the ground in defeat.

"I've found it," she repeated more loudly, still barely able to believe that the object of their quest was right in front of her eyes.

David picked himself and knelt down beside her. Rachel traced the symbol again with her finger. "Look, the Templar cross and crown – but this time with a sword replacing the cross. Remember Bigou's cryptic message? 'Note where the sword is put.' And here it is – through the crown worn by the Madeleine."

David examined the symbol, carefully. She was right: it was clearly not Visigoth artwork, although they had later converted to Christianity. But it was one of several signs with which the Templars were closely associated. And judging from the discolouration, it had been there a long time.

"It looks pretty genuine," he admitted, standing up. "There's only one problem: this altar is a solid slab of rock."

Rachel stood up and realised that what he said was true. It was hewn from a solid piece of limestone. It didn't even have a lid like the sarcophagi. So near, yet so far. Disappointment crashed through her, and she sank back down on her haunches, her hands clasped to her face to hide the tears that pricked her eyes. No, this would not do. Fighting to keep her emotions in check, she sat back and tried to look at the altar dispassionately. There had to be something else – something they hadn't yet figured out. Then she noticed a slight discolouration on the left-hand side of the stone, and leaned forward to get a closer look.

"David!" she said urgently. "Take a look at this! We're definitely on the right track – there's an identical symbol on the other side of the altar!"

"You're right," he said, stepping forward and peering closely. "But we're still no closer to finding the answer."

They stared at the two symbols in frustration. Then Rachel, tilting her head to one side, noticed something odd. Her eyes travelled to the bottom of the stone, and she gave a gasp of disbelief.

"What is it?"

"The two symbols!" exclaimed Rachel. "They're mirror images of each other. The swords are both on the diagonal through the crown, but they're pointing towards each other – and downwards. And there, at the bottom, in the centre…" she reached forward and scooped away the accumulation of debris on the cave floor, to confirm her suspicions "...there between them, at ground level, is a third, identical symbol – except this time, the sword is pointing straight down vertically. And look what new symbol the three create together – the V, the womb, the sacred feminine, just as in The Last Supper, pointing the way!"

"I think you're jumping to conclusions ..."

His words fell on deaf ears as Rachel continued to scrabble away in the dust.

"There's a hollow in the rock here; it's been filled with stone dust," she muttered, clawing at the ground with her bare fingers, not waiting to grab a trowel. Then her fingers touched something hard, something with a shape, something warmer than the surrounding stone.

"There's something made of wood here," she said excitedly.

"For heaven's sake, Rachel, don't touch it – whatever you've found could be more than 1,000 years old – if you're not careful it will just crumble to dust!" David rapidly unbuckled his rucksack and pulled out a brush and a trowel. Rachel moved aside as he knelt down and carefully began to move the debris to one side, little by little, until a fragment of wood appeared. He continued to sift the dust from around the edges, until it was clear they were looking at the corner of a small wooden box, tilted slightly to one side. Now he could see the shape and alignment, David started removing the debris more rapidly until the whole of the box lid was visible.

He gently brushed the surface of the rough wooden container with his fingers – it was roughly six inches long by four inches wide. "It feels fairly solid, thankfully," he said. "Unlike the passageway, this floor's fairly dry, and the wood is probably oak or elm. We can't be sure about whatever's inside, though," he added. "It will probably need the same treatment as the parchment scroll."

Rachel watched in silence as David used his trowel to scrape away the dirt around the box until the bottom edge was visible, then inserting the point of his trowel underneath, he eased the box clear of the hole. He picked it up gingerly. "We're lucky," he said over his shoulder. "The box looks pretty sound..."

He broke off as he saw Pierre suddenly sprint for the far side of the cave. A gunshot ricocheted across the chamber. Spinning round, David saw a column of figures in black hooded robes filing into the cavern from the far end. One of the men had broken away and stood, smoking gun in hand, over the slumped body of Pierre, whose lifeblood was rapidly spilling out onto the stone floor.

The man turned and strode towards them, lowering his hood. It was Dubois. And now he was pointing the gun directly at Rachel, who was kneeling over Pierre with tears running down her face, her hand over her mouth in disbelief.

"If either of you move, she dies too," he said icily.

"What do you want, Dubois?" asked David quietly.

"I want the Madeleine. Nothing more, nothing less. And for that, you can keep your precious little gospel – don't think I don't know about it. Theologians will argue over it for decades; it proves nothing. But the Madeleine is different."

"What do you want with her?"

"Her life," said Dubois, simply. "Christianity is dying, my friend. The churches are empty. People are returning to the old ways, the old gods. She alone has the power to revive it. I cannot allow that to happen. Those of us who follow other paths are emerging from centuries of persecution. Countless thousands of our brethren were burned at the stake by her kind. She is a necessary sacrifice."

"Her kind were burned at the stake, too, Dubois," said Rachel furiously, recovering from her initial shock. "Or slaughtered in their beds, in towns like Béziers! Didn't they teach you about the Cathars at school?"

Dubois bowed his head in acknowledgement. "Indeed, I can empathise with their fate. But regardless of history, the unveiling of the Madeleine at this hour would, I fear, bring new persecution on our heads. By sacrificing the bride of Christ, we will appease the ancient gods and pay the debt owed by those who killed in his name."

"Do you seriously think the Madeleine would give herself up to you?" said David savagely, getting to his feet. "Even if she were naive enough to come, there is no way her people would allow her anywhere near this place."

"Ah, you speak of the Rosicrucians, I think. We know they have been protecting her. Well, you must find ways to persuade them – and her," said Dubois suavely. "Assuming, that is, you want to see your 'friend' alive again."

"If you kill Rachel you lose your bargaining chip."

"She is expendable. And given that she helped to discover the Madeleine, a fair sacrifice."

"And if the Madeleine gives herself up, what guarantees do I have that you will free Rachel?"

Rachel stared at David in horror. "For God's sake, David, don't even think about it! Marianne is far more important than me! It's vital her message gets out."

"Religion has caused enough death and destruction," said David, looking at her steadily. "I wish Marianne no ill, but you're much more important to me."

Rachel stared at him with a confused mixture of anger and tenderness. "Just don't do it," she said finally in an unsteady voice, looking away to hide her tears.

"Well, much as I hate to interrupt this charming show of affection, we really do need to make a decision, don't we, Mr Tranter?" said Dubois sarcastically. "What is it to be? The Madeleine or your girlfriend?"

"And if I refuse to make a choice?"

"Then regretfully I will have to kill both of you."

David's mind raced as he stalled for time. Refusing to cooperate was clearly not an option, but he had no intention of handing over Marianne on a platter for these deranged cultists to have their way with.

"And the gospel?" he asked.

"Stays here," said Dubois firmly. "Consider it an incentive."

"What guarantees do I have you won't destroy it?"

"You will just have to trust me."

David was still standing several feet behind Rachel. He had to act quickly if he were to act at all. Though in his mind the gospel was of small importance compared to the lives of Rachel or Marianne, he was damned if he was handing over to Dubois something that so many had died to protect.

"OK, Dubois you win," said David reluctantly.

"NO!" screamed Rachel, her voice strangled with grief.

"I'm going to put this box down slowly on the ground, and walk out of here. Keep Rachel safe and I'll try to broker a deal. But if you harm a hair on her head, I swear to God I'll hunt you down and kill you with my bare hands."

He knelt down, lowering the box, but as his hand reached the ground he grabbed a nearby lump of rock, threw back his arm, and hurled it at Dubois with all his might. Not for nothing had David played cricket for Oxford – he could hit the wicket from 50 yards. Dubois was too surprised to move. The stone hit him square between the eyes, and he went down as if he had been felled.

"Run Rachel, run," bellowed David, grabbing her by the arm and dragging her to her feet before sprinting towards the tunnel entrance, twisting and weaving as gunfire echoed around the cavern. A cultist lunged at him, then dropped to the ground screaming, caught in the hail of bullets. Others close by backed away, anxious to avoid the same fate.

Another scream of pain echoed through his head; this time a woman's. David glanced over his shoulder to see Rachel lying horribly still on the ground, then the tunnel was upon him.

He had no way of knowing if she was alive or dead, but there was no going back now; he could do nothing to help her. Clutching the box tightly, he ran as fast as he dare through the downward-leading fissure, ducking under projecting rocks, his feet slithering on the smooth, damp stone. He could hear the sounds of pursuit, running feet punctuated by curses as Dubois' men banged heads, knees and elbows on the unyielding stone.

He rounded a corner to see the roof-fall just yards ahead. Without stopping to think, he clawed his way over the pile of mud and stones, then quickly shuffled across the tiny ledge beside the gaping maw of the chasm, clutching the rope as he went. As he reached the far side, he spun round, yanked out his climbing knife and slashed the fixed line. Two quick strokes of the sharp blade was all it took, then he was running again, not looking, not caring about what happened to his pursuers. As he hurtled headlong down the tunnel, he heard a horrible scrabbling sound behind him, a desperate shout, cut off abruptly in mid-cry, then a babble of voices. Slowly the sounds receded as he continued his flight through the passage, then suddenly he was scrambling out into the warm night air.

"It's OK, Marcel, it's me," he gasped as a shape loomed in front of him. "Let's get out of here. Vite!"

Chapter 46

"I will not leave Rachel to die!" said Marianne furiously, banging her fist on the green-baize desk, her dark eyes flashing dangerously. "I will not!"

"I cannot allow you to go there," said the Count, quietly. "You don't know she will be killed – we can alert the gendarmerie…"

"The gendarmerie? That's a joke – that would be a death sentence! They will be in somebody's pay, if not the cult then the Church."

"Surely we can go back with some of your men, Gilles?" asked David. "She's put her life at stake for Marianne. You owe her that much. I'm not suggesting Marianne goes herself…"

"And you think Dubois will just hand her over? Or were you planning some kind of 'Gunfight at the O.K. Corral' down there?"

The three sat stony-faced in the Count's study the following morning, conducting a council of war. After the events of the night before, everyone's nerves were frayed.

"I still don't understand how they found you there…" Marianne turned to the Count in frustration. "Has someone betrayed us, Gilles?"

"I think it's more a case of 'the enemy of my enemy is my friend'. The cult is a poorly kept secret around here. What better way for the Church to be rid of both you and the gospel? However, I will make inquiries – it is possible there was a leak somewhere in our organisation."

Silence fell again, broken only by the ticking of an ornate gold Napoleon III ormalu clock on the mantelpiece.

"Well, I agree we have to do something," said the Count eventually. "But we don't even know if Rachel is still alive, horrible though that thought may be. I suggest we wait until they contact us, then David and I will go back with some men and try to force their hand."

"And probably all get killed," said Marianne stubbornly.

The Count sighed in exasperation, before turning to David. "Changing the subject briefly, how long will it be before we can start getting the gospel translated?"

"It's in better condition than the scroll we found in Mary's tomb. It looks like an early medieval copy of a much older document, but there are only a few pages, sadly. Still, it's written in vulgate Latin, so translation shouldn't be difficult, and though we need to stabilise the paper, it's less fragile than the scroll. I would say two to three weeks."

"It's disappointing it's only medieval. And a few pages? I understood it to be a complete gospel," said Marianne, clearly disappointed.

"I agree, but given the turbulent times when it disappeared, it's hardly surprising if copies were made. The wording is quite archaic – the source document was almost certainly from a much earlier period. Still, we'll let the manuscript experts decide on that one."

He paused, drumming his fingers on the table. "Well, we're not accomplishing much sitting here. I agree with the Count, let's wait until we hear something – we've no idea where to start looking for her anyway. If they want to make an exchange, they will be in touch soon enough. Then we can decide on a course of action. Though I agree, Marianne mustn't come with us."

She glared at him, and he looked away, shame-faced. It was bad enough that he had left Rachel to her fate; he couldn't countenance endangering Marianne's life, too, whatever he may have told Dubois.

* * * * *

It was another 48 hours before they heard about Rachel; 48 hours of nervous strain that left everyone tense and irritable. The mood wasn't helped by the onset of torrential rain that fell in seemingly limitless quantities, with no sign of abating.

Finally Hélène's network of contacts in Rennes-le-Château relayed a message that Rachel was still alive, having suffered only a flesh wound, though nothing more was known. The news lifted a huge burden from David's mind, but her ultimate fate, and that of Marianne, still weighed heavily.

Then came instructions from the sect, delivered to the château by post and addressed to the Count. It was a shock to them all that the approach was so brazen.

"They know about you, then, Gilles," remarked Marianne, as they convened once more in his study to discuss the news. "Perhaps there is a traitor in our midst, after all."

"It's possible," he admitted, "though given the clandestine nature of our organisation, I still think it more likely the Church is behind this. The sect has only just become involved, yet both David and Rachel have been targeted before. Those cranks are just being used as a convenient tool."

"The fact remains this 'safe house' has been compromised," said David. "We can't stay here now – but first we have to extract Rachel. What are their demands?"

"We are to meet them tomorrow night in the undercroft. They will let Rachel go unharmed, in return for Marianne. Who, of course, they won't get."

Marianne glared at him, but said nothing.

"That goddamn place again!" snorted David. "How many men can you put together?"

"Half a dozen, maybe," replied the Count.

"Is that all?"

"We are not an army, David. The Rosicrucians' mission is to help people on the path to spiritual development. Our involvement with the Madeleine is a part of that process, to preserve a vital truth that will bring new meaning to mankind. Over the years that has evolved into a protective role, but we do not have infinite resources."

"OK. So we go in there with maybe a couple of guys, while the rest hold back for some kind of surprise attack. But what then? What's to stop them putting a bullet in Rachel's head as soon as they see we don't have the Madeleine?" David stared gloomily out of the window at the grey, wind-swept skies as the rain lashed the windows. It seemed even the weather was conspiring against them.

"There's no way around this," said Marianne, after a long pause. "I'm going, and there's nothing you can do to stop me, Gilles. You can put me in a bullet-proof vest or take any other precautions you like, but if I'm not there, Rachel will die, and I'm not prepared to have that on my conscience. It's one thing being prepared to risk your life to save something precious, as we have all done. But deliberately sacrificing someone else to save my life... I can't allow that. It's not what Christ stood for."

"And I simply can't allow you, my dear, to put yourself in harm's way..."

Marianne pulled herself up to her full height and defiantly tossed back her mane of raven black hair. "I am the Madeleine, descendant of Christ!" she said, her eyes blazing. "You will not order me what to do! The hour has come. Events are moving quickly, and I must play my part, whatever that may be. We have the gospel. I must take my chances for my own safety. We are nothing if we are not prepared to risk our lives to help our fellow men and women. To abandon Rachel would betray the very cause my ancestors fought so hard to protect."

The Count looked at her steadily for a moment, then nodded his head. "So be it, my lady. I suppose I have always known this moment would come. I will make the necessary arrangements." He turned to walk out of the room, before pausing. "But you are right; you will wear a vest," he said, with a wry expression.

She smiled and nodded her head. "Thank you, Gilles. I'm sorry; you know you have always been like a father to me. But it is time."

Chapter 47

Rachel woke with a sick ache in her head and a vicious throbbing in her thigh. She tried to sit up, but the room swam before her eyes and she slumped back on the bed, willing the vertiginous spinning to stop.

Where the hell was she? She cudgelled her brains, trying desperately to remember what had happened. She had been in the Visigoth chamber with David; they had found the gospel, and then… Then the terrible images of the previous night flooded back in a kaleidoscope of shock and pain: the gunshot; the slumped and bloodied body of Pierre; Dubois' cat-and-mouse game; David's sudden, desperate act – hurling a rock and felling Dubois; her feet turning to lead as she tried to follow him out of the cavern, a slow-motion sequence that felt like wading through treacle. Another gunshot, followed by searing pain, then… nothing. From that point on, her mind was blank.

She tried to sit up, more slowly this time, the rickety iron bedstead squeaking in protest. Dim light filtered through a grating in an ancient oak door next to the bed. In the gloom, she could just make out that she was in a small room, perhaps no more than 10ft square, that appeared to have been hewn out of solid rock. She swung her legs over the edge of the bed and tried to stand up, only to crash to the floor as her left leg gave way in an explosion of pain.

She heard movement outside the door, and a few minutes later it swung open. Dubois stood framed in the doorway, this time dressed in his more familiar jacket and cravat, looking for all the world like some ageing history professor.

"Please, let me help you," he said with seemingly genuine concern, kneeling down beside her.

"Get away from me, you sick bastard," said Rachel vehemently. "I don't want your filthy hands anywhere near me. And to think I tried to persuade David to trust you!"

"As you wish," said Dubois, backing away.

Rachel manoeuvred herself onto the bed and sat clutching herself tightly.

"I'm not a monster, you know," said Dubois, attempting to lighten the atmosphere.

"Oh really?" muttered Rachel sarcastically.

"I am merely standing up for my religion; to correct centuries of bloody persecution by the Catholic Church."

"I'll judge you by your actions, not your words. You killed Pierre in cold blood. You're nothing more than a terrorist."

"Ah, but one man's terrorist is another man's freedom fighter, non? As for Pierre, it was a shame, but he would not have hesitated to do the same thing

– I knew the man. He had a gun. If he had shot me, then who would be the monster?"

Rachel fell silent. There was no point engaging with the man's twisted logic.

Dubois tried to change tack. "I am sorry about your leg. If it is any comfort to you, it was not I who pulled the trigger – your boyfriend saw to that." He put his hand to a livid bruise on his forehead.

"Yes, that was a pretty good shot, wasn't it?" said Rachel smugly. "He used to play cricket for Oxford."

"Really," said Dubois, anger flashing across his face. He struggled to regain his composure. "Still, we have patched your leg as best we can. Luckily, one of our brethren is a doctor. It seems the bullet passed straight through without hitting anything vital. You lost some blood, nothing more – apart from that nasty bump on your head, of course, where you hit the ground. I have some antibiotics for you here, though of course it's up to you if you take them."

He tossed a plastic container of pills onto the bed next to Rachel, who looked at them with extreme suspicion.

"No doubt you think they are something nasty, but I assure you they are not. It's up to you – I don't want to force you to take them, but I do want you to recover."

"What's the point if you're planning to kill me? You don't seriously think the Count will agree to hand Marianne over, do you?"

"Who knows? I believe the Madeleine to be an honourable woman. You are only here because of her."

"Her line has survived for 2,000 years, endured centuries of persecution – just as you say your own followers have done. Yet you just want to destroy her?"

"It is a necessary price, I am afraid. With her gone, there will be nothing to prevent the return of the ancient ways; a religion that honours the gods and goddesses of the Earth, and celebrates the cycles of nature – birth, death and rebirth."

"That's just crazy! I know some Pagans, and I respect their beliefs – they would be appalled by your actions. Do you really think killing her is going to bring your fringe cult, whatever it is, into the mainstream?"

"Pah – Pagans. Just a bunch of ageing hippies," retorted Dubois. "I am talking of the old religion; the religion of the Visigoths and the Celts. A religion that requires sacrifice. Nature is a fierce mistress, but she maintains balance and order. Christianity has put Man on a pedestal, let him believe he can master the planet – and now he is destroying it. By offering the Madeleine's blood, the gods will be appeased, and it will strengthen our power to create change. We are not a fringe cult, as you put it; there are many who believe in the old ways – deities whose roots go back to Greece and Rome, and beyond. We have different names for our gods, but we have the same aim: taking up arms to save Mother Earth, and all life upon her, from extinction. We are many, and we have disciples in all quarters of government."

"A religion, it would seem, that indulges in blood sacrifice – judging from the altar. Marianne would not be your first victim, I suspect."

"The Jewish faith, among many others, practised ritual sacrifice. God even commanded Abraham to kill his own son, Isaac, to test his faith."

"Yes, but Christ came to change all that, didn't he? To bring the message that people should be ruled by love, not fear; by compassion, not hatred."

"And where has that got the world? Centuries of warfare and bloodshed. I don't doubt his good intentions, but it hasn't worked very well, has it?"

"Which is precisely why the Madeleine needs to live, to open people's eyes to the false dogma of the Church and reawaken Christ's true message," said Rachel furiously. "A message that tells us that our journey in life is to find the Christ within ourselves."

"A noble sentiment, but one, I fear, that will be lost on most people."

"No, it won't. There is growing spiritual awareness in the world – it just needs a focus; a focus that isn't bound up in dogma about 'being saved' or going to hell, but rather built on an understanding that each and every one of us has a spiritual identity that we must discover and reconcile in our daily lives." Rachel fell silent, surprised by the vehemence of her outburst. Her long conversations with Marianne at the château had clearly found their mark.

Dubois gave her an odd look.

"Anyway," said Rachel, hurriedly, "where the hell are we?" Further discussion was futile, but she needed information.

"We are still in the cave system under Rennes. There are a number of small chambers that were created down here over the centuries. Don't try to escape – it's a complex maze and there are many chasms. You could easily fall to your death."

With that, he rapped on the door to summon the jailer, and abruptly left the cell.

Endless days seemed to pass, though deprived of nearly all sensory input, it may only have been two or three. Other than a visit from the doctor, who persuaded her to take the meds, and the food brought by her guard, she saw no-one. She became deeply depressed, racked with guilt at allowing herself to become so ensnared in the Rennes mystery when she should have been spending time back home with Emma. She had abandoned her to embark on a wild goose chase that might, quite literally, be the death of her.

Sleep became the norm. Sleep punctuated by deep, disturbing dreams: of darkness and demons; of a terrifying vision of the plane crash that killed her father; but most of all of Emma, locked in a darkened room, calling out her name, again and again and again…

* * * * *

She was brutally awoken, dragged from her sleep, blindfolded, bound and gagged, then frogmarched by hooded figures through dimly lit passages. Limping painfully and desperately scared, she tried to take in her surroundings – at first the ground underfoot was ankle-deep in mud, and water dripped steadily onto her head. At one point she could hear the sound of running water falling into what sounded like a vast tank. Then the ground under her bare feet turned to hard, unyielding stone. Finally the blindfold was ripped away and she screwed up her eyes as the light from an array of flaming torches flooded her retinas. She was back in the Visigoth chamber.

Terrified, struggling to get free, she was half-carried to the altar where the goat's head loomed horribly large, and laid roughly on top. Her blouse was ripped open, and she was tied spreadeagled to the iron spikes at each corner of the stone.

Dubois walked over and leered at her, toying with a richly jewelled dagger. "Quite the pretty thing, aren't you?" he said, lasciviously. "A fitting gift for the gods."

Chapter 48

The cave system that led from the hillside below Rennes to the Visigoth burial chamber was wet and slippery after the torrential rain of the previous few days, and the small group took great care as they scrambled up the steep passageway. Water oozed and trickled through the myriad cracks and fissures in the sculpted walls of the former underground river, the hollowed, white, lichen-covered stone glistening in the harsh white light of their LED head-torches.

The party was under instruction to maintain silence, save in an emergency, but there was little mood for idle chatter; rather, a deep sense of foreboding. No-one knew precisely how events would be resolved, but everyone feared for Marianne's safety. She was a fiercely independent, headstrong young woman with powerful convictions: it would be difficult to prevent her following through her intended course of action. David and the Count had privately agreed they had no intention of letting her give herself up, but there was no disguising that they were embarked on a highly risky undertaking. The best they could hope for was a stand-off that would somehow allow them to rescue Rachel, but the odds were high that someone would be killed or seriously injured.

They had managed to muster eight men in the end, all of whom were armed. Two were left at the entrance to the tunnel to guard their backs and make sure no-one tried to interfere with their vehicles. The remaining six accompanied David, the Count and Marianne; three in the lead, with the remainder bringing up the rear.

After 15 minutes of difficult progress through the treacherous tunnel, slipping frequently, they finally halted at the chimney where one of the cult members had met his death. The leading bodyguard put on a safety line and threw a grappling hook across the gaping chasm, snagging it on the rock-fall on the far side at the second attempt, before using it to steady himself as he edged across the void.

The rope was quickly tied off at both ends to create a new hand-line, and each member of the party put on a safety harness before crossing in turn. David shuddered to think how cavalier he and Rachel had been on their first couple of visits – with the rock-face now wet, they could ill afford to take chances.

After another quarter of an hour or so, a dim luminescence emerged from the blackness beyond the reach of their torches, a light that grew steadily brighter. Then the chamber was upon them, its grim tableau exposed for all to see. Twelve hooded figures garbed in jet black robes encircled the chamber ahead of them, each carrying a flaming pitch torch, casting dark and tortured shadows across the cave. A 13th hooded cultist stood in front of the altar, arms crossed and head bowed.

But it was the shocking scene on the altar itself that transfixed the rescuers. For on it lay Rachel, bound and gagged, her half-naked body shuddering with fear, a blood-soaked bandage around one leg, her bruised face streaked with tears. Dubois stood looking at them, his ornately jewelled dagger idly tracing patterns on Rachel's bare midriff.

David's eyes misted red as a surge of bloodlust pumped through his veins. There was only one thought in his mind, now: vengeance.

"I am glad to see you kept your bargain, Monsieur le Comte," said Dubois, ignoring David's presence.

"You gave us little choice," replied the Count icily. "And it is only because we value human life more highly than do you that we are here at all. Against my better judgement, I might add – I don't trust any of you heathen."

"You do us a disservice, Monsieur le Comte. I bear you no ill will; your organisation and ours are not dissimilar. We both seek enlightenment."

The Count snorted in derision. "You stand there, dagger poised over a stripped and bound woman, and claim enlightenment? Only we follow the light; you go deep into the dark entrails of the night, Dubois. You seek to revive savage, evil customs. In their day your gods were harsh and cruel – there is no place for them in a civilised world."

"A civilised world, Monsieur le Comte? When mankind ravages the planet and denies the very existence of a supreme being? Eh bien, we do not have time to debate metaphysics. Do you have the sacrifice? As you can see, I have prepared an alternative lest you have a change of heart, so please, do nothing rash. I wish her no harm."

"You wish her no harm, yet you would gladly take the life of another?"

"As I explained to your new friends on our previous meeting, it is not something I do gladly, but rather born of necessity. She carries the sins of the Church on her shoulders. All those who have died at the hands of Rome will be avenged. And what greater sign of devotion could we show to the Dark Lord than offering up the Bride of Christ? So now, let us make the exchange – unless you would rather…." he paused and dragged the tip of the dagger around Rachel's throat, leaving a raw scratch.

"Over your dead body, Dubois," snarled David, breaking free from the group and charging towards the altar.

In a swift movement, Dubois raised the knife high and brought it arcing down on Rachel's chest until the tip was embedded in her flesh. He paused and looked directly at David as the blood welled up around the mirrored steel blade. Rachel convulsed in terror, too petrified to utter a sound. "Don't push me," he growled menacingly, as blood trickled down onto the tattered remains of Rachel's white blouse. "I will carry out my threat."

David froze in mid-stride, his desperate urge to rip out Dubois' throat countered only by the imminent threat to Rachel's life.

Then, with a scream of anger and frustration, Marianne wrenched free from her bodyguards and threw herself at the feet of Dubois.

"Don't do this," she said through clenched teeth. "I have kept my side of the bargain."

Two of the Count's men leapt forward, but gunshots crashed deafeningly around the cave. The men fell to the ground, one ominously still, the other writhing in pain.

Seconds passed, the scene frozen like a video on pause, though to David it seemed like an eternity. "Very well," said Dubois after a while. "It seems I finally have your attention."

He withdrew the knife and turned to the silent figure of Marianne kneeling at his feet. "My lady, forgive my lack of courtesy, but it seems your friends wish to renege on our arrangement."

Marianne rose to her feet, threw back the hood of her coat and flung loose her mane of dark hair, staring defiantly at the man before her. "I am the Madeleine," she said with quiet authority. "Is this what you really want? To kill the last descendant of Christ, the holiest man ever to walk this earth?"

In an unexpected gesture, Dubois bowed deeply and reverently before her. "My lady, you do us a great honour. I have sought you for many years, but in my heart, I never dared believe this moment would come. One day, when our souls meet in the afterlife, I hope you can forgive me for what I now must do."

"There is always room for forgiveness, as Christ forgave those who crucified him," said Marianne steadily, her eyes holding Dubois. "But first there must be repentance."

She paused and leaned forward slowly, putting her hand to his face, her eyes probing deeply. "You lie, Dubois. You have no regret. Know this: in the afterlife, this moment will haunt you for all eternity. I speak not of Hell, for the master you think to serve has no power over anyone's eternal soul. I speak of an absence from God; a terrible, inescapable gulf between you and that of which we are all a part. You will never become a part of God; you will, forever, be a-part. You will experience an eternity of sorrow and emptiness. Even then, you could repent, and be welcomed back to God's awe-inspiring love, but for you there will no turning back, for your soul is irrevocably tainted by hate and a lust for power."

Dubois coloured, but said nothing, held rigid by her gaze.

"So, now, we come to this," said Marianne gravely. "Release her."

Dubois gave a startled look as he came out of the trance.

"Release her," repeated Marianne sternly.

Confused and uncertain, Dubois moved to the altar and cut Rachel's bonds with the bloodstained knife.

"David," said Marianne commandingly. "Come forward and take her away – just you," she added quickly. "And don't try any heroics."

David walked forward shakily, and bending over the altar, brushed Rachel's face with his lips. "Don't worry, it's over now," he whispered softly, then scooping up her quivering body in his arms, he turned and walked back to the Count.

Marianne turned to face Dubois once more. "One last time: do you really wish to follow this through, despite all that I have told you?"

For a moment his eyes flickered with hesitation, then his face hardened. "I have no choice, my lady," he said stiffly.

"Everyone has a choice," she said, turning to the altar. She sat on the edge and swung her legs onto the rough-hewn slab. Two cult members moved forward eagerly to tie her, but she turned to them in anger, her eyes ablaze. "Don't think to touch me!" she said furiously. "Do you doubt the word of the Madeleine?"

The men froze, a startled expression on their faces, and Dubois waved them away angrily, bowing briefly once more to Marianne. "Indeed, I do not," he said gravely. "Forgive their insolence. And because of my respect for your sacrifice, I will make this as painless as I can."

Marianne gave him a long, hard look, then slowly lay back on the slab, her arms at her sides, her long black hair cascading over the edge.

Dubois began to chant; a long, slow, guttural ululation that chilled the soul. At first he sung on his own, then the mantra was taken up by his followers, gaining in crescendo until it echoed around the chamber like a cacophony from hell.

Dubois moved to the altar, and grasping one of Marianne's arms, slashed the knife quickly across her wrist. She bit her lip in pain, but made no sound. Dubois picked up her other arm and ripped the blade across that wrist, too. Blood splashed down over the altar as Marianne's life began to ebb away.

211

Chapter 49

It came slowly at first; a trickle of water meandering across the floor, mingling with Marianne's blood to form a tear-shaped pool beneath the altar, as if the very stone itself were weeping. Seconds later a violent cracking shook the ground beneath their feet. The thunder of crashing water reverberated in their ears as a torrent of white foam hurtled into the chamber, knocking everyone off their feet with its ferocity. As the water gained in force and volume with terrifying speed, the Count struggled towards to the altar, where Marianne lay white and unmoving. Ripping off his shirt-sleeves, he tore them into strips and tied tourniquets tightly around her wrists before picking up her limp body and throwing her over his shoulder.

"Let's go," he shouted urgently to David, who had struggled across behind him, still clutching Rachel's limp body.

"We can't go back that way," he bellowed back over the noise of the water. "Look!"

The torrent had crashed down from the far end of the cave where the cultists had been mostly gathered, and the sheer force of the water had swept them into the passageway from which the rescue party had emerged. The rescuers, for the most part, had been given but seconds to brace themselves against the rock wall behind them before the water struck. One man was knocked off his feet towards the tunnel, but a colleague reached out and grabbed him, at considerable risk to his own life.

"The tunnel will be under water soon," yelled David. "And there's no way we would make it past the chimney – it's certain death. We have to find another way out."

"But where?"

"There are at least two other exits – we found them during the dig. One comes out in the crypt, and I'm pretty sure the other comes out under the château." David looked anxiously at the rapidly rising floodwater. "The Vatican has sealed the crypt door, but we might just make it through to the château. There's a trapdoor at the end of the passage – we couldn't open it, but we might be able to shift it with some help. It's our only chance."

The Count nodded his assent, and waving his men forward, they waded waist-deep across the flooded chamber, struggling against the raging current. The water was cascading through a gaping maw in the cave wall directly in their path.

"Make for the far wall, and work round from there," yelled David. "Just watch out for the tombs along the side." Two of the bodyguards caught up with them, and linking arms, they struggled sideways across the chamber.

Once at the wall they were able to keep away from the worst of the current, and started edging towards the passageway through which David and Rachel had first entered the cavern. On reaching the entrance the going became easier, but the water level was still rising rapidly.

"I'm pretty sure the passage starts to go uphill soon – we should leave this behind," shouted David, trying to make himself heard above the thundering noise of the water.

"Let's hope so," said the Count grimly, shifting his grip on Marianne's comatose body. One of the bodyguards stepped forward to take her, but he refused to release his burden. Rachel had recovered consciousness, but was weak from shock.

In almost total darkness they slowly felt their way along the narrow passage, and soon came to a fork. "Does anyone have a torch?" asked David, and after some brief fumbling, a light penetrated the blackness.

"I think we turn right here," said David, taking stock of their situation. Just a few yards further up, however, they were confronted by a rock-fall. "I remember this," he muttered. "If we retrace our steps to the fork and keep going, we should come to another fork. I think I can remember the way from there."

They trudged back to the original passage and pressed on, the floodwater slowly receding as the passageway twisted and turned its way up a slight incline. After a short while they came to the second fork. "This is it," said David. "One of these passages leads to the château, the other to the crypt." He stared at them blankly, desperately trying to remember which one to take. Marianne had lost a lot of blood; they could not afford delays.

Then he saw it: the thread from Rachel's jumper, clinging to the wall of the passage. "Ariadne's thread!" he exclaimed. The Count looked bewildered, but there was no time to explain. "That thread leads back to the crypt – we used it when we were first exploring the place. If we take the other turning, we should come up under the château."

The new passage appeared to double-back on itself almost immediately, then continued to twist and turn until they lost all sense of direction. Suddenly they rounded a corner and emerged in a small, square chamber carved into the rock. A trap-door was set into the ceiling.

"This is it," he said confidently. "Recognise this from our illicit expedition, Rachel?" He turned and grinned at her, and was rewarded with a weak but winning smile. He turned to the Count. "There's something holding that door shut – let's hope we can make it budge."

One of the Count's bodyguards knelt down on the floor to make a platform, while a colleague stood on his back and pushed hard at the small wooden door. It moved a little with each shove, but something heavy was clearly holding it down. "It's not shifting," muttered the man in Occitan.

"What if we try banging on it?" said David. "It might attract attention."

213

"The man who lives here is a recluse," said the Count. "Only a few rooms in the château are habitable – I doubt he would hear the sound. Still, I suppose we have nothing to lose by trying." He spoke briefly to the man at the trapdoor, who proceeded to thump on it loudly.

They waited desperately, willing someone to appear, but there was utter silence.

"This is grim," said the Count, looking anxiously at Marianne's chalky white face in the torchlight. "I don't know how much longer she will last."

"We can try the crypt, but I don't hold out much hope," said David. "The cardinal's men made a pretty good job of sealing it."

They retraced their steps, and started to follow the woollen thread toward the crypt.

"Wait a minute," said Rachel, beginning to regain her senses. "That turning back there looks familiar."

"We came down here on our first visit, Rachel," said David patiently.

"That's not what I meant! When I was being dragged from my cell, I tried to get a sense of where I was in the cave system. I could hear water falling into what sounded like a huge reservoir – and the ground underfoot was ankle-deep in mud. When we passed that turning just now, there was enough light to see what looked like thick mud on the floor."

"Do you know if we can actually get out that way?"

"Well, the men were coming and going quite freely – they sent a doctor to dress my wound."

David turned to look at the Count. "It's got to be worth a try."

"We'll go faster if I walk," said Rachel.

David made to protest, but she held up her hand to silence him. "I can manage if I put my arm round your shoulder."

"OK – let's go."

They walked back a few paces to the narrow side-turning they had missed – little more than a large cleft in the rock. The torchlight revealed a narrow passageway hacked into the rock; clearly man-made this time, rather than carved by an underground river. On one side the limestone wall was smooth, apart from encrustations caused by water seeping down from the ceiling, as if part of the foundations of a building. The other was uneven, where picks and shovels had hacked at the rock-face in centuries past.

The ground underfoot was six inches deep in mud, and the rock floor beneath the slime only a foot wide in places. The men slipped and slithered their way along it with difficulty, the Count reluctantly accepting help as he struggled to carry Marianne.

"This is definitely it," said Rachel, as they reached a fork. "Down there is the cell where I was being held."

"OK, let's keep going and see where it leads," said David.

They stumbled on for another 100 yards or so, and then the passageway started to become wider and more regular. In a few moments, they emerged into a large stone chamber, the sides of which had been rendered smooth with some type of mortar. In one corner stood an aluminium ladder.

"It's an old cistern," pronounced the Count, examining the walls with interest. "We have one like this at the château – we can't be far from the surface now." He spoke briefly to one of his men, who quickly disappeared up the ladder, and thence on to the bottom of a spiral stone staircase.

"Il y a une porte extérieure!" he exclaimed. "Je peux voir les étoiles!"

"He says he can see the stars!" said the Count, relief flooding over his face. "Try giving the door a shove," he shouted to the man in Occitan. They heard various banging sounds, then a shouted conversation ensued.

"The door is chained shut, but he says he can see through a crack and the whole thing looks pretty flimsy." He turned to a burly guard, who with his height and bulk could have been a twin to Pierre, shot so brutally by Dubois. "Henri – go and give him a hand."

The man shinned up the ladder with surprising speed for his size, and shortly afterwards they could feel the vibrations as his 300lb weight slammed into the thin aluminium door. Twice more Henri attacked the door with all the ferocity of a rugby scrum, and then, suddenly, it gave way, swaying drunkenly on its chain, the hinges ripped from the frame.

They clambered up the ladder, gently passing up the still unconscious body of Marianne. Elbowing past the metal door, they emerged into the night, one of the château's ruined towers creating a ghostly silhouette as it loomed high over their heads.

215

Chapter 50

"What's the latest on Marianne?" asked David, walking into the Count's study.

"Rapidly regaining her strength, thanks to the blood transfusion," he replied. His face was pale and lined, with dark, heavy rings under his eyes. He seemed to have aged ten years in the 48 hours that had elapsed since their escape from the cavern. "They operated this morning. They've had to stitch a tendon that was cut in the attack, and that will take months to heal – but it's her right wrist, thankfully. She will still be able to write with her left hand. She's under 24-hour surveillance by the police – I've pulled quite a few strings and brought down some top guys from Paris; the DCRI, the French equivalent of the FBI, not some bumbling local gendarme." He paused wearily to wipe his forehead with a handkerchief plucked from his top jacket pocket. "Has Doctor Fougère some encouraging news on Rachel?"

Rachel had refused to stay in hospital after her rescue. She had been treated in Casualty alongside Marianne, where the doctors confirmed the bullet-hole in her leg was a clean flesh wound, the slug having passed through the back of her thigh without hitting anything vital. Thankfully the chest wound was only superficial, though a rib had been chipped, such was the power of the blow. Everyone tried to make her stay in for further checks, but Rachel had point blank refused, insisting on returning to the château with David and the Count. After two attempts on her life, she wanted to be somewhere safe and secure, with people she knew she could trust. She was duly discharged with a course of powerful antibiotics, and instructions for the Count's personal physician on changing the dressings.

"She's good, thanks – no sign of a fever, which is the main thing. It will take a few weeks for the bullet wound to completely heal. I think your decision to continue to stay here was the right one, though, Gilles. Our enemies know we're here, it's true, but at least we've got a secure perimeter – no-one's going to get near this place without us knowing about it, thanks to the CCTV."

"Have you made any progress on the gospel?"

"Some. I have had some preliminary results back from the photographic files I've sent to the lab – only four pages so far, but the results are interesting, to put it mildly. It's certainly nothing I recognise as being in either the Bible or the Gnostic gospels. I've sent the translation to a theological expert I know at Oxford."

"Can you give me any clues to pass on to Marianne?"

David hesitated. "It's early days yet, and I'm no scholar…"

"But?"

"As I initially thought, the use of language – grammar, syntax etc – is much older than you would expect for a document of purely medieval origin. It also seems to lack a narrative form: in other words, it's not in story form, as you might expect from reading Matthew, Mark, Luke and John. It's more a collection of events, sayings and theological discourses. It's not dissimilar, in that respect, to *The Gospel of Thomas* – the Gnostic text that some scholars believe may be 'Q', the lost source material – along with Mark – used by the authors of *Matthew* and *Luke*."

A look of disappointment shadowed the Count's face. "Not quite what we were hoping for, then?"

"On the contrary, I would say the style strongly suggests the original text was of very early origin, written down by someone who knew Jesus closely during his lifetime – or at least, very shortly afterwards."

The Count studied David's face closely. "There's something you're holding back, isn't there?" he said.

David smiled. "You've come to know me well in our short time together. Yes, there is something else; something potentially so controversial and ground-breaking that I want to be absolutely sure before discussing it even with Marianne. But if my theory turns out to be true, it will be one of the most momentous discoveries of the Christian era."

"That would be tremendous," beamed the Count.

"A word of caution, however," continued David.

"Yes?"

"However revelatory this discovery may prove to be, as you know, what we found is incomplete – it appears to be just one chapter. And unless we can find and carbon-date the original document from which it was copied, I'm afraid no-one will take it seriously. It will make great TV, but that's about it."

Chapter 51

Two more days passed before Rachel was well enough to be allowed out of bed by the Count's doctor; two days in which she fretted and nagged so much that Dr Fougère finally gave up trying to make her take things quietly. "You may as well be up and around, for all the rest you're getting," he told her. "You have obviously got a strong constitution. David told me about your rapid recovery from the car accident earlier this year."

"It takes more than cars and bullets to put her down – she's as tough as an ox," joked David, earning himself a glare of disapproval. "If you're feeling up to it, Rachel, we could do with talking about where we go next in this quest."

"I agree totally," said Rachel, climbing out of bed. "We need to find the original source of the gospel or it will be a five-minute wonder. As will Marianne. It would give the whole story so much more authenticity. From what she's said so far, the implication is that both the gospel and the body of Mary Magdalene were moved during the crusade. So is it stretching a point to suggest they may have been kept together?"

"Not necessarily. Two priceless holy relics, removed for safekeeping – it would make sense to keep them together. The question is, where?"

"I've a gut feeling it's something to do with the Templars," said Rachel.

"Why does every medieval mystery have to revolve around the Templars?" groaned David.

"Stop being such a bloody cynic. We've heard from Marianne herself that the Templars were closely linked to the Cathars, and helped protect the Madeleine during the crusade. Is it that much of a leap to suggest they may have helped smuggle the gospel and Mary Magdalene's body to safety?"

"I suppose not. But let's stick to what we know, and what we can discover through research, before embarking on a wild goose chase."

"I seem to remember you thinking this whole venture was a wild goose chase when we started out. So while I agree about the need for research, let's not lose sight of the fact that sometimes truth is stranger than fiction."

"OK. Why don't we start by going back to the original research we carried out in Rennes-le-Château and see if Saunière has left us any clues on this one? There is so much information scattered around the church, and so far we have only focused on the search for the original tomb of the Magdalene. Saunière was priest of Rennes from 1885-1917 – he had more than 30 years to carry out research and accumulate evidence. We've had just six months."

"It's as good as place as any," agreed Rachel. "And we still haven't exhausted all those books in the library. It's time to get our brains in gear again. Now, if the two of you wouldn't mind getting out of my bedroom, I would like to take a shower."

Half an hour later Rachel and David were ensconced in the library, sifting once more through all the evidence. David fired up his MacBook and began browsing through the photos he had taken in and around the church, while Rachel thumbed through some of the books left on the table from their earlier brainstorming sessions.

"Here's something we've missed," said David after a few minutes. "The paintings of the Stations of the Cross – we've never had the chance to go through these in detail. Like everything else to do with the church restoration, the content was rigidly controlled by Saunière." He picked up a reference book on the Stations of the Cross, and flipped it open. "And, I seem to remember, one of them gave you the insight about a reference to Mary Magdalene coming to France. Chances are there may be other clues in here." He opened the picture file of Station I. "Not much there," he mused after studying the photo for a while.

"I agree, though it does seems rather odd that Pontius Pilate is wearing a veil... Unless it's symbolic – a hidden truth, that sort of thing."

"The words 'clutching' and 'straws' come to mind..."

"You're probably right," said Rachel quickly, anxious to avoid an argument. "What about Station II?"

"Jesus receiving the cross," said David. "Seems pretty run of the mill. Though what's that young boy picking up off the ground? He looks pretty pleased with himself."

"Could it be a reference to the shepherd boy who found the gold coins?"

"That is an idea; you could be right – I certainly can't think of any religious significance. Just as with the rest of the church, it looks as if Saunière is dropping little clues all over the place. This is starting to get interesting. OK, let's look at Station III – Jesus falls for the first time."

They studied the picture for a while, but nothing seemed out of the ordinary for a religiously themed painting "There really isn't much there," said Rachel disappointedly. "Just a soldier blowing some kind of horn..."

"That's a buccina – a Roman war horn. But as you say, no obvious link. Station IV – Jesus meets his mother. That's the one with what looks like a sail, a nod to the legend of Mary coming to France. I'm assuming the other woman in the picture is Mary Magdalene."

"Can we compare it with the crucifixion scene?" said Rachel.

"OK... Here we go: Station XII. Yes – we've got a matronly, older woman here, whom I assume is meant to be the Virgin Mary, and the same woman in yellow as in Station IV, kneeling at Jesus's feet. That's got to be the Magdalene. OK, let's keep these in order – just in case the clues are arranged sequentially. Next, Station V – Simon of Cyrene carrying the cross. See anything there?"

They pored over the image, but again neither could see anything obvious.

219

"Well, I guess he didn't necessarily put clues in all the stations," said Rachel. "Next!"

"Right, Station VI. Something to do with Saint Veronica, I believe."

"Legend has it that on the way to Golgotha, she offered her veil to Jesus to wipe his face. When he gave it back, his face was imprinted on it. Needless to say, thanks to this miracle, she was canonised. Can't see anything special there," said Rachel.

"How about Station VII – Jesus falls for the second time? That spear has a very unusual haft to it, with an elaborate spiral design. It's obviously symbolic in some way."

"It looks like the clock-tower of a church, though not one I recognise. Intriguing. Just another nod to Mary Magdalene, perhaps."

"OK, here's Station VIII – Jesus meets the women of Jerusalem."

"I've read about this – some people claim the child's tartan robe shows a link to the Templars," said Rachel.

"The Da Vinci Code rears its head once more – I suppose your talking about Rosslyn Chapel, the alleged Scottish connection."

"For once I agree with you – it's a bit of a stretch to suggest the Templars, who were outlawed in 1314, mysteriously reappeared in Scotland more than a century later. Building work on Rosslyn Chapel didn't start until around 1450. Still, it's worth bearing in mind; Saunière must have included the tartan for a reason."

"True," said David. "Station IX – Jesus falls the third time. The obvious thing about this one is that has someone has hacked Jesus's head off the fresco. A souvenir hunter? A mindless vandal? Or some other reason?"

"Probably just a souvenir hunter, judging from what Hélène's told us about the place. She said someone actually stole the head of the Devil from the statue by the door – the one there now is just a copy, apparently. Can't see much else that stands out… Although having said that, the soldier on a rearing horse framed behind the cross could symbolise a knight. And the cross is on its side, forming a diagonal St Andrew's Cross. Another reference to the Templars?"

"I buy the knight imagery. I guess it's important to distinguish between what we think is plausible, and what Saunière believed to be true. OK, next up is Station X – Jesus is stripped of his garments – the scene where the soldiers gamble for Jesus's clothes. Another missing body part, by the look of it – see how that man's arm has been chiselled off?"

"I agree it's odd," said Rachel, squinting at the screen. "But in this case the background is painted behind the missing arm."

"Perhaps it's been retouched."

"Possibly – or maybe there's another reason. Anything strike you as odd about those dice, directly underneath?"

"Not particularly."

"I can't put my finger on it, but they jar for some reason." Rachel paused.

"I wonder what the numbers add up to… Three and four are showing on the first dice, five on the second. Even with my appalling arithmetic, I make that 12. Any dice round here?"

"What?"

"Have you come across any dice around here? I've got an odd feeling on this one."

"I think the Count said there was a box in the corner there with a few old games in it – I was looking for something to keep you occupied in your sick bed…"

"Here we are!" said Rachel triumphantly, dragging out an ancient, battered box of what was evidently a French version of Ludo. She opened the lid and pulled out the dice. "OK, here's the five, and here's the…" Her voice trailed off, and look of astonishment crossed her face. "I don't believe it," she said finally, turning the dice over in her hand. "The three and the four are on opposite sides of the dice – yet this painting shows them on adjacent faces! Whatd'ya make of that, Sherlock?"

"Gobsmacked, to use your vernacular," said David, a look of puzzlement on his face. "How on earth did you know there was something odd about those dice?"

"Feminine intuition," said Rachel, with a superior smile.

David grunted. "Of course. How silly of me. But how do these dice fit into the picture, if you will forgive the pun?"

"That I don't know – but let's remember those numbers; particularly the three and the four. OK, what's next?"

"Right, nearly there. Station XI – Jesus is nailed to the cross."

"Wow, this one's a bit creepy," said Rachel. "Look at the dark, stormy background. That looks like a mountain of some sorts in the background, right in the middle of the picture. I wonder if it has any significance?"

"Perhaps it's meant to be Golgotha…"

"No, they're on Golgotha, you ninny – he's being nailed to the cross!"

"Sorry, you're right – not thinking."

"And those weird silver discs on the end of that Roman soldier's spear? It's almost as if they're pointing straight at the mountain! It looks as though they've got some kind of inscription on them."

"I think the word you're looking for is phalerae. Those discs are war medals – decorations for service and bravery. Centurions would normally have worn them, though they were sometimes mounted on poles." David magnified the image and peered hard at the screen. "It's really hard to make out, but it looks like another spiral design of some kind – the sort of thing you might find in a Neolithic tomb. Normally phalerae would be decorated with the head of a god, an emperor, a lion or something. Right, moving on… Station XII – Jesus dies on the cross – the one we looked at before."

"You were right about viewing them in order," observed Rachel. "Look at the difference in the backdrop! In Station XI we had a mountainous landscape, but here, in the same crucifixion scene, we have the city of Jersualem in the background, as you would expect. Flip back to the other one for a minute… Look at that – completely different. Saunière must have been trying to tell us something in Station XI. Those mountains don't even look like they belong in Palestine – they're way too green, and the sky is really murky. More north European than anything, if you ask me."

"I think you're right… There's definitely something going on here – it's a question of trying to pull together the threads. OK, penultimate picture. Station XIII – Jesus's body is removed from the cross. Still no hills – again, it looks pretty urban; Station XI is definitely a one-off in that respect. Mary Magdalene is still there – something all the gospels agree on. Anything else?"

"Not that I can see…"

"And so to the final painting – Station XIV – the body of Jesus is laid in the tomb." David looked at intently at the painting. "They're burying him at night," he said at length. "Look at the moon."

"What's so odd about that?"

"It's Jewish custom to bury the dead before nightfall – so why are they doing it under cover of darkness?"

"Intriguing… Hey, there it is again!" said Rachel excitedly.

"What?"

"Zoom out – look at the top. It's that damn mountain again! The one in Station XI!"

"Hmm." David opened Station XI once more, and positioned the picture next to the first on the screen. "Well, there's some similarity, I grant you – particularly the volcanic peak – but the flanks look different."

"It's a different perspective," said Rachel. "They didn't bury his body on Golgotha."

"No. So you think the scene in Station XI is looking across to the burial site?"

"Well, I suppose that's possible, but that wasn't what I meant."

"What, then?"

"Well, clearly the mountain is being viewed from a different perspective; but I don't think in either case it's in Palestine. Look at the lichen on the rocks, and the stones around that grotto, glistening with water…"

Her voice trailed off and she stared at David with disbelief. "Are you thinking what I'm thinking?" she whispered, her eyes registering total shock. "It seems sacrilegious to even think it, but is it possible that Jesus's body was brought here, to France, with Mary, and buried in that cave? That would account for why the body was missing from the tomb in the Biblical account. And remember, Mary was the first to find the empty tomb – maybe her account of meeting the Jesus in the garden was just a cover story."

"But why move the body?"

"Maybe she didn't want it to become a martyr's shrine – remember, many of his followers thought of him as the Messiah who would overthrow the Roman occupation and rebuild the Jewish state. Maybe she was worried they would steal the body and use it for propaganda – that his message would be lost."

"But isn't the point that people believe he rose from the dead in bodily form?" queried David.

"Yes, that's what most Christians still believe. But if you accept the idea that the soul survives death, a body is… well, just a body, isn't it? Anyway, I'm probably getting carried away here. There are so many ifs and ands and maybes. Let's go back to that hill in these Stations of the Cross – I'm convinced it's got something to do with all this. Maybe Saunière was simply trying to hint at the place where Mary herself was actually buried. Why don't we look at the other photos to see if there are any more clues?"

"There aren't many we haven't seen. Still, I suppose we could have another look at the statues of the saints and the altar."

"Let's do the altar first. That's where this whole mystery started, with Saunière knocking down the old one. We've already found references on it to the tomb of the Magdalene; it was one of the clues that pointed us in the right direction. And you discovered the sword and the gold, which turned out to be the Visigoth treasure in the undercroft. Maybe there are other clues in there."

"It's certainly possible," said David, scrolling through the folder of Rennes photos until he came across the file he was looking for. "Right, here we are." The altar painting flashed up on screen, brightly lit thanks to his earlier work in Photoshop.

"This is just too much to take in," said Rachel, shaking her head in utter disbelief. "There it is again."

"What?"

"Are you blind? That darned hill! The one in the Stations of the Cross – supposedly in Palestine!"

"It does look pretty similar, I'll admit…"

"Similar! You need your eyes testing. It's obviously the same one, right next to the ruined castle in the shape of an 'M' for Magdalene, which we spotted earlier, and the cross – which we assumed was a symbolic reference to Jesus and the bloodline."

"That's quite convincing actually," admitted David.

"Why thank you, kind sir," said Rachel, in her best British accent.

"OK, let's reprise the rest of the painting – which, we should remember, Saunière painted himself. Mary Magdalene is in her grotto, with a wooden cross, made out of two sticks tied together. There is the Bible – although, of course, from what we now know, it could be the Lost Gospel. And there is the skull, traditionally supposed to symbolise man's mortality, from which only the word of God can save us. But could it mean more than that?"

"And then there are those strangely crossed hands, with interlocking fingers, that some people think is another Freemasonry symbol," put in Rachel.

"That one is very obvious. There are certainly lots of references to Freemasonry in these."

"And given some of the other clues, it's possible Saunière believed the Freemasons were linked to the Templars, even if we know it's not true. Then we've got the sword, and possible treasure. We've found the treasure, but not a sword, as yet… I can't see anything else obvious in the painting itself…"

"What about the inscription? *'Jesu medela vulnerum, spes una poenitentium.'*"

"Is that all?" queried Rachel, peering at the laptop screen.

"What do you mean, 'all'?"

"From what I read in my research, I thought the inscription was longer than that."

"That's all there is here."

"You haven't cut off the photo?"

"No!"

"OK, keep your hair on. Hang on a minute." She grabbed the book she had bought in Rennes and thumbed through it. "Here we are," she said triumphantly. "It seems there was a second line, but at some point it was removed. That's weird!"

"Nothing surprises me about this place any more."

"Agreed. Anyway, the missing line reads: *'Per Magdalene lacrymas, peccata nostra diluas.'*"

David was busy scribbling on a piece of scrap paper. "OK, well what we've roughly got is something like, 'Jesus, you remedy for our ills and only hope for repentance, through Magdalene's tears you wash away our sins.'

"Hmm."

"Now what?"

"Your Latin is a lot better than mine, but couldn't the word 'vulnerum' be linked, grammatically, to Jesus? In other words, could it read something like, 'Wounded Jesus, our remedy and one hope of penance…'"

"I'm no expert, either, but I suppose it's possible – especially if Saunière were trying to make a point. And those crosses that interrupt the inscription do separate the first three words from the next three."

"You know it's a little odd when you think about it, actually," mused Rachel. "Surely Jesus died on the cross to wash away people's sins; at least, that's the conventional Christian belief. But here, it's saying that through the Magdalene's tears our sins will be washed away. Moreover, as we've discussed, the version of events in which Mary is actually named, in John's gospel, Christ's feet are anointed with oil, rather than washed with her tears."

"So what's that got to do with the inscription being erased?"

"Saunière himself clearly believed the anointing version – you can seen the vase of oil in the stained glass window behind the altar – the biggest feature in the church. That being the case, why does he make reference to Mary's tears washing away sins in the altar inscription – Luke's later version of events? Maybe there's a cryptic message hidden in there... that through Magdalene's tears you will find Christ's redemption. Someone removed the part of the inscription for a reason. And actually, in doing so, they have given us a much bigger clue."

"I must admit under normal circumstances I wouldn't have thought twice about the wording. But the fact it's been hacked off does make it pretty suspicious," agreed David. "Unless it's just the work of another treasure hunter, I suppose."

"Well that's always a possibility, given what else they've gone off with, but in this case it seems a little far-fetched to think a collector would chisel off a line of inscription – I mean, how could they remove it without destroying it?"

"True. So what else has Abbé Saunière got in store for us here? I suppose next on the list has to be this piece of confection," said David, opening up the picture of the vast, brightly painted relief of the Sermon on the Mount, at the opposite end of the church. "As we said the first time we saw it, nothing much unusual about it other than the somewhat incongruous torn bag of money in the foreground – that and a woman who could be Mary clinging to Jesus."

"Everyone says it's a bag of money. But whatever's sticking out of that bag doesn't look much like a coin, or any other object I recognise. It looks more like a piece of rock – or even bone!"

"I hadn't noticed that before." David paused to enhance the picture, drawing around the object before boosting the contrast. "That's a bit clearer," he said when he had finished.

"You know what it reminds me of?" said Rachel. "That damned hill again!"

"You've got that hill on the brain."

"Hardly surprising since it crops up so often in both the Stations of the Cross and the altar painting. I wonder if there's anything in here – it mentions several local landmarks connected to the mystery." She idly picked up an English language tourist booklet, A Traveller's Guide to the Mystery of Rennes-le-Château, which she had glanced at earlier, and started leafing through it. Half-way through her face went ashen, and she stared at the page in disbelief. "I don't believe it!" she said slowly.

"What?" said David, irritatedly.

Rachel slowly turned the booklet round and pointed at the picture that was showing, scarcely able to believe what she had seen.

David pulled the booklet towards him and then did an astonished double-take. "That bloody hill!" he said in a strangled voice. There, before his eyes, was the hill in the altar painting, the hill in the Stations of the Cross. Not something that just looked like it; it was the hill. "Mount Cardou," he breathed.

Chapter 52

Rachel snatched the booklet and started to read out the entry. *"Of all the stories connected to the mystery of Rennes-le-Château, the ones linked to this imposing site are the most astonishing. The Knights Templar certainly took an interest in this mountain. It is believed that in the middle of the 12th century they shipped in a contingent of German-speaking miners to carry out excavation works on the slopes of Cardou. The workers were subjected to rigid discipline and were under strict orders not to talk or fraternise with the locals."*

"I hate to pour cold water on all this, but are any source materials cited for these wild claims?"

"No, but I'm assuming the authors are basing this on some kind of oral tradition."

"Possibly. But it's all highly speculative."

"Hey, get this," said Rachel, ignoring him and reading on excitedly. *"This has led to speculation that the Templars may have buried items of extreme importance deep inside Mount Cardou. One of the legends surrounding the knights is that they were in possession of a sacred relic from the Holy Land."*

David laughed. "Don't buy into all that gobbledegook that Dubois was spouting. The Templars may have had a base on the Temple Mount, but there's no evidence they found any treasure – there was nothing there to take. The Romans took most of it when they sacked Jerusalem in 70AD – you can see the sacred Menorah engraved on the triumphal Arch of Titus in Rome to this day."

"Still, the Templars were linked to sacred relics," persisted Rachel. "Some people think the Shroud of Turin was in their possession for a while. And there's the Templar painting found in England just after the Second World War, which bears an uncanny resemblance to the shroud. Templecombe, I think the place is called – You were on a Time Team dig there, weren't you?"

"Yes, I was, and the painting certainly dates to that period – but no earlier. Let's get back to Mount Cardou, before heading off up a blind alley. We do know the Templars were active in this area, and Marianne tells us they have helped safeguard the Magadalenic line – perhaps that was their 'secret treasure'. There are Templar remains all over the Languedoc, including the Château de Blanchefort – which, if memory serves me correctly, is on the opposite side of the valley to Mount Cardou. So despite my scepticism, it's worth exploring the Cardou link – based on what Saunière has given us so far, it's as good a place to start as any. But let's not forget that what we really want to find is the original gospel, and Mary's mortal remains. Mitochondrial DNA testing will prove once and for all whether Marianne is related to her, which would be pretty strong evidence that she is who she claims to be. The gospel may help to back that up. So let's focus. For now we'll follow Saunière's lead, and if that means taking Mount Cardou apart to find it, so be it."

He paused and started poring over a large-scale map. "This is ridiculous," he muttered. "It's enormous – where the hell do we start?"

"Old Nick!" exclaimed Rachel, lunging for David's laptop and pulling it towards her.

"What on earth – have you taken leave of your senses?"

"Old Nick! Lucifer! The statue by the door – the Devil is in the detail…"

"OK, what have you found?"

Rachel paused for a while, staring at the grotesque statue of the Devil that stood inside the church door at Rennes, his horned head surmounted by the Holy Water stoup, and above that an ornate crest displaying twin salamanders, semi-mythical lizards symbolically impervious to fire. The top half of the statue was given over to a group of female saints, standing on a plinth inscribed with the now familiar saying, Par ce signe tu le vaincras. Pride of place, visually, at the centre of the work, was given to a vivid crimson seal bearing the initials 'BS'.

"I know we've gone over this before, but I'm not convinced those are just Bérenger Saunière's initials," she said. "Given what else we've discovered in the church, isn't it more likely to be another clue – superficially, perhaps, just his initials, but in reality, a pointer to something else?"

"I suppose it's possible."

Rachel had a sudden flash of inspiration. "There's a rock called Le Fauteuil du Diable – the Devil's Armchair – near the chambre d'hôte at Rennes-les-Bain, isn't there?" she said brightly. "I remember the owner talking about it. And aren't the two rivers that meet nearby called the Blanque and the Sals?"

"I'm not sure where this is heading," said David, still studying the map. "That's a mile or so south of Mount Cardou."

"Yes, but it's a clue – can't you see, he's giving us a series of prompts. And who knows precisely where the Templars were digging their mine. Give me the map. Look! There's Rennes-les-Bains, and the rivers Sals and Blanque come together just below it. And… I can't believe I've not seen this before!"

"What, for God's sake?"

"There's a spring called La Source de la Madeleine right next door – and Mount Cardou is immediately to the north!" She fell silent for a moment, deep in thought, then a look of understanding dawned on her face, and she grabbed David excitedly. "The Sals is a salt river, isn't it? Through Magdalene's tears… This is the answer! He's giving us a map, dropping in as many geographic clues as he can! Look at the salamander crest – see how the two plumes below the BS seal join together in a V-shape, just like the confluence of the rivers? And they're painted blue. Isn't that a bit of a coincidence? Come to think of

227

it, I think that crest appears above all the Stations of the Cross. And those plumes emerge from a gold crown."

"I like the link to 'Magdalene's tears'. But that still doesn't pinpoint the exact location."

"I know, I know – we're so tantalisingly close…" She paused, racking her brain for ideas. "It's got to be something to do with the Devil," she said finally. "As we've said before, why put him just inside the door of the church – the first thing people see when they go inside a building dedicated to Christ is a statue of Old Nick! And the inscription: Par ce signe tu le vaincras. Why the addition of the word 'le'? Saunière was so meticulous. Was it another reference to the Magdalene, with the number 22, as we thought earlier – or is it that just a red herring? Maybe it was simpler than that; maybe he was referring directly to the statue of the Devil; a pointer that he's an important clue in the trail."

"Under the circumstances, that seems more likely. I think you were on the right track with that heraldic device above the Devil's head. If we're going to continue with this wild goose chase, it seems to me the first place to start looking is the Devil's Armchair."

"Agreed," said Rachel. "God, it's going to be hard to sleep tonight." She stood up, clasping her hands to her head momentarily as she was overcome by a wave of vertigo. "My brain is racing out of control – where does all this stop?"

David moved closer to hold her, his hands resting gently on her slim hips. He looked into her eyes tenderly. "I don't know the answer to that, but I do know we're riding the dragon. Going back to Rennes will attract unwanted attention. You've had a pretty damn close brush with death twice, now – you've still got a hole in your leg, for God's sake. I don't want it to be third time unlucky."

"I don't think there's any going back now," said Rachel softly, touched by his concern. "We're all potential targets. Our most sacred duty is to protect Marianne, and she won't be safe until the truth is out."

"Anyway," she said, pinching his bottom playfully, "You seem to forget I'm quite capable of looking after myself."

Chapter 53

They waited a few more days for Rachel's leg to start healing, but she was champing at the bit to get on with the search and refused to listen to David's pleas to lie low for a couple of weeks before continuing with their mission.

"It will only give them time to regroup – we must keep going," she insisted vehemently. In the end her argument had won the day, and they set off at the crack of dawn the following Sunday; a time when they hoped most people would still be in bed. They took some basic precautions, David growing a beard during the enforced wait, while Rachel, using a hiking stick to disguise her limp, put her hair up and wore a scarf over her head.

"That puts ten years on you," said David, with a sly grin, earning himself an evil glare.

"If it keeps me safe, I don't care," she said sniffily. "Suffice it to say you won't be getting much attention from the opposite sex with that goatee beard."

With Hélène and a driver as escort, they headed to a small car park on the outskirts of Rennes-les-Bains, where they left the Citroen and started out on foot up a small side-turning. The tarmac ended abruptly in a farmyard, where a well-worn path led steeply up the hillside beyond, disappearing into a dense chestnut forest.

As they followed the track up through the sun-dappled woodland, the trauma of the past few weeks seemed to slip away. Golden light filtered through the leaves, flickering on their faces, and the sound of a small brook was never far from their ears as it tumbled down the craggy hillside. It all seemed a million miles away from the dark violence of the Visigoth burial chamber.

Eventually the track emerged in a small woodland glade on the edge of the hill, bounded on one side by a steep ravine. In front of them, overlooking the valley below, lay a square grey slab of rock, encrusted with green-grey lichen.

"Behold, Le Fauteuil du Diable," said Hélène, smiling, with a dramatic flourish, gesturing for them to join her.

"So this is it!" said Rachel. "I can see why everyone has been getting excited about it – it really does look like an armchair."

The huge chair-shaped rock had obviously been hollowed out by human hand – and carved with great precision. They walked around it slowly, examining it from every angle.

"What's this, Hélène?" asked Rachel, pointing to a nearby pool about the size of small wash-hand basin, that was clearly man-made. It was fed from an open conduit carved into the horizontal stone slab that lay behind it.

"That is La Source du Cercle. It is a sacred spring and has been revered for centuries. Many believe it has healing properties – some people claim to have had miraculous cures from it."

"Hmm," said Rachel, her interest piqued. "It seems a little odd to have a sacred spring next to the Devil's Armchair, doesn't it?"

"It wasn't always named this way," said Hélène. "It was originally known as Le Fauteuil d'Isis."

"The armchair of Isis?" said David, startled. "The Templars were heavily influenced by Middle Eastern mythology – their ceremonies have strong similarities to the Roman cult of Mithras. The cult of Isis started in Egypt, of course, but spread throughout the Greco-Roman world. It even features a resurrection story in which Isis brings her brother Osiris back to life after he is killed by Seth. Some experts believe the early Church, in its attempt to eradicate paganism, used Mary Magdalene as a replacement for Isis, encouraging people to venerate her. It was only later, when her following became too great, that the Church put out the smear story that she was a prostitute. Instead, they encouraged people to pay homage to the Virgin Mary; someone who played no religious role in Jesus's life, and therefore posed no threat to the male hierarchy."

"Wow – the links just keep getting stronger," said Rachel. "But would Saunière have known it as Le Fauteuil de Diable? It could be an important clue."

"Oui, certainement," said Hélène. "It was renamed in the Middle Ages, but he lived here for many years. He would have known the older name, too." She walked around to the back of the seat. "Observe!" she said, pointing.

"A Templar cross!" exclaimed Rachel.

"So some say," said Hélène. "It has certainly driven the treasure-hunters crazy over the years – but who knows? Perhaps it was just a mischief-maker."

"What makes you so sure it's a Templar cross?" said David dubiously.

"It's a classic eight-pointed cross," said Rachel.

"Yes, I know that – but as Hélène said, it could have been drawn by anyone."

"And, of course, there is this, too," said Hélène, her eyes sparkling with mischief. She gestured to another symbol on the seat of the chair.

"How the hell did I miss that?" said Rachel in disbelief. Carved into the stone in front of her was an ankh, the ancient Egyptian symbol for immortality and eternal life – a cross surmounted by a circle.

"That looks about as genuine as the Templar cross," said David scathingly.

"Why the crossed swords on the stem of the ankh, I wonder?" asked Rachel.

"Assuming it's not the carvings of some New Age treasure hunter, you mean?"

"You're probably right," she sighed. "There's something we're missing here… We're so close, I know it. I suppose he's giving the Devil's Armchair as a clue, since it's such a well-known local landmark, linking in to Old Nick in the church doorway. Then there's the BS sign, together with the two converging blue plumes in the heraldry, and the 22 letters in the inscription, *Par ce signe tu le vaincras*, two more than usual, giving us the date of Mary Magdalene's feast day. And then there are the possible Templar links, again… I'm pretty damn sure the BS stands for the Blanque and the Sals rivers, though."

She wandered over to the edge of the steeply sloping hillside and looked out through the canopy of trees across the steep valley of the Sals below, soaking up the astonishing beauty of the hills, folding away into the distance in grey-green ripples. Then a thought came into her head, and she turned abruptly to Hélène. "Where is La Source de la Madeleine, exactly? Can you see it from here?"

"It's across the other side of the gorge, away to the south-west – near where the rivers join. Not far as the bird flies," said Hélène, pointing.

"Near where the rivers join," repeated Rachel slowly. "The Blanque and the Sals. "And that's the way the armchair is facing… Le Fauteuil d'Isis is looking across the water at La Source de la Madeleine. Is that a coincidence? Maybe this is just like a treasure hunt, with one clue leading to another. The statuary in the church, the rose window – they all led us to the empty tomb of the pregnant Mary Magdalene. Now perhaps the Devil symbolism is leading us on to the next set of clues."

"So we go to La Source de la Madeleine?" queried Hélène.

"We sure do," said Rachel emphatically.

They retraced their steps back down the winding track, past the old farm buildings and then onto the road that led back to Rennes-les-Bains, where the driver was waiting with the car.

"Alain, allez au pont prochain, si vous plaît," instructed Hélène. "The track starts from the next bridge," she explained. "It's not far up the road, but we must keep the car as close as possible in case…"

"Yes, we get the picture," said David.

231

Chapter 54

The waymarked trail – one of several set up by the local tourism department – led across the river Sals close to its confluence with the Blanque via a series of stepping stones, then started winding up the steep flank of the valley, doubling back on itself as it rapidly gained height above the river.

"It can't be much further," said David, poring over the map while they stopped to catch their breath. "Have you ever been here, Hélène?"

"No – I've been to the fauteuil, but never here. Everyone knows where it is, but few visit – only the tourists."

"I find that strange," said David. "You're related to Marianne, so you're part of the family; her family, since that's the assumption we're working on now. Why haven't you been here before?"

"You live in London, David. When did you last visit St Paul's Cathedral or Westminster Abbey?"

David reddened. "When I was a boy."

"You see, we often take for granted the things closest to us, however important or beautiful they are. They're so close we look right past them."

"Hey, that's pretty prophetic," said Rachel, stepping back to the edge of the path and staring past them. "I think we've just found it – look behind you!"

Hélène and David turned round to look at the hillside rising steeply behind them. A jumble of rocks lay at the edge of the path, cutting into the leaf-strewn earth bank. At the rear stood a small, grass-covered knoll with an exposed face of bare rock, and at its base a dark cleft. As their eyes took in the apparent chaos of rock, covered with lichen and layer upon layer of fallen leaves, they were able to make out a crude semi-circle of stones enclosing a small pool, almost dry despite the torrential rain a week earlier. The more they looked, the more obvious the shape became.

Rachel knelt down to peer at the cleft in the rock. "You're going to think I'm sounding off again, but does that shape remind you of anything, David?"

"What in particular?"

"The V-shaped opening with that narrow cleft above?"

"You're on about the sacred feminine, again."

"It's pretty hard to ignore, don't you think?"

"Now you've pointed it out, yes, but you can see shapes in anything if you stare hard enough."

"Maybe. But I'm betting this is an ancient pagan site, presumably to some kind of mother goddess. Interesting that it's been renamed for the Madeleine – not the Virgin Mary. I wish we could enlarge the opening somehow, but we can't just start digging up an ancient monument. Wait a minute – what are those markings on that projection of rock at the top…" She leaned in to get a closer look. "It's a head – complete with moustache. And more importantly, a helmet. It looks ancient – this isn't recent. In fact, this place looks completely neglected. But I'm guessing Saunière found this and…" She stopped dead in her tracks and spun round, her eyes dancing. "You're right about the carvings on Le Fauteuil du Diable, David, they're not genuine – Saunière put them there! He left an elaborate trail of clues that led us to the Fauteuil, and now here!

"Well if he did it's not much help to us," said David. "As you say, this is the French equivalent of a scheduled ancient monument. We can't dig here without a permit, and that could take months to arrange."

"But what if the trail doesn't stop here? Maybe it's just another signpost along the way."

"And maybe this is a cul-de-sac," said David gently. "But let's not give up on it just yet. Help me get rid of this debris so we can get a more thorough look at the site. The best archaeological finds are often well hidden. If nothing else, it would be respectful to tidy the place up a little."

They set to work, removing armfuls of leaves and twigs that had accumulated over the years, together with a few broken branches and lumps of rock that had fallen in from the hillside above. When they had finished, the shape of the basin in front of the source was much more defined.

Rachel left David studying the layout and clambered up above the pool, where a break in the dense foliage gave a commanding view over the valley of the river Blanque far below. She stood staring over the precipitous drop, lost in thought. All the clues Saunière had so carefully laid… The solution felt tantalisingly close, yet just out of reach. She ran back over their research, desperately cudgelling her brains for something they had missed.

Then a flash of inspiration burst in her mind, and she scrambled back down the hillside as fast as she was able, only just keeping her footing as she slithered on the loose scree. She cannoned into David, still standing by the pool. "Hey, go easy with that leg." he said, grabbing her to stop her falling. "Are you OK? You look as though you've seen a ghost."

"Remember that booklet we read in the château library? The one that mentioned Templar excavations on Mount Cardou – and the German miners they brought in?"

"I do, but…"

Rachel spun round to face Hélène.

"Are there any old mine-workings around here that you know of?"

Hélène paused for thought. "Possibly. I remember hearing about some old workings up here somewhere, as a child," she said. "Of course, we were told not go near them, but we still went looking. We never found them, though."

Rachel gave David a meaningful glance. "Do you know when the mine dates back to?"

"I believe it was last used in the 19th century, but people have been mining Pech Cardou for hundreds of years – the rocks are rich in copper and lead."

"We've got to see it," said Rachel, emphatically. "We can't afford to ignore any leads, however unlikely they may seem. Can you take us there?"

"As I said, I do not know exactly where it is – but it is supposed to be somewhere near an old shrine on the side of the mountain. I remember Anne-Marie telling me about it."

"Can you take us to the shrine?"

"Oui, I have been there as a child. It is not far from here. We need to take the car to Montferrand, a small village above Rennes-les-Bains, and we can walk from there. It is about 45 minutes on foot."

"Great. Let's go!"

They retraced their steps to the car, and then returned to Rennes-les-Bains, where Alain, the driver, turned across one of the town's two ancient bridges high over the river Sals, negotiating the tiny little back-streets at a speed that made Rachel cover her eyes in horror – at one point squeezing the car through a gap between two houses that was so small the wing-mirrors almost brushed the stonework.

From there it was a five-minute drive up a steep mountain lane to Montferrand. Just outside the village, the driver turned off down a badly rutted track and pulled in behind a derelict farmhouse.

"The path starts back there, but we don't want to advertise our presence," said Hélène.

They walked back up the muddy lane, then took a small, almost hidden path that disappeared through the brambles, following the course of a stream. After a hundred yards or so, the path gave way onto an ancient, grassy track that started gently winding its way up the tree-covered flank of Mount Cardou. The track had been well engineered, cut into the side of the hill, and in many places the remains of an old stone retaining wall could still be seen.

"It must have taken some work to build this," said David. "Looks pretty industrial."

After half an hour or so, the track abruptly gave way to dense undergrowth, while a small path led off to one side, climbing its way up the flank of Mount Cardou, now towering high above them.

"Well if this did lead to the mine, it's impassable now," observed David. "I guess we've no option but to take the higher route and try striking back down the hillside a little further on."

After 15 minutes' hard climbing up the tortuous footpath, Hélène stopped where it crossed a steep slope littered with rocks and loose stones. "I think the shrine is somewhere near here," she said hesitantly. "I was only nine or ten when I came here; it's hard to remember."

"Don't worry," said Rachel. "Why don't we spread out? There are four of us – that gives us a much better chance of finding it. If one of us sees it, just holler. And if anyone gets separated, make your way back up to the path and wait here."

Alain looked uncomfortable and muttered something in Occitan to Hélène. Neither David nor Rachel could follow the conversation, but her sharp tone spoke volumes. He shrugged his shoulders in typically Gallic fashion, and she turned back to face them. "He is not happy about us splitting up, but we have no choice. Let's go."

They scrambled down the hillside, slithering across the loose scree, making their way crab-wise across the 45-degree slope. On one occasion Rachel slipped, skidding down the slope on her backside, saving herself at the last moment by grabbing a handful of shrubs sprouting from the chaotic jumble of rock.

"Ouch, that hurt," she said, rubbing the friction burns on her palms where the plant had braked her descent.

"Are you OK?" asked David. "You really shouldn't be doing this with that injured leg."

"I'll live," she responded.

After 50 yards the slope levelled off and they were able to scramble through the dense vegetation without much difficulty. Suddenly there was a shout from Rachel. Spinning on his heels, David turned in the direction he had last seen her and started crashing through the undergrowth towards the sound of her voice. Then he was at her side, standing in the middle of a small clearing.

"This has got to be the grotto," said Rachel, pointing. In front of them was a shallow cave hollowed out of a large, discoloured outcrop of rock that formed a natural arch above the opening. "It's not very deep," she continued, as the others came running. "Quite dramatic, though. Could this have been the shrine your grandmère told you about?" she queried, turning to Hélène.

"Oui, certainement," she said excitedly. "This is where we came as young children – it is, as you say, quite impressive. I seem to remember there was a small statue of Our Lady inside."

Rachel wandered into the entrance. "Well there's no statue now. It's way too shallow for a hermit's cave, and the walls are completely blind, but it could have been a shrine, I guess."

"What now?" said David.

"We look for the entrance to the mine."

"Have you seen the size of this mountain? It could be anywhere, and with all the vegetation we could just as easily fall down an old mine-shaft. It's going to be like looking for a needle in a haystack."

"Hélène said it was supposed to be nearby. We found this place, didn't we? So let's spread out and see what we discover."

They split up and continued their way down, sliding across patches of loose shale that still punctuated the steep hillside. Rachel found herself scrambling through some thick bushes, and managed to find a small path – little more than a sheep track – that made the going easier. After 50 yards the path become more clearly defined, but it was now heading straight down towards the valley floor. She hesitated. At this rate, she would be at the bottom in 15 minutes, and it would be a long, steep climb back up again. She was about to turn around when an instinct – whether intuitive or sheer bloody mindedness, she was never sure – made her plunge on downwards. Another 50 yards, no more, she told herself.

The path led down the side of a large outcrop with a steep drop to one side and ended on a small plateau, where she stood looking around her. It wasn't dissimilar, in some ways, to the grotto above, but there wasn't much to see. She pushed through a clump of dense bushes sprouting up in front of the rock-face – and there it was. Hidden behind a small tree was the gaping entrance to a deep cave, some eight feet in diameter. She tiptoed closer, scarcely able to believe her luck. A rusty steel girder with a chain wrapped around it, just inside the entrance, gave the game away. This was most definitely a mine, and one that had been in use within the last 100 years or so. Further inside was a step down to a small ledge; below that a 20-foot vertical drop. In the dim light she could just make out a sizeable passageway leading off to the right.

She knew she should tell the others straight away, but she couldn't resist the temptation. And besides, she had to make sure it was the real thing. Unslinging her climbing rope, she threw it around the steel girder and attached it back onto herself using a simple belay. Then, tentatively, she lowered herself little by little inside the shaft.

Once at the bottom, she donned her head-torch and scoured the chamber. There were actually two passageways leading away from the foot of the shaft; the one she had seen from the entrance, and another, hidden from above, that led away to her left. She started walking down the right-hand tunnel, a wide shaft about four feet across and six feet high. It appeared to be some kind of main artery within the mine, for as she progressed further into the hillside, she noticed several smaller galleries leading off on either side. Eventually, however, it came to an abrupt end in a solid rock-face.

Rachel looked at her watch – the others would be getting worried, and she certainly didn't want to start exploring the smaller galleries on her own. She returned to the chamber at the mine entrance, and glanced at the second passageway. It was smaller, and appeared to have been more neatly cut, as if by small hand tools. To the untrained eye, at least, it looked older. She hesitated again, then quickly walked a short way along the shaft. It, too, seemed to be heading straight for the centre of the mountain, but after no more than 100 yards she came up against a large rock-fall.

Disappointed, she turned and retraced her steps, only to stop, rooted to the spot. On the wall in front of her, thrown into sharp relief by the glare of her head-torch, was a symbol carved into the rock. It was a horse with two riders; the same image they had seen on the Dalle des Chevaliers that Saunière had lifted more than a century before – the ancient seal of the Templars.

Her heart pounding, she exerted every ounce of strength to pull herself quickly back up the main shaft on the rope belay. She undid her harness and walked out into the sunlight, her mind racing. She was brought abruptly out of her reverie by a shout from close by.

"Rachel – are you OK?"

"I'm fine – I've found it!" she yelled.

"Rachel!" David's voice echoed across the hillside once more, edged with anxiety.

Exasperated at having to leave her discovery, she scrambled back up towards him.

"There you are!" exclaimed David, as she appeared through a tangle of branches. "We've been looking everywhere for you – where the hell have you been? I was worried sick about you."

Her eyes sparkling mischievously. "Nice to know you still care," she said. "Wait till you see what I've found."

Chapter 55

The Templars' German engineers had done their work well. The mineshaft had been cut straight and true, with only the occasional deviation to avoid fault-lines in the rock; the walls square-cut and chiselled.

The rock-fall was less of a deterrent than they feared, and half an hour's hard work created a large enough opening to squeeze through. Leaving Hélène on the outside as a precaution, and with Alain guarding the entrance up above, Rachel and David followed the shaft as it led onwards like an arrow.

Down and down it went, deep into the heart of the mountain that some believed held the secret to the origins of mankind. For both of them, having seen the tombs of the pharaohs in Egypt's Valley of the Kings, it bore all the hallmarks of an entrance passage to a royal mausoleum.

Rachel's mind buzzed with anticipation as she sensed the imminent denouement of their quest. Finally, as the corridor turned slightly uphill, their head-torches picked out something dark blocking the way ahead. As they drew closer they could see an immense studded oak door ahead of them.

"This is it, I guess!" she said, barely able to contain her excitement.

"Hopefully. But how on earth are we supposed to open this thing?"

Rachel walked up to the door and gave it a shove. "Hmm – good question. There's no keyhole that I can see," she said, running her hands over the aged surface of the wood, searching for an opening. "Wait a minute – what's this?" Her fingers closed over something smooth and circular that moved under her touch. "What on earth?" she exclaimed, shining her head-lamp on the area. "David, take a look at this!"

He stepped forward, and in the combined light of their lamps a row of three metal tumblers could be seen on the right-hand side of the door. "I don't believe it!" said Rachel. "It looks like some kind of combination lock – surely they didn't have this kind of technology back then?"

"Actually, they did," corrected David. "The earliest known combination lock dates back to the Roman period. Then during the Islamic Golden Age, which saw huge advances in science and mathematics, a Muslim engineer by the name of Al-Jazari outlined how to build a combination lock in the wonderfully-named Book of Knowledge of Ingenious Mechanical Devices. Right about the time the Templars built this place."

"So the Templars brought this knowledge back with them from Palestine?"

"It certainly looks that way. They were renowned for their scholarly, if somewhat esoteric, beliefs, and they would have been exposed to Islamic culture, and all it had to offer. It begs the question, however, as to what the combination actually is."

"I think I know that," said Rachel, her eyes dancing.

"You do?"

"Remember the dice in the Stations of the Cross? The three and the four on adjacent sides of the same dice? And a five on the other? It's another clue from Saunière – he must have found this place."

"Rachel, you're a genius! What are you waiting for?"

With a trembling hand she slowly turned the tumblers, on which faded Roman numerals could still be seen. Then she gave the door a hard shove and with a groan of protest it slowly swung open.

A small, man-made chamber stood before them, roughly twenty feet by ten, hewn out of the solid rock. Facing them, on a dais at the far end of the room, was a stone altar inlaid with vividly painted wooden panels edged with gold leaf. In the centre was a carved, embossed shield bearing the familiar red Templar cross pattée on a white background. Above the altar was an ornate golden canopy, the front of which depicted a dove in delicate gold filigree, with wings outstretched, rising into the heavens. Above the dove, in the very apex of the canopy so that it formed a small pyramid, was an eye with lines radiating out from it like the rays of the sun. The top of the altar itself was devoid of ornamentation save for a small, bare marble plinth placed in the centre, around which ran a delicate golden rail, supported on small gold posts.

On either side of the altar were the statues of two women: one, younger, holding a baby, with an alabaster jar in her free hand. At her feet lay a skull and an open book. On the other side stood a more mature woman.

In front of this tableau, forming a large 'T', stood a huge stone sarcophagus, its lid bearing an unusual but strangely familiar effigy of Christ in mortuary repose, his hands crossed over his groin. To the left and right of the sarcophagus, completing an arc to the altar, stood the statues of six saints.

Rachel and David stood in silence, overwhelmed with awe at what lay before them.

"So we've uncovered the final resting place of Jesus Christ," said Rachel finally, her voice faltering. "This is just too much…" Tears welled as she knelt before the holiest shrine in Christendom – tears for the loss of her father; tears for the pain of her divorce; tears for the absence of her daughter, who she missed so much; tears for the horrors she had so recently endured. And finally, as the sorrow drained away from her, her tears turned to an inexplicable and indefinable joy; an uplifting of the spirit and an indescribable feeling of Oneness.

David reached out to squeeze her hand. "Don't worry," he said in a choked voice. "I feel the same way."

Several minutes passed before Rachel rose slowly to her feet. "I don't know what to say. I never thought that one day I would see… this," she said, gesticulating, unable to find the words to describe what lay before them. "Or react to it like that."

"Nor me," said David. He paused, lost in the moment. So this was the secret the Templars had been guarding. But there was something about the effigy on the sarcophagus lid that nagged at him, a hard-to-reach memory at the back of his mind that tugged at the edges of his consciousness.

"I've got it," he announced suddenly.

"What?" queried Rachel, turning to him in astonishment.

"The effigy on the lid – the face in particular. Have you seen the Turin Shroud?"

"Not in person, but in pictures, of course..." Her voice trailed off. "You're right – it's a carbon copy of the Shroud, at least, as I remember it. It certainly doesn't look like any other image of Christ I've seen."

"Note there's no halo – refusing to use a halo in their art was part of the evidence laid against the Templars that they did not believe Christ was divine." David paused, looking around the chamber, taking in the architectural detail. He gave a start. "Have you seen the other tomb?" he asked.

"Other tomb?" queried Rachel.

"To your right."

Rachel looked to her side. Just inside the door was a simple stone sarcophagus that had gone unnoticed amongst all the grandeur of the mausoleum. It had obviously been carved in haste, and was rudely finished, but bore the effigy of a woman.

They moved into the chamber and knelt at the side of the coffin, trying to decipher the crude inscription chiselled into the side. David read slowly: "Hic iacet corpus Maria, vocatur Magdalene, sponsa Christi, apostola apostolorum. Hic sepultus anno domini nostri MCCIX. That means..."

"Here lies the body of Mary, called the Magdalene, bride of Christ, apostle to the apostles. Buried here in the year of Our Lord 1209," translated Rachel. "I can manage that much Latin – a little less flowery than the inscription on the tomb at Rennes, but then I guess they were in a hurry. The year 1209 rings a bell, for some reason."

"The start of Pope Innocent's crusade against the Cathars. They obviously moved her body here for safekeeping as soon as the massacres started. So if the body was moved in haste at the start of the crusade, that means there are no guarantees the original version of the gospel is buried here with her."

"I think the Madeleine at the time had a hand in all this. It's unlikely the Templars would have moved the body without her approval. As for the tomb of Jesus, that's a complete revelation. Marianne hinted there was something she was holding back, something that was clearly very important."

"I remember," said David grimly. "It might have saved us some time if she had shared that."

"I agree, though I can understand her reasons for not mentioning it. I don't think she knew the location – I'm sure she would have told us if she had – but she didn't want to over-complicate an already difficult situation."

"You're not kidding! This thing is suddenly a whole order of magnitude bigger. Do you realise the theological implications? It's one thing to suggest Jesus was married – even that his bloodline has continued; it's quite another to say he didn't rise again from the dead. It means there was no Resurrection – it puts an end to Christianity as we know it."

"I totally disagree," said Rachel stubbornly. "Historically, there have been several branches of Christianity that didn't believe in a bodily resurrection, but rather a spiritual one – the most famous being the so-called Aryan Heresy, and, of course, the Cathars. The medieval idea of a bodily resurrection is way past its sell-by date. The reason why none of the early Christians – in fact, right through to the Middle Ages and beyond – did not believe in cremation was because they thought they would physically rise from the grave, just as Jesus had done; or so they thought. Yet few modern Christians buy into that idea. The vast majority of people are cremated when they die – so why do they still hang on to the belief that Jesus physically rose from the dead?"

"Perhaps they don't understand the inconsistency."

"Maybe you're right. But in an age when more and more people of all faiths believe in some kind of spiritual afterlife, with no bodily existence, does it really matter if Jesus didn't physically rise from the dead? If his spirit transcended death, surely that's all that matters? Didn't Jesus say in the gospel of Luke, to the criminal crucified alongside him, 'Today thou shalt be with me in paradise'? That suggests Jesus believed he would ascend to heaven that very day, the day of the Crucifixion, not three days later in some form of bodily resurrection – though he might have appeared to Mary in spirit form. Anyway, I don't see how it alters his message – or even, from an evangelical perspective, that he died for our sins, if that's what you believe. Though personally I think that's a superficial way of looking at things. Maybe, just maybe, this is just what Christianity needs to drag it kicking and screaming into the 21st century."

"Still, that debate will no doubt rage across the world for decades to come, but it doesn't help us now," said David. "So far we haven't seen any evidence of the Lost Gospel. The obvious place to look would be her tomb, but I'm reluctant – and I hesitate to use the word – to 'violate' it."

"You didn't show such scruples at Rennes."

"That was before... all this," muttered David.

Rachel raised her eyebrows in surprise. "A conversion on the road to Damascus?"

"Not exactly – let's just say a reappraisal."

Rachel smiled. How like David to hedge his bets – but coming from him, quite an admission. "You know what I think?" she said after a while.

"What?"

"I think that even if a gospel wasn't interred here with the body, back in those dark days of the crusade, when she saw how things were turning out,

241

the Madeleine would have made every effort to hide that precious relic, the gospel written by Mary Magdalene. And where better than here? Perhaps those medieval fragments in the undercroft were just a decoy to put the Inquisition off the scent. Or maybe it was left there by one of the faithful, and found later by the Blancheforts, or Abbé Bigou. Who knows? But remember the treasure that was smuggled out of Montségur, just before the surrender? I think it was the gospel. I always thought it was the Madeleine herself, and maybe in part it was. But in some ways this is even more precious: the words of Christ, from the person who knew him best: his wife. And as for opening the tomb, if Marianne thinks it's OK, it's fine with me too. She told us to find the gospel, remember?"

She sat back on her haunches and smiled at the strange reversal of roles – her pushing for the tomb to be opened, David holding back, not from some arcane archaeological perspective, but out of respect for the remains of one of the central characters of the Christian faith.

Then, slowly and reverently, she reached forward and grasped the lid of the sarcophagus. Silently, David joined her, and together they heaved the stone a few inches to one side. There, lying on top of a figure wrapped in a white funerary shroud, was a small, round case of ancient leather that looked as if it had once served as a arrow quiver. Gingerly, David picked it up and peered inside the open end. Tightly bound inside were a series of scrolls.

He turned to Rachel, his eyes burning. "The Lost Gospel," he breathed.

Chapter 56

"So here we are, on Christmas Eve, with a ground-breaking programme that could change forever the way we view Christianity."

Suzanne Schneider looked around herself nervously. America was a God-fearing nation. As far as her career was concerned, what was about to go down could make her – or break her. Not to mention the death threats she was certain to receive.

"Naturally, before airing a show like this on live TV, we go to great lengths to make sure there is a solid foundation in fact. This isn't Oprah!" She paused for effect, forcing herself to smile.

"I have to confess that when the people I am about to introduce first came to me a few weeks ago, I found their story hard to believe. But the evidence they have put forward – hard evidence – has been verified by experts as authentic. That evidence is none other than a complete, intact version of a gospel written by Mary Magdalene, which not only throws new light on her relationship with Jesus, but more importantly, suggests that our interpretation of Christ's teachings is completely wrong." She paused again as a murmur went up from the studio audience. That had them going – for better or worse.

"This is a complete gospel that has been dated to the middle of the 1st century, making it probably the first book ever written about Christ – by the person who knew him best; Mary Magdalene. And the contents are earth-shattering…"

Suzanne paused, wetting her lips. "Among other things, it appears to be the source material for the Gospel of John…" More voices spoke out in the audience, and she held up her hand again. "We also have evidence, from both this gospel and a stunning archaeological find, that Mary Magdalene was indeed married to Jesus, and bore his children… One of whom is with us tonight."

They had deliberately tried to downplay that one, tacking the big headline on the end of the build-up, fearing a backlash – but now there was real anger out there, with people standing up, shouting, while studio staff desperately tried to shepherd them back to their seats.

Suzanne swallowed hard and tried to steel herself. "Ladies and gentleman, please welcome National Geographic researcher Rachel Spencer, archaeologist David Tranter, and the woman at the heart of this sensational discovery, the descendant of the Magdalene – Marianne de Blanchefort!"

The cameras panned to the wings as Rachel, David and Marianne walked onto the set. They smiled and raised their hands to acknowledge the applause. Then, as Rachel stepped behind Marianne to take her seat, a gunshot punched through the air, and Rachel slumped to the floor, a vivid red stain spreading across her blouse.

For a split second there was stunned silence as the audience tried to grasp what had happened, then silence turned to screams. Pandemonium ensued as people stampeded for the gangways, while security guards desperately tried to pinpoint the source of the gunshot. But all that remained was a small cloud of blue smoke drifting upwards in the hot studio air and the sharp smell of cordite.

After what seemed like an eternity, the station's security chief appeared and signalled that the studio was secure. Suzanne slowly emerged from behind a camera where she had been cowering, rearranging the earpiece that had come adrift in the mayhem. Trembling, she looked across at the floor manager. He cycled his hands around each other to indicate the cameras were still rolling – this was headline-making news.

David was kneeling beside Rachel, cradling her limp body in his arms, his face wet with tears. Suzanne crouched down beside him as paramedics rushed onto the set. "I'm so sorry," she started to say, but they were both bundled out of the way as the medics took charge and started the CPR routine, pumping Rachel's chest, pausing periodically to give artificial respiration.

David and Marianne stood clutching each other, unable to tear their gaze from the scene. The CPR went on for what seemed like minutes. As sirens wailed in the distance, one of the medics working on Rachel paused to look up at Suzanne, and shook her head. Marianne saw the sign and a spasm of nausea seized her. She pushed past a guard and ran to where Rachel was lying.

"Move out of the way, please," she said quietly but firmly. "Now." The medics looked startled, but there was something about her presence that commanded respect, and they moved away from the body. Marianne knelt at Rachel's side, fighting back the tears. This was the woman who had endured such hardships to help her bring Mary's message to the world. She had taken a bullet intended for her. She could not die; it was not her time or place.

Gently, she laid her hands on Rachel's blood-stained blouse and bowed her head in prayer, her long dark hair spilling over Rachel's pallid face. As the seconds passed, an ethereal aura seemed to surround Marianne, the air around her body shimmering in the harsh studio lights. It seemed, for a while, as if time itself stood still. Then, slowly, the glow faded and Marianne's head slumped, her body swaying with exhaustion.

Suzanne could only look on dumbstruck as the scene continued to unfold. For as David moved across to support Marianne, Rachel's eyes jerked open and she began to cough. She sat up slowly, clutching her chest, momentarily unaware of her surroundings. "I feel like I've been run over by a train," she groaned. Then she saw Marianne's tired smile, and the look of frozen disbelief on Suzanne Schneider's face.

The floor manager caught the presenter's eye and gesticulated frantically.

Suzanne turned to Camera 1. "Ladies and gentlemen," she said shakily. "I think we have just witnessed a miracle."

Epilogue

"So what is it, exactly, that you are claiming, Marianne?" Ten minutes had elapsed since the shooting; ten minutes in which the medics had confirmed that Rachel, whom they had believed dead, was now alive and unhurt, and insisting they continue with the programme. "If we don't get this out now, we may as well all be dead," she told them. "There are too many people out there who want to keep us quiet."

The studio audience had not been allowed back, save for a few VIPs, and Suzanne and her guests had resumed their places. The raked bank of studio seating may have been mostly empty, but the cameras were still very much rolling – and the contents now being beamed live to every channel in the States.

"I appreciate this may be difficult for some people to deal with," said Marianne. "But first let me assure you that what I am about to tell you in no way undermines the basic tenets of the Christian faith – that Christ was the son of God, and that he died and rose again from the dead. However, what is crucial – and what's been quite literally lost in translation over the centuries – is his message.

"That's why I'm sitting here in front of you here today, to reveal the truth about Christ, and what he really came to tell us. It's a message that has been twisted and distorted over the past two millennia, sometimes deliberately, sometimes due to the passage of time, and sometimes due to an all-too simplistic interpretation of the gospels.

"I can tell you this with conviction for one very good reason. To many this may sound far-fetched, but it is the truth, nonetheless: I am a direct descendant of the union of Jesus Christ and Mary Magdalene."

"Well, you've just performed a miracle," put in Suzanne Schneider, hurriedly, nervous of the reaction this was going to get from America's millions of evangelicals.

Marianne looked embarrassed. "That was God working through me, as he can through all of us if we have sufficient faith," she said.

"Getting back to my point, why anyone should find a marriage between Jesus and Mary sacrilegious, I really don't know. We may call Jesus the 'son' of God, but he was mortal while on Earth; he was also a Jewish rabbi, who were expected to marry.

"There is plenty of evidence, if you look for it – even in the only four gospels that the tyrannical bishop Athanasius allowed to be included in the Bible. For example, why was Mary permitted to join Jesus's mother and his sister Salome in preparing his body for burial after the Crucifixion? No-one outside the family would have been permitted to do that – it would have been scandalous for any other woman to see, let alone touch, a man's naked body, even after death – much as it is in Islamic cultures today.

"And earlier, when Jesus arrived at the tomb of Lazarus – Mary's brother – the gospel of John tells us that while Martha ran ahead to meet Jesus, Mary waited at the house to be summoned by 'the Master' – precisely the protocol that would have been observed by an orthodox Jewish wife at the time. When Jesus sees her crying, John says he is 'deeply moved' and agrees to help Lazarus.

"Shortly afterwards, Mary anoints Jesus's feet with expensive oil and wipes them with her hair. Again, at the time, for an unmarried woman to wear her hair loose in the company of anyone other than her husband or immediate family would have been completely taboo. Jewish women of that era would have worn the equivalent of an Islamic niqab at all other times.

"I will come back to this later, but first let me tell you how I came to be here today. My family has lived in southern France more or less permanently since Mary Magdalene fled there soon after the Crucifixion. In the past few weeks, archaeologists in the Languedoc working for National Geographic, under the supervision of Rachel Spencer and David Tranter..." she gestured to where Rachel and David were sitting "...have discovered a mountain tomb, built by the Knights Templar to house the holiest relics of Christ – brought back from Palestine during the Crusades. A tomb that also contains the body of my ancestor, Mary Magdalene.

"Now there will be sceptics among you who will still doubt. But let me tell you this: there is a tradition of Mary Magdalene fleeing to France dating back many, many centuries – there is even archival evidence in England to that effect from one of the few monastic libraries to escape destruction by King Henry VIII. It's really not that strange; Gaul was, after all, part of the Roman Empire – King Herod, who features in the New Testament, was later exiled to Gaul by Caligula.

"Carbon-dating shows the remains in Mary's tomb date back to the 1st century AD. Mitochondrial DNA, which as you may know can prove female lineage over many millennia, has shown not only that she was born in the Middle East, but also that I am her direct descendant."

David leaned in to catch Suzanne's attention. "Can I add something here?"

"Of course, go ahead," said Suzanne.

"I think it's important to say something here on the subject of DNA testing..."

"No David, please," interrupted Marianne. "We discussed this, and we agreed..."

"That was before..." he hesitated "...Whatever it was that we saw earlier," he finished, unable to find the words to describe what he had witnessed. "I think people have a right to know. So, here goes. That same DNA testing showed that Marianne's genome contains a segment of DNA from a species currently unknown to science."

There was an audible gasp from the assembled throng of VIPs and TV management that had now gathered on the edge of the set.

"A species unknown to science?" queried Suzanne in a shocked voice. "What are you saying, exactly?"

"That, perhaps, this is the first physical proof we have had that Jesus – from whom Marianne is descended – was not of this world; not just spiritually, but physically. His genome was different to ours. It moves the idea of God from being just an arcane philosophical concept to something more tangible; something we can relate to. He came from somewhere outside of this world, outside of this planet – at least, in part. Make of that what you will."

The studio was utterly silent, save for the ticking of a clock.

After what seemed like an eternity, Marianne started to speak. "When we first found the sarcophagus, we assumed, given the other evidence in the chamber, that we had indeed found the last resting place of Jesus Christ – but the tomb was empty. However, there were a few botanical fragments that have been identified as coming from the jujube tree, or ziziphus spina-christi… In other words, they may be from the Crown of Thorns. The fragments are still being examined, but it looks as though we may be able to salvage some DNA from them. If that matches mine, then… As David says, it adds a different dimension to this story."

"You can say that again," said Suzanne. "Is there anything else you can tell us about the sarcophagus?"

"Well, one thing worth mentioning is that the effigy of Christ on the lid is identical to the image on the Shroud of Turin. It's possible the tomb discovered by David Tranter and Rachel Spencer once contained the Shroud, together with the Crown of Thorns and other relics, and they were moved when the Templars were outlawed for fear the hiding place would be revealed under torture. If the Templars were guardians of the Shroud, it would explain why it first appears historically in 1353 in the keeping of Geoffroi de Charney, thought to have been a nephew of a Knight Templar of the same name who was burned at the stake in 1314."

"But hasn't the Shroud of Turin been exposed as a medieval forgery?"

Marianne shook her head. "It's true that carbon-dating carried out on the Shroud in the 1980s appeared to show it was made in the Middle Ages. However, it's possible the fabric used for testing was from one of the many repairs carried out, or that the sample was contaminated. What's really interesting is that more recent tests carried out by Giulio Fanti at Padua University have placed the Shroud at between 300BC and 400AD. Furthermore, no known method has yet been put forward for the Shroud's 'photographic negative' image; for the nail wounds to the wrists and feet; for the pinpricks of blood from a crown of thorns; or for the numerous tear marks to the skin caused by the Roman flagellum, or scourge. In addition, the use of paint has been completely ruled out. Professor Fanti says the only possible way the image on the Shroud could have been created is by a burst of exceptionally powerful radiation."

"And on that point, I can report one new finding from the archaeological examination," put in David. "There were a few scraps of burial cloth in the sarcophogus which have been carbon-dated. Not only are they first century, they have also been exposed to an extremely high level of gamma radiation."

There was a loud murmur from the remaining guests watching from the wings.

Marianne waited for the excitement to die down before speaking. "But the biggest revelation, the most tremendous discovery we made in that Templar chamber, was nothing to do with holy relics or my family tree.

"A gospel was found in Mary's tomb: a gospel that predates all other gospels, a gospel that will revolutionise our understanding of Christianity, and may have been the source material from which the other gospels were drawn – the so-called 'Q' gospel, much talked about by scholars.

"While still undergoing forensic analysis and restoration, the gospel has been dated to the 1st century AD. Structural analysis of the text, based on fragments of a medieval copy recovered from another site nearby, shows it to be a very early account, without any of the narrative..." she paused and smiled... "you might say, 'the flowery bits', that make the four Biblical gospels so distinctive.

"The analysis also shows very clearly that this 'Lost Gospel' is the direct source material for the gospel of John, although it may also have been drawn on by the authors of Matthew and Luke. And it clears up a mystery that has confounded experts for many centuries: namely, the identity of the 'beloved disciple' referred to so often in John. Everyone assumes it was a reference to John himself, but it's a most unusual wording.

"The simple answer is that the 'beloved disciple' was none other than Jesus's wife, Mary Magdalene – whom he married at the wedding in Cana. Strange, isn't it, that John is the only gospel to mention this event, at which Jesus is asked to deal with a wine shortage – hardly the role of an honoured guest.

"If you switch the names John and Mary, everything falls into place. You can even see where the editors of John got into such a mess trying to rewrite the original text – for example the Crucifixion scene. Everyone knew Mary had been there, so they couldn't just remove her from the story, as they did elsewhere. They had to insert 'the disciple whom Jesus loved' – not mentioned in any of the other gospel accounts – to try to ensure their fictionalised version of events hung together. Except it doesn't, if you analyse the wording carefully.

"So why go to all this trouble to marginalise Mary? It's not hard to see why.

There were many vying factions within the early Christian Church, but one of the most remarkable things about that period was the important role played by women in some of these groups. You must remember that Israel, Greece and Rome were all highly patriarchal societies; women were considered not just second-class citizens, but an inferior species – the property of their husbands or their fathers. The Jews, and even some Christians today, believe that Woman, in the shape of Eve, was instrumental in getting us thrown out of the Garden of Eden.

"As you might expect, the equal role of women in the early Church did not sit well with its male leaders, and they systematically set about re-writing history, creating a new, all-powerful, male-centric Christian dogma.

"Of course, it also suited Rome's first Christian emperor, Constantine, to have a highly structured, patriarchal religion that could be used to control people. He encouraged the early bishops to 'get on message' and create a new, unified belief system, much like the CEO of a big company might do today.

"Gospels that didn't suite the new doctrine were declared heretical and outlawed. Those that survived the process and made it into the Bible were heavily edited, something Biblical scholars readily acknowledge. In some cases passages were even added later, such as the attempt to stone the adulterous woman in John. Here, the word was even put about by priests that the woman concerned was actually Mary Magdalene – a blatant piece of character assassination, if ever there was one.

"So the misogynists, of whom Peter and Paul were the chief offenders, won the day. It's worth noting that in one of the Gnostic gospels left out of the Bible by the early Church fathers, Peter is quoted as saying that women 'are not even worthy of life'.

"Which brings me to my final point. One of the key themes of the Lost Gospel was actually left out of John, for reasons that will become apparent, although it's hinted at in some of the Gnostic gospels.

"That theme, I'm afraid, will be controversial to some. It flies in the face of what your evangelical pastors are telling you over here in the States." She paused, unsure of how to continue without causing offence.

"The facts are these, as found in the gospel, embraced by the Cathars with whom Mary came into contact, and passed down to me by word of mouth from mother to daughter, through an unbroken line stretching back to the Magdalene herself.

"Firstly, there is no such place as Hell. God created the universe, and everything within it. There is no duality, no evil force. The argument that because there is a force for good, there must also therefore be a force for evil, is completely without logic. The only evil in this world comes from the hand of Man; to suggest otherwise is simply to let us 'off the hook', as you say, for all the terrible things we do to each other, and to the planet.

"It's worth noting that the Torah, the first five books of the Bible and the cornerstone of the Jewish faith, makes no mention of Heaven or Hell. And as I have already mentioned, Jesus was a rabbi. Later traditions mention 'Gehenna' as a place of punishment – but even then, the time a person's soul could spend there was limited to 12 months, before being admitted to 'Gan Eden', or heaven.

"Secondly, because there is no Hell, there is no need to be 'saved' from it. Of the six known theological schools of early Christianity, four actually believed in universal salvation – that all souls would eventually be reunited with God, regardless of their beliefs. Only one church believed in perpetual torment for unbelievers, and you can probably guess which one that was."

"Rome?" said Suzanne.

"Exactement! Do you really think a loving God would condemn his children to eternal damnation, if this mythical place Hell existed, just because they didn't believe in him?" She turned to Suzanne. "Would you? Would you condemn your own children to eternal damnation just because they stopped 'believing' in you?"

Suzanne hesitated, like a rabbit caught in the headlights. "I suppose not," she said, hesitantly.

"And if you wouldn't do that, how much less likely is God to do so!" said Marianne. "Christ did not come to 'save' us from the Devil, nor do we have to be 'born again' to enter the Kingdom of Heaven – unless, perhaps, we need to live another lifetime as part of our spiritual journey.

"You know, that smug badge of honour about being 'saved' really bugs me. It's not what Christ was about. We all transcend death. There may be some souls who still choose to turn their faces away from God, but that will be their choice, not His.

"That phrase 'the Kingdom of Heaven' is really a metaphor for spiritual enlightenment. Christ came to show us the way; to recognise, and to come to know, the 'Christ' within each and every one of us; to fulfil our destiny and become a spiritual being. Did he not say, 'Beware that no-one lead you astray saying "Lo here or Lo there", for the Son of Man is within you'? And did he not also say, 'Ask and it will be given unto you; seek and you will find; knock and the door will be opened unto you'?"

Marianne turned to face the camera. "You know what's really important? Just this: our soul is the most precious, beautiful thing there is. We must nurture it like a flame; we must feed it with love, compassion and forgiveness; for they are the oxygen without which our soul will surely flicker and die.

"If only people realised that every time they hurt another human being, or fail to help someone in need, they are actually damaging their immortal souls, then maybe the world would finally find peace."

There was a long pause as the cameras zoomed in on Marianne's face, before Suzanne Schneider spoke once more. "Well, you've certainly made some pretty mind-boggling claims, there, Marianne. Just to pick up on your point about Hell – if we don't need to be 'saved', what was the point of Christ's death?"

Marianne smiled. "That's a fair question. Christ died and rose again in spirit to prove that our souls transcend death, something, as I have said, not widely recognised at the time – or even now, in this materialistic world," she added, smiling. "He also wanted to drawn a line under the teachings of the Old Testament; the 'angry' God who brought death and destruction down on Israel's enemies was no longer relevant. Christ wanted to show us all a new path; a path of love, compassion and forgiveness: only an act of supreme self-sacrifice could do that. He did, indeed, die to show us the way – he wanted to send a powerful message that we should focus not on our bodies or our physical wellbeing, not on building up treasures on earth, but on 'storing up treasures in heaven' – in other words, spiritual growth; discovering the spark of God within us, the spark that connects us to every other human being that has ever lived, or is yet to live.

"But it's not just about spiritual navel-gazing – we must practise what we preach in our everyday lives. The Church today puts so much emphasis on saving our souls that we have lost sight of the compassion and forgiveness that is at the heart of Christ's teaching. And we must do it not in the hope or expectation of being rewarded, as some of your televangelists suggest, but rather out of love.

"We stand at the threshold of a new age; a new dawn for mankind. Christ's message really can end all wars, eliminate all poverty, eradicate violence and injustice.

"That is the true vision of Christianity that we must all take forward. Not blind belief, not a 'get out of hell free' card, but an understanding of our spiritual identity, and our true relationship with God, and with each other."

FINIS

Afterward

Most of the historical events portrayed in this book are true. The Cathars belonged to a Christian sect that flourished in southern France and northern Italy in the 11-13th centuries. They believed in reincarnation, and also that Earth was a 'hell' from which release was to be fervently prayed for. They were noted for living a simple life, with a rejection of worldly pleasures, and for condemning the greed and corruption of the Church of Rome.

In 1209, Pope Innocent III launched what amounted to an act of ethnic cleansing against the Cathars, with knights from all over Europe joining what would later become known as the Albigensian Crusade. The campaign lasted until 1229, and tens of thousands of Cathars were slaughtered in what can only be described as genocide. But the suffering was not over – that year also saw the launch of a Papal Inquisition to extract confessions as part of the Pope's continuing mission to eradicate what it saw as the Cathar heresy. The Cathars' last stronghold, the mountain-top château of Montségur, fell in 1244 after a long siege, and more than 200 believers were burned alive in a communal pyre. There are contemporary anecdotal, albeit unsubstantiated, stories of something precious being struggled out of Montségur shortly before the inhabitants surrendered. The Cathar characters of Corba de Lanta, her daughter Philippa, and their respective husbands Raymond de Péreille and Pierre-Roger de Mirepoix are all real.

For those interested in reading more about the Cathars, I recommend Stephen O'Shea's *The Perfect Heresy*. I also thoroughly recommend a visit to the Languedoc, and Montségur in particular. Montségur is an achingly beautiful place, though there is always a strange stillness there, as if the hills can never forget the atrocity.

Most of the information – I hesitate to say 'facts' – about Bérenger Saunière and Rennes-le-Château is also as accurate as I have been able to make it. Saunière is documented as having found some gold coins in the church, shut up the building, and employed workmen from another district to continue excavations in secret. He then started digging up the churchyard, to such an extent that villagers complained He did, indeed, come into fabulous wealth, not only renovating and redecorating the church, but building himself a large house next door, where he indulged in lavish entertaining. He was later censured for selling masses, but it is not thought he could have accumulated nearly enough money this way to explain his wealth.

Hundreds of books have been written on the subject, mostly in French, and there are now hundreds of websites, too. It really is difficult for the newcomer to know where to start; even harder to distinguish fact from fiction – or 'faction', where a few facts have been embellished or distorted and copied from one book or website to another as if they were fact. Here my journalistic discipline helped, and I have tried to stick to the accounts that appear to have the most authenticity – though I have used a little dramatic licence here and there to improve the story, so it shouldn't be taken as 'gospel' (if you will forgive the pun). I thoroughly recommend Jean-Luc Robin's *Rennes-le-Château: Saunière's Secret* as a particularly good introduction to the subject, and one that takes a similarly sceptical approach (the English version is not currently available on Amazon, but can be found in the bookshop at Rennes le Château). There really are some pretty wild theories out there!

The observations on the features in the church, including the altar-front and the Stations of the Cross (but not the arrangement of the statues), are largely my own, based on several visits to the area and close analysis using Adobe Photoshop, which I have used in my work as a journalist for many years. There is certainly a mystery waiting to be discovered at Rennes-le-Château, but the answer almost certainly lies in the crypt. There is almost no doubt that there is a crypt, but whether the authorities will ever allow it to be opened up seems unlikely – apart from anything else, an empty crypt would ruin the tourist trade! The enigma is likely to remain for the foreseeable future.

The undercroft beneath the crypt is my invention, but the limestone geology around Rennes is riddled with underground water courses, so it's not too much of a stretch for the imagination. Certainly the tunnels beneath the castle and the village itself are very real – no tourists are allowed to explore them, however.

The Knights Templar is probably one of the most mysterious and fascinating organisations from medieval times, and the subject of much speculation – not to mention fantasy. There seems to be some contemporary evidence that they excavated tunnels under the Temple Mount, and may well have found some archaeological artefacts. They were certainly reputed to be the guardians of a holy relic, but what, precisely, it was we shall probably never know. Again, there are plenty of wild theories masquerading as fact – including the claim, widely repeated on the internet, that the Templars' sixth Grand Master, Bertrand de Blanchefort, was in some way connected to the Blancheforts of Rennes-le-Château. While it was sorely tempting to include this idea in the book for plot purposes, I chose not to, since the claim – made in *Holy Blood, Holy Grail* – has been disproved by French historian Richard Bordes in his book *Les Mérovingiens à Rennes-le-Château, mythes ou réalités. Réponse à Messieurs Plantard, Lincoln, Vazart et Cie.*

I am not the first to suggest that the mysterious 'beloved disciple' in the Gospel of John is, in fact, Mary Magdalene, and if you analyse the wording of John you will see just how tortuous the amendments are – especially the insertion of the John figure into the crucifixion scene, where the other three

Biblical gospels make no mention of him. Nor is it my idea that John is based on a text written by Mary Magdalene – that credit must go to Dr Ian Poole, who makes it the basis of his book *Mary Magdalene and the Gospel of John* (ISBN: 978-0955793301). I have conflated this with the idea of a 'Lost Gospel'; I do believe that, in time, more evidence will come to light as to the true part Mary Magdalene played in Christ's life, as with the recent discovery of the 'Wife' fragment. Like many, I fail to see what is so theologically challenging about the idea of Christ being married. Christianity today has strayed a long way from its roots, and like the Catholic Church in the Middle Ages, has become mired in dogma. To survive in the modern age, it needs to rediscover the spirituality of the gnostics. There is much we could learn from the Cathar approach to life.

As for Da Vinci, linking him to a holy bloodline is purely my invention, but the circumstances of his birth are certainly curious, and the references to his DNA having Middle Eastern origin are based on recent scientific research. The theory that the Mona Lisa is actually a painting of his mother Caterina has also been suggested by some experts. Close analysis of *The Last Supper* makes it impossible for me to believe that the figure to the right of Jesus is anything other than a woman.

And as for the one-fingered gestures in many of Leonardo's religious paintings, that is a whole new opportunity for debate!

Printed by Amazon Italia Logistica S.r.l.
Torrazza Piemonte (TO), Italy